BLOOD GAME

CARLA SIMPSON

OLIVERHEBERBOOKS

PROLOGUE

CALAIS, FRANCE

Headlights slipped in behind her in the stream of traffic, and glared in the rearview mirror. Close, too close.

Those headlights had followed from Paris, not obvious at first, moving through traffic on the motorway as she moved through traffic, like dozens of other automobiles in the fading daylight. It was there again when she stopped for fuel, then returned to the roadway, slipping back into the traffic.

Hiding.

Now those lights appeared again, the silver Audi briefly silhouetted in the headlights of a passing cargo van. Closer now.

She wasn't intimidated. She'd sharpened her driving skills on dangerous roads, through dozens of roadblocks and bombed-out streets in Beirut, then Iraq, going after the story. It was her job. It was what she did, in places where few dared go, let alone women journalists.

But this wasn't Lebanon or Iraq, or Afghanistan. It was the French countryside, and she was after a different story.

She thought of the photograph taken by a young war-time photographer—her father—over seventy years earlier.

France had been a different place then, a country occupied by the German army, determined to destroy anyone who stood in their way during one of the most horrific events in human history.

The photograph, taken in June 1944, was tucked into her notebook, a black-and-white image taken just after the landing at Normandy, like the selfies people took with their cell phones, smiling images taken in front of a church or castle, oblivious to the past, the struggles, the wars.

Was it a diversion from the other photographs Paul Bennett had taken? Of young soldiers with haunted expressions who had faced the horrors of four long years of war, then stormed the beaches of Normandy where so many had died, their names etched on a plaque at one of the memorials, or simply lost forever?

What would historians, centuries from now, think when they discovered those concrete bunkers still in place where the German army had made a last stand? Would mankind have reached a better place a couple of centuries from now, a better understanding that went beyond the greed for power?

Power. History was full of those who had exploited it, killed for it, and had then fallen—the Greeks, Romans, Germans in the last century, and the recent Gulf wars. Old conflicts that reached back into the ancient world, and now terrorists on the streets of cities throughout the world.

She glanced at the rearview mirror again as those headlights suddenly loomed closer and accelerated until the silver sedan was beside her, then suddenly swerved toward her. She swore and tried to steer out of it, the rental car slipping over the edge of the roadway, then felt the tires break loose.

The rental car shot over the embankment, then rolled. Shattered glass and twisted metal exploded in a violent shower, the rental car finally shuddering to a stop.

The wipers flapped like broken wings in the pouring rain on what was left of the shattered windscreen. The steering wheel pinned her as the taste of blood backed into her throat. Pain spiraled through her.

She would have laughed if she could at the irony that after dozens of roadside attacks in the Middle East, hiding from rebels and insurgents in bombed-out buildings and the barren mountains in Afghanistan, she was going to die in a car accident in the French countryside.

Dazed, fighting back darkness at the edge of her vision, she was aware of a shadow that moved through the watery glare of headlights at the edge of the roadway as someone came down the embankment.

Then that shadow fell across the shattered windscreen, and a hand reached past her through the gaping driver's window and grabbed her notebook.

Unable to move, barely able to breathe, blood pumping out onto the rain-soaked upholstery, she stared up at the driver of the silver Audi.

"You...!"

CHAPTER
ONE
EDINBURGH, SCOTLAND

K ris McKenna frowned as her cell phone lit up with an endless stream of messages.

It was just after 12:00 noon, New York time, except she wasn't in New York.

She'd caught the red-eye out of JFK, the only flight available on short notice, and then information blackout since taking off from London—some technical issue with the plane's wi-fi, they were told.

Now messages that she hadn't been able to pick up earlier, were popping through—her publisher, their legal counsel working through the night on damage control, Alec Cameron, red-haired with his bow ties from the London Office, and several calls from Brynn Halliday at Sky News.

She was running on caffeine and two hours' sleep as she scrolled through the stream of messages, other passengers and flight crews cutting around her.

There were a couple of messages she didn't recognize and a few more she chose to ignore, as she passed a pizza bar on her way to ground transportation. Images from the midday news that had become too familiar played on the wide-screen.

"In a developing story, eye-witness accounts support earlier reports that another automobile may have been involved in the tragic accident three days ago that took the life of war-time correspondent and Pulitzer Prize-winning author CB Ross in the French countryside.

"*Catherine Bennett Ross was known for her work over forty years as one of only a handful of female war correspondents, with a career that spanned the Six-Day war in 1967, the Vietnam conflict, the fall of the Berlin wall, as well as countless assignments in the Middle East, followed by a successful publishing career with top-selling political thrillers after retiring to the Scottish countryside.*

"*Condolences have been pouring in to her New York publisher from heads of state, members of the military, and those she worked with in a career that spanned four decades and covered some of most pivotal events in modern history. Catherine Bennett Ross, who redefined the role of women in journalism and then went on to win the Pulitzer Prize, dead at the age of sixty-four.*"

And she was her friend.

She had pushed it back since first hearing the news—the shock and disbelief, everything on auto-pilot, putting together that first press release; calls back and forth with the London office; bringing in their legal team in spite of the fact that it was the middle of the night when they first heard the news; coordinating the marketing teams that were already gearing up for promotion on that next book, then trying to get a flight out.

A passenger from some other flight bumped into her shoulder, then stepped around as she stared at those images now, like so many times Cate had reported from some foreign location she couldn't name because of rebel attacks in the area—" CB Ross reporting from Afghanistan," with a burned-out Humvee and those stark, barren mountains in the background.

"How did you do it?" she had once asked the world-famous correspondent who had become a client with that first book—living out of a suitcase, going to places other people only read about in the middle of some war zone or the next military coup in some other part of the world. Living life on the edge, and sometimes over the edge.

Cate had shrugged in that no-nonsense way she remembered from one of those first conversations, after hours in the London office when she first came on as a new author.

"You have a job to do. You pull up your big-girl panties and put one foot in front of the other."

Kris's hand tightened over the handle of the carry-on as she headed for ground transportation.

One foot in front of the other.

James Morgan scanned the arriving and departing passengers—business types, students, late-season tourists, going on the description and a publicity shot taken a couple years earlier—university education, editor with a prestigious New York and London publisher.

He looked for the stereo-type—the executive suit, heels exchanged for expensive walkers for those midday sprints through Manhattan or London to a local salad bar with dressing on the side; then after-hours drinks with the girls at the latest hotspot or trendy nightclub before heading out to the country for the weekend. But there was just one problem with assumptions. The first three letters of that word said it all.

Kris McKenna could have been just another late-season tourist, or one of those students returning from holiday—the faded jeans, the sweater and denim jacket, sport shoes that looked as if they'd seen some miles, and the canvas bag over her shoulder.

Except for the wave of long auburn hair that brushed her cheek then fell just below her shoulders, glimpsed in one of those publicity shots—the finely carved features that had looked up into the camera, and that dark-blue gaze that had a way of reaching deep into the gut at the same time it said, "go fuck yourself."

Assumptions. He took another drag on the cigarette, as he watched her cross the terminal toward ground transportation.

It was just a glimpse at the edge of his field of vision, that sudden darting movement near a bank of vending machines and kiosks, as a slender figure in a hooded sweatshirt darted through the congestion of travelers. It was quick and too familiar, and enough to tighten his gut.

Instinct—that all the weeks in hospital then rehab, along with the requisite line-up of painkillers hadn't dulled—uneasy in crowded places, always looking for that individual that didn't fit in.

Paranoia? Battle fatigue? PTSD? Everyone had a label for it.

In the crowded airport it wasn't the movement so much as the way the person moved, slipping out from beside one of those machines, darting among passengers, stopping, looking around, then moving again—cautious, determined, the dark sweatshirt with the hood pulled low, slicing through the crowd on a direct track.

He glanced across the terminal, saw the target that hooded figure made and tossed down his cigarette, already on the move.

The blow came from behind and slammed into the back of Kris's shoulder. She stumbled and almost went down, a hand snaking around and locking over the strap of her shoulder bag. She held on.

A woman nearby screamed, then someone shouted a warning over the noise and confusion. She felt that moment when her attacker hesitated, a glimpse from the shadow of the hood, then he suddenly let go, cut past her, and disappeared into the surrounding crowd.

A hand closed around her upper arm and she was pulled back to her feet.

"Bloody fucking parasites!"

That hand locked around her upper arm—long fingers, the worn cuff at the sleeve of the leather jacket, and a glimpse of a tattoo.

"They've gotten bolder and airport security already has their hands full with everything else. But I doubt that one will bother you again. He's off in search of some other victim, unless airport security grabs him first.

"Are you all right, then?"

It was faint, that way of ending a question with 'then' or 'aye.' When in Scotland...

That hand steadied her.

"Are you hurt?"

Kris looked up at the edge in that voice.

She was tall at five feet, ten inches. He was taller, with long dark hair that curled over the collar of the jacket, dark eyes, and lean features, beard-roughened face, good-looking even with the frown.

"They use the crowd to their advantage." He brushed off the sleeve of her jacket, and settled the strap of her bag back at her shoulder. "It could have been worse. You should have let go."

"That's easy for you to say," Kris fired back, irritated more than anything. "My passport, credit cards, and papers are in that bag."

She pushed back the irritation. She wasn't ignorant about street crime or crowded airports. Living in a city like New York, you learned to be careful and alert. But at the moment, she just wanted to get out of the airport.

"Thank you."

Gratitude? Maybe. But the dismissal was obvious, that blue gaze dropping the temperature around them a good thirty degrees. He reached around her and seized the handle of her carry-on.

She stared after him as he walked off with her bag in tow. It was there in the accent that was pure Scots and slipped through with more than a little irritation, before walking off.

James Morgan.

There was no mistaking that dark gaze, the dark hair, or the resemblance to one of Cate's friends—Anne Morgan. She was supposed to meet Anne, and they were to drive up together to Inverness.

It was Anne who had found the Tavern for Cate when she made the decision to retire and write that first book.

"Some place quiet, tucked away, green. I'm done with deserts," Cate had said.

There were several pictures of James Morgan at Anne's office, his arm draped around her shoulders, the uniform, his hair cut military-short, handsome in a reckless sort of way, far different from the man who suddenly stopped, turned, and gave her a long look.

He was older than the young man in that photograph. There were lines that hadn't been there before, and a leanness had replaced the muscular build of the twenty-five-year-old who had been into body-building at the time. The reckless expression was gone too, replaced by something else, something dark and closed.

"I'm not after your passport or your credit cards, so you can lose the attitude," he said by way of explanation.

"Anne had a problem with a client at the last minute. I had to be here anyway taking care of some things, and I'm headed back. It was her idea that we drive up together. She sent you a text." He shrugged with indifference and headed for the exit.

Kris followed him and her carry-on. "I have a reservation for a rental car."

He let stopped, let go of the handle of her bag, and headed out the exit.

"Suit yourself."

She grabbed the handle of the carry-on and followed him out to the line of parked rental cars.

"It probably doesn't make sense to rent two cars for the same trip," she conceded. There was that look again, as he hit the remote trunk release of a white economy model in the near parking space.

"No, it doesn't."

There was a duffle bag in the trunk, jacket, but no garment bag.

"No uniform?" she commented, with more of an edge than she intended, after that 'suit yourself' indifference.

He grabbed her carry-on and threw it into the trunk.

"A uniform makes an easy target."

Blunt, and another hard reality of the world they lived in.

There had been too many terrorist attacks around the world. And anyone in a military uniform was a particularly inviting target.

"I'm sorry, I didn't mean..." she started to apologize.

He cut her off. "Aye, you did mean it."

He knew where the attitude came from—the loss of her brother, the pain of that sort of thing, the helplessness, and the anger—things that couldn't be undone and had to be lived with.

"We'll leave it at that."

He slammed the trunk lid and rounded the car to the driver's side. He leaned against the roof line of the rental.

"I'm not the enemy. So, let's try this one more time. You're welcome for the help back there, although you probably could have taken the bastard down yourself with just a few words."

Direct shot.

She took a deep breath but held back what she would like to have said.

"The military is what I do," he continued. "Because there are dangerous people in the world. I don't get into the politics of it. I let other people do that, even when they fuck it up."

The anger was there, but carefully controlled. She heard it in the way the accent sharpened around the words.

He made a sweeping gesture of the car park. "If you have a problem driving up together, there are plenty of other cars. Help yourself."

Blunt, to the point. And she had to admit that she deserved it. She'd been condescending and judgmental, two things she had little patience for in others, none when it came to herself.

They stood there like a couple of MMA combatants, except he wasn't the enemy, and she didn't want to be. She was past the point of tired, and there was a lot to deal with once she reached Inverness. She slipped into the passenger seat and slammed the door.

CHAPTER
TWO

K ris awakened suddenly, disoriented in that way of waking in strange places when the brain slowly catches up.

It was dark, a thin stream of headlights angling past then disappearing in the distance, and she realized she must have been asleep for quite a while.

Everything gradually came back, along with the realization that they'd left the main roadway. A sign loomed out of the dark and icy rain as James Morgan angled the rental car around a curve in the road.

Kingussie.

It was one of a half-dozen small towns between Edinburgh and Inverness, spread out along the foot of the Cairngorm mountains. In the summer months it was a haven for cyclists and hikers. In the winter, the hikers and cyclists gave way to skiers.

The older part of the town was close to the roadway which had once been the only major coach road that linked the two cities. The newer parts of Kingussie spread back toward the hills with an assortment of inns, hotels, and restaurants.

The lights of a roadside tavern gleamed through the rain. He eased the rental car to the curb at the front of the Red Stag Alehouse beside a half-dozen other cars. He set the brake and cut the motor.

"We're stopping?" she asked.

"I'm hungry, and we've a couple more hours." He got out of the car and pulled on his jacket.

At least that was something they could agree on. She'd had only an energy bar since early morning, and she was suddenly starving. She grabbed her jacket and shoulder bag.

The air was sharp and a light snow had begun to fall as they drove north. Assuming she was going to make a quick trip over and then get back to New York, she'd only brought a light jacket, and shivered against the sudden cold after the heat inside the car.

Inside the alehouse, a fire burned at a hearth, large enough for a man to walk through, with logs piled high. The evening crowd had just started to arrive, along with a couple of older gentlemen who played at dice, one of them slamming the cup down on the table, the other roaring with laughter as he called for another round of ale, an older couple at a table near a street-side window with a black-and-white dog dozing at their feet, and two young couples who looked as if they had been hiking and got caught in the sudden change of weather.

Hats and jackets were lined up in front of the hearth, steaming faintly, while customers warmed themselves on pints of ale and amber-colored drinks that could only be whisky, probably from one of dozens of distilleries throughout Scotland.

The great room had the usual stag and boar heads mounted on walls over dark wood wainscoting. Comfortable-looking, overstuffed chairs sat before the massive fireplace. Framed pictures of sports teams filled the wall behind the bar. There were a half-dozen empty booths tucked beneath street-side windows, with more seating at tables and chairs. James Morgan headed for a table in the corner next to the fireplace.

He pulled the chair out for her, then took the one opposite against the wall. It triggered a memory, and she frowned. Her brother had done the same thing when he was home on leave and they went out to dinner.

"Habit," Mark once said with a shrug, dismissing it. "Crowded places."

She didn't understand at the time. Her friend Angie had explained it to her later. Her husband had served in the first Gulf War and it was one of those things that became so deeply ingrained that it was second nature to anyone who served in a war zone.

"They always want the wall at their back where they can see everything around them. It drove me crazy until I realized he was doing it to keep us safe, even in rural Virginia."

Her brother tried to make light of it. "Sort of like a John Wayne movie, your back against the wall of the saloon so you can see the bad guys coming."

Except that it wasn't a movie. It was all very real. And sometimes the bad guys were women or children who wore explosives hidden in their clothes. Her brother struggled with it. Three tours. Then he was gone.

Food was ordered at the tavern bar, then brought to the table, coffee cups lined up with two brewers going full time.

"They serve a decent hot beef sandwich," James commented. "Or you can order from the menu."

"I'll have whatever you're having," she replied, and caught the slightly surprised look in the angle of a dark brow.

"No mixed green salad with dressing on the side?"

She caught the undercurrent and chose to ignore it.

"I'm hungry."

While he went to the bar to place their order, she scrolled through her text messages, then scrolled back.

There was a message from Cate that had finally come through, sent just before the accident. It was flagged *important* and there was an attachment.

"We need to talk. I've sent you something."

Kris frowned. The attachment appeared to be a black-and-white photograph. But of what?

Noise from the bar had her looking up as a group of young men entered and lined up, throwing orders at the young waitress.

They had the look of locals, probably just off from work. There was pushing and shoving as pints of ale were served up.

"Aye, it's half-past six then," Kris heard the girl behind the bar say.

James returned to their table with two mugs of steaming coffee, but his gaze returned to the bar and the young men lined up there, telling jokes, attempting to flirt with the waitress who simply shook her head and returned to the kitchen to place their order. Some things were the same no matter what country you were in.

He glanced at her phone, the screen lit up.

"New message from Anne?"

She shook her head and tucked her cell phone back into her bag.

"An old message that just came through."

James set a mug in front of her. That dark gaze met hers.

"Technology is great, when it works."

The barrier came down a little, moving them past that first encounter at the airport and the silence afterward as they drove north. He gave her a half smile, the barrier dropping a little further in a temporary truce.

A loud whistle came from the direction of the bar as the group of young men drained their mugs and called for another round.

"Friday night," she commented.

"It's an excuse to do something stupid and say things you'll regret later." He shrugged. "But when you have your mates about, you're especially brave, and especially stupid."

"Says the voice of experience?" she asked.

"Some," he admitted.

"All mouth and no brains?"

"Aye, well, the brain doesn't kick in until around age twenty-five. You've had some experience with that?"

She nodded.

"Boyfriend?"

"My brother."

Although when she thought about it, the same could be said about a couple of boyfriends, one really serious relationship, and a brief marriage.

He nodded. The loss of her brother had been especially hard, according to what Anne had told him. It was there in her eyes, and the way she moved the conversation away.

"It looks like the owner is a serious sports fan."

Awards and trophies lined the wall behind the bar.

He nodded as the waitress brought their order to their table.

"It's impossible not to be when you're in the Highlands."

"You played?"

It fit that first impression of him—lean, athletic.

"Anne thought it was good for all that pent-up energy when I was a lad."

She caught the way he glanced over her shoulder toward the bar as their waitress returned, the loud comments with a few crude remarks thrown in.

"You call her by her name," Kris commented.

His coffee was almost gone. He stared thoughtfully at the cup.

"Aye, well she was very young when I was born," he explained. "As I got older, we looked to be more brother and sister. Other people called her by her name. So did I, she didn't seem to mind."

For the first time since leaving New York, the knot that had throbbed at the base of her skull had begun to unwind. She could have easily slipped into one of those overstuffed chairs in front of the fire and spent the next several hours there. Or possibly days.

"How long will you be at Inverness?"

He had barely touched the food in front of him, accepting another refill of coffee.

"Just a couple of days," Kris replied. "I need to meet with Cate's solicitors, then go out to the Tavern."

It all sounded so business-like.

"Once I have the manuscript she was working on I'll be going back to New York."

Except that it wasn't just business. She took a bite of the sandwich against the all-too-familiar hollow feeling in her stomach that had nothing to do with hunger.

"Anne was hoping you might stay for a while," he commented, watching her, the way she pushed her food around but barely touched it.

"I need to get back. There's a lot to do once I have the manuscript —editing, final decisions about marketing, possibly setting a new release date. It depends on how much work needs to be done." And that text message. Was it something about the book?

He continued to watch the group at the bar as they ate in silence. Kris grabbed the tab when their waitress returned.

"You paid for the car rental," she pointed out, and handed her credit card to the girl.

"I can see why you and Cate got along," James commented, as the girl cleared way their dinner plates. "You're like her."

"Stubborn?"

She'd heard that before, from her brother whenever they got into the usual brother-sister fights growing up. And she and Cate had a few constructive conversations over certain aspects of her books—characters that were too thinly disguised from people who were still living, things that could be revealed about places Cate had been, things she had seen.

Cate usually won, and her publisher had them make the usual disclosures in the front piece of each book after having the manuscripts vetted by their legal department to make certain they weren't exposing anything that would bring on a lawsuit. But she had won her share.

James nodded. "There's that. She had to be strong in her work, sure of herself," he replied, surprising her. "And to hell with anyone who didn't like it." That dark gaze narrowed on her. "You're like that."

Then he was glancing past her toward the bar again, where a disturbance had broken out among the group of young men. They had surrounded the waitress when she returned. When she tried to go around them, she was cut off, one young man reaching out and crudely touching her breast.

It might have been an accident, but her reaction was no accident. She punched him, hard, which only raised the stupid level as he grabbed her by the shoulders, his expression changing to anger.

James pushed his chair back from the table.

"Do you have our receipt, miss?" he asked the girl as he approached the group at the bar.

"Fuck off!" the one who'd grabbed her replied, then turned back to her.

"Enough, lads," James said, barely loud enough to be heard over the laughter and crude comments. "Leave her alone."

"And I said, fuck off!"

The change in him was barely noticeable, but Kris recognized it. She'd seen that same reaction once in her brother, when everything suddenly changed and became dangerous.

One of the other young men glanced in his direction, then made a comment to his companion. Another comment was made and they all laughed.

Kris didn't see him move, only what followed as he grabbed the young man's arm, twisted it behind him, then slammed him face down onto the bar. When the young man's companions would have gone after him, that dark gaze warned them back.

"Stand back or I'll break it off," James told them, in that same low voice that promised he would do exactly that, as he pulled the young man's arm up higher against his back.

"Son-of-a-bitch!" the young man screamed, his face pinned against the bar. "You broke my nose!"

The tavern owner came out of the kitchen behind the bar, a meat cleaver in one hand.

"What's this now?" he demanded, waving the cleaver in their direction.

"I've told you before. I'll not have your trouble in my place. Pay what you owe, then be on your way."

Several seconds passed. The tavern had gone silent except for the hiss of the fire at the fireplace and the clatter of a dish in the kitchen. Money was slapped down on the bar. As the others left, James released the young man who wiped the blood from his face with a tight expression.

"Get out!" the owner repeated.

The door of the Alehouse slammed behind him. The owner turned to the girl.

"Go on your way now, Lexie," he said gently. "You have customers waiting." He looked over at James as he tucked the cleaver under the bar.

"My apologies for the trouble."

"No problem," James assured him, as he picked up Kris's credit card.

It was after nine o'clock when they reached her hotel in Inverness. The snow had followed them, the air sharp with the changing season. He rounded the rental car and pulled her carry-on bag from the trunk, then walked with her across the lobby to the front desk.

She gave the front desk manager her credit card.

"Would you have broken that boy's arm?" she asked. That dark gaze met hers.

"I could have. That's all that matters." He set her bag down.

"I'll let Anne know you arrived safe and sound," he said in parting. "And don't worry about the boy. He'll have a few bruises, but he'll live."

Once inside her room, Kris leaned her carry-on against the wall. Even though it was late, and in the early morning hours New York time, she sent a quick text message to her publisher to let him know that she had arrived, and copied Alex at the London office, then scrolled back to that message from Cate.

She looked at the time it was sent, just hours before the accident but it hadn't come through right away.

"I've sent you something..."

Kris opened the attachment. There had been only that brief glimpse at the tavern at Kingussie. Studying it now, she was even more confused. It appeared to be a black-and-white photograph. But of what? And why had Cate sent it?

The image was blurred as if Cate had quickly taken the shot of the photograph and then sent it off. Studying it closer, it appeared to be a piece of artwork.

"We need to talk..."

Whatever the reason Cate had sent that message it, had been important.

But what did it mean?

CHAPTER
THREE
INVERNESS

The hotel front desk manager arranged a rental car for her the next morning for her appointment with Cate's lawyers and the drive afterward out to the Tavern, where Cate had lived after retiring.

The solicitor's office was located in the city business center a short drive from her hotel. The attorneys for her publisher had cleared all the legal hurdles for her before leaving London. After the meeting, the keys to the Tavern lay on the passenger seat beside her shoulder bag.

She navigated the turnaround at the town center, then caught the roadway north out of the city. The rain and snow were gone, the sun breaking through the clouds. The temperature was in the high forties, the morning air sharp with that blend of rain, earth, and time that was so typical of the Highlands.

Inverness was both old and new, the old castle on the hillside looming over the city, the newer part of the city glimpsed in modern offices and store fronts. As soon as she left the city, the old returned, a thousand years of history in the sprawling hills and glens that spread into the Highlands.

Old places, Cate once said about Scotland.

As a war correspondent on countless assignments, she had traveled to other old places over the years—Israel, the Far East, the

Middle East during both Gulf wars. But this was where she chose to live when she retired, and had started the next part of her life.

Her father, photographer Paul Bennett, whose career started during World War II with those iconic photographs of the bombing of London, battlefields, and then the Normandy invasion, had been born in Scotland. For Cate, it had been like coming home, reconnecting to the places he had told her about as a child.

She had lived almost her entire life in hotel rooms and one-room apartments in city towers with crowded elevators, or sleeping on bunks or cots in some remote location, bags constantly packed, preparing for that next assignment, a gypsy life not made for permanent relationships. It was the remoteness of Scotland that had drawn her. The great quiet of the mountains. After moving to Inverness, she often drove up into the Highlands, hiking some of those distant trails. Getting back to her roots, she called it, usually with a flask of her favorite single-malt tucked into her kit.

Wise, with a wicked sense of humor, C. B. Ross could hold her own interviewing heads of state, a dangerous third-world dictator, or the man on the street. She was completely unpretentious, generous to a fault, but didn't suffer fools. She'd lost her father and numerous friends along the way in that career, some of them on those battlefields. Each one was deeply felt. She had written about it.

"You cry, curse, and shake a fist at God, then you pull up your big-girl panties and get on with it!"

Kris was never certain if the saying was original to Cate, but she certainly embodied it.

The roadway stretched out beyond the city, giving way to rolling fields, stands of old oaks and elm trees, with a sharp pungent fragrance after the storm.

It hit her then, all the moments of the last several days that she'd kept under control, pushed the memories back, refused to think of anything except the book. But as she pulled into the tree-lined drive that had once been part of an old coach road on the outskirts of Inverness, surrounded by towering elms, it all swept over her and the tears came. Slowly at first, then streaming down her cheeks as she stared at the stone walls and the roofline, windows staring blankly back at her.

The scent of rain, wet leaves, the autumn season with winter not far behind, unique to the Highlands, swept over her when she stepped out of the car.

This time was different. The breeze in the branches of the old elm was different, the sound of the stream that ran behind the Tavern was different. The quiet was different.

She slowly walked up the flagstone walkway, half expecting Cate to throw open the door in greeting along with some comment about how long it had been since she was last there.

How long? The question hung in the brisk air.

She had been planning to come over when the book was finished, stay a few days, relax, maybe hike into the highlands.

Her hand was on the latch at the stout oak door.

Too long. She thought of something Cate once wrote in the front of one of her books.

"Every one of us loses something precious; lost opportunities, lost possibilities, feelings we can never get back. We have to hold onto the things that matter."

Feelings she could never get back—respect for someone who had shaped the way people viewed the world around them, admiration for someone who had never compromised even though it had cost her important assignments, then a successful author, and the friendship over the past eight years that came from working together on her books.

Tears? Cate would have laughed, that rich full-throated sound.

"Good God, girl! We'll have a drink. And then get on with it."

The iron latch at the oak door was original to the Tavern. Cate had insisted on keeping it. It had rusted into place. She'd had it restored by a craftsman in Inverness who specialized in restoring old fixtures. The key too was iron, heavy in her hand. Cate had it made, specially cut for the massive lock at the door.

"Get on with it," she told herself, turning the key.

The mustiness of old places, blended with the familiar smell of over two hundred-fifty years of whisky and ale made her smile. That too had been a big part of its appeal to Cate when she and Anne Morgan first set out to find her a place to call home.

"I've been in my share of bars. It feels like home."

Of course, it looked somewhat different from the pictures she had seen when Anne first discovered that it was for sale. There had been substantial restoration to bring it to what it looked like now, a fully functional tavern.

A sound greeted her, the meow of the resident cat, a black-and-white tuxedo the size of small dog, that had showed up on Cate's doorstep and then moved in. Cate had named him Rob Roy—Robbie for short.

"He robs the food off my plate when he should be catching mice, but we get along," Cate explained. She'd never been in one place long enough to have a pet, and hadn't expected him to hang around.

"He likes an occasional nip of ale, and warms the bed. My kind of male!"

But Robbie the cat had stayed, wandering in an out of the Tavern like a regular customer. Whenever Kris had stayed at the Tavern, he somehow found his way onto her bed in the guest room. He was a great foot-warmer.

She bent down and picked him up. He curled over her shoulder and started purring.

"What are you doing in here?"

It wasn't like Cate to leave him locked inside when she left for a few days. There was usually a large food bowl left at the back landing, or he scrounged for himself outside until she got back. The only answer she got was that loud rumbling in her ear.

"You miss her," she said, rubbing a cheek against the soft fur.

She had grown up with an assortment of pets—a succession of dogs, cats, a couple of hamsters, and the usual assortment of goldfish that seemed to survive everything.

It was only when she got older that she learned the goldfish regularly went on to fish heaven and were replaced without her knowing it. That had been a rude awakening at the age of nine.

The cat made himself comfortable on her shoulder as she walked through the Tavern.

Cate had it restored, using as much of the original fixtures and materials that could be salvaged. She had contacted a local historian, learned as much as she could about the history of the Tavern, then hired local carpenters and craftsmen for the work. It had taken over three years.

The wood floor had been beyond salvage, caved in to the dirt underneath, with all sorts of rodents living there. The new flooring was milled locally, and glass for windows was reproduced the same as it was two hundred years earlier. The only concessions to modern technology were electricity and plumbing. The fixtures were all authentic, simply restored with wiring for lights instead of whale oil or candles.

Cate had rented an apartment in town and drove out daily from Inverness to check on the progress. When it was finished, the Tavern had been restored to its former glory, right down to the original bar that had been salvaged, complete with nicks and gouges no doubt made by some regulator's pistol or highwayman's knife.

Just as it had almost three hundred years ago, shelves lined the wall behind the bar, stocked with ale and whisky, in bottles instead of casks, with labels from local distilleries. But a special place was reserved for her favorite—a forty-year single malt. They had opened a bottle and toasted the completion of the restoration on the Tavern, then again when her first book sold over a million copies.

The main room of the Tavern became a gathering place for friends from her days as a correspondent reporting for major networks from war-torn countries, and celebrations with Anne Morgan and friends she'd made after moving to Inverness. An interview by the BBC had once taken place there. But it was the taproom through the doorway at the end of the bar that had become Cate's creative haven.

A couple hundred years earlier, the tap room had provided storage for casks of ale and whisky for travelers to quench their thirst on their journey to and from the Highlands. The casks were still there, empty, except for a couple that occupied the shelves behind the desk with Cate's computer, printer, satellite receiver, and widescreen television, and the wall, symbolic of another wall—the Berlin Wall.

Cate, along with her cameraman, was one of a handful of journalists assigned to cover the fall of the Berlin Wall. She had interviewed dozens of Berliners in the days leading up to that historic event, candid interviews that had brought the world into that divided city, like so many other historic events Cate had been part of. At the top of her wall was the date the Wall had come down and a stone retrieved from the rubble.

Like the Berlin Wall, it was covered with Cate's own graffiti—notes, pieces of paper with dates and other reminders, a plot diagram for the next book she was planning, receipts, newspaper and magazine articles, and the date at the very top: November 9, 1989.

The 'wall' had fascinated Kris, filled with newspaper and magazine articles about prominent heads of state, the assassination of a third-world dictator, or the bombing of a remote target in Afghanistan —history in the making.

"I interviewed the son-of-a-bitch!" Cate had pointed out the picture of the cave opening in that remote hideout in the mountains of Afghanistan, the last known hiding place of one of the terrorists in the months after the first Trade Center attack.

"He was educated, articulate, and an absolutely crazy bastard."

But she had gotten the story, little realizing until years later that she had interviewed one of the most notorious terrorists in history.

Now Kris thought back over the past few years and wondered how many times they had sat across from each other in the main room. Or in the taproom, discussing Cate's latest book, arguing some plot point that needed to be changed to protect the innocent, and not-so-innocent.

She was going to miss that—the conversations, the stories, the laughter, but most of all she was going to miss Cate; her strength, that go-to-hell attitude that had won her a Pulitzer for her work as a journalist who always looked for the truth.

"*Firinn*, the Scots call it." Cate once told her, as she saw the profession of journalism changing.

"God knows it's in short supply these days."

She set Robbie down. She rounded the end of the bar and felt along the wall inside the doorway to the taproom for the light switch. She flipped on the lights and stopped just inside the doorway.

"Damn."

CHAPTER
FOUR

The taproom had been ransacked.

Drawers at the desk had been emptied, papers scattered everywhere. Black-and-white photographs, hundreds of them taken by Cate's father over his career as a photographer, had been pulled from old library card file drawers that Cate had salvaged, and were strewn across the floor. The laptop computer lay in the corner, the screen broken and skewed at an angle.

The back door of the taproom stood ajar and creaked faintly at a gust of afternoon wind. The latch had been pried away, and the lock with it.

"Damn," she swore again, then spun around at a faint tapping sound.

It came again, a shadow falling across the taproom window, then again, as the wind stirred a branch of the elm tree outside against the glass. She slowly let out the breath she'd been holding.

She'd been through this before, once in college, returning from classes to find her room ransacked, her computer, CD player, television, and anything else that could be turned for easy cash or drugs, gone.

The usual police report had followed, along with an extra set of locks, but nothing eased that feeling that she'd been violated, that someone had gone through her things, and taken anything of value. She'd cleaned the room from top to bottom, replaced everything with insurance money, but it did little for that feeling of helplessness, that feeling that it didn't matter how many locks she put on the door, someone would get past them.

She felt a little better after she had moved, but that feeling never completely went away. It was there now, even though it wasn't her home or apartment that had been broken into—helplessness, then anger.

At the doorway, Rob Roy peered at her curiously, then set about washing his face with cat-nonchalance.

"You go right ahead with what you're doing," she told the cat.

Somehow it made the Tavern feel not so empty to hear a voice, even if it was her own.

She picked up the desk phone, momentarily struck by a memory when Cate had it installed.

"No cell coverage! Don't you love it! I wonder if they come in colors. We had one on the wall when I was growing up—harvest gold."

The phone was black and looked as if it might have been sitting on a shelf since World War II, but it worked, the tone reassuring as she dialed the number. There was no answer at Anne's office. She hesitated, then called James Morgan.

He surveyed the damage, picking up a black-and-white photograph, then setting it down.

A Leica camera with several very expensive lenses, that had belonged to Paul Bennett, sat on the shelf behind the desk next to another camera that he had used to take those iconic photographs during World War II.

Both cameras were probably considered collector items, no doubt all the more valuable because of their connection to Bennett. Other photographs, hundreds of them, a record of his career and countless awards over the years, were scattered across the floor.

Who went to all the trouble to break into a place, he thought; ransacked it no doubt in search of money or anything of value that could be quickly turned to buy drugs or black-market video games, then left two extremely valuable cameras—one highly collectible, as well as the flat screen television, computer, and other equipment?

"What about jewelry, money, credit cards?"

Kris shook her head. "She had a few pieces of jewelry from her father, but she didn't wear them. She kept those in a safe deposit box. Money, credit cards, she would have had those on her when..."

He caught the hesitation.

"Aye, that makes sense," he replied.

"Other things," she went on, "mementoes from places she went on assignment, things she was given..." She made a sweeping gesture of the taproom.

"I don't think there was anything of real value."

She picked up a small statue of the Virgin Mary that had been swept to the floor along with the laptop computer, a gift from the Holy See after a story she did on the Vatican and its somewhat colorful history.

No holds barred, Cate hadn't avoided the controversial issue of the role of the Vatican during World War II, but she hadn't sensationalized it either. Out of gratitude or perhaps mutual understanding, she had been presented with a St. Christopher's medal on behalf of the Pope at that time, for protection. Then years later for one of those books, she was given unprecedented access to the Vatican archives.

The book became a bestseller, condemned by the Pope then in residence, for the questions it raised based on centuries-old doctrine that had come full circle to the present, history repeating itself because of the actions and decisions of powerful men in the Church. She had met and interviewed some of those men during her long career.

She and Cate once talked about it, about fate, and the fact that nothing was by coincidence, a long conversation in front of a fire in the hearth at the Tavern.

"You don't live as long and see as many things as I have without realizing that nothing is coincidence, or by chance," Cate had said at the time. "We all have a role to play, a path to follow. We're put in certain situations for a reason." She had laughed then—laughter filled with irony.

"I was going to be a teacher, a nice, respectable profession. My generation, that's what women did—nurses or teachers. That's what my father wanted—a nice, stable profession, meet someone, settle down with a family." That laugh again.

"He didn't exactly follow his own advice. Neither did I. "

A chance encounter at a university lecture had set Catherine Bennett Ross in a different direction. She worked for a brief time under Tom Wolfe, but journalism was changing in the radical 60's.

The new journalism movement became involved in the action of a story. Because she had been raised out of a suitcase on her father's assignments that took them all over the world, the new movement whetted her appetite for the stories about people and places that weren't reached from a desk in London or New York.

There were roadblocks and controversies along the way that were all part of her—knowledgeable, driven, principled, trusted, tough when she had to be, and included a brief stay in jail for refusing to reveal a source. All of it went into the person she became, but always that laugh, sometimes ironic, sometimes self-deprecating, often with a meaning that left the other person or the viewing audience wondering what she wasn't telling them.

Then there was the serious side, where viewers kept tuned in, and readers later found in her books—integrity, hard truths, strength. Only once had viewers ever seen the other side of her, the person who had handed over a meal to a boy who was starving in Anbar province, or a few favors called in when she had arranged for a truckload of food to be diverted to a village in Africa where the inhabitants were starving after warring factions had destroyed their crops and livestock—the same person who held an American soldier who lay dying and had pushed away the camera so that his family wouldn't see his death on the nightly news.

Months later, she had paid a visit to his family at her own expense, with no press, no cameraman, just the last words he had spoken.

"I owed him and his family that much," she said about it then. "He wasn't afraid at the end, just sad that he couldn't go home. It helped me understand things about what my father had gone through during the war, the things he had seen, the photographs he took. That boy gave me a helluva lot more in those last moments, than I gave him."

It was that part of Catherine Bennett Ross that had shown through in her books, stories of people caught in incredible times, the games powerful people played, and the humanity that often came out of nowhere and changed the course of events.

James stayed with her until the police arrived.

Some things were the same no matter where you were. She showed them her identification along with the authorization letter to retrieve the manuscript from Cate's solicitors.

"Everything appears to be in order," the lead officer, Inspector Simson commented after he'd read through the paperwork.

"You're from New York?" he asked.

She nodded. "I was Ms. Ross's editor."

There was a comment that was more a sound, as he took pictures of the documents with his phone.

"We'll need to check this out. And what is your interest in this, Morgan?"

They had made eye contact, and a brief nod of acknowledgment when the police constables first arrived.

"Didn't know you were back," the inspector said, a sliding glance at James Morgan.

"A short stay," James replied. "Nothing for you to be concerned about."

Inspector Simson looked up, met that dark gaze, then quickly went back to his notes, hastily entered into the I-pad.

"We'll need your contact information, Miss McKenna, if we should have more questions." Then, with a look about the taproom, "We've seen an increase in crime the past few years. Unfortunate business burglary."

"Friend of yours?" Kris asked as they left the Tavern.

"One of our finest," James commented drily. "We attended St. Luke's together, then second levels. He'll file his report and make a statement to the media because that's what he's good at. Then, because of the media coverage, he'll reassure the public that every-thing is being done to find the person who's responsible. But the truth is, he couldn't find his arse with both hands—the perfect public servant."

"Little Dickie Simson?" Anne replied. There was something in her voice, not quite disapproval but close enough.

"As I remember, he was always such a disagreeable child,

throwing tantrums, banging his head on the floor as a toddler when the two of you were in day care."

"The same," James replied, over a cup of coffee.

They'd met Anne Morgan at her office. An appointment had run late and she had just finished signing up a property for a holiday rental.

"He always was a bit of a..." Anne paused, searching for the right word.

"Wanker?" James filled in the blank. "The sort who always does the minimum required, but likes to take full credit," he explained.

Kris was familiar with the term. Obviously there was no love lost between them.

Anne gave him one of those looks, that held for a moment and said volumes, then a faint smile. She was reserved, the sort who listened rather than jumped into a conversation, an admirable quality in her line of business dealing with clients and rental properties, both local and foreign travelers.

Over the years, she had built up a successful property management business and knew the importance of building strong business relationships. She had worked with Cate to find just the right place to live after she decided to retire to Scotland. The two women were a study in contrasts.

Cate had traveled the world, reporting from war zones, remote outposts, and mountain encampments. She was medium height, outspoken, wore khaki and boots, with blue eyes that could cut a person down to size, her hair classically short gone to silver, a look she was famous for in hundreds of interviews from those remote places. She had grown up in a man's world paving the way for other women journalists and correspondents, learned to hold her own, and never backed down from a good argument, or a good bottle of Scotch.

Anne Morgan was refined, understated in wool sweaters and skirts, with either a string of pearls or a simple gold chain and a flash of color in a neck scarf, her thick, dark hair like her son's, with a natural wave and worn chin-length with layers that softly framed her face. She had been married once.

It was a bottle of forty-year-old single malt that had bonded two women so different from each other on the surface. Anne had given the bottle to Cate as a gift to celebrate the purchase of the Tavern after a year of looking for just the right place.

As Cate told it, the two women sat in the main room of the Tavern, both with feet propped up on one of the few tables still remaining— one in hiking boots, the other in three-inch heels, with a fire burning at the stone hearth, the roof sagging over their heads, weeds growing up through the floorboards—and polished off the whisky and another bottle Cate had stored in the bar.

They were as different as two people could be in background and life experiences, but connected in the way that opposites often connect, and discovered they were not so very different after all. Two girls getting together over a bottle of very fine Scotch.

It was a party Kris would like to have attended, just to sit in the corner and watch the two of them.

"Well, I suppose he's good enough at what he does. Burglary, you said?" Anne shook her head.

"It wasn't just burglary," James commented. "Someone was looking for something."

Kris frowned. "A famous person dies, no one home, an easy target..."

It was common, and made sense, as much as she hated to admit it. He gave her a hard look—you're a smart girl, think about it.

"Nothing was taken—cameras, her computer, or this," he held up the St. Christopher's medal. He dropped it into her hand, then pushed away from the desk.

"Enjoy yourselves."

"You're leaving?" Anne said with surprise. "I was hoping you'd have supper with us."

"I'm off to the gym, and then over to Will's place for some hard labor."

She saw the worried expression on Anne's face. "I ran into Karen at market a few days ago. It seems Will has a new motorbike."

James crumpled his cup and tossed it into the wastebasket.

"How is Tom Jeffries, by the way?" he asked, changing the subject.

Kris glanced from one to the other, aware that somewhere in this conversation was a topic he chose not to discuss.

"Tom is quite well, thank you," Anne replied.

"You should know that he asked for my approval, last time I was home," he commented.

Anne was startled. "Approval? For what?"

He leaned across the desk. "For whatever is going on between the two of you."

"I don't believe I need your approval," she replied.

His expression shifted.

"Tom does."

He grabbed his jacket from the back of the chair. "He's a good man. Don't be hard on him. Say yes, the next time he asks."

"You'll be careful?" Anne said.

He flashed her a smile as he left the office.

"Always."

"Damn," she swore softly when he'd gone.

Anne had made reservations at the River House. It was cozy, intimate, with tables that looked out on the River Ness. Kris had come there once before with Cate and her London publishers.

"You must know that Cate was very fond of you," Anne said as their orders were taken.

"Not in so many words, of course, that wasn't her way. It was in the other things she did say," Anne went on to explain. "About how you fought for her first book when the publisher wanted her to write her memoirs—he thought it would be more marketable, more sales; how you went to the distributors and convinced them to increase their orders because you were certain it was going to be a bestseller; and how you convinced her that she needed to go with a certain cover design that set the tone for the other books that followed. It's probably the only time that I heard her admit that she was wrong about something." That smile again.

"She was a bit put-off about that. But she admitted that you were right, and admired the fact that you stood up to her."

Kris smiled to herself. That was putting it mildly. Cate had threatened to pull her book from Ellison Publishing and take it someplace else where she didn't have to argue over every point.

The point Kris finally made was that it was Cate's job to write the book, it was her job to get it published.

"I think a better description would be pissed off," Kris admitted, taking a sip of wine, remembering the arguments.

"You were right though," Anne replied. "And she trusted you because of it." She was thoughtful. "She would trust you now to see it through with this last book."

See it through. Her brother Mark had said that once, before he went back the last time.

"The others are still over there," he had told her. "I have to see it through. I owe it to them."

"How do you do it?" Kris asked, trying to figure out how to say something that was so deeply personal.

"How do you deal with the possibility that he might not...?" She hesitated and decided against asking it.

"That he might not come back?" Anne suggested, taking up the question.

She said nothing for several moments, her expression thoughtful. Then, she set her glass of wine down and folded her hands before her on the linen tablecloth.

"It's not the wounds, although that gave me quite a turn when they brought him back this last time, to see your child like that." Another expression then, not quite a smile.

"Except that he's not a child." Anne looked over at her. "You didn't notice? I'm not surprised. He doesn't let on, you see. It's not his way, never has been. I suppose it has to do with the way he was raised, stoic Scottish attitude, carry on, and all that.

"And he always felt that he had to be the strong one, the man of the house with just the two of us when he was growing up, he was always taking care of me and everyone else." She was thoughtful.

"It's been almost four months since I received the call from his friend Danny. I don't know the details, of course. You're not allowed to know, military secrets and all that. He was in hospital for a long time after arriving from Germany. It was a bit rough there for a while." She took a deep breath and another sip of wine.

"Their unit was attacked. That much I do know. You don't hear about that in the news reports. He lost several on his team, and James was badly wounded." She paused, staring off at some distant point.

"His shoulder was the worst of it. They had to re-build it. There was a lot of damage to the muscles and tendons, that sort of thing.

Four surgeries later, they've sent him home for a bit with frequent trips back to London to check on progress, and a lot of physical therapy. He has to go back in a few days." She angled a look at Kris.

"Don't get me wrong, I love having him home but it has changed him. That and the time before. The wounds were...different, deep inside. He struggled with that, and I felt him slipping away, into a place where I couldn't reach him. Cate was here then. It was right after she bought the Tavern.

"He spent a great deal of time there, working on the Tavern. It's worse, I think, than physical wounds. Physical wounds heal, eventually. But the other wounds..." She looked off again.

"To this day he's never spoken of it, but I know that time out at the Tavern changed him. What he went through is still inside, just beneath the surface, a part of him. It comes out every once in a while, a look, something that's said, then he hides it all away again." She stared down into her wine glass.

"He works out at the health club when he's home, getting his strength back. It's been slow progress, but he's determined..."

Kris knew the rest of it, the way it had been with her brother. "To go back."

Anne nodded. "Yes, you see he feels responsible for the ones who didn't make it."

She knew about that too, the bond where rank disappeared when things got ugly. Her brother had spoken about it, lines that disappeared when the man, or woman, next to you was someone you counted on, someone who might save your life. Or you might save theirs.

"It's just very difficult knowing the danger, knowing how he is about things. He feels that he let his teammates down. You saw a bit of that at the office. And there are other things. He doesn't let anyone in, doesn't let anyone get close." She was thoughtful again.

"You asked how I deal with it," Anne continued. "With a great deal of hair color to cover the gray, and a lot of sleepless nights." She took a sip of wine.

"Wine helps." Then she was serious again.

"It's not up to me, you see. It's who he is, who I raised him to be. If he has the courage to make the hard choice, then I have to have the courage to accept it."

Kris looked over at her. She'd never thought of it that way and realized there were all kinds of courage.

"So, what's next?" Anne asked, changing the subject. "What will you do about the manuscript? It will be a few days before Inspector Simson will have his report ready, trust me on that. And then there will be the insurance claims to be submitted."

She had been thinking about that on the drive back to Inverness.

Not just a burglary, James Morgan had said, but someone looking for something. But what? The manuscript?

Stealing it made no sense. There had been enough publicity about Cate's next book, that it would easily be recognized, and any attempt to sell it would bring down a criminal investigation and numerous lawsuits.

What then? Money? Anything that could be easily turned on the street for drugs? But, as James pointed out, it didn't appear that anything of real value had been taken.

"I need to let my publisher know everything that's happened," she replied as their server arrived with their supper. She wasn't looking forward to that conversation.

"And I still need to find the manuscript."

"What about Cate's computer?" Anne asked over a second glass of wine.

"The police have it for evidence. It was badly damaged. I don't know if anything can be retrieved."

Anne was thoughtful for several moments. "There's someone who might be able to help with that. He owns an internet café in the old part of town," she explained.

"He does computer programming, web hosting, and some other kind of work on the side that he's rather vague about. He's bit of a character," she went on.

"But once you get past the eye shadow and all the tattoos, he really is very talented. There was a bit of a dust-up last year with the authorities about someone who was one of the regulars at the café, some sort of illegal activity. The authorities made a bit of a to-do about it, but nothing ever came of it." She took another sip of wine.

"He did some work for Cate last year when her old computer crashed. He was able to retrieve everything for her, and then set her up with off-site storage in case it ever happened again. They got along famously, but then Cate had a way about her. She was working with him on an archive of her father's work for a gallery in London. I have his number if you'd like to ring him up."

It was two bottles of wine and late when she got back to her hotel. She checked her phone messages and frowned as she scrolled through a half dozen from her publisher. It was after office hours in New York, everyone would have already gone home for the weekend. And she had no answers.

She scrolled through the contacts until she found the number Anne had given her. It was after midnight, but some places never closed. She pressed the icon on her phone.

"You've reached the Internet Café," a young woman's voice came on the message. "It's Gamer Night. If you've reached this message, it means we are off to another universe, fighting battles, and slaying dragons. Do stop by or leave your number, we'll get back to you."

Gamer Night. She ended the call without leaving a message.

One of the assistants at her office was into internet gaming, and had invited her along to one of their sessions. At the time, her publisher was putting out a book on the widespread popularity of internet gaming, and she had accepted the invitation to verify first-hand some of the information that was included, and out of curiosity over something she'd heard a lot about but had only limited experience with. It had been fascinating, and intense.

The usual gamer night bore no resemblance to World of War or other video games found on the commercial market. Their world was an underground network of players that spanned the country and beyond, and participants took everything very seriously to the point of stalking other gamers and sabotaging them in an attempt to take them out of play, all with alter identities. Throw in the occasional investigation by the FCC or NSA, and she decided this part of the cyber world was a little too dangerous for comfort.

She'd opted out of the next invitation, even though the experience helped validate the book, which sold well within the gaming community.

Eye shadow and tattoos.

She didn't care if Innis had blue hair, if he was able to help her find Cate's manuscript.

CHAPTER
FIVE

The Internet Café was in the part of the city that dated back to the days of good old Prince Charlie and the '45 Rebellion, surrounded by three-hundred-year-old buildings that had been converted into an eclectic blend of boutiques, specialty shops, art galleries, pubs, and cafés.

It was Saturday, and in spite of the late season, there were a lot of tourists out on a cold morning, students, and locals dressed in sweatshirts and jeans, woolen sweaters, and Macs.

She had been a theology major at college with a history minor, then changed her major her third year. She had never lost her passion for history, though, and had spent days in the old part of the city on earlier visits over, exploring narrow cobbled streets and other old places, poking about churches with gravestones that told their own stories.

Old places, as Cate called them, and stories waiting to be discovered.

It was early, but the phone message when she called simply stated, "We're open."

She turned at the next corner and eased the rental car to the curb next to a gleaming black motorcycle. She cut the motor and grabbed her shoulder bag. At the end of the cobbled sidewalk, James Morgan leaned against the saddle of a gleaming black BMW, a to-go cup of coffee in one hand.

"Dangerous," she commented, gesturing to the powerful motorcycle, and recalling her conversation with Anne Morgan the night before, and the worried expression on her face at the thought he might re-injure himself.

He shrugged a shoulder. "It's only my second cup. It's not dangerous until the fourth or fifth one."

"I meant the motorcycle."

He knew exactly what she meant. "We all have to die sometime."

As soon as he said it, he knew he'd touched a nerve. He saw it in her eyes as they darkened, the tiny frown lines that appeared as she fought back unwanted emotion.

"I was thinking of Anne."

Direct shot, and not the first time. He'd tapped into something she didn't usually let anyone see. He recognized it. Wounds, that had yet to heal. He knew a little about that.

"Let's start over," he said. "Anne asked me to stop by." He cut a glance to the Internet Café.

"This place attracts a lot of different sorts, and Innis can be..."

"A real wanker?" she replied.

Truce. He nodded.

"Aye, well, he can be a bit of a hooligan, even though Cate apparently got along well enough with him. But Cate had a way about her."

"Meaning?"

"She didn't take any shit off anyone."

She grabbed the handle on the door. "Neither do I."

Innis was everything Anne had described, and more. Tattoos covered every inch of his body, at least all the visible parts. She could only guess at the parts that weren't visible. And the various colors of eye shadow had been applied in layers over light blue eyes. It was striking, and set off the blue hair. And he was in costume—camouflage pants, t-shirt, combat boots, and the headband.

"It's a bit wild in here this morning," he explained after introductions were made.

"Most of the gang have been up for two days straight. It's that way when you go to war."

By *war*, he obviously meant the gamers who were wired in at different computer stations around the café, planning strategies, launching attacks, fighting off counter-attacks, the streets in chaos, smoke billowing from a burned-out military vehicle—the usual chaos and destruction that lured both men and women to the world of internet gaming.

She caught the expression on James' face as he stepped into that make-believe world that was far removed from the real world that he and so many others fought in each day, a world where there were no breaks to eat, smoke a joint, or go to the restroom. A world of real blood and death.

Wanker. She thought of that as she spoke with Innis and explained the reason she was there.

"Cate's editor," he exclaimed. "All the way from New York! I've got this great idea for a book. A thriller, lots of action with some great sex thrown in...!"

She smiled. If she had a dollar for every time she heard that. "When you have something put together, I'd be happy to take a look," she replied, then brought them back to the reason they were there.

"You did some work for Cate when her computer crashed last year."

He shrugged. "I help a lot of customers. Yer mum is one of them." He threw a smile at James.

"I set up her website for her rental company. That sort of thing. Simple stuff."

"You also set up off-site storage for Cate on her own server."

He shrugged again. "Basic stuff, secure, in case her computer crashed again."

"I need access to that site."

Blue eyebrows disappeared into the purple headband. Before he could respond, a young woman appeared at his elbow. She was small with short-cropped black hair spiked up all over her head, zombie make-up, and also dressed for combat.

"What about her computer?" he suggested. "Anything she was working on would probably be there."

She and James exchanged a look. "That's not an option." She explained about the break-in at the Tavern.

"That's raw," he replied. "I suppose it takes all sorts in this world."

The young woman gave them both a look. "Kim needs your help," she said insistently, indicating a young Asian man at one of the computer terminals.

"Look, I'm sorry about Cate," Innis started to explain. It was the typical brush-off.

"I'd really like to help, but I have customers waiting."

"And I have a court order," Kris informed him.

Blue eye shadow was vivid against suddenly pale skin. "Look, I don't want any trouble from the authorities."

"Innis!" the young woman insisted impatiently.

"Bugger off, Luna!" he snapped. "I'll be there in a minute." He turned to Kris.

"I don't know if I can help," he said hesitantly. "Everything is protected. Only Cate had the password. Security and all that."

Three excuses rolled into one, his voice climbing with each one.

James leaned across the counter. "Then, go in through the back door."

She didn't know who was more surprised, herself or Innis.

"I don't know..."

"You set up the server," James cut him off. "There's always the usual access built in with a particular code sequence. You created it, you can break in."

Kris glanced at Innis, dressed in camo, combat boots, with blue eye shadow, then at James Morgan in jeans and sweatshirt. The pretend soldier, and the other who had no need to pretend.

"Well, I suppose if you have an order from the court." Innis replied. "But not out here. My computer is in back."

"Go in through the back door?" she whispered as they followed him to a workstation in an office at the back of the café.

"All servers have them. It sort of blows the theory about security. But then you Yanks have your own issues with secure servers."

She stared at him as he followed Innis. He stopped at the door to the office.

"Are you just going to stand there? You'll miss the show. This should be interesting."

Innis closed the door and then sat down at the computer at the desk. "I set this up for her last year." He made several key strokes, scrolled through a screen of codes, then entered more key strokes.

"She wanted it for personal information, banking, the usual sort of thing."

"What about the book she was working on?" Kris asked.

"Aye, that too." He entered more information, scrolled through again, then entered additional information.

Watching him work, Kris was reminded about the old saying—anything someone could build or encrypt, someone else could hack into.

He found what he was looking for, entered more information, hesitated, then hit two final keys on the keyboard. The screen lit up with rows of data.

"We're in," he announced.

Kris rounded the desk and leaned over his shoulder, scanning through the files that came up. There were the usual—banking, bills, tax information, copies of media releases, files for topics she had been researching, along with files of sources, interviews over the years, articles that had appeared in newspapers, and taped interviews throughout her career, separate files for each of her previous books, and then a file name that Kris recognized, the working title of Cate's next book.

"Open that one."

She spent the next three hours going through the file, reading through chapter after chapter, then searching through other files. A sandwich Innis had brought in earlier was untouched as she sat back at the workstation.

"Did you find it?" James asked.

He'd left earlier to take the motorcycle back to his friend Will, who was doing work on James' car. He'd spent the last hour exploring the café. She shook her head.

"Just an earlier draft that I saw several months ago. We discussed changes and I know Cate was working on them. But they're not here." The latest back-up that she'd saved was almost two months earlier.

She thought of the damaged computer. Was it possible Cate simply hadn't backed up more recent work? Had she gone off on a brief getaway to clear her head after working on the book for the past year? Some time off to connect with old friends? Writer's block?

It happened to the most successful writers. Or was it something else? She looked up as Innis came back into the office.

"You were doing some other work for Cate for a gallery showing of her father's photographs in London." She recalled what Cate had mentioned months earlier. And she had connected with a gallery in London for the showing.

Paul Bennett's work was known world-wide, iconic pictures that had documented world events and appeared in magazines for over fifty years. It was said that his photographs often showed a side of those events that might never otherwise have been seen—the human side. Cate had been more excited about the gallery showing than the release of her next book.

"I didn't find any photographs on the server."

"What about the store room," James suggested.

Innis looked at both of them. "I was going to get to that." He gave James a narrow look, then stepped past them both.

"I usually keep it locked." And with a look at James. "I never know who's going to come snooping about." He pushed the door open, reached a hand along the inside wall, and flipped a switch to a bank of overhead lights.

The room was long and narrow, and spanned the width of the café at the back. It was lined with the usual steel racks and shelves on one side, and a work counter with a sink along the opposite wall. Several trays sat side-by-side on the counter. A wire line had been strung over the counter. He'd obviously been working recently. Several photographs hung from the wire. The wall behind it was lined with photographs that had been enlarged and displayed under special lighting. There must have been at least fifty of them, black-and-white images from another time and place. Paul Bennett's photographs.

"She brought me the film to archive, and then enhance for the exhibit—Bankside Gallery in London. She wanted certain photos enlarged and the detail sharpened. A lot of detail can get lost when enlarging from a small image, and some of the film was so old it was beginning to deteriorate. She was afraid it would be lost forever.

"It took a lot of work to restore the photographs. There were a few where there was no film, just the finished photograph. Those I had to take digital prints, then work with the images. Painstaking shit. But it was worth it."

And a great deal of very expensive equipment by the looks of it. Kris stared up at those photographs, a lifetime's work, pictures of the

Allied landings at Normandy, soldiers caught in those moments of life and death, expressions haunted as they shared a cigarette. And others—a young Frenchwoman with a cat leaning out of a second-story window, the building scarred by bombardment, a single flower in the pot on the windowsill, struggling, surviving against the larger subject of scarred buildings and the street below filled with tanks and soldiers.

She'd seen some of Paul Bennett's work before, images that appeared in the media years before when he passed away, again on the seventieth anniversary of the end of the war, and in photographs Cate had displayed at the Tavern. But those photographs didn't compare to the ones she saw now.

The detail was so much sharper. Background images seemed to leap out at her, and those other images, the faces, their eyes seemed to look straight at her, each one like a haunting work of art.

"This is incredible," she whispered.

Innis was an artist, with an eye for the emotion to be found in those photographs.

"I've played around with photography for years," he explained. "The way a shift in the light changes everything, a single image that can bring out so much. Firinn, Cate called it."

"Truth," Kris recalled.

Like father, like daughter, she thought. Truth, in the images captured in Paul Bennett's photographs, and truth in Cate's career and the stories she had told and then written. She stopped in front of the next photograph and stared at the enlarged photograph.

Like the others, it was a simple black-and-white photograph. There was nothing remarkable about it. Nothing and everything. It was identical to the photograph attached to the message Cate had sent.

"I've sent you something. We need to talk."

"What do you know about this photograph?" she asked Innis.

He shrugged. "When I first saw it, I thought it was very like a photograph a tourist might take—you know, on holiday, castles, ruins, paintings, things like that. It didn't fit with the others he had taken. And it was one of the ones with no film, just the photograph. But Cate was quite taken by it. She tucked a print of it in her notebook."

There were other photos, British troops, landing craft, German bunkers above the beaches, civilians caught in everyday life trying to survive, a young man with a rifle hung over one shoulder, and a young woman with dark hair and equally dark eyes, dressed in a heavy coat, her hair windblown. But it was her gaze that caught Kris's attention as she stared over her shoulder, something the camera caught in that moment when the photograph was taken. Something almost intimate.

"French Resistance," James said, staring at the image over her shoulder. "There were a great number of them who worked with the Allies during the war, providing information, even doing some of the dirty work themselves. The outcome might have been different without their help."

"You know your history," Kris said, with more than a little surprise.

He shook his head. "Required study. I didn't care to have Sister Margaret Alice twist my ear off for not paying attention. She was a tyrant about history."

She tried to visualize that as they left the dark room. Somehow the image of James Morgan, dutiful student, and Catholic school didn't exactly come together.

It was after seven in the evening. She'd spent the better part of the day at the café, and she had nothing. Except that photograph, no clue what it meant, or the reason Cate had sent it.

The evening crowd had begun to arrive—couples, singles, groups of others, Luna intense at a computer as she challenged another player and sent all her warriors into battle, while Innis coached another customer on gaming strategies.

It always amazed her the time spent in gaming rooms like the café. Didn't people have lives?

As they left the café, she caught a glimpse of the evening news on an overhead screen. Brynn Halliday, who dominated the evening news in London, had just finished her previous segment.

She was Sky News' rising star in a tough, no-holds-barred business, and polar opposite of Cate in both talent and reputation. Tabloid journalism was more her style, where anything was fair game, even if it meant stretching the truth, twisting it, or no truth at all. Video images flashed across the screen about a train wreck outside Brussels, several cars derailed, passengers dazed and bleeding.

Sensationalism. The tabloid press and the internet.

"The woman is a shark," James commented. "Anything for a story."

Kris heard the disgust in his voice. "You don't like her."

"It's the smell of blood, and she doesn't care whose blood, as long as it boosts her career. She did a piece last year on military families who've lost sons and daughters in the Gulf War, causing more pain for people who were already in a lot of pain."

They stepped out into the cold night air. She had declined supper at a nearby pub with the excuse that she would grab something at her hotel. She had calls to make. It was after hours in London, but still early in New York. She couldn't put her publisher off any longer. She hit the door lock on the key fob, then suddenly stopped as she rounded the front of the rental car.

"Well, isn't that just about perfect," she muttered. The front tire on the driver's side was flat.

Everything was fine when she left the hotel—the rental agent had even gone around the car for the usual inspection before handing her the keys. She must have run over something on her way over to the café.

James knelt beside the car and ran a hand over the tread, looking for the usual piece of road debris that might have caused the flat. He frowned as he felt the cut in the tread, probably from a knife, and easily made as someone walked past. All it took was one cut not easily seen but the result was the same. A momentary thrill by some local punk and then laugh it off.

He and his mates had their moments, but not destructive, flashes of rebellion that came and went as those years came and went. But a glance at the other cars lined up along the pedestrian walk didn't reveal any damage.

A single hit?

Why the rental car, when there was an expensive number parked two down the row, a more meaningful statement if someone was out to make one, take a swipe at a high-priced number. He stood and brushed his hands off.

"We'll make a call. The rental agency can take care of it. My car is around the corner. I'll take you to your hotel."

They caught the cross-town roadway toward the river. Her hotel was one of the larger hotels in Inverness, with easy access to the historic parts of the city as well as the business center. He parked in guest parking and walked with her to the front entrance.

"What about the manuscript?" James asked. "Can you work with what you have?"

She'd already thought about that. "It needs a lot of work."

"Could you bring someone in to finish it? A collaboration, or a ghost writer?"

It wouldn't be the first time a book was put out after a well-known author died—written by someone else under special arrangement.

She'd bet her publisher had already thought about that, including meetings with their legal department. Getting the next book out was always top priority, and the fact that it was the last book written by a best-selling author made it even more important.

"That would be for my publisher to decide, and work out with Cate's estate."

Several guests were on their way out of the hotel for the evening. She stepped aside as they moved past—late season tourists including a young couple in parkas and hiking books, and two older men in windbreakers with sports logos possibly there to take advantage of the fall fishing season. A guest brushed past, head down, obviously in a hurry as he cut through the other guests on their way to parking area.

It was probably just her imagination after everything that had happened, but she hesitated and glanced at the parking area where the guest had disappeared.

James caught the hesitation, then followed that brief glance, and the question came back at him. Who parked on the street when there were parking spaces close to the hotel entrance?

"Thanks for the ride," Kris was saying as she walked ahead of him. "I can handle it from here." She stopped as she realized that he still stood at the entrance.

"What is it?"

He shook it off and followed her to the front desk. She let the manager know the location of the rental car. He apologized for the inconvenience and made a note to contact the rental agency in the morning. She frowned as James walked with her across the hotel lobby.

"I can find my way to the elevator."

He ignored the comment and reached around her to hit the call button. He leaned against the wall, arms folded across the front of his jacket.

"Tell me about the photograph."

CHAPTER
SIX

He saw the surprise in that dark-blue gaze.

"And before you tell me that it was nothing, just an interesting picture that Paul Bennett took years ago along with hundreds of others he took during the war, come up with something better than that. You recognized it." That dark gaze met hers.

She wasn't ready to tell him, or anyone, about the photograph Cate had sent, wasn't even certain that it meant anything other than the fact that Cate had stumbled across it and had been equally taken with a picture that seemed so out of place among all the others that her father had taken during the Allied landing. She shrugged it off, as the elevator arrived.

"Like Innis said, probably a typical tourist shot—churches, castles, that sort of thing. It was interesting, that's all." The doors slid open.

"Thanks for the ride back to the hotel. I appreciate it." A hand stopped the doors as they swept closed. He stepped into the elevator with her.

"It's not necessary for you to see me to my door, Captain Morgan," she said with growing irritation.

The doors closed behind him. Those dark eyes narrowed, that same look she'd seen the day before at the tavern on the drive from Edinburgh. He followed her out of the elevator.

"Give me your key card."

"It's late," she replied. Then, "If you think..." That dark gaze shifted. She could have sworn she saw amusement there.

"The thought is interesting," he had to admit.

It was even a little intriguing, then dismissed it. Too much work with a woman like her—complicated, cool on the outside, too many layers on the inside, analyzing everything, all business, emotions carefully hidden, and then there was the resentment.

He knew where it came from. She'd lost her brother in Afghanistan. Obviously they'd been close, but a lot of people had lost someone over in the sand box. He'd seen that at the airport and then again out at the Tavern. She had a wall around her emotions. He leaned in close.

"You're not my type." Then he repeated, "Give me the key card."

She thrust it into his hand at the same time she took a step back.

He inserted it into the lock on the door, and pushed it open. He swept a hand along the inside wall, and lights came on in the living area.

"Stay here."

That dark gaze stopped her when she would have pushed past him. More than a little irritated, she waited just outside the entrance to the room.

It was automatic, the visual sweep, then back to the bedroom door. He crossed the room, instinctively moving along the edge of the room, then pushed open the door to the bedroom, another light switch, and he was moving through to the adjoining bathroom. When he returned, she was standing in the middle of the living room.

"They went that way," she announced, jabbing the air with a thumb in the direction of the hallway. "You just missed them."

Smart ass, he thought.

"Then you're safe," he commented, dropping the key card on the entry table. "Unless they decide to come back. In that case you can just explain that you're from New York. That ought to scare them off."

She could have sworn she saw a faint smile, or smirk might be more accurate.

"Thank you so much."

"You're tired, get some sleep. And be sure to lock the door."

"I think I can handle that," she replied.

When he had gone, Kris poured herself a glass of Scotch from the courtesy bar. She skipped the ice and the usual splash of water as she pulled her cell phone from her shoulder bag. Cell coverage had been sketchy over the past few days, but she had a strong connection on the hotel wi-fi. David Ellison answered on the third ring.

She took a long drink of the single malt, the smoothness of it reminding her of other trips, sitting before a fire in the heat from the stone hearth at the Tavern, Cate sitting back in her chair, feet propped at the edge of a scarred table.

The call lasted over an hour. She explained everything that had happened over the past two days, including the break-in at the Tavern, and the fact that Anne was handling everything through Cate's solicitors and the insurance agency. And then the inevitable question.

"What about the manuscript?"

There was a long pause afterward. She heard the fatigue in his voice, along with the frustration, but she also knew that his thoughts were already past the fact that she hadn't been able to find the finished manuscript.

"There's nothing more you can do there," David finally said. "I need you here. Get back as soon as possible."

Back to New York, she thought frowning as the call ended. Meetings, the inevitable legal wrangling with Cate's attorneys, re-negotiation, new terms, and the inevitable question about who was to be brought in for a collaboration. Then more meetings.

They needed an author with good credentials, someone with a similar style who could take what they had in that partial draft and seamlessly work through the back half of the book. A couple of names came to mind. One was already one of their authors. The other had published with Ellison before moving on two years earlier—the better of the two, but probably harder to get, if he was even interested.

It was a tall order, stepping in to ghost-write a New York Times best-selling author. And then there was the whole issue of that author's own work and publishing obligations under contract. More complications, more delays, and not even the certainty that they could pull off a collaboration, she thought, her eyes narrowing as she came off the bed and crossed the room to the dressing table.

She was tired. The whisky had taken away the chill in her stomach. A hot shower was next, as she pulled the top drawer open, and then hesitated as she reached for the silk night shirt.

She had been in a hurry that morning and hadn't put everything away before leaving to meet with Innis at the café. But there was something about the way everything in the drawer had been pushed aside, as if someone was looking for something. She spun around, scanning the room for anything else that seemed out of place—drawers, the closet, her bag.

It didn't appear that anything had been taken. Her portfolio, clothes hung in the closet, personal items in the bathroom—everything seemed just as she'd left it that morning. Except for that drawer and the clothes inside. She pulled out the night-shirt then closed the drawer.

It had been a long day. She was tired. There was probably nothing to it. But before heading for the shower she double-checked the lock on the door and made certain the safety bar was in place.

The digital readout on the clock glowed through the darkness of the one-room flat.

James Morgan leaned against the window frame and slowly blew out a stream of cigarette smoke, the narcotic of choice at just after 4:00 a.m., when sleep had disappeared several hours earlier, scattered with the usual dreams that seemed to take a perverse pleasure in waking him.

He'd quit smoking, several times, then decided that nicotine was better than the pain killers the doctors prescribed. He'd weaned himself off of them when he realized they were becoming a habit, taking over, and taking him to places he didn't want to go. It was too easy to numb the physical pain, and the other pain that sliced through his brain when he let himself remember.

That was when he'd rented the small flat in the city from one of Anne's clients, month-to-month, during convalescence and the rounds of appointments in London that held his fate in their hands. Four surgeries, hundreds of hours of therapy, physical evaluations, then the psychic evaluations.

Was he depressed? Did he have recurring nightmares? Any sleeplessness? Did he experience feelings of being out of control?

How about 'E'—all of the above, James thought, as he stubbed out the cigarette. And in that perverse way of turning things back around, had wondered if the psychiatrist behind the glasses with the computer analysis in his hands ever had a friend cut down beside him, unrecognizable for the bloody mass that was all that was left after the smoke cleared, or watched a mother escort her young child into a marketplace with bombs strapped to his body, both of them blown to pieces along with a few dozen others, or was forced to knee-cap a boy in front of his father in order to get information that meant the difference between life or death for his team.

How about that, he thought, shoving the images back into the box, forcing himself past the memories, slamming the lid shut as the ring tone sliced through the darkness and the memories.

"Are you there, man?"

Innis.

"I was at it most of the night!" He spoke low, but the excitement was there, along with something else.

"I've found something. This is crazy shit! You've got to get over here! Hello?"

"I heard you." James rubbed the ache in his shoulder. "What is it?"

"Not over the phone. Get over here as soon as you can." The call went dead.

"Fucking lunatic," he cursed as he headed for the shower.

His mood hadn't improved when he parked at the back of the café a little after six. He was running on four cups of coffee, black and strong, and in no mood for emotional hysterics with blue eye shadow.

The café was empty, the crowd having thinned out after the usual late-night tech wars and invasion of some imaginary foreign country. The local 'mercenaries' had all gone home for a few hours' sleep before their day jobs at the local bank, investment firm, or hospital, and they'd all mess themselves if they were ever actually in combat.

The back door was locked. He knocked, aware that he was scoped out through a peep-hole, then a bolt was thrown back. Innis motioned him inside.

"Did anyone see you come round the back?"

"The garbage collector, the meter reader for the electric, and two dogs fighting over a take-out container," James replied.

Innis did a quick look around then stepped aside. He slammed the steel door and threw the bolt.

James followed him through the storage area into the office at the back of the café. The computer station was littered with half-smoked cigarettes stubbed out in ashtrays, along with a half-full coffee cup. Innis crossed the office, checked the front of the café, then closed and bolted the door, before returning to the computer station.

"This whole thing really pissed me off," he was saying, fingers flying over the keyboard. "What I mean is, I have companies that come to me to set up their servers, websites, all the secure shit! Like the work I did for Cate."

He continued entering strings of numbers, codes, then more strings of numbers, fingers flying.

"I should have seen it!"

"Seen what?" James demanded.

Innis entered several more strings of numbers, then hit the enter key. "This."

The screen lit up with rows of numbers, logs, symbols, the usual tech language for coding and encryption.

"Translation?"

"Here," Innis indicated a string of numbers, a break, and then another string. "And again, here." He scrolled down.

"What am I looking at?"

"SQL Injection."

"Come again," James replied. He was trying to lose the headache behind his eyes. Innis wasn't helping.

"An outside user opens a web interface and attempts to log in by searching for a string that hasn't been properly terminated. Then they look for any URL that ends in a certain code. He looks for the number of information columns, finds which ones accept inquiries, then changes the ID to a code that he creates. Then he injects a SQL statement into the code string."

James gave him a look that had him backing up in his chair.

"All right. All right. It wasn't obvious at first. Whoever did this is good, really good." Innis took a breath.

"Cate's server has been hacked. Once I found it and knew what to look for, there are footprints all over the place. I called Kris, I thought she'd want to know. But there was no answer."

James studied the display.

"This string of codes, a space, then this combination of letters," Innis pointed out.

"Here again. And here."

"Can you tell when these occurred?"

"It goes back at least two months. The most recent was four days ago."

"How many times?"

"At least a half dozen over the past two months?"

"Was it meant to sabotage the server?"

That blue-shadowed gaze met his. Innis shook his head.

"Whoever is behind this was looking for something."

He spent the next two hours looking over Innis's shoulder, along with a crash course on hacking. Whoever had accessed Cate's server had methodically opened every file, including the last draft of the book she'd been working on. As Innis put it, there were footprints everywhere.

Four days ago. That put it the same day as the accident in France, and just before Kris had arrived from London.

"Is there any way to identify the hacker? Some chain of information that leads back."

"That's the hard part. If it's some of the well-known hackers out there, they have a tendency to sprinkle breadcrumbs."

"Keep it simple," James told him.

"They have certain techniques that are almost like a fingerprint," Innis explained. "You can't prove anything but it's pretty obvious which are the better-known hackers around the world. It's the lone wolf that's harder to find. You have to put bait in the trap." At the look James gave him, he went on to explain.

"You make a change in the server protocol that signals that something has been uploaded recently."

"Like staking out a rabbit to lure the wolf."

"Exactly. Then when the wolf catches the scent and moves in, you spring the trap. In this case the trap would be a ghost that follows the wolf after it leaves—a unique protocol that leaves a trail. The tricky part is getting away with it so that the wolf doesn't know that he's been tagged."

James frowned. Someone looking for something. But what? The manuscript?

The finished manuscript, if it existed, wasn't there. That would have been discovered the first time the server was hacked. Then what? Try to sell it back to the publisher?

It didn't make sense. And then several more instances where the server had been hacked. Innis was right, someone was looking for something, but apparently hadn't found it.

"Do you think that's the reason the Tavern was broken into?" Innis asked.

The Tavern, the incident at the airport, then again at the hotel, something that had bothered him about the person he saw. And now the discovery that Cate's server had been hacked into, and it wasn't random.

He called Kris's cell phone. When she didn't answer, he called Anne.

"I spoke with her this morning," Anne replied. "Apparently her publisher was pretty adamant about her returning to New York as soon as possible. She had a meeting with the police first thing this morning about the break-in at the Tavern, and then caught an early flight to London."

CHAPTER
SEVEN

The conference call with New York had ended a little over an hour earlier. Everything had now changed.

Plan B, determine their legal position with just the partial manuscript. It was out of her hands.

She returned other calls, met with the director of marketing at the London office, and then made another call.

"I have your flight Ms. McKenna," Alec's assistant poked her head into the office.

Jewel was young, fresh out of university, literature major, glossy blunt-cut hair, and wearing retro 60's flower-child tunic and leggings.

"Eight-thirty tomorrow morning from Heathrow will put you into New York by midafternoon. And I've arranged transportation for the morning from your hotel. I hope that's not too early, but it was the best to be done on short notice."

"That's fine."

"And Alec...Mr. Cameron asked about supper this evening?"

Kris smiled. She heard the hesitance, and subtle change in Jewel's voice.

"And Brynn Halliday with Sky News returned your call. She'll meet you at seven at the Blue Oyster."

She'd made the appointment with Jonathan Callish at the Bankside Gallery. Cate had been working with him on a showing of her father's photographs. He was obviously surprised by her call, but had agreed to meet with her at the gallery. The appointment afterward with Brynn Halliday was public relations on behalf of the publisher.

Kris had been putting her off. But if she didn't give her something, she'd just invent her next story about Cate and the accident. She was a shark, and like a shark, she was looking for a story by dropping bait of her own in the form of information she had supposedly received from one of her sources about the accident in France.

Kris had mixed feelings about meeting with her but she had her own reasons. She wanted to find out what Brynn Halliday knew.

She slipped on her jacket and grabbed her shoulder bag. With all the meetings and phone conferences there hadn't been time to go to her hotel earlier in the afternoon, and she was still wearing the jeans and sweater she'd put on that morning.

"Oh, and security called a little while ago." Jewel commented from the doorway of the office.

"There's a man downstairs asking for you."

Kris frowned. Beyond the staff at the publishers and Brynn Halliday, no one else knew that she was in London.

"Is there a name?"

"Didn't say. Don't forget your phone," Jewel reminded her, a little too anxious to be rid of her.

Alec Cameron had his hands full with this one, Kris thought, as she headed out the door.

The elevator bumped down at the ground floor lobby and she stepped out. She looked up in surprise.

James Morgan took her by the arm and walked out of the building with her.

"We need to talk."

⸻

Kris frowned as she stared out the rain-beaded window of the rental car outside the Bankside Gallery.

James cut the motor and sat back against the driver door. "It's real, and whoever is doing this is more than your average hacker or rank amateur."

"You sound as if you've had some experience with this sort of thing."

"Required training."

Her gaze met his. He didn't elaborate, and she didn't ask.

"Innis may be a bit of a wanker," he continued. "But he's good, and not above taking a quick look at secure sites. Bloody hell, nothing is secure. But what he saw, the method they used, scared the shit out of him. According to Innis it was real high-level, sophisticated, the sort that is almost impossible to detect unless you've done it yourself."

"Cate was well known. She'd had a lot of success and exposure, a celebrity with her first book optioned to film. There's been a lot of publicity about the accident. It could be just some hacker trying to find out about her next book."

He didn't say anything and she knew he didn't believe it. Neither did she. But she was still trying to wrap her head around the fact that someone had hacked into Cate's server, looking for something.

What?

She thought of the break-in at the Tavern. The local authorities had written it off as just another robbery, easy target with no one home. But as far as she could tell, nothing of value had been taken. And what about the files and photographs that were scattered across the floor of the taproom? James had been certain then that someone was looking for something.

She grabbed the door lever. An attendant met them at the entrance to the gallery, her gaze sliding over them with cool appraisal. They were escorted into the main gallery, past displays and movable walls beneath strategically placed lighting that created a visual experience of an artist's work. Jonathan Callish was supervising the placement of a painting, standing back chin propped on his hand.

"Just there," he instructed the young man who moved the painting an imperceptible micro-millimeter. Then, "We just need to adjust the lighting and it will be perfect." Callish turned to greet them.

Jonathan Callish was the owner of Bankside Gallery, one of several small but well-known galleries near the Tate Modern on the bank of the Thames River. He was in his early fifties, slender, with thinning gray hair, and impeccably dressed. Kris guessed Saville Row by the cut of his suit, that fit as if it had been made for him, with gleaming leather shoes, and polished nails. His father had served with Paul Bennett during World War II.

"Thank you for agreeing to meet with me." Kris held out her hand, aware of his faintly surprised expression as she introduced James Morgan.

"Of course," he replied. "Such a tragedy about Ms. Ross. And of course, I was hoping to have a showing of her father's work in the coming months. Dreadful news."

"That's what I want to speak to you about," Kris replied.

They accompanied him through the gallery with high ceilings and glass-domed lighting, white walls, gleaming hardwood floors, and polished chrome light fixtures strategically located on suspended overhead tracks that could be repositioned depending on the layout of the art being displayed.

They passed a display of contemporary art, the images in bold slashes of black and red against a stark white background, the series titled "War and Aftermath."

Several of the canvases depicted war in graphic blood-red and stark black images. The last canvas in the grouping was sharp contrast—"Aftermath," in slashes of startling black images where nothing of life remained.

"This particular exhibit has been somewhat controversial," Callish explained, almost apologetically, then added, "But the artist has gained quite a following."

She studied the images. They were cold, void of any feeling, and yet filled with an almost brutal reality, the eyes of those in the first canvases—"War"—streaming blood-red tears, while those of "Aftermath" were only contorted, lifeless shapes.

"There's a lot of anger there," James commented.

"You see it," Sir Jonathan turned and looked at him with excitement. "The message the artist was trying to convey. You have an eye for art."

"Blood, death, nothing," James replied. "It's all there, if you know what to look for."

Kris glanced over at him with more than a little surprise. The realities of war that most people never saw, except in a video game or movie?

She looked back at the series of paintings. There was also sorrow and despair in the bent and twisted forms.

"Very interesting," Kris commented, forcing herself to study the images in spite of the fact that they evoked emotions she'd worked hard to move past.

She had attended several showings in New York and London over the years. Everyone had their own perspective on a certain subject. The approach this artist had taken with the collection seemed to closely resemble the Futurism movement of the past century in its abstract symbolism. It had also enjoyed a recent revival among collectors in New York.

"I am always interested in people's reactions."

A young woman joined them. She was slender, dressed in black, with slashes of vivid color in the scarf she wore about her shoulders, not unlike the paintings, her dark hair pulled back into a long braid. She wasn't beautiful—that was too easy a description. Striking was more accurate, with dark, almond-shaped eyes, exotic, with the vivid color of the scarf against the emotionless canvas of her face.

"This is the artist," Callish introduced them, his expression shifting to some other emotion.

"Alyia."

Dark eyes fastened on Kris, then angled toward James Morgan. "Symbolism is important, don't you think?" she asked.

"It can mean many different things to different people."

"I once heard it explained that the medium is the voice the artist chooses to express an idea," Kris replied.

Alyia nodded. "You have studied art?"

"Mostly the Renaissance period."

"Ah, the period of enlightenment." A faint smile curved her lips, as though she found that amusing. She turned to Callish.

"You will excuse me. There is still much work to do."

She turned to Kris with that dark gaze. "It was a pleasure meeting you, Miss McKenna."

"We are very busy," Sir Jonathan explained as she left. "The show is only a few days away."

"I won't take much of your time," Kris explained. "I was hoping you might be able to tell me something about the gallery showing you were planning for Cate's father, Paul Bennett."

He gave her a too-quick smile, the professional mask firmly back in place.

"Of course." He gestured in the direction of his office. "I was very curious when you contacted me."

"I'm interested in a particular photograph you may have seen when you met with Cate. I understand that she selected the photographs she wanted for the gallery showing."

"Oh, yes," Jonathan commented as they followed him to the office. "She was most insistent that the photographs represent work that he'd done, but might not have been previously seen. And of course I agreed with her. I was excited to work with her on the exhibit." He rounded the desk, indicating the two chairs across from it.

Kris handed him the scanned photograph Cate had sent her. "Do you remember this particular photograph?"

He frowned as he stared down at it. "I'm usually very good at remembering different pieces, paintings, photographs, but I don't remember this one."

"I'm told that it was among the photographs Cate brought to you."

The look he gave her was more than curious. He looked startled, then quickly recovered, and shook his head. "It's most unusual—I would have remembered it. It wasn't among the ones she chose for the exhibit."

"Unusual in what way?" James asked, curious what his answer would be. Until that moment he had been content to listen and watch.

He'd learned a long time ago that people talked too much. It was what they didn't say that often revealed far more, and it was about body language—the way the artist refused to make eye contact, except when she was introduced to Kris, the way Callish kept folding then unfolding his hands, the smile that came too easily.

They were lessons hard-learned in encounters with insurgents, sources embedded behind enemy lines or where there were no lines—something in the voice, a glance, in the shift of the body, a gesture that was too convincing with a far different meaning behind it. There were messages in all of it, if you knew what to look for.

"Well for one thing, it's completely out of place with his other work from that period," Callish replied. "Pictures of the war, soldiers, people in the streets, the photographs that people are familiar with, that sort of thing." He handed the photograph back to her.

"I would remember it if I'd seen it before."

They walked back to the car together after leaving the gallery. Kris didn't bother to hide her disappointment. She had hoped he might be able to tell her something about the photograph.

"He's lying," James said. "And not very good at it."

"Why do you say that?"

"He talked around everything, and kept repeating himself."

Kris frowned. Callish had no reason to lie about the photograph. It was possible he simply didn't want to be bothered with questions about an obscure photograph, especially since the gallery showing wasn't going to happen now.

He had obviously put a lot of time and effort into the exhibit. Never before seen photographs from the war, with the recent anniversary, would have been a very lucrative draw. Now, with the accident, all of that time and effort was wasted.

She glanced down at her phone. It was later than she realized.

"I have a meeting. I can take a cab from here."

"Brynn Halliday of Sky News," he replied. And then at her surprised expression, "A young woman by the name of Jewel at your office mentioned it."

"Supposedly she has new information about the accident from one of her sources."

"Whom she wouldn't name over the phone," James finished the thought. "Did it occur that she's playing you?"

"We're playing each other. If she has information, then I want to know. I can handle Brynn Halliday." She stepped to the curb and waved down a cab.

"Where are you meeting her?"

"A club called the Blue Oyster."

He waved the driver off and caught the flash of anger in those blue eyes.

"We don't want to keep Ms. Halliday waiting."

End of conversation.

The Blue Oyster was like other popular outdoor clubs, even in the middle of a London drizzle.

It was Friday evening, crowded, and music pumped out into the night, crowded tables under umbrellas, servers with trays of drinks weaving through the obstacle course of bodies under the overhead canopy, a blend of young professionals, singles, and those who pretended to be. It could have been any popular New York night scene. The players were all the same, just a different place, different day.

It was on the corner with cross streets on two sides that fed from the city center, the river flowing behind, with lights strung along the roofline. People wandered in from the street or tied their boats up along the dock at the river's edge. Tables were full, while others gathered on the dance floor under a canopy. Leave it to Londoners to carry on even in that weather. James pulled to the curb along the frontage street.

Brynn Halliday was seated at a curbside table across the patio, that trademark mane of blonde hair worn loose and tossed over one shoulder. Journalism-lite, Cate had said of her. Tabloid journalism in a world where opinion took precedent over actual reporting of facts.

"Put her in combat boots in the middle of Anbar province, no beauty salons or designer boutiques, but with unlimited tanning opportunities. Now, that would be a story!" Cate once said.

There had been a temporary fall from grace the year before. Sky News' star reporter had exaggerated—call it invented—the details of a story about a pleasure cruise hostage situation in the Mediterranean.

She claimed to be in danger trying to reach the hostages with the rescue team. It turned out she missed the boat, literally, remaining safely ashore then joining the rescue team after they returned with all the hostages safe. She had scooped the story, but in the rush to be the first on-air, she had stretched the facts and her role in all of it.

An on-hour apology to the rescue team as well as the families involved was issued by the network when details were leaked to another network. If she hadn't been the star at Sky News, she might have found herself out on the street, hustling Star magazines. Instead, she took an extended vacation, then returned to a new assignment covering human interest stories.

Kris had no illusions about the purpose of the meeting. A scoop about author Catherine Bennett Ross might go a long way toward re-establishing Brynn Halliday's credibility, and getting back a prime-time slot with the network. She caught a glance, and Brynn waved like they were old friends.

"I'll wait here," James told her.

That caught her by surprise, since he'd pushed his way into her meeting with Callish, not to mention insisting on driving her to the Blue Oyster.

"You don't want to meet Brynn Halliday?" she said with exaggerated surprise.

He leaned back against the car, and lit a cigarette. "I'm not into crowded places."

There was something in the way he said it—a memory, something she'd heard before when her brother came back from one of his tours in the Middle East, changed into someone she hardly knew.

"You're a difficult person to reach," Brynn Halliday said, looping an arm through Kris's as she crossed the street and joined her.

"This is one of my favorite places," she added conversationally. "Would you like a drink?"

"Whisky neat," she told the waiter as she took a chair sat at the table. "You have information about the accident?" Kris reminded her.

Dark blonde brows arched.

"You are direct," Brynn commented, then, "I like that."

Like hell you do, Kris thought to herself. Now what exactly have your sources told you?

James squinted through a stream of cigarette smoke, as she crossed the street.

It was instinctive—the sweep of the street, the intersection, the venue, everyone who came and went, drinks in hand, looking to score, or just looking. The evening rush hour was on and it included Brynn Halliday in a black, full-length leather coat that was stark contrast to the blonde hair that spilled past her shoulders.

The screech of tires on wet pavement brought his head up, instinct tightening at his gut. Then he heard the rev of the engine. Headlights swung around the corner, a white van careening through traffic. It was headed straight for the Blue Oyster.

He was already moving. The cigarette exploded in a shower of embers as it hit the pavement. There were startled glances, someone cursed as he pushed past, then a scream as the van jumped the curb, slammed into the half wall at the edge of the patio, and kept coming.

Kris turned toward that sound, then heard her name somewhere among the shouts and screams. A table went over. Headlights came straight at her.

CHAPTER
EIGHT

O nce, on a trip home from Virginia during college, the commuter train she was on was in an accident.

There was no warning, just a sudden sickening lurch, the sensation of speed, too fast, the sound of steel against steel as the engineer braked too late, a bone-jarring shudder, then the sensation of hurtling out of control, helpless, amid the chaos of shattered glass and terrified screams, passengers flung about like broken dolls. Afterwards, there was an even more terrifying silence, pinned under a seat that had torn loose, staring up at the floor of the car overhead in a world that was suddenly upside down.

She had been one of the lucky ones, escaping with only a few minor scrapes and bruises, but in those moments afterward, pinned in the wreckage as smoke filled the car, instinct was all she had left as she fought her way up out of the debris and twisted metal.

It was like that now—that explosion of light, shattered tables, umbrellas scattered like toys, the smell of oil from the patio lanterns like the smell of fuel oil, and the blood. The patio of the Blue Oyster had been reduced to a killing zone.

James had taken the worst of it, reaching her as the van plunged across the patio, taking her with him on the run, both of them thrown, then rolling as the van scattered tables, chairs, and bodies.

It was over in seconds, the van gone, jumping the steps at the opposite end of the patio, disappearing down the adjacent street.

He kicked a chair away, pushing through the pain in his shoulder, then instinctively rolled to his feet. Keep moving, he told himself. It might not be over.

She was curled on her side, barely moving. He grabbed her by the shoulders.

"Are you hurt?" And when she didn't answer him right away, "Kris!"

She was pale, wild-eyed, stunned, clutching the front of his jacket. He shook her gently. That blue gaze met his, dark, confused, as she fought her way past the shock, past the horror.

"Are you hurt?

Goddammit! She wanted to scream at him, but the words wouldn't come. She shook her head.

"Can you stand?"

What sort of fucking stupid question was that? Then as she tried to stand, she realized it wasn't such a stupid question.

"I've got you," he told her. "Hold on to me."

His arm went around her waist, holding onto her, pulling her to her feet as the first sounds of sirens pierced the silence.

All around them, were the first movements of others, while still others lay unmoving, lifeless, a nearby shoe lost in the chaos, a man with blood on the side of his head.

She tried to take it all in, tried to understand. But as soon as a thought was there, it slipped away, refusing to stay in one place, replaced by another that slipped away.

Who would do this? Who would deliberately drive through the patio, then disappear?

"Look at me!" James demanded.

He needed her to focus, to be clear-headed, to think.

"We need to leave, now!"

Her hand shook as she shoved her hair back. All around her were broken chairs and tables, the wounded, and others who weren't moving. In an instant, the usual Friday evening club scene had been shattered. Then she saw that mane of blonde hair, Brynn Halliday's frozen expression, staring blankly back at her only a few feet away.

"Oh, God..." she whispered.

He pulled her away, around tables and chairs, past a young man who struggled, dazed, to his feet.

She tried to stop him, pulled back. "We can't just leave...Brynn...?"

He held onto her. "You can't help her now."

She stumbled, almost went down, and he was pulling her back to her feet. No amount of arguing stopped him.

At that moment she hated James Morgan.

Lights flashed by—streetlights, headlights from other automobiles, emergency vehicles—glaring off the rain-spattered windscreen as they drove through the business district, shooting past shops and pubs, nightclubs. Then across a roadway, down several more streets, eventually slowing down, the heating system in the car cranking out heat. It wasn't enough, not nearly enough.

She sat huddled in the passenger seat, arms wrapped around her as if trying to physically hold herself together. She had no idea how long they'd been driving, or where they were going. She couldn't think, didn't want to think about what had happened. Her brain wouldn't go there, as the streets of London passed by in a blur of flashing blue, red, and yellow lights.

Then, only the occasional glow of a streetlamp, before it slipped away into the darkness. Down another street, vaguely aware of a street sign. They'd stopped.

It was the sudden stillness that had her looking up, then the closing of the car door. It was still raining. Then he was pulling her from the car.

They were both soaking wet as he slipped the key into the lock and pulled her inside the ground-floor flat.

He moved through the steeped darkness of the living room, drawing the window shades down before reaching for the light switch.

She hadn't moved but stood just inside the doorway, arms wrapped around herself, staring down, holding on. It was something he knew only too well. Shock, and the natural instinct to fight past it. To hold on to something, the brain trying to process what had happened, make some sense of it, when it was impossible to make any sense of it, and that edge, like standing over a precipice, wanting to let go and just fall into some dark oblivion, yet refusing to let go.

"Sit down, before you fall down," he said gently, pulling her over to the couch. He pulled off her jacket.

"I'm all right," she said, then clamped her teeth together to keep them from chattering.

It was just the cold, she told herself. But every time she closed her eyes, she saw Brynn Halliday's body, the blood, her sightless eyes staring back at her and that helpless sensation swept back over her.

"Of course you are," he replied, tossing her jacket aside and grabbing a sofa blanket. He wrapped it around her shoulders. She was pale, and there were dark smudges under her eyes. Then there was the scrape at one cheek, red against white with blue starting around the edges from that first tumble when he grabbed her.

He could almost see the bones beneath her skin. But it was her eyes and the dark, haunted expression in them that tightened his gut.

"I'll get the furnace going."

She heard the pop and hiss as it came alive. She focused on it. Then, there were other sounds, a cupboard being opened, the clink of a glass, more sounds, then he was handing her a glass.

"Drink it. All of it," he said gently. "It will help."

Drink me!

She felt like Alice who had tumbled down the rabbit hole. She would have laughed at the thought except for the bloody images that refused to go away. This was no fairy tale.

She did drink all of it. Then another, the whisky warming through her belly, then into her hands, a faint glow wrapping around her, around that single light at the table, and James Morgan as he moved about the flat.

He found towels in the bathroom, and cleaned her hands with a wet cloth, then worked the towel through her hair.

"Every time I close my eyes…" she whispered.

"I know."

She looked at him then, eyes still dark, filled with shadows.

"I keep seeing her lying there, the look on her face. If I hadn't agreed to meet her…"

If was a word that haunted him. *If* only they hadn't gone on that last mission; *if* he'd checked intelligence reports just one more time, even though he'd checked them a half dozen times before they left; *if* one of his team hadn't hesitated when that woman came out of the darkness, running toward them.

"Does it ever go away?" she asked.

He heard the tears in her voice and stroked her wet hair and lied, because at the moment that was what she needed.

"In time. Just hold on. Hold onto me."

"You've seen it before."

They both knew what she meant.

"Aye."

"How do you make it go away?"

He thought about that, the conversations with fellow soldiers, his mates, with people who had been there and lived through it, and other people with a list of degrees behind their name who thought they understood but didn't have a clue.

"You tuck it away deep inside," he told her. "You lock it in a box, and keep it there."

And pray to God the box doesn't open, he thought. Because if it did, it would consume you, piece by piece, until there was nothing left.

"After a while, it's something you remember," he brushed a strand of hair back at her cheek.

"But it's not the first thing you remember. And then, it's not the second or third thing. It's as if it happened to someone else." Another lie.

The flat was silent except for the faint hum of the furnace. Her head was heavy at his shoulder and he realized that she was asleep. He eased her down onto the couch and tucked the wool blanket around her.

There would be dreams. It was impossible to escape them, but he would be there, awake, unable to sleep...fighting back his own demons.

It was half past one in the morning.

He tapped the number on his cell phone, abruptly ended the call, and stared at the clock. He entered the number again, this time waiting for the ringtone.

How many times, Jonathan Callish thought, had he dialed that number late at night, only to end it before she picked up? Knowing that it made her angry. Then, coming through the entry from the garage eventually, safe.

The evening news channel had carried the broadcast—the latest terrorist attack in London they were calling it. A local nightspot this time, popular with young professionals at week's end, gathering to toss back the latest cocktails while unwinding from the work week, execs from the latest start-up, entertainment types from theatre, and the assortment that seemed to gather in places like that.

The photos from the Blue Oyster had been ghastly. Among the dead—Brynn Halliday of Sky News, a video of her being carried into an ambulance, a lifeless hand slipping from under the blanket over her body.

He'd glanced at the clock then and watched the newscast with growing anxiety, terrified to see the carnage, terrified what he might see, terrified to change the channel.

She's not there, he told himself. She's alright. But still he watched, scanning the faces of the injured, those who had survived, the chaos.

There was no answer.

Where are you? screamed through his thoughts as the images on the screen played like a macabre horror film. He ended the call and hit the auto dial key again as a sound at the latch came from the door.

"Where have you been?" he demanded as she came through the entry hall.

"Working," she replied, throwing down keys and a shoulder bag. "I told you I would be working late."

"The news..."

She looked past him to the wide-screen on the wall.

"Yes, it was on all the channels. Have they said how many casualties?"

"Several were taken to hospital..." he started to explained. "You know how I worry."

"They blocked everything around it," she explained. "I had to take the long way home." She stopped, eyes soft.

"But as you can see, I am safe."

"But if something should happen..."

"I'm always careful," she assured him. "And I needed to finish the piece. I can't just stop. You know that."

He did know, even though his own efforts had never attained the following that hers had. He did understand. He just wished that she did.

"You should not worry." She pressed a hand against his cheek and kissed him.

"I must get out of these clothes. I have paint all over everything."

He followed her to the upstairs bedroom. "You might have called."

He saw the shrug of a slender shoulder and knew it fell on deaf ears. When she was working, she refused to stop for anything.

"You're finished, then?"

She untied the shoulder strap and stepped out of the designer overalls that accentuated every curve.

"It is finished." She turned, the sheer peasant blouse she had worn underneath revealing more than it concealed, her breasts full, dark, her nipples erect.

She walked toward him then, smoothing back the lock of hair that had fallen over his forehead...like a little boy.

"I thought we might go over to France, take a holiday," he suggested. It had been a while since they'd had taken time together.

He wanted to touch her, but hesitated. She'd been working practically non-stop; she was probably tired. That was often the case. Instead, she surprised him, taking his hand and bringing it to her breast.

She was warm, the dark nipple pressing through the fabric against his palm as her other hand moved low at the opening to his trousers.

"Alyia..."

She pulled him down for another kiss, different this time, hungry, her tongue wrapping around his even as she unbuttoned the front of his pants, those slender fingers wrapping around his flesh, stroking him until he was fully aroused.

How many times had it started this way? A kiss, soft words, taking him to the edge only to plead that she was too tired.

But this was different. Tonight, she was different, her hands moving over him, impatient at the buttons of his shirt, pushing it back, her mouth skimming over him, nipping, taking him with her to the bed.

She sprawled across the satin coverlet, pulling him down to her, her dusky body like warm honey glowing before him. She arched as his mouth closed over her breast, pushing back the last of his clothes, then a slender hand moved low between them.

This too was part of it, her fingers stroking her own flesh, slipping inside, again and again until she was breathless beneath him. But this time she brought her hand up, eyes dark, and offered him a taste.

Everything was forgotten—the images on the screen, the tragedy of the evening, the chaos of another terrorist attack, even the hours he'd waited.

There was only her body, the taste of her, her slender legs wrapping around him.

CHAPTER
NINE

T he smell of coffee was strong, sharp, the kind her brother used to say you could stand a spoon in.

Kris followed it, pushing her way up out of sleep, pushing back the chaos and sounds from the nightmare.

The world gradually righted itself in simple, familiar things—the sound of water running, the distant hum of the furnace, the gurgling of the coffee brewer. She slowly sat up, taking in the unfamiliar surroundings.

A coffee mug appeared in front of her. She took it, wrapping her hands around the stoneware mug.

"How do you feel?"

Sore, bruised, every part of her hurt, and then there was the bruise on her cheek that throbbed.

"I'll let you know in a minute," she replied, taking that first sip, pushing back the nightmare of the previous evening, frowning at a memory as she closed the lid on that imaginary box.

That came from somewhere. Something he'd said?

She was vaguely aware of that dark gaze, the brush of his fingers across hers as he handed her the mug, intimate, as if they were any two people sharing that first cup of coffee the morning after. She took another sip, closing her eyes as the coffee worked its way to her belly, caffeine gradually kicking in.

She looked around. It was still dark outside, the flat filled with shadows except for a single light in the small kitchen.

"Where are we?"

He saw the frown that struggled past the memories of the night before, then when there were no memories, only the residual of the Scotch he'd given her.

"The flat belongs to a friend," he explained, brushing her hair back from her cheek, his fingers gently probing the bruise.

"I stay here when I'm in London—appointments, doctors, psychologists trying to decide if I'm a danger to humanity."

"Did you get any sleep?" she asked. She'd obviously spent the night on the couch. Had he stayed up all night?

Sleeplessness. She knew it came with the rest of things guys who had been in the Middle East carried around with them. Her brother had gone through it—"*I get enough.*" Two hours, three?

"Some," James replied, that dark gaze angling away from hers.

He was shirtless, barefoot. The jeans rode low at his hips, enough to draw any healthy female's attention.

Get over it, she told herself. He's a handsome guy, you're a healthy female. Basic chemistry. There were whole ad campaigns that celebrated the male body—lean, muscular in all the right places, flat belly. And the way those jeans fit. Book covers they put out were all in on that sort of thing. It was all about sex.

James Morgan had it, there was no argument there. The scar on his shoulder somehow added to the appeal, along with those dark eyes that had a way of taking everything in with just a glance. And then there was the tattoo.

It seemed everyone had one—personal statements, a way to establish one's identity—skulls, symbols, a name. Not something she was usually attracted to.

She thought of Innis, tattoos down the length of both arms, covering his hands, neck, and God knows where else. But this was simple, beautiful, almost elegant, and frightening at the same time in the sweeping lines.

It was a stag's head that covered the entire upper half of his body in shades of blue and black, the head bowed, the animal's eyes staring at her, antlers wrapped around ribs and up over both shoulders, one twisted over the scar on his shoulder, and another word added itself to that first impression—fierce. And she realized it was his own statement.

She'd seen it at the roadside tavern on that long drive from Edinburgh, glimpsed it in conversations, the way he had of watching everything around him, that dark gaze, and the thought came again. Fierce.

"Some of Innis's artwork?" she asked, putting conversation between them.

He shook his head. "An artist in Manila a few years back. But don't tell Innis. It would hurt his feelings."

"Why the stag?" She needed the conversation, anything to keep from thinking about what had happened the night before.

He shrugged. "Certain cultures are very superstitious. They believe the stag has supernatural powers," he explained. "Others believe that death takes the form of the stag."

Like a good luck charm to keep him safe?

"Do you believe it?"

"It doesn't matter what I believe, only that the other person believes, even for a moment."

She realized what he meant—an advantage, just a few seconds in a confrontation that might make a difference. Life or death.

"That bruise is just getting started," he commented. "Have you ever had a black eye?"

She nodded. "A couple."

"Your brother?"

"When I was twelve. He decided I needed to know self-defense. He landed a good one, and then in college it was soccer.

He was impressed. "Aye, that can be rough," he admitted, watching her.

She was grateful when he let it go, and didn't ask more questions about Mark.

"Are you certain your friend won't mind bringing someone home?" She made a sweeping gesture of the flat with the coffee mug.

He shrugged, his fingers moving down across her jaw as he checked for any unusual swelling. They'd both landed hard the night before. It hadn't done his shoulder any good either.

"I usually call first, just to make certain," he explained. "But Danny won't mind." He caught the surprise in her expression, and realized the assumption she'd made about the flat and the person who lived there.

"Is Danny also in the military?"

"We went through our first training together. Then we went in different directions. When I came back, I needed to be in London for a while. He let me stay here when I was released from hospital. I had therapy and weekly appointments, so this worked out."

She glanced over at a poster on the wall at the edge of the kitchen. It was a concert poster from a Jackson Browne concert.

"Who's the fan?" she asked.

"That would be Danny. He collects rock and roll memorabilia, mostly from the 60's and 70's, American artists, some country artists, Charlie Daniels." He gestured to the poster.

"Jackson Browne is a favorite." He caught the edge of a faint smile below the bruise on her cheek.

"Running on Empty."

"You know it?" he was surprised. He wouldn't have guessed her to be a fan.

"We had an author who used it for the title of one of her books. We had a group come in and they did a cover of it at the book launch. "

Running on empty. Now there was a metaphor for a lot of things, she thought.

"You'll live," he announced, tossing down the cloth he'd used to clean the scrape on her cheek.

"There's no other swelling, but you're probably going to feel it the next couple of days. A hot shower would help, then some ice."

Next couple of days? she thought, already feeling it in every muscle. He pulled her to her feet.

"The shower is at the end of the hall. There are towels on the shelf. And there's a kit with some salve for the scrape on your cheek."

Kris stood under the stream of hot water long after she'd rinsed off, the water beating the knots out of sore muscles until she felt like a wet noodle and her skin was like a prune. She could have just stayed there for the next two or three days, except that the hot water would probably turn cold, and Danny wouldn't appreciate the next electric bill.

She found the t-shirt on the counter by the sink, black, neatly folded, and realized that James must have put it there while she was in the shower. It hung to her knees, but it was clean compared to her pullover that had streaks of blood and grime down the front from the night before.

The early morning news was on the wide-screen as she came out of the bathroom. One news segment had finished and another came on about the incident the previous evening at the Blue Oyster.

She watched as those images played over and over—emergency vehicles, people traumatized, others interviewed in scenes that had become too familiar the last few years—a bomb set off at the Boston Marathon, the devastation of 9/11.

He saw the expression on her face. It was there in her eyes, the way they had gone dark, her face pale, staring at those images.

"There are four known fatalities with dozens more injured and taken to hospital," the newscaster informed viewers. "Among the dead, Brynn Halliday of Sky News.

"According to sources, who asked not to be identified as they were not authorized to speak on the matter, Ms. Halliday was meeting someone in connection with the recent death of best-selling author Catherine Bennett Ross, who was killed in a tragic car accident in France.

"There is little information at this time regarding the assailant, who was reportedly driving a white van," the broadcast continued. "However, a cameraman who had accompanied Ms. Halliday, managed to get this video footage. Some of the images are graphic, and may be disturbing for the younger viewing audience."

The camera moved suddenly, footage showing the van as it tore across the patio, patrons scrambling, including the cameraman, others caught in the chaos of overturned tables and chairs, and Brynn Halliday, suddenly turning with a perfect screen-shot of the person she'd gone to meet in those last moments as the van barreled toward them.

"Metropolitan police are requesting that anyone with information about the van or the driver, contact the number displayed at the bottom of your screen. There are concerns throughout London that this was a new terrorist attack, like so many seen across the UK and Europe."

The broadcast ended with additional footage of the carnage at the Blue Oyster. She closed her eyes, but it was still there.

"It wasn't a terrorist attack," James said, his voice low as he stared down into his coffee cup. He knew a thing to two about that sort of thing. Then he looked up, watching her.

"And it wasn't random. Whoever was driving that van had a target."

CHAPTER
TEN

t was crazy, insane. She wanted to laugh, but her emotions were too raw and she was too tired.

"You don't know what you're talking about," she replied.

He didn't argue, that dark gaze watching her.

"You can't possibly know that," she told him. Except that it sounded as if she was arguing with herself, trying to convince herself that it was another random accident, someone over the edge trying to prove something, crying out for help, or some relationship gone south, or a terrorist attack. It had all the markings of it that had become all too familiar.

He watched the way her eyes darkened, the denial that the idea was just too ridiculous, but the words never came.

"The encounter at the airport in Edinburgh," he reminded her, the faint accent surfacing. "The break-in at the Tavern."

It could have just been a coincidence.

"The tires slashed on your rental car outside the Internet Café." He walked it all the way back, each incident since she'd arrived.

"A coincidence? Just some street punk out for a thrill? The guest leaving your hotel last night? First impressions are usually correct," he added.

He saw it too! What she hadn't mentioned was the certainty that someone had been in her hotel room before she returned that night.

"Cate's server hacked into," he went down the list. "Someone looking for something."

Each one, by itself might be easily explained, then dismissed. His friend, Dickie Simson, the police inspector in Inverness, said as much. It was unfortunate but when a place like the Tavern sat empty it became an easy target for robbery, vandalism. Easy assumptions. Too easy, and she knew it.

"What information did Brynn Halliday have about Cate's accident?" He kept pushing.

She took a deep breath, going back to those few moments before the van came crashing toward them. She closed her eyes against the image that came next, Brynn Halliday's crumpled body, sightless eyes staring back at her.

"According to her sources...there were witnesses who claimed there was another car involved in Cate's accident."

Someone looking for something. A target?

He waited. She was smart with a couple of college degrees, and tough when she had to be. She'd handled herself with solicitors, insurance people, the media, and Inverness's finest, not to mention she was CB Ross's editor and friend.

That alone told him a lot about her. As the saying went, Cate didn't suffer fools, and she'd undoubtedly met a lot of them throughout her career.

She'd had a reputation for being tough. She had to be in a male-dominated world, spending most of that career in the field covering wars, third-world conflicts, the fall of foreign governments.

Now, he watched the way Kris turned everything over, thought it through, in spite of the fact that she'd had only a few hours' sleep, was bruised and exhausted. It was all there if she was willing to see it.

"That's crazy," she whispered.

He helped her take that next step. "Brynn Halliday wasn't the target. She simply got in the way."

"*We need to talk.*" Cate's last message.

She sat down on the couch, going back through everything that had happened, back to that last text message, back to those first images of the accident, and the newscast.

"*I've sent you something.*"

It was all there. The encounter at the airport, dismissed as nothing more than the usual airport crowd, someone trying to make a quick grab; the break-in at the Tavern, hundreds of photographs scattered across the floor of the taproom; the front tire of her rental car slashed outside the Internet Café, dismissed as the usual street vandalism; the encounter at her hotel, a passing glimpse, but that sense that most people experienced of having met someone before; and the night before after their meeting with Jonathan Callish.

It was there for someone who was willing to look at it.

Oh, God! She felt physically ill.

If Brynn Halliday's sources were right and there had been another car involved in Cate's accident in France and the driver had driven off, what did it mean? Why would someone just drive off?

The rest of it was there, something she didn't want to admit, but made perfect sense.

"I've sent you something."

What was Cate after on that trip to France? What had she gotten herself into?

She looked up, her gaze meeting James Morgan's. He was right, about all of it. Except she had no idea what it was, or the reason someone was willing to kill because of it.

He saw it in the expression on her face—the struggle to understand, and the pain as reality set in. And there was one link to all of it, something that someone had been searching for at the Tavern; something they thought she had.

James set a plate of eggs and sausage down on the small kitchen table.

He could cook. Who knew? she thought.

She pushed the eggs around and made a half-hearted attempt to eat. Her hand shook as she set the fork down.

He sat down across from her and poured more coffee. It had grown cold in the flat as the first snow of the season threatened, and he'd kicked the heat up several degrees, but the shaking of her hand had nothing to do with the cold and everything to do with raw nerves.

There had been no argument, no attempt to explain everything away, just that look in her eyes and the expression on her face. It was there now, reminding him of women and children he'd seen in Afghanistan—silent, shell-shocked, trying to make sense of everything in a world that made no sense, desperately needing something or someone to hold onto.

"Tell me about the photograph."

She had explained how she got the photograph and the text message Cate had sent. Now she tried to explain what it was.

"It appears to be a photograph of a painting or possibly a tapestry, early 14th century would be my guess. They were common during that period, usually found in chateaus and homes of the nobility. The most well-known is the Bayeaux Tapestry with the images of the Battle of Hastings."

"William the Conqueror," he commented. "There was a bloody, power-hungry son of a bitch."

She nodded. "Tapestries were like an archive of important events —marriages, births, deaths, war. I first saw the Bayeaux Tapestry when I was on a trip to France during summer break." She took another sip of coffee.

"Then a few years ago, my publisher put out a coffee table book about the tapestry. The history of the Bayeaux is incredible. During the French Revolution it was confiscated and used to cover a horse cart, of all things. The only reason it survived was because a private citizen recognized it and hid it. Since then, it's gone through a remarkable restoration. That it survived the Middle Ages is incredible."

"What about the tapestry in the photograph?"

She shook her head. "I don't know what it is."

"Why would Cate send it to you?"

"I don't know," she replied again, exhaustion pulling at her. "I don't know. I don't...know!"

He heard the frustration and exhaustion, saw it in the way she shoved back a handful of hair that fell across her eyes.

He said nothing. He didn't have to. The truth was, the more she found out, the less she knew about any of this, including the reason that someone was willing to kill over the photograph.

"About last night," she eventually said, and caught the look as he cleared away the plate of eggs that had grown cold.

"Thank you."

She was grateful. The truth was, if he hadn't been there...

He scraped the dishes off at the sink, then shoved them into the small under-counter dishwasher.

"It seemed the thing to do at the time." He poured more coffee, his gaze moving past her to the wide-screen in the living area.

Images on the television, the sound muted off, pulled her back to the night before at the Blue Oyster. It was like a nightmare that kept playing over and over—the chaos, panic, terror, and the bodies.

"Whoever is doing this isn't going to stop, are they." As much as she wanted to believe it, she knew better.

"No, they won't stop. The question is, what are you going to do about it?" Still shirtless, he headed for the hallway.

"I'm going to take a shower. Don't open the door for anyone."

A door closed, then the unmistakable sound of the shower. She turned on the audio to the wide-screen.

She's seen it all earlier, but the images from the Blue Oyster were no less startling, making her want to look away at the same time it was impossible to look away.

It was much like the terrorist attacks in France over the past several months, the stunned expressions of patrons and employees, the glaring lights of emergency vehicles, military blockades set up on the street, emergency vehicles, helicopters overhead, and overall, the Sky News report.

A montage of live video and still-shots played across the screen, some taken by Sky News, and others obviously taken by bystanders with cell phones.

"In a statement released by Sky News, Ms. Halliday was following recent developments in the death of news correspondent and best-selling author Catherine Bennett Ross, who was killed in a tragic automobile accident in the French countryside."

The segment then went to the now familiar footage from the accident, followed by an interview segment from two years earlier when Cate's last book had been released.

"This particular book met with quite a bit of controversy due to the storyline and your characterizations that closely mirrored well-known political figures, and yet early sales figures indicate another best-seller. Can you comment on that?"

Kris smiled to herself, remembering the interview that was so typically Cate. Blunt, fearless. Honest.

"People will make their own conclusions, but the most important thing that I always strive for, whether it was in my reporting from the field or in my novels, is truth. You can cover it up, dress it up, or ignore it, but truth will always find its way, and people want that. They may not always like it, but they want the truth. I was raised on it. It was very much a part of my father's work."

"Famed war-time photographer, Paul Bennett," the interviewer had provided. "And his iconic photographs from a career that spanned over forty years."

"In the early years, it was all black-and-white photographs," Cate had replied. "Then color photography. He worked with that too, but he always came back to that earlier medium. He said there was more to be seen in the black-and-white photographs, that they forced people to take a longer look, to find the truth in each one.

"He was one of the best, right up there with earlier photographers Matthew Brady and Ansel Adams, in photographs that portrayed images people had never seen before, as well as Joe Rosenthal, and Margaret Bourke-White, who was a great friend, with their straight photography, and a handful of others whose images still evoke such strong emotions without manipulating the images that is so prevalent today," Cate explained, against a background of her father's iconic photographs.

"Truth," the interviewer wrapped up the segment. "At times controversial, always amazing—the hallmark of an award-winning career in journalism, and now as best-selling author, C. B. Ross. Ironically," he added, "Brynn Halliday had struggled with that very topic during her career. More coverage of the devastating attack last night in London at the noon hour."

Kris turned off the wide-screen. But those last images were still there.

Firinn—truth.

She picked up her cell phone and scrolled through her contacts. The number came up, one of the last she'd called. It rang several times. Then Alec Cameron picked up.

"Bloody Christ!" he exclaimed on the other end of the call. "Where are you? Have you seen the news? What the hell happened?" Then, again, "Where are you? The old man has been taking calls from the media. New York called right after everything hit the news." He took a breath. "Are you all right?"

She explained as much as she could.

"Yes, I know. I saw the news. I can't go into that now. I need your help, and no more questions."

The call went silent for a few seconds. "All right."

"I need information," she replied. "And I need you to keep this just between the two of us."

"Of course, but I hope you'll be able to explain everything, say over a drink, or supper?"

She smiled in spite of the fact that her face hurt. "Absolutely, but I need you to keep quiet about this. Not a word to anyone, especially not Jewel." There was a pause at the other end of the call.

"How do you know about that?"

"Senior editor, ambitious young woman, long days, working weekends..." She filled in the blanks.

"Right. We'll just keep that to ourselves."

Kris explained what she needed.

"The contact information for the woman who was the primary consultant on the Bayeaux Tapestry for the book that was published a few years ago. She's an expert on Medieval tapestries." She envisioned him shoving a hand back through spiked red hair.

"That may take some digging."

"Then dig," she told him. "It's important. Call me back when you have it."

It had been almost six years since the book was put out. She had come in late on the project, with most of the research and background information already in place.

The book, with over a hundred color plates, had been the project of Senior Editor Nina Blanchard and had taken almost two years to put together and publish, the most complete and authoritative book on the Bayeaux Tapestry, with the expertise and knowledge of a woman who had spent her entire adult life not only researching the history of the tapestry, but was an authority on the fabrics, yarns, dyes, and techniques that had been used at the time and the most recent restoration.

She picked up the call on the first ring tone.

"You are such a pain in the ass," Alec told her.

"What have you got?"

According to the information he was able to come up with, Diana Jodion lived in France and taught at the University at Caen in Normandy. He provided the number they had at the time.

"I owe you." As soon as she said, she knew exactly how Alec took it.

"Yes, you do."

She placed a call to that number at the university. Diana Jodion was just leaving for her next class. Kris heard the interest in her voice.

"Yes, of course," Diana replied. "I would be happy to meet with you. I am here late the rest of the week, an afternoon lecture series."

When the call ended, she looked up and found James Morgan leaning against the doorway to the bedroom, wet hair shoved back, wearing a sweatshirt over that tattoo, handsome and intimidating all at the same time.

He heard the end of the conversation, and knew what she was thinking. Part of it came from the relationship she'd had with Cate, a bond that came from working closely together over four bestselling novels, and friendship, believing in that first book that the publisher wanted to change, fighting with the marketing departments. He'd heard all about it from Anne.

Another part of it was who she was—smart. She knew how to think her way through things, he knew that from Cate, with a whole lot of stubborn thrown in. She didn't like giving up, or being told no. He'd seen that more than once since that first encounter at the airport. And the last part was the simple fact that she was more like Cate than she probably knew. She didn't quit.

"Diana Jodion?"

He'd apparently heard most of the conversation.

"She's an authority on Medieval tapestries," she explained. "She was the consultant on a book we published a few years ago. She may be able to tell me something about the tapestry in the photograph. Cate had contacted her several times."

"In France."

She heard the disapproval in his voice.

"She's agreed to meet with me. She may be able to tell me something about the tapestry that will provide some clue why someone is after the photograph."

"Let the authorities do their job," he told her. "Go back to New York."

He went into the kitchen and poured another cup of coffee. End of conversation.

Not quite.

"I'm not going back. Not yet."

He leaned back against the counter, cup in hand. "You've done your job. It didn't work out. There's nothing more you can do."

"It's not about the job." She didn't expect him to understand.

"It's about finding the truth—the reason someone drove a van into the nightclub, what someone was looking for." And the other part of it, the reason Cate had been driven off the roadway in France.

"The truth?" he threw back at her, temper slipping. "The truth is Cate was into something that ended badly." He needed to make her understand.

"The truth," his voice had gone quiet but no less angry, "is that there are some very bad people out there who are willing to go to extreme lengths to get what they want. The truth is that whoever is behind this is willing to kill whoever gets in their way."

"You think I don't know that?" she threw back at him. "Every time I close my eyes, I see Brynn Halliday and the others at the Blue Oyster, the blood. I hear those sounds..."

Her color had returned, eyes filled with the pain of those memories, her voice raw with it.

"My choice, my decision. I'm not going back until I know what happened."

He swore, the words whipping at her, then threw the coffee mug in the sink. It shattered, coffee exploding in a dozen directions.

"It's too dangerous! You could get hurt...You haven't a clue what you're dealing with." Neither of them did, and that was the hell of it.

Her voice shook with anger. "I'm willing to take the risk."

"I'm not!"

It slipped out of the box, a cold sweat breaking out between his shoulder blades. He tried to push it back, but it refused to go back— that raw, naked fear that he had let others down, that he shouldn't have been the one to make it out alive, that he couldn't keep them safe...

He grabbed keys and slammed out the door of the flat.

His hands shook as he slid behind the wheel of the rental car. He tried to hold on, but it was there, dragging him back—the pain, the rage, the blood, and the loss, blocking out everything else, like a wound that had been re-opened. He slammed the shift lever into gear, shot out of the parking slot in front of the flat, and hit the accelerator, the rental car fishtailing in the pouring rain.

"What have you done?" Jonathan Callish demanded, staring at the news coverage on the television, when the call was finally picked up.

"She has to be stopped."

"We didn't talk about this!"

"It was necessary."

"Necessary?" Callish replied. "Five people are dead, including Cate Ross and that woman from Sky News! You said it would be taken care of. It's not taken care of. You've made a mess of everything. I don't want anything more to do with this. I'm done!"

"You are not done. She was seen entering your gallery. Eventually it will come out that the accident in France was no accident. How long do you think it will take London's finest to connect everything and come knocking on your door?"

CHAPTER
ELEVEN

The English Channel boiled, waves rising up, then crashing down.

The ferry shuddered as it rolled to the bottom of another wave, then climbed up out of the steel gray water, sea spray slamming against the triple-thick glass on the passenger deck before whipping away on a brutal wind.

It was a lonely feeling, the expanse of the channel ahead, the fading lights of Dover off the stern.

Kris stared out across the bow, hands wrapped around the polished steel railing. Other passengers—couples, singles, and obvious late-season tourists—reclined in passenger chairs or fled to bathrooms, faces drained of color only to return a short while later, paler, if that was possible, fresh bag in hand courtesy of the concierge crew, while the ocean beyond the bow rose up to meet a leaden sky.

"The seventh wave is usually the most powerful."

Cease fire, she thought.

"Or the ninth," she replied. "Depending on coastal land mass and wind conditions."

"You know your waves," James replied.

"My brother taught me to sail."

"Unusual..."

"For a girl?" she finished the thought.

He refused to let her bait him. "Most people like the speed of fast boats. Sailing is almost a lost art."

"Mark crewed when he was in college, and competed in a couple of regattas the summer before he went into the military. "

It was the first they'd spoken since leaving Hempstead earlier that morning. After their argument, he'd returned to the flat. He'd thrown things into a backpack and then headed for the door.

"It's a couple of hours drive to Dover, then another hour or so across the channel." Then he walked out of the flat slamming the door behind him.

Bloody, damned Scot!

"Why theology?" he asked now, and when she looked at him in surprise as the ferry cut through another wave, "Anne mentioned it was your college major, before you went into publishing."

Safe territory for conversation, she thought.

"I suppose I was looking for answers. I wanted to understand different faiths and the reason people hold onto it when things change around them, the power it creates, and the reason people were willing to die for it."

"Pretty heavy subject," he commented, watching the flow of passengers around them, the rental car several decks below.

The choice would have been because of her brother, looking for answers in that logical way of hers when there were no easy answers. He knew all about that.

"Do you believe in God?" he asked.

"We were raised on it," she replied. "My mother was determined that we have a good Protestant upbringing."

"But no longer?" he speculated. "Because of what happened to your brother?"

Cate had mentioned it once. That loss had obviously affected her deeply. It revealed a lot about her. Painful loss, wounds that hadn't healed. He knew about that too.

She stared out the sea window. "It was his last tour. He didn't have to go back. But he felt that it was important. He could be stubborn."

"Family trait."

She looked over at him then, those blue eyes going dark on a memory.

"They went in to rescue hostages, but they'd been moved days earlier. They were ambushed, only three of them got out alive, one of the rebels who was providing them information, one of the guys on his team, and Mark." And then he went back.

It was too familiar. Out there, they were constantly re-inventing the mission, dealing with bad intel, making things up as they went along. And then the details, read from a press report that came afterward, the edited version the military put out to the media, or no explanation at all.

More often than not, the families never knew the truth. All they knew was the heartbreak of lost sons, daughters, fathers, husbands. And brothers.

He remembered the calls he made afterward, off-the-record, unauthorized, a conversation that meant nothing to those higher up, but meant everything to a mother, father, or wife, trying to understand the last days or hours of a life that had meant everything to them. And it meant something to him, to carry those last words home, and find some way of understanding it himself.

The bigger question that came back in the long hours of the night —did he believe in God? Out there, when things got bad, everything came back to that.

Please God, give me the courage not to let the others down. Please don't let this young man suffer...

"Why did you change your major?"

She shrugged. "Theology didn't have great career potential," she admitted. "Beyond teaching, writing a book, or entering a convent. Journalism offered more choices, and I liked the idea of taking something from idea to finished product, something that could inspire people or take them on a journey they might never have taken."

"You're not the convent type," he pointed out.

She laughed at the thought. "That option was off the table my senior year of high school—courtesy of Craig Martin."

"Ah, first boyfriend," he commented.

She would have had plenty of them. It was the eyes. A man, or a boy hoping to become one, could get lost in them and never want to find his way out again.

"The love of my life," she admitted with another self-deprecating laugh. "Then, he was the love of Misty Anderson's life. He became a dentist." She shook her head, not certain why she was telling him all this.

"Don't get me wrong, I don't have anything against dentists. I just could never be married to one." She paused, thoughtful.

"What would dinner conversations be like? *How many root canals did you do today, dear?* "I've been grateful to Misty Anderson ever since."

She caught the sideways look he gave her, a half-smile.

"Why the military?" she asked, watching the way he glanced past her, watching everything and everyone.

"Nothing as lofty as your reasons for choosing theology, or journalism. I wasn't exactly priest material." He leaned over as if he was about to share some deep, dark secret.

"It was a school trip when I was fourteen years old."

She'd expected something along the same lines that had influenced her brother to follow their father's military career—growing up in that environment, family tradition, the thrill for adventure that had turned into something far different in the real world of war and death.

He rubbed a hand across his chin as if considering how much to confess. "I was a bit of a handful then, and my marks at school showed it."

"I can't imagine."

She could though. He would have had some of that height then, with those dark brooding eyes, raised by a single mother who worked and couldn't know where he was all the time, and with the questions all adolescents have about life, hormones, and how they can get out of that next math test.

"Ah well, it was a trip to the Memorial at Lochaber in the Highlands. I almost didn't get to go." He shrugged. "My marks weren't high enough and something about my attitude at the time."

"Really?"

He ignored the sarcasm. "I wanted to go in the worst way, if nothing else for the chance to get away from the classroom. To Anne's surprise, I managed to pull my marks up at the last minute." He made a confession.

"I copied Julie Hennessey's paper, changed it around a bit so our teacher, Sister Margaret Alice, wouldn't be suspicious."

"Imagine that." She listened, and caught a glimpse of something besides the pain and loss, the uneasiness of crowded places, the hard, dark things that he'd seen and things he'd done.

"At first it was all about a day off from school," he explained. "The memorial is impressive enough, this massive statue of three soldiers out there in the middle of nowhere. Simon Fraser, Lord Lovat, had the first commandoes of World War II train there in that God-forsaken place.

"But the thing that stayed with me was the people who came from all over to see it. Ordinary people—young, old, men, women, and some who had served in the military, all quiet like in a church. It didn't matter the age, there was a respect, along with sadness, pride, and memories.

"They brought things to lay at the memorial in remembrance— flowers, pictures, or a token of some kind. Some of them were so young not even knowing the reason they were there. Others scattered ashes of a loved one, like they were bringing them home to join their brothers who had served. There was something in each of them, sadness to be sure, but pride as well, something to hold onto, to believe in."

He looked over at her then. "There are things that change you, set you on a certain path that you're not even aware of at the time. Then one day, it's there, and you look back and see how the way was set, the things that mattered."

Things that mattered.

He had found that at a memorial to fallen soldiers, and the things that mattered became the people he fought for and the men he served with.

"Did Anne ever find out that you copied Julie Hennessey's paper?"

"I told her about it years after." He shook his head. "Strange, I received a higher grade on that paper." Then he gestured to the over-head video display.

They were only ten minutes away from the port at Calais.

It was impossible not to search the crowd as passengers made their way back to their automobiles when the announcement went out. He kept a tight hold on her hand as they descended the stairs to the car deck.

Her cell phone went off as they reached the rental car, a text message popping up on the read-out.

"Diana Jodion will meet with us after her last class at the university."

"That gives us just enough time to reach Caen," he replied, a drive of just over three hours, as they felt the faint bump of the ferry as it docked.

The landing bridge was secured as the ferry eased against the pier. Massive doors opened. Overhead lights at each lane changed from red to yellow as automobiles slowly eased forward.

They followed the stream of cars, buses, and motorcycles that filled the double lanes that wound up the hillside, then sped onto the main roadway toward Caen.

Traffic was a nightmare, one that she'd never gotten use to on that earlier trip. Instead she and her friends had relied on public transportation. James Morgan wasn't intimidated by the late afternoon swarm of cars that clogged the motorway. He cut across traffic with the efficiency of someone who had done it before, with horns blaring and hand gestures from other drivers.

Most of the old part of Caen had been destroyed during the war. The abbey was all that survived, with most of the city, including the university, re-built after the war.

The university was a sprawling campus that was actually three campuses divided into eleven colleges, all linked by a tramway. The art school was part of the fine arts college. Diana Jodion had sent directions to her office, once they arrived on campus.

They passed through a gated entry and parked near the building with a fountain and elaborate modern sculpture—a phoenix rising from the ashes, symbolic of the rebuilding of the university after the war.

"She spoke with Cate the day before the accident." She told him what Diana Jodion had mentioned, as they walked up the steps to the entrance of the building.

"They were supposed to meet the following day." The same day Cate had sent the photograph, and that last text message.

Diana Jodion was the foremost expert on the Bayeaux Tapestry, and she had been instrumental in the restoration that had begun several years earlier.

"It was a painstaking process," Kris explained. "But she was able to coordinate the work with the historical societies for the funding that was needed. She was the main consultant for the book."

It was well after six in the evening when they entered the building, walking through the main foyer where different mediums of art were displayed—metal and clay sculptures, blown glass, paintings, papier-mâché figures that were amazingly lifelike, along with fiber art pieces, against a backdrop along the wall with life-size photographs of that iconic piece of fiber art—the Bayeaux Tapestry.

The original was displayed at the museum in Bayeaux, and while no photograph could possibly do justice to the beautiful intricate figures portrayed in the original panels, the photographs that covered the entire length of the wall along the hallway provided an astonishing glimpse of the size and complexity of a priceless piece of art that had been years in the making, depicting thousand-year-old events that had changed the course of history in Britain and France.

"There's no documentation to authenticate the Bayeaux Tapestry." Kris went on to explain what she had learned during the publishing process of the book. "But there are references to it that suggest it was originally commissioned by Bishop Odo, William the Conqueror's brother."

They walked the length of the hallway to the reception counter at the far end, where a young man sat behind a counter at the work station.

"That was later in the eleventh century. It was a way of documenting important events since most people at the time couldn't read or write."

"Or, put out political propaganda to the masses?" James suggested, studying one of the panels that depicted William's invasion of England.

She couldn't argue with that. Whether it was 1066, the year of the Norman Conquest, or present day, events had a way of being shown according to a political agenda, whether it was in wool yarn on a massive scale, or the media of the twenty-first century. Some things never changed.

"Medieval news at six," she replied.

"Et fuga verterunt Angli—the English left fleeing," James translated the Latin text above the images at the next panel.

She looked at him in surprise. "You know Latin?"

"Some." He angled her a look as if sharing a secret, and a look of genuine pain. "Catholic school. It was required study. There are some things you don't forget with a nun standing over you with a ruler in her hand."

"You were a bit of a handful." She mentioned what he had confessed earlier.

"It was more that I couldn't see the point of all of it. Who spoke Latin in the real world? And there was that other thing."

"That other thing?" she asked, curious, as they reached the reception counter.

"I think Sister Margaret Alice paid more attention to me."

Kris couldn't help it. It was just too good to pass up. "Some latent, virginal lust on her part?"

It didn't take too much imagination for that one. When he wasn't angry, or in one of those dark places where he had a habit of retreating, she could see the attraction—those dark eyes, that brooding expression and that old expression about still waters running deep. A young girl, or a full-grown woman, would probably want to dive in.

He shook his head. "I suppose that it had more to do with my own lustful ways." He smiled faintly at the memory.

"Julie Hennessey," he confessed. "She changed quite a bit over those last couple of years in secondary school. Some of us used to hang out in the car park, smoke a few, and commit a few other sins. Sister Margaret caught us. A couple of the lads got a good thump across the knuckles with the ruler for that one."

"But you didn't," she guessed. It would have been that expression she was seeing now that would have persuaded Sister Margaret.

"Aye, well, she did have her favorites," he admitted. "She also played a mean game of football—much like your soccer. In full dress habit—goalie," he added.

Go figure, Kris thought. "And you got off with a warning about your lustful ways."

"Something like that."

"May I help you, please?" the student attendant asked as they reached the reception counter.

He directed them to the stairwell that led to the second-floor class-rooms and instructors offices.

Diana Jodion was small and slender, streaks of gray highlighting dark, shoulder-length hair swept back from her face and secured with a clip. Soft grey eyes held the expression of the teacher—calm, intelligent, but with a passion for her work.

"I was most surprised when I received your call, and curious," Diana greeted them.

They spoke briefly about the book that Ellison had published on the Bayeaux Tapestry.

"I was a junior editor at the time," Kris explained. "But I was fascinated by the history of the tapestry, and the enormous amount of work that went into it—the dyes, the intricate needlework, the number of seamstresses who worked on it over the years, and the political climate of the time. Not to mention the fact that it survived over hundreds of years."

Ms. Jodion inclined her head slightly, her expression thoughtful.

"I think you are not here to discuss the Bayeaux."

Kris took out the photograph Cate had sent her. "I was hoping you might be able to tell me something about this."

Diana Jodion studied the scan of the photograph Cate had sent, her expression softening.

"Ah, yes, the Raveneau Tapestry," she replied, almost with reverence.

Kris exchanged a look with James. She had hoped that Diana Jodion might be able to tell them something about it, but this was more than she expected.

"You recognize it?"

"It is from the Medieval period, fourteenth century." Diana looked up then, her expression almost wistful.

"Where did you get this?"

"Cate Ross sent it to me. What do you know about it?"

Diana nodded. "She too had questions when she contacted me. She said that she needed my expertise. That is all she told me. I had no idea what it was about." She was visibly taken aback, then smiled.

"You must forgive me. I have spent a lifetime studying and teaching about these magnificent pieces of art, not unlike a curator of a museum with the great masters before him—the techniques, the history, the unbelievable details, perhaps not appreciated like a Van

Gogh or Renoir, but unique and so very beautiful in their own way. And this," she gestured to the photograph, "is like seeing a ghost."

"A ghost?"

Diana smiled. "The Raveneau tapestry was lesser known than the Bayeaux," she began.

"But it was unique in that it was supposedly created by just one person over several years—a lifetime, according to what little is known about it."

"Why is it called the Raveneau tapestry?" James asked.

Diana frowned. "There are always stories about such things, particularly about famous artwork—who was the woman in the Mona Lisa? Van Gogh's self-portrait? Did he really cut off an ear in a fit of madness? Most are just that—stories, because there is so little factual information that has survived.

"We do know that it was named for the woman who supposedly created it, Isabel Raveneau, a young noblewoman."

Kris sat back in the chair. Not only did it have a name but it had been named for someone, like the Bayeaux Tapestry that had been created to celebrate an event—the conquest of Britain.

But what was important about an obscure, seven-hundred-year-old Medieval tapestry? And why had Cate been interested in it?

"You have questions," Diana commented.

"What can you tell us about it?"

Diana Jodion sat back at the desk. "As we know from the history of the Bayeaux Tapestry, very often they were an archive of important events—marriages, family life, celebrations, and war," she added.

"There was a time they could be found in most of the great houses of Europe, but they have disappeared over time so that now there are only a handful in museums that have survived."

The Bayeaux had survived for hundreds of years and was saved from destruction. The Raveneau Tapestry had also survived. The photograph was proof of that, but that still didn't explain the reason Cate had abandoned work on her latest book and come in search of information about it.

"Where is the tapestry now?" Kris asked. If she could see it, maybe that would provide some answers.

"Sadly, it was lost during the war, like so many artifacts when the Germans occupied France," Diana explained. "The photograph you have is quite possibly the last one that was taken before it disappeared."

Stolen, looted by the Germans, or destroyed in the Allied bombings. It was well-known that some of the great Masters' paintings had been confiscated by the Nazis. Some had been recovered after the war and now hung in museums like the Louvre, but many, numbering in the hundreds, were never found and presumed lost forever. Over the past few years there had been reports of lost art discovered in an attic or apartment after the owner died, hidden for over seventy years. And there was the recent publicity over a lost 'gold train,' supposedly filled with looted gold and artifacts that disappeared in Poland in the last months of the war. So far, no gold train had been found.

"Are there any other photographs of it?" Kris asked.

"Some have survived, taken before the war," Diana replied. "Let me show you."

She turned to a computer screen and entered search information. Several images came up.

"These color photographs are from an early documentary. The lighting was not good, as you see, and the color technology was not what it is today, but this photograph will give you an idea of the size and scope of the tapestry. This was taken in 1937. Sadly, there are not more photographs of the individual panels but you can see some of the images." She turned the computer screen so they could both see the images that came up.

"You see the hunt scene, a very common theme in Medieval tapestries, and then the scene of a young knight going off to war. This was during the last of the Crusades so it was not uncommon to find these images in artwork. Although you will see something very unusual in the next image if you look closely. It has caused much speculation over the years," she pointed out.

"It is a young woman in a knight's tunic and armor. See the braid of long hair she is wearing?"

"Who was she?" Kris asked.

"It is thought that it might very well be Isabel Raveneau, a young noblewoman of the time, and so the name of the tapestry. Her family name was Montfort, a very prominent family during this period, very wealthy. Raveneau was the name of her mother's family."

"Why would she take her mother's name?"

Diana shrugged. "There could be any number of reasons. History is filled with such stories. It is said that she was her grandfather's only heir to the Raveneau fortunes."

"Where was this photograph taken?" James asked, leaning across the desk to study it more closely.

"At the Abbey Mont St. Michel," Diana replied. "You can see in the background. It hung in the sacristy of the abbey before the war, supposedly a gift from Isabel Raveneau. It is said that she lived there for many years."

"She was a nun?" James asked.

Diana shook her head. "She was a patron of the abbey, and for whatever reason chose to live there."

It wasn't uncommon, Kris knew. Many wealthy and influential families of the Medieval period became patrons of churches throughout Europe. Atonement, absolution of sins, or possibly as a way to buy their way into heaven—religion and power.

"What would it be worth today?" James asked.

"That would depend on its condition. Your friend asked the same question. I told her the same—it is impossible to know. A mystery, no?" she added. She looked over at Kris.

"Are these not the things that novels are written about?"

Kris had come hoping to find answers. She had only more questions.

"You said there were stories about the tapestry? What sort of stories?"

"The most common one is that there was a secret in the tapestry, woven in the images."

"What secret?"

Diana shrugged. "There was one story that Isabel Raveneau defied her father in his choice of the man she was to marry."

"An arranged marriage."

"Just so," Diana nodded. "And you see the first young knight riding away? An adopted son of Montfort. It is said that he was her lover."

"What about these other images? Isabel Raveneau in knight's armor?"

"There are those who believe that she was showing her defiance at her father's choice of a husband, and what she would have done if she was free to do so. Not unlike Joan d' Arc, who believed that God had sent her to defend the people and put the rightful king on the throne of France."

And was then burned at the stake, because of those who feared her, or feared what she believed. Kris had studied it in her theology classes.

"What are these letters?" She could barely make them out for the poor lighting available when that photograph was taken. "Fili?"

"There are several Latin words stitched into the tapestry," Diana explained. "It was a way of documenting important events. You must remember that the tapestry dates back to the 14th century. "

"It means son." James translated the text.

"Yes," Diana replied. "However the exact meaning is not known, since John of Montfort had no true sons. Only two daughters."

But he had an adopted son, Kris thought. If the stories were true.

"Messages, puzzles, secrets," Kris commented.

Diana nodded. "Just as they say there is another painting behind the Mona Lisa, perhaps a hidden message, or another portrait."

"Is there any other information about the family?" Kris asked. "Descendants, records, anything that might explain something about the tapestry?"

"Several years ago, during restoration at the Abbey at Mont St. Michel, a series of articles was written about the history of the abbey.

"There was a woman who claimed to be a descendant of Isabel Raveneau. She had no proof of this, but it made an interesting story." Diana smiled.

"She was an actress of some minor talent in the late 1930's with a very vivid imagination. I have the article." She scanned through another computer file.

"Her name was Vilette Moreau. There was quite a bit of publicity about the tapestry then, and speculation about what might have happened to it. That was over ten years ago. She would be very old now."

"May I have a copy of the photographs and that article?"

It was late when they left Diana Jodion's office, an icy rain pelting down as they crossed the car park.

She had a half-dozen color print-outs of the tapestry that Diana had made for them, along with a print-out of the magazine article about the restoration at the abbey ten years earlier.

Photographs, an old magazine article, an eccentric woman who claimed to be a descendant of Isabel Raveneau. Stories, secrets, messages stitched into a seven-hundred-year-old tapestry. And it told her nothing about the reason Cate had been there.

It was after nine in the evening. A production at the campus theatre had ended. Patrons, students from evening classes, professors at the end of a long day, streamed across campus to nearby apartments or autos.

The parking area emptied, cars exiting to different parts of the city, returning home, or in the direction of the nearest tavern. All except one.

The late model Audi that sat idling, a cloud of exhaust in the cold night air, amber parking lights glowing through the misty rain.

It was a feeling that never went away, as James watched the Audi in the rearview mirror.

It might be nothing, he thought. Someone making a cell call before leaving.

"What is it?" Kris asked.

Headlights came on, and the Audi backed out of the parking space, then crossed the parking area in the opposite direction. He shook his head.

"Nothing."

CHAPTER
TWELVE

The hotel was one of several along the main thoroughfare in Caen, built after the war to accommodate the growing tourist industry, the room decorated in 1970's plastic, with a turquoise shower curtain with half-moons on it in the bathroom, and street-side windows that looked out on the street below from the second floor, with two vinyl-covered chairs across from the bed. But the sheets were freshly laundered and black-out shades blocked out the neon lights that gleamed beyond the windows, advertising off-season rates.

It was after midnight when they checked in. She wouldn't have cared if it was a bunk bed with a sleeping bag in one of those hostels from her college days.

James paid with cash instead of the plastic she had in her hand. She didn't argue. She was running on less than four hours' sleep, and that saying about the second day being worse after an accident, was setting in. She hurt all over from the attack at the Blue Oyster.

"All the comforts of home," James commented as he closed the door.

"I wouldn't walk barefoot on the carpet," he commented, noticing a stain by the coffee bar.

"No problem," she replied, not even certain she would last long enough to take off her boots.

He set the lock and safety chain at the door, then crossed to the windows. He scanned the street below at the front of the hotel, then both directions. The area was well-lit, and there was still traffic, even this late in the season. He pulled down the shade.

"Do you always do that?" she asked from the edge of the bed that was as far as she'd gotten. He'd checked the closet and the door to an adjoining room—also locked and bolted.

"I don't like surprises."

He set the backpack on the table between the two chairs, and laid the sack with the other half of her sandwich on the coffee bar.

"Paper cups," he commented, gesturing to what passed for a small kitchen. "But there's coffee for the morning." It was one of those small compact brewers with individual brewing cups. He looked over at her.

She sat at the edge of the bed, dark circles under her eyes, legs splayed in front of her, and looked more like an exhausted child. Her thick, dark hair swept forward over her shoulders.

"Lie down before you fall down," he told her, reaching around her and pulling back the coverlet and blankets. There was just one bed, a double.

"I'm fine. It was just the heat in the car," she covered a yawn. "And the food..." She couldn't even remember what it was—a sandwich of some kind on a croissant, cold, mostly tasteless, the last choice in the cold case at an all-night market.

He swung those long legs up onto the bed and gently pushed her down onto the pillows, then pulled off first one boot then the other, thought about the jeans, then decided against it.

"I don't need you to take care of me," she murmured.

He angled a dark brow. "Of course not." He pulled the blankets up, tucked them around her, and cut the light on the bedside table.

"There's enough room," she said through another yawn.

It was simple enough, practical under the circumstances, share the one bed, they could both get a decent night's sleep. Anything but simple.

"I'll take the chair," he replied.

She listened as he moved around the room in the dark, the scrape of one of those chairs dragged across the room. He pulled an extra blanket from the foot of the bed, then settled in the chair.

It should have been easy, just close her eyes. But she lay there, unable to sleep, thoughts crowding in, thinking about what they'd learned from Diana Jodion as rain pelted the window, the pulse of the lights from the street slipping past the edges of the shade.

"Do you believe in God?" she asked, staring through the shadows.

From what he'd shared about his early school years, it was a natural assumption. But there was a saying about the first three letters of the word—*ass*umptions were easy and too often wrong.

His head was tilted back on the chair, his profile outlined in the sliver of light that slipped past the edge of the window shade.

"I didn't for the longest time," he finally replied. "Probably something to do with youthful rebellion on my part."

"Sister Margaret?" she asked, thinking that might be reason enough to rebel.

There was that thoughtful silence again. She could almost see him shrug, the way he had of dismissing something.

"You question things, the purpose of everything, trying to find your own way and the meaning of things."

Her brother had gone through that phase, hormones kicking in, stubborn, certain he was invincible.

"And then things happen."

She lay there, listening through the darkness, thinking about what he had been through, what her brother had been through.

Things that changed you, he'd said earlier.

It was the closest he'd come to opening the door on what he'd been through, a glimpse of the doubt that haunted him, the painful losses that Anne had mentioned.

"There are moments where everything else is stripped away," he said softly, almost a whisper.

"And faith is all you have left."

He leaned against the window frame, the edge of the shade pulled back, staring out into the night. A sound had him turning back into the shadows of the hotel room. It came again, something murmured, then the sort of restless movement that came from dreams. She stirred again, mumbled something, an arm thrown across the bed.

Bad dreams.

He knew all too well how dangerous they could be. They took you places you didn't want to go, and then all too often pushed you over a cliff into that dark abyss. They made no sense, a jumble of images and experiences that could leave you in a cold sweat, clawing your way up out of them.

She made another sound, moving restlessly in that dark place as he crossed the room and sat on the edge of the bed.

There were tears, he heard them in the tangled words that wrapped around a name—her brother. And he was reminded that there were all kinds of casualties, not just those lost in some nameless corner of the world.

"Teiris," he whispered in Gaelic, brushing a tear from her cheek—something Anne used to say to comfort him as a child.

The words were old, spoken in dozens of languages over a scraped knee or something that frightened. And it all meant the same —Everything is all right. You're safe.

"Go back to sleep," he whispered.

He should have tucked the blanket around her and gone back to his make-shift bed. He'd slept in enough chairs, at an airport waiting to go out, on floors in a dozen places that all blended together. Hard places.

Instead he lay down on the bed and pulled her against him. She sighed, a soft, broken sound, then turned into him and burrowed deeper, her head on his shoulder.

She smelled faintly of soap from the shower that morning at Danny's flat, rain and wind in her hair, the saltiness of tears, and something else that was all woman.

It was more than sex. It was that something that came after two people made love, something warm that whispered of something that every human being needed. He pulled her closer, and slept.

She sat up, memories mixed with traces of dreams. She hadn't been alone in that bed, but she was alone now. The hotel room was quiet, except for the distant sound of a door slamming somewhere down the hallway. She swung her legs over the edge of the bed, and another memory returned from the night before. She glanced back at the bed.

Under any other circumstances she would have had a good laugh at herself. James Morgan was not her type, completely opposite of the men she connected with, including that brief arrangement that had ended up nothing more than paperwork a year later. Married and divorced in twelve months, more or less—most of it less.

The physical attraction was there. She had to admit that James Morgan in jeans, without a shirt, and that tattoo, had tapped into something that could only be described as physical. But there was the other side of what that tattoo and the scars on his shoulder represented.

Given half the chance, he would go back to Afghanistan or Iraq, or some other hot spot in the world that was broadcast on the evening news. The same as her brother.

She found the hastily scribbled note beside the coffee brewer.

"Back in thirty."

Less than twenty minutes later, she stepped out of the bathroom, the smell of coffee, dark and strong. She caught the look, the surprise when he caught the fact that she was dressed in nothing but a towel, then the frown. She ignored all three as she went straight for the coffee.

"The clerk at the front desk said there's a store not far, some sort of cyber café." He closed the flap on the backpack, trying to ignore the towel and the woman in it.

Sleeping together fully clothed was one thing. Simple. Standing that close to a woman wrapped only in a towel—a very small towel—was anything but simple. It pushed at him. He pushed it away.

"I called Innis. He's going to take a look at Cate's cell phone account." Among other things, he thought. The frown tightened, but he didn't say anything. Not yet. He wanted to see what Innis found. If he was right, it was a game changer.

"He'll get back to us."

"When does the cyber café down the street open?"

He looked up, then glanced at his watch. "It's one of those all-night places. Innis's sort of place."

She nodded. Under any other circumstances she would have objected to hacking into cell phone accounts. These weren't other circumstances.

"I can be ready in ten minutes."

The cyber café sold everything from wide-screens to the latest I-phone and everything in between, a French version of the Internet Café, with a coffee bar.

She spent the morning searching for information about Vilette Moreau. She finally found the reference to the magazine article Diana Jodion had showed them, then another link on a person search.

"Gerard was the name in the article. That's the reason I couldn't find anything! Moreau was her stage name."

"Probably the name of a husband who was passing through at the time," James commented, leaning over her shoulder.

She ignored the comment and read the information that came up on the next screen. "Born in 1923 or 1925 according to different accounts, married four times. She made several art films before the war." She looked up and caught the expression on his face.

"She would only have been sixteen, maybe seventeen years old when the war started, depending on the birth date."

"Art films?" He made one of those typically Scottish sounds at the back of his throat.

"Who would have guessed, looking at the photograph of that sweet little old lady?"

She continued reading. "After the war, she resumed her film career and starred in several well-known French films, including a production on the life of Joan of Arc."

There was that sound again as he looked over her shoulder. "Adult films to martyrdom, quite a repertoire."

"She made several more films through the 1950's," she read. "She retired in 1965, after playing the mother of a well-known French actress in her first film."

Kris recognized the well-known French actress from the blonde hair and that famous pout. There was a newspaper clipping from a French newspaper about the film.

"Apparently they didn't get along," she continued. The newspaper clipping showed Vilette Moreau with a handful of blonde hair and a furious expression. The article was in French.

"You speak French?" he asked, leaning over her shoulder.

"Enough to get me around the country on summer break when I came over the first time during college—'How much does it cost? Where is the train station? Where is the bathroom?' That sort of thing."

"Or, get into trouble," he commented. "Let me guess, spoilt girl on her own for the first time, staying in hostels, everything stuffed into a backpack. No one telling you what to do or warning you about curfews, or Frenchmen. And they wouldn't have been able to resist the long hair." Or those eyes, he thought.

"Go to hell," she told him good-naturedly. "I worked my ass off four summers in a row and saved every dime so that I could make that trip." And Mark had thrown in the extra few hundred dollars she needed, she thought, remembering. Not to mention that smile he gave her at the time, and a wink.

"Don't tell Dad. It'll be our secret."

That was right before 9/11. Four years later she stood with her father when the military transport touched down, wanting to run away, to be anywhere else as that flag-draped coffin was slowly carried off, wanting to scream through the anger and tears, at the same time holding it all in. Still holding it all in.

"Here's the interview for the article Diana mentioned, during the restoration at the abbey. Vilette recalled seeing the tapestry as a child. According to the article it was exactly as her great-grandmother had described it."

"*I was fascinated about the story of my ancestor, Isa Raveneau, who made the tapestry, and the story that the tapestry told. Of course, it was not surprising that I was part of the French partisans during the war, and then later played the role of Joan of Arc. I was meant to play that role.*"

"Among other less noteworthy acting credits," James pointed out. "All those art films."

"It is all there in the tapestry," Kris continued reading the quote from the article. "The secret Isa Raveneau promised to keep."

She scanned the rest of the article. When it was written, Vilette Moreau lived with her son and his wife.

"At the time the article was written, she lived in the village of Giverny in a house she purchased after the war."

She sat back, staring at the computer screen.

She had been born in 1923. That article was over ten years old. Vilette Moreau would be over ninety years old, if she was still alive.

Diana Jodion had mentioned a secret in the tapestry. But history was full of secrets, old stories handed down by word of mouth, like lost Nazi gold trains that sent archeologists and treasure hunters scrambling all over the European countryside. And like most old stories, nothing was ever found.

Had Vilette heard stories about a secret, and then simply added them to her own story? Tales told by an eccentric old woman who craved the spotlight?

And what about Isabel Raveneau?

Who was she? Why had she taken her mother's family name and then apparently lived most of her life in relative obscurity at the abbey at Mont St. Michel?

She entered the name, Montfort, in the search box. Several entries came up, among them, John of Montfort, from Brittany. She read through the Montfort genealogy, the family history linked to the King of France and the dowager queen of Scotland through a second marriage to the Duke of Brittany, a prominent and powerful family.

She skimmed other references, then suddenly stopped as a name stood out.

"Diana told us that Montfort was Isabel Raveneau's family name, but she took her mother's family name. Here's an entry. Isabel of Montfort was the first-born daughter of John of Montfort and his wife, Genevieve. Genevieve's family name was Raveneau. Her father was prominent in trade and shipping."

It was all there. Her birth had been recorded in church archives in Brittany, France, June 1318. But there was no other information about her life, if she had married, had a family, only that single reference that she later became a patron of the Abbey at Mont St. Michel. There was an additional mention about a young sister that had not survived. The Montfort family holdings eventually passed to a great-nephew in Scotland.

"She died at the abbey in 1379," Kris continued to read. "But there's no mention of it in the Montfort family genealogy. It's as if she didn't exist."

"Or, she was deliberately left out," James suggested.

The picture that emerged wasn't unusual—a wealthy nobleman who had no sons, in a time and place where sons were vital in preserving family wealth, inherited titles and lands, carrying on the family name, while daughters were considered an asset in the marriage alliances they made and the wealth that came with it. Wealth and power.

She studied the color prints Diana Jodion had made for them from those images that had been taken decades earlier, particularly the one of a young woman in knight's armor. The banner she carried overhead was a jet-black raven on a red background, wings spread as it soared with a blade clenched in its talons. The raven. A symbol for the Raveneau name?

What exactly was she looking at?

Something out of a young woman's imagination, perhaps rebellion at her place in her family and history? Not unlike Joan of Arc?

Had the young woman in knight's armor and tunic simply been the work of an over-active imagination? Or did it have some other meaning? There had obviously been some reason for her to take the Raveneau name.

"Her family was apparently very wealthy," she commented. "Large land holdings, the family chateau, business interests tied to holdings in Britain. But she took the Raveneau name." She looked over at James. "And then lived most of her life in seclusion at the abbey."

She pushed back her hair in frustration as she studied the photograph Cate had sent just before the accident.

It was typical of a woman who had built a career chasing 'the story,' then a second career telling the story in four best-selling novels.

"We need to talk."

But what was the story behind the photograph? What had Cate uncovered that she had thought important to send that last text message?

"Innis sent this." James showed her the text message on his phone. It was a web address, and a log-in.

Kris entered it into the computer. The site came up, then immediately linked to another site. It was a Skype session. Innis popped onto the computer screen.

"Where are you?" he asked.

"A cyber café in Caen."

"Who else is there?"

She exchanged a look with James. "Just the clerk."

Innis nodded. "You might want to keep the audio down on this."

A list came up on the screen. It took a moment before she realized it was a list of phone numbers.

"These are the calls Cate made and received beginning several days before her trip to France, and including the day of the accident."

There were over two dozen calls, at least a half dozen to two different numbers. One she recognized—Diana Jodion's number at the university.

It wasn't surprising that Diana's number came up more than once.

"What about these other numbers?" Kris asked. There were several more over several days, according to the log times and length of calls shown.

"That will take a bit more work. They fall into different areas, and some of them may be private."

"I need names," Kris replied. The numbers by themselves meant nothing, unless she called each one to find out who they belonged to.

"And a map of all the locations, along with the dates and times of the calls," James added.

There was no response from Innis, then, "I don't think I can do that...There's a lot of built-in security, especially after everything that's happened all over Europe the past few years, encryption, security devices."

James reached around her and entered a series of letters and numbers at the keyboard.

"Use this," he told Innis. "It will help you get the information."

Innis made a sound on the other end of the call.

"This is crazy shit!" he exclaimed. "This is spook stuff. The mates I know won't go near this stuff after that whole political leak thing with the Yanks. How do you know about this?"

"Don't ask, and don't stay on the site too long. Get out as soon as you've got the information." Then he added, "And cover your tracks. You don't want strangers paying you a visit in the middle of the night."

There was another expletive. "Right," Innis finally managed. "Print the list," he told them. "It has a timed destruct as a precaution."

"How do you know about this?" she asked as she hit the print key.

"I pick things up here and there," James explained as he headed for the printer at the counter across from her, grabbed the print-out when it came through, and then folded it and stuck it in his jacket. On-screen, the list suddenly burst into cyber flames, and was gone.

"There's something else," Innis added. "It looks as if someone else has been taking a look at Cate's phone account."

"What have you got?" James asked.

"I found something when I was taking a look around, a break-in and an information string. It might be nothing, an anomaly..."

James frowned. "Take another look, check it out. I want everything."

"I'll get back to you," Innis replied.

"Not at this location. Use my cell number when you have something."

"We need to go," he told her when the call ended, glancing toward the clerk.

CHAPTER
THIRTEEN

"What is it? What's happened?" Kris demanded as they left the café.

"Give me your cell phone." James told her as they crossed the street.

It was mid-week, well after the early morning commute. A local tram stopped, passengers disembarking as others boarded, the driver waiting for a sanitation truck to move ahead before entering traffic.

"What are you doing?" she demanded as he dropped her cell phone to the sidewalk and then drove a boot heel into it. It shattered, the screen splintering into dozens of pieces.

"Insurance," he replied.

"All my contacts are in there!"

"Exactly."

She grabbed him by the sleeve. "Exactly what?"

There was something in his expression that she'd seen before, on that long drive from the airport at Edinburgh, something just beneath the surface, something dark and edgy that had her taking a half step back.

"Your contacts," he explained. "Every call, every text message you've made and received—your London office, Brynn Halliday, dates, times, appointments, every person you've spoken with, every place you've been since you first arrived, including that first text message from Cate."

She stared at him. "You think my phone has been hacked?"

"Someone has been following you from the beginning. The airport, the Tavern, your meeting with Brynn Halliday."

"There are other people who had that information," she pointed out.

It was weak and she knew it. She was still trying to take in everything he was telling her as the uniformed crew returned to the sanitation truck.

"Insurance," he repeated as he picked up the shattered phone and pitched it into the back of the sanitation truck.

"Let them follow that for a while."

Was it possible?

She knew the answer.

Cell phones. E-mails. Anything and everything on-line, access at a keystroke. It was possible. And if Cate's phone had been hacked into, how difficult was it to hack into hers?

Just follow the link, the calls Cate made, the messages she sent. Her stomach knotted at the thought.

"Where are we going?" she asked as they returned to the rental car.

"We need to get off the street for a while," he replied, hitting the door lock of the rental car.

"Some place out of the way until Innis gets back to us with that information."

He slid behind the wheel. "We're going to play tourist for a while."

She looked at him as if he'd taken a serious step away from sanity as she buckled the seat belt.

"Tourist?" she asked as he angled the car through traffic at the center of the Caen.

When the spires of the Gothic church came into view, she was certain he'd lost it. They rounded the park across from the church and parked along a side street.

"Feeling the need for confession?" she asked as he cut the motor, still trying to deal with the possibility that whoever had tried to run her down at the Blue Oyster might have followed them to France. Possibly the university, and the hotel.

"Haven't you heard," he replied as he got out of the car. "Confession can be good for the soul. How is your soul, Kris McKenna?" he asked, then answered his own question.

"That's right, you don't believe in such things."

All right, shot taken, she thought, as they approached the carved doors of Eglise Saint-Pierre.

Photographs displayed at the entrance showed the recent history of the church, along with photographs of the damage that had been done during the Allied bombings of World War II. The massive restoration after the war had included recreating ornate stone work, a new façade and new stained glass. The carved cornerstone revealed that original construction had begun in 990 AD, with expansion from the 13th to 16th centuries.

"That was during a great expansion of power by the Church in Rome," Kris explained. "Power and wealth." She made no attempt to disguise her contempt.

"Medieval powerbrokers—kings who paid loyalty to the Church, expansion of the Church into the Middle East, playground for the Templars and the Crusades, and the conquest of Jerusalem." A war that was still being fought in the Middle East, and on the streets of the western world centuries later.

"Step inside," she commented. "Confess your sins, and all will be forgiven." She pushed open the ornately carved door and stepped inside the church.

Times were posted outside for tours of the cathedral. The last tour had just ended and it was quiet inside, in that way of old stone castles and churches, the nave steeped in shadows that reached up toward the barrel vaults, then glowed in a sudden burst of color as sunlight poured in through stained-glass windows that had replaced those destroyed during the war.

The architecture was a combination of Gothic and Italian Renaissance from those later expansions, while the original choir was two levels of large arcades from the earlier Norman period, with arches that reached up into a clerestory. Centuries of faith, wars, and conquest in stone walls.

One hour, two. The peaceful stillness of the church wrapped around them as they walked through the nave, and she thought of the countless people who had knelt on those stone floors, believing in the truth of an all-powerful God, needing to believe in their darkest moments, and possibly looking up through those Gothic stained-glass spires and finding something they could believe in.

They passed through the nave and into the main chapel, rows of chairs empty that time of day, candles lit by the faithful, glowing beside the altar. They paused in front of a marble grave slab—William of Normandy, whose conquest of England had changed the course of history, some believed, for all of Europe and the known world. A man of faith and war had built the first part of the church and was then buried there. At least part of him, the rest lost over time.

"We need to go," James whispered, indicating his phone.

"Innis?" she asked as they left the church.

He nodded as they returned to the car. He put the call on speaker so they could both hear what he had to say.

"What have you got?"

"You know how it is when you're looking for something, you go through all the usual steps, and you can't find it. You finally say fuck it, and there it is right in front of you."

"What did you find?" James repeated, with an eye onto the street.

"Well here's the thing, I was looking for the usual tricks—codes, strings of information hackers use for access. There's always something that pops up—a gap in a chain sequence, or it might be some meaningless string of information, but it's there if you know what to look for.

"It's like trying to find a ghost. You keep hunting and eventually something pops up. Even the best in the business leave fingerprints. It's sort of like unwanted relatives dropping in at the holidays."

"The short version," James told him.

"It's there, and it's sophisticated. Whoever hacked into Cate's cell phone was good, very good. Not as good as me, of course, but good nonetheless. My guess is that they operate rogue."

Kris looked over at James, and mouthed the word. Rogue?

"Under the radar," he explained. "They sell their services to anyone who has the right amount of money, drugs, or something else of value. Security companies, foreign governments, terrorists." He didn't go into details about what they'd seen in the Middle East among some of the more radical hackers and jihadis, the scores of children sold into trafficking.

"They're usually techies who did some time with the big companies, but didn't like the structure. They're talented and don't care about what is legal or illegal. The best kept secret is that your government and mine use their services."

"They're like pirates," Innis went onto explain. "They hide out, operating underground. They all have a certain style, a way of getting in and getting the information, then corrupting a file or server. They love chaos. These guys are really wanked out. The thing is, once I knew what to look for, sort of like a call sign, I also tapped into Kris's cell account."

She exchanged a look with James.

"What did you find?"

"At least a half dozen breaches, all with the same signature. The same person hacked into both accounts."

That's what James was afraid of. "When was the most recent?"

Innis hesitated. "Around three this morning."

She caught the look James gave her. Just a few hours after they met with Diana Jodion.

"What can they track?" she asked.

"Everything—calls and text messages you made, and everything you received, as well as anything that's stored."

Every call, including the call to Diana before that, the text message from Cate, and every call or message she'd made and received—every move she made, every place they'd gone.

It was like being stalked, except whoever was doing the stalking was invisible, sitting in some apartment or techie enclave, watching everything she was doing.

She slammed out of the car, fighting the anger and the fear that someone—the same person who had stalked Cate—was following them. Her hands shook. She jammed them into the pockets of her jacket.

"I've got the information you wanted," Innis continued, as James watched her through the windscreen—the anger, the frustration, the way she drove a hand back through her hair.

"There were several calls to Gerard Martel in Lisieux."

James made mental notes, and kept an eye on her as she leaned against the car, hands shoved into the pockets of her jacket, her hair sweeping forward. He couldn't see the expression on her face, but he read the body language.

"What about the hacks into both accounts?" he asked.

"I'm working on it." There was a pause. "If you need a place to hang out over there..." Innis added when he'd given him the information he'd tapped from both phones.

"There's this gamer I know. He lives in Paris, under the radar if you know what I mean. He's an all-right sort when you get past the tattoos and the dreadlocks."

This from someone who wore blue eye shadow. James wrote down the address, then told him, "Be careful. If you can find them, they can find you."

"Me?" Innis replied. "Not a chance. I know all the tricks."

"There's something else I'd like you to check out," he added. "Jonathan Callish—see what you can find out about him."

"Callish? The art wonk? What's up?"

"Just a feeling. He's in the high-rent district, but not a lot of inventory. I'm not into that sort of thing, maybe it's the way of things. But I'd like you to check him out."

"I'll see what I can find out."

"Be careful, my friend. These are not nice people."

"Aye," Innis replied, then added, "You know where to find me."

He studied the list after Innis ended the call. There were at least a dozen numbers. A handful were businesses—fuel stations or markets, and two hotels where Cate had stayed. The rest were private numbers, cell phones, and a couple of land lines, a road map of dates and times where Cate had been those last days.

She had covered a lot of territory in a short period of time. It was obvious that the trip over hadn't been a casual vacation or weekend getaway from the pressure of finishing the book. In fact, the whole idea of Cate buckling under pressure was laughable. He'd never known anyone tougher, smarter, more focused, and capable of sorting through the bullshit.

Unless it was the woman he watched now through the windscreen of the rental car. She was just as smart, and she had a toughness all her own, whether she realized it or not. She had to after what had happened in London. Anyone else would have crumbled and taken the first flight back to New York. He saw it at the flat afterward, when that first shock had worn off—the denial, disbelief, then the truth that came crashing in on her.

People he'd known, hardened teammates out on a mission, often lost it in those seconds after an attack when there was nothing but the silence and the body count. Then instinct kicked in. Mental toughness. Grit. Call it what you like. She had it, and that damned, bloody stubbornness. She looked up as he stepped out the car. He handed her the list, then reached for the pack of cigarettes inside his jacket.

"He's good," he told her. "Once you get past the eye shadow."

He lit a cigarette and blew a stream of smoke into the cold morning air.

"Every place Cate went, every call she made—names, places. It's all there."

She saw it halfway down the list, then saw it again. Cate had made the first call two days before the accident. The second call was made the same day she had sent that text message! She looked up.

"Gerard Martel, in Lisieux."

He saw the expression at her face, the excitement mixed with determination.

"It might not mean anything," he cautioned. "According to the information you found, Vilette Moreau would be over ninety years old, if she's still alive."

She knew where he was going, his feelings from the beginning—the risk, the danger. He'd made no secret of it. He also knew her feelings about it. She held out the list.

"Cate called that number twice. Both calls lasted several minutes. The last one was made just hours before she sent me that text message." Just before she died in that car accident.

"She spoke to someone at that number. I need to know what she found out."

He threw the cigarette down onto the sidewalk and crushed it out.

She should go back to London. At least there she could get protection, let the authorities handle everything. But he knew exactly where that argument would go, and he wasn't about to let her go on alone

Not after the information Innis had given them.

CHAPTER
FOURTEEN

Even in late fall, Lisieux was like a painting, the sky sliding into a pale shade of gray as clouds lowered over the Basilica, trees and gardens that surrounded stone houses that had stood for two hundred years and survived the Allied bombings of World War II, in shades of yellow, amber, and gold, while other parts of the town dated from after the war like so many other places in France that had found itself under German occupation and then Allied liberation.

What had Cate found there?

The woman at the local market, one of those typically provincial markets that sold spices from crockery jars, and late fall vegetables in baskets, was less than accommodating. She shook her head with the mumbled excuse that she spoke no English when asked about Vilette Moreau. But the man at the meat counter was curious, emerging in his white apron. In her limited French, Kris explained whom they were looking for.

Yes, he replied in slightly accented but perfect English and with a frown at the woman. Vilette Moreau lived nearby with her son and his wife on the outskirts of Lisieux, although she was very old and frail. He made a familiar gesture—not right in the head. It was to be expected, he said with a shrug, for someone who was that old.

He sent beef bones each week to the house for her son's wife to make the soup that was all she could eat now. He had called the house then. There was a brief conversation, then he nodded.

"Take these with you." He put several fresh pastries in a box. "They are a favorite," he explained, and patted her hand.

"Chocolate. Madame Moreau was a very famous actress, you know."

The woman behind the counter made a sound of disgust and disappeared into the back of the market. He simply shrugged again and smiled.

"Famous," James said, with more than a little sarcasm as they left the market.

The house at the address he gave them was in the typical Normandy style, two-story, stone and plaster with a slate roof, and surrounded by gardens enclosed by a white fence.

The last of the season's flowers were gone, bare vines hanging from the arbor, flagstones lining the walk. But Kris could imagine the setting in the Spring like one of those Monet paintings—peonies blooming along the walkway, water gurgling in the fountain now filled with dried leaves, wisteria hanging from the arbor.

Celine Martel met them at the door of the kitchen to the house. She was in her early fifties, slender, with chin-length dark-brown hair that she tucked behind her ear. She wore a simple, long-sleeved blouse and skirt with an apron over it. Instead of provincial, the look was more 'guardian at the gate' in the sharp eyes over a long nose and a thin mouth.

"You are the publisher?" she asked, with a sliding glance over both of them at the introduction the butcher at the market had given over the phone. There was the curiosity behind a cool expression.

"I'm with Ellison Publishing," Kris introduced herself, giving the same reason for being there that she'd given the owner of the market.

"I was hoping to meet with Vilette Moreau. A friend spoke with her a few weeks ago."

In for a penny, in for a pound, as the old saying went, Kris thought, ignoring the look James gave her. She would know soon enough if Cate had been there.

"The woman, the journalist, who was killed in the automobile accident," Celine replied.

"We were working on a project together," Kris explained. She didn't elaborate that Cate's latest book had nothing to do with the reason they were there.

"She was hoping to find information about her father, from the war," Celine Martel commented, then added with an indifferent shrug, "With the anniversary of the war they are always wanting to know about it."

So, Cate had been there, not just a couple of phone conversations.

"Is Vilette here now? Would it be possible to speak with her?"

Celine Martel stepped back and motioned for them to come in.

"Yes, but you must understand, my husband's mother is very frail. Her mind wanders. I told the other woman the same." She closed the door and followed them into the house.

"She is in the garden room—it is warmer there."

They followed her through the house with its low ceilings, dark wood floors, and white-washed walls. The room looked out to the gardens at the back of the house. In the spring, the wall of glass would look out on a scene that would have been like a painting. Now, late fall, the willows were stripped of their leaves and looked like bent old women huddled against the cold. A fire burned in the stone fireplace.

Small, no larger than a child, Vilette Moreau sat before the fire in a high-backed wheelchair, a lap robe over her legs. Her daughter-in-law crossed the room, gently touching her shoulder.

"Maman?" she said, rousing her. "These people have come to see you."

Vilette stirred, looking up at her daughter-in-law, slightly confused in that way when first waking.

"These people have come to talk to you about the woman who came to see you, the author," Celine Martel explained in a loud voice. Vilette smiled faintly, then nodded.

"She is hard of hearing," she told them in passing. "And she frequently dozes off. I will bring coffee."

At first, Kris was certain that Vilette had dozed off again, eyes closed, her head bent slightly forward. She exchanged a look with James, uncertain whether to try waking her, or to wait until her daughter-in-law returned.

"Can you speak?" Vilette suddenly asked, angling a glance at them both with sharp eyes.

Come closer so that I can see you," she said in heavily accented English. "What is your name?"

"Kris McKenna," she replied, raising her voice as her daughter-in-law had told them. "You spoke with a friend of mine." She gave Cate's name.

"Why are you shouting?" Vilette demanded.

Kris exchanged another slightly amused look with James.

"Who is this man with you?" Vilette demanded again, before Kris had fully recovered from the fact that, in spite of her daughter-in-law's description, apparently Vilette Moreau was not at all hard of hearing. Selective hearing was more like it.

"A friend," Kris made the introduction.

Sharp blue eyes narrowed as Vilette stared past her. She slowly nodded.

"What is that?" she demanded. A thin, blue-veined hand pointed to the pastry box.

Kris set the box on the table beside her. "Monsieur Dumont from the market said they were a favorite of yours."

"Open it," Vilette said, ignoring everything else.

James retrieved the knife from his belt and stepped around Kris. He cut the string around the box.

Vilette Moreau watched him with avid curiosity. He went to fold the knife and she reached out a hand with surprising quickness. Her fingers closed around his hand. She slowly nodded, studying the tattoo of a sword on the inside of his wrist with the number below it.

"The warrior," she said softly, then patted his hand. "What did Monsieur Dumont send?"

"Chocolate crème pastry," he replied, lifting the lid.

Vilette clapped her hands together like an excited child. She took hold of his hand again, smiling as she looked up at him. Kris would have sworn she was flirting with him.

"We will have a party," Vilette declared.

"Sister Margaret Alice, Julie Hennessey, and Vilette Moreau," Kris whispered.

"Nuns to ninety-year-old women," she commented as he passed the box to her. "Impressive."

He made a sound that was probably slightly more civil that what he could have said.

"A party," Vilette again exclaimed excitedly, then began singing to herself in French.

Was this what Cate found when she was here? A frail old woman, who drifted between fantasy and reality?

The frail old woman angled a look at her.

"Have you slept with him yet?" she asked. She turned, cocking her head, those blue eyes glinting with humor.

"We're...friends." Kris was too surprised to come back with anything more.

"Sleep with him," Vilette said with a wink. "You will not regret it."

Kris sat back in the chair at the other side of the table. Vilette was old, her mind wandered? Now she knew where. She ignored the look James gave her.

"I'll think about it," was the best she could come up.

"No!" Vilette scolded, then smiled again. "Do not think! Just do!" Those sharp eyes narrowed.

"But I think you are not here to bring me chocolate pastry. You have questions, like the other one who came here."

Questions, that had to wait until the pastries had been set out on thin china plates with cups of steaming black coffee, and Celine Gerard had left them alone once more.

"You are like her," Vilette commented, taking a bite of pastry. "The other one—with all your questions. She was also a friend?"

Kris nodded. "We worked together."

Vilette nodded. "There was an accident. My daughter-in-law spoke of it." She shook her head.

"So very sad. I liked your friend very much, a strong woman. There was so much more to talk about."

The fire hissed faintly at the hearth. James placed more wood on it as rain washed the garden room windows. It was like a cocoon, the cold, watery world outside, the warm glow of the fire inside.

"You were interviewed for a magazine article several years ago," Kris began with what Diana Jodion had told them, hoping she would remember. "When restoration work was done at the abbey at Mont St. Michel."

Vilette nodded. "There are many stories." She gave her a look. "Some people do not believe them." She smiled faintly. "The wanderings of the mind of a foolish old woman, eh?"

She made a gesture, a thin index finger laid alongside her nose. "But I know what is true. What do you want to know?"

Kris took out the photograph Cate had sent her and handed it to her.

"Tell me about the tapestry."

Vilette studied the photograph for a long time, a faint smile on her lips.

"To tell you about the tapestry I must tell you what I told your friend about my ancestor, Isabel Raveneau, as my grandmother told it to me, and her grandmother told it to her.

"Historians always think that something must be written—written proof for it to be true. But long before stories were written down, they were handed down from one generation to the next—stories that perhaps hold more truth."

She settled back into her chair and smoothed the lap robe about her.

Whom was Kris seeing now? A descendant of Isabel Raveneau, or the actress playing some part in a story of her own imagination?

"She was called Isa by her father, the Duke of Montfort, a very wealthy and powerful man," she began.

"There were two daughters. Isa was the oldest, strong-willed, independent with a mind of her own, unusual for a young girl of that time. She was his favorite and perhaps much like the son he had always hoped for.

"She was well educated by private tutors," she continued. "And the Duke took her with him on his travels, for he had many estates and holdings in both Normandy and Britain. But to tell you about her, I must also tell you about him." She looked over at James.

"There is cognac in the cabinet," she angled her head toward a fine old wood cabinet across the room.

"James." She repeated his name with a look that lingered on him.

"Chocolate and cognac. You must pour it. My hands shake and I would not want to spill it."

He opened the cabinet and found the decanter, along with a half-dozen small tumblers. His expression was doubtful at the wisdom of the cognac, a dark brow angling up.

Vilette laughed. "You are like him, and the same name—James," she said with a knowing look.

"Always looking out for others—the protector, guardian, young James of Montfort."

"You said there were no sons," Kris reminded her.

"No true sons, but a bastard born to a father who could not acknowledge him, and a debt paid with the favor by another, the Duke of Montfort, who took him in spite of his bastard birth. And from the moment the Duke brought young James into the family, their lives were all changed." Vilette motioned to James to pour the cognac.

"My daughter-in-law does not approve," she said with wink. "I am an old woman. What is the worst that could happen? That I might die?" she laughed again, and gestured to the tumbler.

James poured a small amount and her eyes sharpened. He poured another half inch in the glass. She patted his hand.

"How were their lives changed?" Kris asked, forced to wait for an answer as Vilette smiled with obvious pleasure as she took a sip, eyes closed for a few moments. Then they opened and her gaze was sharp.

"Isa was just a child when he was brought to live with them. He was older by a few years, and very handsome," she added, with a wink at James.

"And aware of his lowly status. Therefore, his fate was whatever he made of himself, and the opportunities given him."

"Opportunities?"

"He was educated at the university at Notre Dame."

"A priest?" Kris asked with surprise.

It wasn't uncommon. Throughout history offspring of noble families, usually second sons, devoted themselves to the Church. William the Conqueror's brother, Bishop Odo, had risen through the Church and founded the abbey at Mont St. Michel. Other titled families of Europe, including royalty, were filled with accounts of those who had given their lives to the Catholic Church, including women who became patrons of a particular church and devoted their lives to that calling. But what little she knew about Isa Raveneau didn't mesh with a life of devotion to the Church.

Vilette shook her head. "Not a priest. He was given a commission. It is there in the images she stitched into the tapestry," she explained. "A knighthood."

"But how was that possible, considering...?"

"That he was a bastard?" Vilette finished the question.

"It was purchased by his natural father?" James took a guess, causing both women to look over at him.

"It would have been a way of getting rid of him, without the guilt." He added, "Catholic school—Sister Margaret was an authority on medieval history."

"Just so," Vilette replied. "It is said that the commission of knighthood was provided by his natural father, and James was sent to Spain with many others, including two sons of a man called St. Clair on one of the last Crusades to Jerusalem in 1345."

"They were sent to take the heart of Robert the Bruce to Jerusalem after his death." James commented with a look from Kris.

"A failed journey that cost many lives, including the two sons of St. Clair," Vilette added.

St. Clair, or as history along with several books and a well-known film came to know them, the Sinclairs of Roslyn, near Edinburgh.

"1345," Kris said thoughtfully, remembering studies of the Crusades from college. "Isa Raveneau would have been a young woman then."

Vilette nodded. "A young woman grown, and very wealthy through both her father's and her mother's families."

Kris took out the printouts she'd made along with the ones Diana Jodion had provided. She studied the color images of the tapestry.

She was familiar with ambiguities in famous pieces of artwork. That had been part of her early studies in theology. The Mona Lisa came to mind, along with several others from the Renaissance period —images within images, or images that appeared to be one thing but were in fact another, religious images wrapped in alabaster and marble that conveyed an altogether different meaning.

"What about this image?" she pointed out, handing it to Vilette. "This appears to be a woman in knight's armor."

Vilette nodded. "So you see, and you understand, I think."

Images within images, or those that appeared to be one thing but were another? A young woman dressed in knight's armor; headstrong, stubborn. Kris realized the only possibility for what she was looking at.

"Isa and James were lovers," Vilette explained. "But a marriage would not have been accepted by her father. Wealth and titles are power, and he arranged her marriage to another, and sent James away to Spain."

That was what she was looking at—strength and courage in the expression of the young woman astride the horse. The tapestry was like a series of photographs of a defiant young woman. The question was, what was the truth? Or was the image just the willful imagination of a young woman determined to defy her father. Some things never changed, no matter what century they were in.

"What about the Raveneau name?"

"Her mother's name," Vilette nodded. "She took her name out of anger when James was sent away. The tapestry was her way of telling the world that she defied her father."

Did it also explain the reason she lived out most of her life at the abbey once she turned her back on her own family?

Vilette took another sip of cognac. She smiled. "You see the image of a rebellious young woman, like a book or the part in a film, acting out her anger, but it is far more. You see here, this scene." She pointed to the one with the arbor and the images of the young man and woman.

"You think it is a simple garden scene!" she said emphatically. "And then the young woman kneeling and praying? But no! They spoke vows even though there was no priest to bless them before he was sent to Spain with the others. She defied both her father and the church."

And the panel with the young woman in knight's armor came after. Not just rebellion against her father, but something more?

"The knights who went there never reached Jerusalem," Vilette continued. "It is well known that all but a few perished in Spain." She looked over at James.

"He was taken prisoner there with others, to be ransomed for gold, or left to die."

Diana Jodion had spoken of it—a story within a story. A young woman of great wealth who rebelled against her father and took her mother's family name, then lived out the rest of her life in seclusion at a remote abbey?

But that wasn't all of it. There was more, in that panel with Isa Raveneau in knight's armor.

"She went after him?"

It was the sort of thing written about in romance novels that they published. But was it real?

Vilette nodded. "She had the means and the ability, and a companion. Supposedly he was a distant cousin of James' who had gone with him to Spain. He was loyal to James, a Scot," she turned and looked over at James Morgan.

"He escaped and brought word to Isa, and then returned with her to Spain to free him."

"She bought his freedom?"

Again Vilette nodded. "According to the story my grandmother told, a very dangerous enterprise." The old woman sat back, the tumbler now empty.

She was tired. It showed in the lines on her face.

"When they returned from Spain, Isa took him to the Abbey Mont St. Michel. The wounds he had received in Spain had not healed. They had a little time together there at the abbey." She was silent for a long time, her expression sad.

"When he died, she was determined that he would be buried in his own land, in spite of the father who would never claim him, and so she took him home."

"To Scotland," James commented.

"Just so."

"But she returned to the abbey," Kris added what was known about the history of the tapestry.

Vilette nodded. "Yes, and became a patron out of gratitude for the care they were given by the monks when they returned from Spain. It was there her only child was born, his child." She pointed to the printouts. "My ancestor."

"It is all there," she continued. "In the tapestry—her story, and his."

This was what Cate had learned after finding that photograph. A lost tapestry, history captured in a black-and-white photograph in those last desperate days of World War II.

"I was told there's a secret in the tapestry."

Beyond the historic value of the tapestry as an archive, like the Bayeaux tapestry, there was nothing she had told them that was worth the lives of two people. There had to be more. Obviously, Cate had thought so.

Those blue eyes narrowed on her. "Myths, legends, secrets—so many questions, like your friend."

"Is there a secret?" Kris asked.

Vilette smiled. "It is there in the tapestry, stitched into the fabric, the secret brought back from Spain all those years ago." That blue gaze watched her.

"What do you believe?" She smiled faintly. "Do you believe in God?"

A question that she'd asked herself many times over the past few years. James Morgan had asked her the same question.

"I don't know," Kris answered truthfully. "I did, once." She exchanged a look with him. The truth was she had turned her back on it when Mark died. She felt betrayed by everything she had once believed, by the God she had believed in.

"But not now?" Vilette asked. "Is it not possible that you were sent here when your friend could not return?"

"Sent?" Kris replied. "You talking about destiny? Divine providence?"

"The path you were chosen to follow," the old woman suggested, sitting back in her chair.

"For your friend, for yourself." The sharp blue eyes were watchful.

"I am an old woman. I do not have much time left," she said with a thoughtful expression.

"My son, the others, they do not believe what I know. They think it is only the ramblings of a foolish old woman." She leaned forward. "You must ask yourself—what do you believe."

She wanted to believe, all of it, but the fact was the print-outs only showed a portion of the tapestry. Nothing that she'd seen indicated anything about a secret.

"Bring me the box on the table." Vilette gestured to a small round table beside the hearth. A porcelain box sat beside a vase with a bouquet of dried flowers. It was the size of a small jewelry case, the lid hand-painted with red roses, and looked very old. James handed it to Vilette.

"This was given to me by my grandmother. It is all that I have left of her, but you will see."

Vilette opened the box, talking to herself in French, impatiently pushing aside several newspaper clippings, one with a photograph of a beautiful young woman, folded letters from a different time when people still wrote letters, and notes yellowed around the edges, the sort of things collected over a lifetime and four husbands, not to mention a career in film, including those early 'art films.' She finally found what she was looking for.

She took Kris's hand and placed a small medallion in her palm. It was the size of a coin and appeared to be very old, the edges worn smooth. An image was embossed in the soft metal that might have been gold.

"I was going to give it to your friend when she returned," Vilette explained.

Kris stared at the embossed image on the pendant. It was identical to the images that had been painstakingly hand-stitched into the tapestry, a trinity knot wrapped around a Scottish thistle.

"It has been passed down for many generations," Vilette said in a soft voice. "James gave it to her. It was all he had from his father. And now, I give it to you."

There was a sound as the garden room door opened and Celine Martel returned.

"Maman, it is late," she scolded. "And it is time for your medications." Vilette frowned.

"Bah! Medication to wake me up, medication to help me sleep, medication to keep me alive. Always it is so." Vilette winked at them both. "But I prefer the chocolate and cognac." She laid a hand over Kris's hand.

"You will tell Isa's story so that it is not lost," she whispered. Then as her daughter-in-law persisted, she smiled at Kris.

"Did I tell you that I was an actress? In Paris, before the war. Such a wonderful time. So many handsome young men." And then, "You must come again and we will have pastries from Monsieur Dumont." A thin hand waved back at them as Celine Martel wheeled her from the garden room.

"Do you believe her?" James asked, as they left the house in Lisieux, the lights of the small enclave amid those infamous hedgerows from a century earlier glistening through the misty rain.

Did she? Or was it all a product of a vivid imagination? Another role Vilette was playing for those last moments in the spotlight? And what about the pendant?

"It doesn't matter what I believe." Her fingers brushed the cool metal of the medallion in her pocket as they returned to the rental car.

"It's what Cate believed."

The story.

But what was the story, she thought, as they left the village and returned to the roadway. A forbidden affair? A headstrong young woman determined to go after the man she loved? And a secret that James of Montfort, a bastard by birth, had brought back from that ill-fated last Crusade?

History was full of such stories. Like King Arthur and the knights of the Round Table, stories handed down but never proven. She brushed the cool metal of the medallion, the raised thistle over the trinity knot in gold.

Faith.

Centuries earlier it had dominated people's lives, giving them something to hold onto, something to believe in and somehow make sense of their world in those early centuries.

Religion had held power—in Rome, the Muslim world, and other cultures. She had studied it in college. In some places, it still held power.

What had the medallion meant to Isa Raveneau? Was it nothing more than a token of lost love? An image she had added to other images in the tapestry?

'True son,' Vilette had called James of Montfort. A true son of a father who refused to acknowledge him, a true son who returned from Spain—from that failed last Crusade, with a secret.

Was that the story Cate was after?

A story in a photograph, like hundreds of other photographs taken during the war.

CHAPTER
FIFTEEN
JUNE 6, 1944, NORMANDY, COAST OF FRANCE

"What is your name, soldier?" Brigadier Lord Lovat demanded as the transport lurched beneath them.

"Private Paul Bennett, sir."

"Ah, the photographer. Do you have a weapon other than that bloody camera?"

"Yes, sir." He adjusted the rifle at his shoulder, the camera secured around his neck.

"You're Scot?" Lord Lovat asked.

"Aye, sir. Inverness."

"Thought as much. Are you any good with that camera?"

"I've had some experience, sir. The Daily Mirror." He mentioned the London newspaper he'd gotten on with three years before, after submitting those photos—life in the midst of chaos in London, the bombed-out buildings, men, and women huddled in underground rail stations, children on evacuation trains to the English countryside, even one of the young Princess Royal, Elizabeth, in her uniform, a driver for the emergency services.

His contact at the Mirror had given him a doubtful look when he told him that he'd signed on with the military in spite of a boyhood injury that had left him with a limp. He'd laid a hand on his shoulder.

"Have you told your family?"

There were just his mother and sister, safe in Scotland. He nodded. He'd posted the letter just that morning. In twenty-four hours he was on his way. That was all they'd given all of them attached to the press corps, and sworn to secrecy. Everything, the flat he shared with a staff writer, his other equipment, was left as if he were planning on returning at the end of the day. Absolute secrecy was required.

"I went over during the first war, you see," his editor had told him. "Too old to go this time around." He was part of the Home Guard.

"Keep your head down lad and keep moving. Did they tell you that rounds always come at you in bursts? Remember that. When they stop, move. And don't stop to think, just keep going."

He'd thanked him for the advice and swallowed past the tightness in his throat, heading into the unknown.

Twenty-four hours later they were lining up to board the transport under cover of darkness. There had been speculation for weeks about when they might leave, along with the build-up, decoys constructed at bases to throw the Germans off while everything and anything that could float was pressed into service.

He and a young man named Callish, whom he'd taken training with, found themselves assigned to the same transport, along with the 84th.

Lovat grunted now at his response as the French coastline of Calais suddenly appeared through the early morning fog.

"Well this isn't your usual garden party, young man."

As if to remind them all of that, an explosion rocked the transport off to their starboard, men and bodies thrown into the water—one of the mines they'd been warned about, waiting underwater, one of the German measures against a coastal invasion.

"No, sir," Paul replied as they swept past, and couldn't help but wonder if the same fate awaited them.

He glanced past Lovat, past the armored vehicle anchored into the bay of the transport, past the specially trained commandoes of the 1st Special Service Brigade, through the clouds of fog and smoke that engulfed the beach ahead.

The landing craft lurched on another wave, churning toward that beachhead and the cliffs beyond. The others aboard, Callish beside him, steadied themselves, expressions grim, waiting, waiting.

What were they thinking, Paul wondered as he took several shots with the 35mm Leica, ironically produced in Germany before the war, that had set him back a couple months' wages. But it had been worth it. That and the three lenses he purchased just a few weeks earlier—a mark-down sale from a London merchant whose store had been bombed and left in ruins. People weren't buying cameras to take on holiday.

"How old are you?" Lovat asked.

"Twenty-four this past April, sir."

There'd been no party, no birthday songs, only the blessing from the priest—"May God guide and protect you." And a bit of stale cake sent weeks earlier from his mother.

"Ah, well, you'll be an old man before this is over," Lovat added. "We all will be."

"Aye, sir."

He already felt like an old man, after living in London since the bombings began in '39, with the air raids, scrambling to get into one of the underground shelters, bodies crammed together...and bodies on the streets. People, just trying to live their lives. And dying. He'd taken pictures of it all—images and scenes that came back in the night in dreams.

Lovat motioned to a man behind him.

"Come along then, William," he told him. "I want a picture as we go ashore, bloody proof that we made it, you see?"

A man stepped past him and joined Lovat at the bow doors of the landing craft.

"Bloody crazy maniac," Callish whispered beside him, just out of earshot. "Brings along his own personal piper."

They were closer now, those around them checking their equipment and weapons one last time, to a man their expressions fixed in what he would later describe as their 'war faces,' and the thought occurred to him as he took another shot with his camera, that it was all the same—centuries apart, but these twentieth-century warriors were much the same as those before them, in other places, other wars, about to step off into the unknown.

"They're called hedgehogs." Callish pointed out the beach barricades, the Germans line of defense against a sea landing, steel crossmembers like jacks in a line along the beach. But this was a deadly toy.

"They say there are mines strapped to each one," Callish added.

How many would still be alive at the end of the day? Or the next day? Paul wondered.

"Take my picture," one soldier had told him before leaving Dover, and had given his name—Ian Campbell. A good Scottish name.

"That way they'll be able to identify me if I don't make it back."

If any of them made it back.

"Make yourself ready," Lovat told the man beside him. "I want a good rousing piece for the lads."

Click, click of the camera. Lovat's personal piper pumped up the bag with the pipes secured across his chest.

He made quite a sight, the bagpipes at his chest, the field pack at his back, like a beached turtle, legs and arms sticking out from the ponderous shape, and Paul wondered if he would be able to make it ashore through the churning surf that was as dark and dangerous looking as any he'd seen on holiday on the north coast of Scotland.

The man winked at him as he tuned up the pipes. "Stay with me, lads. If they take a shot at me, it won't make it past this rig I've got on." He pumped and tuned over the whine of the engines as they rolled toward the beachhead, closer now.

"Hail Mary, full of grace," another man beside them prayed. "Protect us in our hour of need."

Click, click, click. A half dozen more shots of those around him, faces that needed to be remembered. And then he was stowing the camera in the waterproof pouch. The landing craft lurched and the engines slowed then reversed. Only a hundred yards from that beach now.

"Have a care, lads," Lovat said one last time.

The bow doors opened, commandoes jostled around them, then moved past, jumping into the rolling surf, then plunging toward the beach. They followed Lovat, his piper right behind him like the Pied Piper.

Bullets exploded all around them, popping on the surface of the water, whizzing past, and the churning surf turned blood red.

"Bloody Christ!" Callish swore beside him as they hit the water, scrabbling for a foothold on the sandy bottom.

Plop, plop, plop. Bullets rained down around them. They kept moving, past a body floating in the surf, then another rolling back toward them on a receding wave. A hand reached up out of the water and Callish instinctively grabbed for it. Just moments before he'd been sharing a cigarette with the man. The body bobbed in the water.

"Leave him!" Paul shouted. "You can't help him now." He grabbed Callish by the collar and shoved him forward.

They kept moving, stumbling, pushing back to their feet, past another body floating in the surf, sightless eyes staring.

"Hail Mary, full of grace," the man had whispered only moments earlier. Now he was dead.

He counted bursts of rounds that hit the water, then the interval between. Four maybe six seconds.

"Move!" he shouted to Callish, then hit the water just as another burst opened on them. He counted and they were on the move again, clawing their way toward the beach.

Several yards ahead, Lovat with his piper close behind, stormed the beachhead, bullets from machinegun fire in those rocky emplacements beyond the beach popping all around him in a macabre accompaniment to the pipes.

Lying in the sand, the freezing water of the channel washing around him, Paul Bennett took out the camera as others raced past, hit the beach, then died.

It was still Tuesday, June 6, the longest day of all their lives. And for so many, the last day.

He counted again as the rounds whizzed past. Then came the silence between, even as chaos swarmed around them. He used the camera like a weapon, catching the determination, desperation, fear, in their faces, taking cover behind another body as Callish crawled behind him.

One word came to mind—Armageddon.

There were no words spoken as they crawled across the beach, ironically took shelter behind one of those steel hedgehogs the Germans had installed, then lunged ahead, past bodies, then parts of bodies, and followed others as they made for the base of those cliffs with those gun emplacements above. Keep moving, he reminded himself.

They were scattered among the rocks, common soldiers side-by-side with green lieutenants who'd studied war and now found themselves in the midst of something no one could study for.

He suspected there was no book that prepared them for the

carnage, looking back at the beach they'd crossed, out across the channel with every boat imaginable deployed, dirigibles hovering overhead, a communication lifeline with a bird's-eye view of those emplacements and the countryside of Normandy that stretched in both directions while aircraft swept over their heads, flying inland, raining death down on a tough, determined enemy.

The enemy.

He hadn't understood it, the ruthless German push into Poland, then Czechoslovakia and a half dozen other countries, and the horror stories that came out of it.

Then the bombings in London. Even then, he didn't understand. Not until he was sent out by the newspaper to capture pictures of the devastation at a school, children's bodies scattered about like dolls, images that would haunt him for the rest of his life.

"Take your pictures, kid," a soldier beside him said as he struggled to comprehend man's inhumanity against man.

"Someone has to show what happened here."

He nodded, because he couldn't speak, his throat raw from the salt water, the smoke, from yelling, from retching his guts out at the sight of a man's head half blown away. His hands shook, but he kept shooting with the camera, barely taking time to focus, catching a shot, then another.

Click, click, click.

"Smoke?" A soldier next to them offered a cigarette.

He didn't but he took one anyone. The accent was pure American, a Yank, his face smudged black.

"They say tomorrow will be worse."

He glanced back at the surf that rolled in and the bodies that bobbed beside tanks and transports, the channel beyond crowded with tankers and landing craft while Allied aircraft swept overhead. He swallowed past the tightness in his throat.

He took more pictures, because he had to. Would anyone believe this?

They were trapped, exchanging gunfire, trying to find a way up that slope. Then, others were rushing past, commandoes along with Yanks, all clustered together, their units scattered, in a desperate surge to take the bunkers above, success by attrition.

Explosions rocked the hillside, sending rock and shattered

concrete down the slope. Then the bunkers were silent except for scattered rifle shots, and they were all moving up that hill.

"Bloody Christ!" Callish swore again as the order went out and they scrabbled up the embankment, trying to get a foothold, swarming like bees to a hive, exposed like targets in a shooting gallery, except they were now doing the shooting.

They reached the summit, and stared at the carnage, the bodies of Germans who'd made a last stand in those bunkers along with those who had charged past them.

"Keep moving! Keep moving!" The order went out as bombers swept overhead.

Their unit was scattered, a handful here, a handful there among Yanks and Canadians. They had no idea where the main body of their unit was, or if it existed any longer.

The view of the beaches below and the channel beyond was organized chaos as waves of infantry continued to wade ashore now accompanied by military armament, trucks, more landing craft, transports with equipment, while farther out in the channel seven thousand ships and other craft off-loaded more equipment.

It was amazing, incredible, and at the same time horrific. He was seeing history through the lens of his camera, loading, shooting, reloading, then reloading again even as they were ordered into a sort of formation. They were headed inland on the heels of retreating Germans.

"They say, we're for St. Malo with the Yanks," Callish whispered beside him. "One of the lads said they're eager to have the port, but the Germans have been holed up in the city."

"Where did you hear this?"

Callish shrugged. "Overheard one of the Yanks."

It made sense. With that many ships offshore, they needed control of the ports—St. Malo, Calais, and others along the French coast.

Callish gestured to a half dozen civilians gathered with the officers.

"French Underground. I overheard them speaking in French." He shrugged. "My mother made me study the language. The boy says they can get us to St. Malo. They know where all the German roadblocks and checkpoints are. The girl is pretty, once you get past the men's pants and jacket, couldn't be more than fifteen or sixteen. What should we do?"

Paul Bennett looked around. There were a handful who wore the same insignia on their sleeves, but the rest of their unit was either down on that beach, or had gone ashore and were someplace else, and there was no sign of their group leader. There had been instructions—if they were separated, join up with the nearest unit until you reach a base camp, then re-group. Staying on that beach below or setting off attempting to find their unit on their own wasn't an option under the current conditions.

"Looks like we're headed for St. Malo."

CHAPTER
SIXTEEN
PRESENT DAY, THE INTERNET CAFÉ, INVERNESS

The coffee was hot and strong. Innis had lost count how many cups as he scrolled through information, eyes raw from the cigarette smoke, and a gaming crowd that had stayed into the early hours of the morning.

It was always that way on game night, the café jammed with gamers in front of a dozen terminals, playing against each other and an additional unknown number who linked up off-site.

The competition had been intense, players in costumes appropriate to the game they were involved with, others in jeans and t-shirts.

He had Luna decorate the café for game nights, themes that went with the games so that it seemed like the players were stepping into a scene right out of the game—pirates, commandoes, zombies, that sort of thing, with food appropriate to the scenario for the night—skulls made out of French bread loaves with gummy eyeballs hanging out, meatballs in red sauce that looked like eyeballs swimming in blood, and an assortment of para-military gear, all plastic but so authentic looking that he had a visit one night from the authorities about having weapons on the premises.

Bloody cock-suckers! Innis thought. Now they wanted him to pay for a permit on game nights.

"Like bloody hell!" he muttered, with a glance to the entrance as a customer came in.

There was the usual glance around, those themed decorations from the night before still hanging on the walls and from the ceiling, Luna in full makeup of the living dead as she went about gathering paper cups and picking up empty energy drink containers, and an assortment of ash trays overflowing with cigarette butts and the stubs of other home-grown varieties in spite of house rules.

No drugs, not even the medicinal kind. Not that he was into telling other people how to live their lives, but the last thing he needed was the authorities storming the doors and busting his nuts because some little old lady saw or smelled something funny at his shop. He took a swallow, nerves humming as he skimmed through the banking information, financial statements, and other personal information.

Beyond the glass of the office window that looked out onto the main floor, business had slowed to the usual midday crawl, a couple of teenagers at gaming stations who'd ditched school, Night Crawler —his part-time employee who more or less lived at the café (another city ordinance violation)—presently assisting an older woman who reminded Innis of his grandmother. He concentrated on the screen in front of him.

He wasn't into freelance hacking; he left that to others. There was too much risk—you never really knew who the client was. He had done some work for a few select clients, mostly corporate types who preferred to stay away from the big well-known firms that were into security and provided 'cyber investigation' as a side benefit for some of the biggest names on the planet. Those clients preferred to stay off the radar, and rotated among some talented private individuals for some impressive fees. The crew in Paris did some work for others, who were over the edge and existed only in the shadows.

The fees for those one-offs had provided the seed money for the Internet Café. But this was different. It was personal. Cate had been a friend, and it bloody well looked like she'd been run off the road in the French countryside and left to die.

An unfortunate accident, the media called it, authorities looking into reports another car had been involved, then that whole fucking business in London the night before.

Terrorist attack?

Well looky here, Innis thought.

"Knock, knock," he said with a sort of macabre humor, and keyed in a series of common codes. There were times it was too fucking easy.

"Let's see who's there."

The hack was fairly routine, wait for a data upload, then slip in during the handoff to another bank of servers—child's play. Then, enter the information, play around with a few of the more common passwords. He shook his head at the passwords some people chose and a full screen display of information on Jonathan Callish—that he was undoubtedly certain was secure and paid an arm and leg for—came up on the screen.

"Everything you want to know," he said with satisfaction. "Financial statements, banking, dining habits, several entries for club fees. Let's see what that is all about. Well, look what we have here," he said to himself with a sort of perverse pleasure.

"You just never know about some people." He linked up to other sites, pulling up government data, official records, city permits and licenses for the gallery, credit card accounts. Something caught his eye and he scrolled back.

"Marriage license?" Well that wasn't unusual. But the name on the license was definitely of the female persuasion.

"So the wanker goes both ways. Each to his own personal taste I always say."

He continued his search. As he suspected, information for the gallery and most of Callish's personal information was supposedly protected by the usual well-known security programs and firewalls. If the average person realized how weak the average internet security measures were, they'd have a freaking coronary.

The simple truth was, there was no such thing as security. It was commonly known in the cyber world—whatever a security company or some rogue individual could put out there, someone else could break into—find a hole, a gap in the wall, then slip in. They were all playing the same game, it was just a matter of speed—get in, get the information, then get out. And everything was for sale.

He scanned the next screen, same boring shit. Then, "Hello?"

There were several drafts of funds labeled business development. The destination was an account at an international bank in Paris.

Business development? There were at least two dozen entries over the last two years. He did the mental math and whistled. There was almost twenty million dollars in transfers, not exactly pocket change.

It appeared the transfers had been made by two different identities. He followed several links, then searched the name that came up on the receiving end of all those transfers—Le Noir.

Foreign language had never been his best subject. In fact he'd dropped out. But he didn't have to be a language expert to figure this one out.

Le Noir, loosely translated, The Dark Side. Not exactly what he would have chosen for the name of a gallery.

"All right," he said to himself. "Let's see what we can find out about this new business enterprise." He entered several search words, the name of the gallery and cross-linked it to Callish.

The usual public information came up. The gallery had opened the year before. There had been an extravagant opening with media reviews about the 'eclectic' blend of art and artifacts offered at the gallery. There were pictures—Callish, an attractive young woman, the artist Alyia, an assortment of guests, artist-types, and a man who showed up in the background of several photographs.

"Let's take a closer look."

He saved one of the shots, then opened it in the program he'd used to enhance the photographs Cate had brought him of her father's war-time work.

This character was dark, dark hair and eyes, definitely Mediterranean type, he thought. Or possibly Middle Eastern?

Artist? Or just an art wonk who hung around galleries?

He definitely wasn't the artist type, not that this character had a sign hung around his neck, and not that he was an expert. He just didn't look the type.

Collector? Not old enough.

They were usually short, pudgy, balding, like Callish, with some artsy type on their arm, and more money than they knew what to do with, the type who purchased according to a financial portfolio, or just because, and then hid the treasure away where it was found fifty years later when the person died. Like the old wanker who dropped dead the year before. No heirs, the authorities open up the residence and discover two Van Goghs, a Monet, and a Picasso that hadn't been seen for decades.

Again, just an observation.

He scrolled through several more photographs from the opening night, lots of fanfare, accolades about the success of the London gallery, names of some of the attendees, apparently big names in the art world.

"Blah, blah, blah."

He went back to Callish's financial portfolio, cruised through several files. There was a lot of money moving through the London Gallery that just didn't add up to the opening of a second gallery. He started a search on the artist, Alyia.

She had apparently come on the London art scene two years earlier, critical acclaim, some good reviews. Others did a pass on her work. Bottom line, the art world was unimpressed, but still she had the showings at Callish's Bankside Gallery. It paid to be sleeping with the gallery owner.

He dug a little deeper—education, family, known associations, that sort of thing. Everything came up perfect. But the information only went back five years.

"No such thing as perfect," he muttered.

He cross-referenced the information to school records—educational institutions were easy to break into. He came up with a blank. According to those records, a student by the name of A. Malik had been removed from the school register—deceased!

"Then who the hell is Callish married to?" He went back to the date of the marriage and brought up more records. There was the usual identification for both. He tried another search and came up empty.

The screen went blank.

"What the fuck!"

He brought the search back up. The screen suddenly exploded with row after row of strings of information. At a glance he knew he'd been caught, and those strings of code meant just one thing—the server on the other end was sending corrupt codes back to his server.

"Bloody hell!"

Whoever was doing this was no amateur. It was too sophisticated.

"Two can play this game." He flexed his fingers and attacked the keyboard. He entered a string of codes, blocking the incoming information. Then went on the attack.

His fingers flew over the keyboard, blocking incoming code, then launching his own code. It was like a game of war, as another code came in, he fired back, sending a string of code that replicated itself over and over—strike, then counterstrike, corrupting that rogue server as it went along.

"Checkmate, you slimy bugger." He watched with grim satisfaction as link after link in that rogue server flashed an error message, then he headed for the exit, covering his tracks along the way. But whoever was behind the attempted hack into his server wouldn't make the same mistake twice. They would try again.

When he was out, he sat back.

Christ! he thought. Who was doing this? And what were they after?

Cate's accident, the break-in at the Tavern, then the incident in London. Someone was playing for keeps and they were willing to kill to get what they wanted. But what?

He looked up, only just aware that Luna stood in the doorway of the office.

"What?" he demanded.

"A customer. He wants to know if you could help him."

He frowned. "What customer?"

"At the front. He's new, haven't seen him before. He was asking about you."

He looked past her, to the front of the café. He knew all the local gamers and computer geeks. At one time or another they found their way into his shop. He didn't know this one, though he looked the part—jeans, sweatshirt, some brand-name sport shoe, long hair. Still...

"Tell him we're closed."

She stared at him. "It's only half past, and there's the group coming in this evening."

He glanced past her to the new customer. It was probably nothing to worry about.

He was always saying they needed new customers, and the coincidence of someone new walking into the café right in the middle of his game of sabotage was probably just that—a coincidence. Still...

"I've been thinking, luv. We need a little vacay."

She looked at him as if he'd taken a hard right turn away from reality.

"A vacation? In the middle of winter?"

CHAPTER
SEVENTEEN
MONT ST. MICHEL, COAST OF FRANCE

The last tour of the day had arrived, tourists and day travelers boarding shuttles at the car park for the ride over the causeway. A display screen at the information center announced that the last tour departed at 5:00 p.m. for the island.

They boarded the shuttle and found seats near the front, the driver welcoming everyone board in both French and English as the door closed.

"Good afternoon and welcome to Mont St. Michel."

The driver, a woman, was both tour guide and historian, reciting information Kris remembered from an earlier visit years before.

"The abbey has been a holy site since the year seven hundred and eight," their driver began.

"What you see now was built over several centuries, culminating in the dome with the gilded statue of Saint Michael."

"According to legend, the Archangel Michael told the good bishop to build a church," Kris whispered. "The bishop ignored the angel and he burned a hole in the bishop's skull. The Saint's skull, with a hole in it, can be seen in one of the churches."

"It's never good to piss off an archangel," James commented, as the driver continued her introduction to the abbey.

"The abbey has been a fortress, a sanctuary, a hospital, and prison. The ramparts were built to defend against the English. It should be noted that it has never been conquered.

"In later centuries, the Benedictine monks lived here in several private chambers that you will see, depending on the tour you take. At the base of the abbey is the town of Mont St. Michel, where you will find food, and accommodations for those staying on the island. The omelets are an island specialty, once served to pilgrims who required a quick meal—their own fast food—before continuing their travels." This brought laughter among the tourists.

"The causeway that connects the island is under water at certain times during the day. Unfortunately," she continued, "many have lost their lives to the quicksand and unpredictable tides. We ask that you do not attempt to cross over to the mainland on foot across the tidal basin, especially at night. It can be very treacherous."

They crossed the mile-long causeway, the shuttle slowing as it reached the island terminal, and the driver announced the last departure time.

"The last shuttle of the evening departs the island at nine o'clock this evening. Several tours of the island and abbey are offered. The abbey is open until eight pm. There are private residences that date from the 13th and 14th centuries that are now part of the museum tours. Please check the tour schedule. Enjoy your stay."

Years before, when the abbey had been on Kris's list of places to visit that summer after college, it had seemed just one more gothic church on a list of several. There had been the usual tour, the curator —very much like a docent of a museum—pointing out the usual points of interest, and providing the usual history of sea battles, assaults by the English across the channel, and the construction by William the Conqueror as a fortress almost a thousand years ago.

There was the usual display of cannon along the rampart and the various residences that dated back to the fourteenth century, but there was no mention of another story that was part of the history of the abbey, about a young woman who had defied her father, retreated to the island fortress, and created a tapestry that held a secret almost seven hundred years later.

They stopped at the tourist office, and asked for the director. Cate had made two calls to the tour office. The director remembered speaking with her.

"Yes, of course. Most unfortunate about the accident. Ms. Ross met with Brother Thomas when she was here. It was for a book she was thinking of writing. He is an authority on the abbey and the history of the island. "

She and James exchanged a look.

"Is he here today?" she asked.

"He is conducting evening mass. It started just a short while ago. I can let him know that you want to speak with him."

He took out a cell phone and sent a text message—new age meets the old world, Kris thought, thanking him.

With a little less than an hour until evening mass ended, they followed visitors on the Grand Rue, the main street with shop and restaurants, then along the sea wall, the lane climbing steadily toward private residences and the island museums.

According to the tour they followed, there were four museums on the island—a maritime museum that explored the tidal phenomenon that had protected the island fortress for over a thousand years, the archeoscope where visitors could view a stunning technological presentation that explained the convergence of faith, history, and legend in a light show, according to the promotional brochure, and the history museum that was like taking several steps back in time, with life-size wax models, true-to-life reconstructions, displays of weapons of the time including those used for torture.

"Just your average day at the office," Kris remarked at the grisly scenes that had been recreated and left little to the imagination.

They followed the tour as they wound their way along a narrow lane that slowly climbed to a row of private residences.

According to the signage at the entrance of a two-story residence, it was almost completely intact as it had been in the 14th century, including furnishings, crockery, and wall hangings. A young woman dressed in period costume provided visitors with the narrative of what life was like on the island in the 14th century.

"Everything you see about the island, everything needed for the households of the time, inns, the abbey, had to be brought over from the mainland by cart, including all the granite stonework you see that was quarried on the mainland and then brought over the causeway that was nothing more than ocean bed when the tide went out. Construction of the abbey began in the eleventh century, and has been rebuilt over the centuries due to loss from fire of the early wood structures, poor early construction, and expansion to include the abbey.

"The island fortress was originally commissioned by William the Conqueror, who was Norman," she continued. "And you will find many carvings, motifs, and original weaponry that has survived. Construction over the centuries include Norman, Gothic, and Romanesque architecture. This residence was built in the mid fourteenth century. We ask that you stay behind the rope barriers in the interest of preservation of the artifacts and furnishings."

They followed the tour from the main room with the carved stone at the threshold that gave the year 1342 as the year the residence was built. According to what Vilette Moreau had told them, that would have been after Isa Raveneau returned from Spain.

The residence had dark wood floors with mahogany window casements, the windows looking out onto the gardens they had passed. The furnishings were also mahogany, a large corner cabinet, armchairs with leather seats and backs, all the wood painstakingly carved with elaborate designs—scrollwork, floral motifs, carvings of birds and animals. This was no common worker's residence.

The kitchen had been painstakingly preserved with wood counters, a large stone hearth and oven, a huge copper pot that hung over the raised hearth, and crockery that lined the shelves. Fake vegetables lay on the countertop along with several fake plucked chickens, and added to the imagination of what it might have been like centuries past.

The rooms on the main floor were common rooms, fascinating with their period furnishings and utensils that provided a glimpse into the everyday life of the residents of the island. But the private bedchamber on the second floor was far more intimate.

The walls were those same granite stones and the floor was wood, but a large area rug filled the center of the room. The bed and other furnishings had been roped off.

As with the furnishings in the common rooms, the furniture was rich, dark mahogany, including the large, canopied bed with bed hangings. The headboard and bed frame had all been carved with delicate designs from nature. A cabinet that stood in the corner was also mahogany with a floral design carved into the doors.

An arched stone doorway was opposite the bed, and an arched window casement included a large brass urn at the window seat. The windows looked out on the gardens below and the bay beyond. A large hearth filled the opposite wall of the room.

"The large pot you see hanging at the hearth would have been used to heat water for bathing, although many believed that bathing too often wasn't healthy," their guide explained with a faint smile.

"The table with the mirror above is original to the residence. You will see that the mirror is made of polished metal, and there is an assortment of personal items." She pointed out a brush, combs, and several porcelain containers.

There was nothing masculine about the room, Kris thought. Nothing to indicate that a man had ever occupied the chamber. Except for the suit of armor that stood in one corner. Was it original to the residence or had it been added to add to the tourist experience?

"The house has been in the same family for over four hundred years. They maintained it as it was originally. It has only recently passed from the last private owner to the heritage foundation that oversees the entire island as an historical site. There are stories that it was originally built by a very wealthy patron of the abbey who lived here for several years."

Kris exchanged a look with James. According to Vilette, Isa Raveneau had lived at the abbey the rest of her life after James' death. Was it possible she might have been that wealthy patron?

"As a point of interest," their guide added, as they left the room, "you may want to visit the abbey archive, which contains documents and manuscripts written by the Benedictine monks who have lived here over the years. There are translations from Latin and copies are available for purchase and provide an interesting glimpse of daily life at the abbey."

Kris stayed behind as the tour moved on.

"What are you doing?" James whispered.

"Vilette said that Isa Raveneau lived at the abbey after James' death, and never returned to her family."

She wanted to see more of the chamber, the furnishings, something that might tell them if Isa Raveneau might have lived there.

"Kris..."

"You don't believe it." She heard the doubt, saw it in the expression at his face.

"I believe that Vilette believes it."

"What about the medallion?" she asked.

"A medallion that somehow survived over seven hundred years?" he pointed out. "A trinket that could have been found in any antique shop."

"Cate believed the story." Believed it enough that she had come here, following that story. And now two people were dead.

"What are you looking for?" he demanded.

She shook her head. "I don't know..."

What was she looking for? A sign that said *Isa Raveneau slept here*?

A wealthy patron had built the house, and everything in it indicated wealth with a feminine touch in the choice of wall hangings in the great room, in the delicate porcelain dinnerware, and other artifacts.

The keystone over the entrance to the home had been carved with the year 1342. According to Vilette, Isa Raveneau had gone to Spain to ransom James Montfort after the disastrous battle at Teba in 1335. Also according to her story, they had returned and sought refuge at the abbey, known for giving sanctuary to pilgrims traveling across Europe. And then Isa Raveneau had supposedly returned to the abbey and stayed there after that trip to take James' body back to Scotland.

Like so many old houses, chateaus, and castles that she'd seen on earlier trips, the room had the smell of old wood, the pungent smell of the ocean that surrounded Mont St. Michel, and the faint smokiness of the fireplace that was large enough for a person to stand in.

The craftsmanship never failed to amaze her, seen in the countless cathedrals and castles with their vaulted ceilings, each stone precisely placed to support the next, and the next, like the stones over the opening of the fireplace with the keystone that locked all the others in place.

The furnishings had been roped off, but not the window casements, a tall wardrobe, or the fireplace.

Seven hundred years of soot had accumulated on the granite stones in the hearth, all but obscuring the images that had been carved on each one—flowers and leaves that draped the arch of the fireplace in the design cut into the stones.

Symbols, letters, numbers were often cut into stones to mark something significant—the year a slab was poured for a new building, a family crest, or emblem.

The great houses of Europe were filled with carvings meant to convey a date, a family name, or some important event. The Egyptians had been noted for their carvings and paintings inside palaces and tombs. The Romans had their own symbols, statues, and letters.

"The raven?" he suggested.

According to Vilette, it was part of the Raveneau family crest.

"Possibly," she replied, tracing the image on the keystone with her fingers.

It was caked with soot and grime over the centuries. She scrubbed at it with the sleeve of her sweatshirt and bottled water.

"Defacing an historic artifact?" James asked. "There's undoubtedly a stiff fine for that, possibly a little prison time."

"A little light housekeeping." She scrubbed the jagged cuts, each one precisely made to form a unique design.

It might be nothing more than leaves like the carved garland that ran up the sides of the hearth, or it might be the mark of the stonemason who had set the stones or the artisan who had carved the images, like signing a painting.

She scrubbed harder, the image slowly emerging.

"Everything Vilette told us is true," she said, taking a half step back, staring at the image.

"What is it?"

"Isa Raveneau lived in this house." They exchanged a look.

They heard voices approaching. Kris pulled her phone from her pocket and took several shots of the keystone, and the image that was carved in the surface—a trinity knot wrapped around a Scottish thistle.

"Evening mass should be over now," James commented as they left the rest of the tour.

They followed signage that indicated the direction to the abbey church at the top of Mont St. Michel.

"A thousand steps, just a walk in the park," James commented as clouds gathered out over the water.

"We might just make it before that storm breaks."

The island fortress had been built over a thousand years earlier with granite rocks mined and cut on the mainland, hauled in carts across the causeway at low tide, and then winched to the top by a sophisticated hoist system, layer upon layer, buttresses and chambers, storerooms, residences for the monks built at the lower level to support the weight of the abbey above, then upward, providing the foundation for the abbey church.

It was an architectural and engineering marvel that had withstood assault and invasion, and provided a haven for pilgrims returning from the Holy Land, that apparently included Isabel Raveneau and James Montfort, according to the story Vilette Moreau had told them.

"Bloody Christ!" James swore as they began yet another flight of stairs carved in granite, the town at the base of the island spreading out below them.

"Careful," she warned, trying to catching her breath before staring the next part of the climb.

"You don't want to piss off Saint Michael."

He made some other comment, lost on the wind at the battlements and the roar of the ocean as it crashed against the rocks below.

CHAPTER
EIGHTEEN
JULY 10, 1944, COAST OF FRANCE

They'd been on the march for over a month, a handful from their company along with Americans and Canadians.

At night, they hid in the fields, barns, and behind stone fences that had stood since the time of the Crusades, with the roar of the ocean when the guns fell silent, an invasion army by day, pursuing a dangerous enemy, exhausted, eating field rations, grabbing a few hours' sleep at night with their rifles beside them.

Paul Bennett had been given no instructions on the pictures he was to take.

"Send us back what you can," the editor of the Daily Mirror had told him. Then, "You come back to us, lad."

He went on instinct, shooting pictures that were stark contrast of an invading army against the French countryside in the midst of summer, that was at times picturesque and at other times heartbreakingly destroyed—the chaos of a looted, burned-out village against the bucolic peacefulness of cattle grazing.

And then there were other shots—the casualties, those who had pushed ahead of them, soldiers from every Allied nation determined to take back seaports, at the same time liberating the people of the French countryside, pushing back the Germans who were determined to destroy everything in their path, and other shots of the men, gaunt-faced, exhausted, resolute, with quiet conversations or no conversations at all over meal rations quickly consumed, weapons braced across their knees, then moving on, always moving.

Home for all of them, no matter where they were from, was a far place that all of them wondered if they would ever see again.

Click, click. Rolls of film carefully wrapped in waterproof pouches. And then a new roll of film. And the boy.

His name was Nico. He had been born in Czechoslovakia, but escaped at the age of eight just before the German invasion of that country. He had no idea if his family was still alive or had been sent to one of the concentration camps. He was now fourteen, painfully thin, with just a sprinkling of hair on his chin. But his eyes were the eyes of someone far older.

He spoke little, but everything was there in dark, haunted eyes that stared back at Paul Bennett's camera. He'd killed his first German when he was nine.

The girl's name was Micheleine. She was fourteen when the war started, from a village north of Paris.

Micheleine had followed her father and brothers into the Resistance. They had been captured and executed. That was four years ago. She wasn't a young girl any longer.

Because she spoke both English and French, and out of necessity had become almost fluent in German, she was a valued member of the Resistance with the ability to move behind enemy lines, carry messages between French and Allied groups, and gain valuable information on German troop movement.

She had been caught once and escaped. There were rumors a high-ranking German officer had died during that escape. She had a price on her head and a name she'd been given by the French people who considered her a hero. Jehanne.

She was just over five feet tall and couldn't have weighed more than a hundred pounds. She carried a rifle with the assurance of someone who knew how to use it, and was their guide through enemy lines.

She was a frequent visitor to their encampment at night. The camera and the pictures Paul took caught her attention and broke down a natural reserve around people who might be dead the next day.

"Do you take photographs for the American Army?" she had

asked one evening as he carefully cleaned the lens that had somehow miraculously survived wading through channel surf, crawling across the beach, and the march inland.

Her usual reserve dropped, curiosity shining in her dark eyes.

He shook his head. "For the newspaper I worked for before being shipped over."

He carefully extracted a roll of film and added it to the half-dozen other rolls he kept in the waterproof pouch to send off when they reached the next Allied post.

"Before the war, I did individual portraits, weddings, christenings, that sort of thing. When the war broke out, I got on with the Mirror. They wanted photographs of things out and about in London, how people were getting on with the bombings, food rationing, inside the shelters, that sort of thing."

"And now you take photographs of bombings in France, towns destroyed, that sort of thing," she had commented with unmistakable sarcasm.

She was entitled to that, he thought.

"Someone said that I need to take the photographs so that no one forgets what has happened here."

He was fast losing the light, and set the aperture at the camera by the glow of a nearby campfire behind her. He adjusted the film speed. Then she looked up, everything she had experienced revealed in the emotion on her face and the look in her eyes, and it touched something inside him.

"Do you believe it will make a difference?" she asked.

"Do you believe that you make a difference?" he replied as the glow of that campfire surrounded her.

Click, click, click.

She frowned into the camera. "If I did not, then all is lost."

He took several more shots of a beautiful young Frenchwoman who had seen too much, had killed, and left innocence far behind. But at that moment, just long enough for the shutter to capture her expression, the young girl peeked out at him.

Click, click.

"Take your pictures, Paul Bennett. They will tell the story," she said as she stood to leave.

"Then perhaps, one day, this will end."

When dawn came the next day, she and Nico were already gone, scouting ahead with a handful of commandoes, sending messages back about German troop movements. But in the days that followed, moving south by day, she sought out their small encampment in spite of the fact they weren't allowed to build a fire and it was pitch dark. She sat with them, eating their cold rations.

"Tell me about your family," she said one night as they finally made camp at the edge of a grove of trees, sentries posted along the perimeter.

He told her about his mother and sister, safe he hoped, in Scotland.

"Tell me about Scotland."

He thought about that for a long time, the way a place imprints itself in the memory and emotions, how to describe it.

"It's green and the mountains in the distance are capped with snow. There are places that have no electric, or need for it. The people there live as they have for hundreds of years. On the outer islands, people still speak the old language and tell stories about the water horses." At her sudden change of expression, he explained. "Legends about shape-shifters that live in the fairy pools and lochs."

She laughed then. "Do you believe in water horses?"

"Ach, well when you look deep into one of the pools with the light moving across the surface, there are things that move about and tease you." He liked the sound of her laughter.

"But it's the smell of the land." He angled a look at her through the shaft of moonlight to see if she was still laughing at him. "It's the smell of wild things and the earth, and ancient places after the rain, that stays with you like a memory. And then there are the fairy glens."

"Fairy glens?"

"Aye," he replied. "Where it's said the ancient ones come from the other world on Samhuinn, and move among the living for just a little while before returning to the spirit world."

She laughed again. She was usually so serious, too serious for one so young. He took several more pictures.

"You are as comfortable with the weapon as you are with the camera," she commented.

"Bird hunting with my grandfather, a long time ago," he replied. "He often took me with him." It was a good memory.

"What about your family?" he asked, and wondered what she would tell him.

She had never shared anything about herself, in the way that conversations often turned to home and family. She kept everything to herself, tucked away, hidden.

"I had two brothers and a sister. My father and brothers joined the Resistance in the beginning, the early days when they knew it was only a matter of time before the Germans came. They were captured." Her voice had gone quiet.

"I was told they were executed. That is when I joined the Resistance."

"And you've been with them ever since."

"Yes," she replied. "I do it for my father and brothers, for those who cannot fight for themselves. I will not stop until the Germans are gone, you see?"

There was an edge in her voice then, grim determination along with the anger.

"What about your mother and sister?"

"They are safe, I pray. The last I knew, they lived with my uncle on his farm."

"What will you do after the war?" he asked. She didn't reply for a long time, and he thought she might not.

"I haven't thought of it. For so long, there has only been today with no promise of tomorrow."

He felt her looking at him then. "Will you go home to your fairy glens?" she asked.

He smiled at the way she said it, not really believing it, yet perhaps needing to.

"I might work for the newspaper again." But human-interest photographs hadn't been all that exciting.

"Will you continue to take your photographs?"

He thought about that, about the shots he'd taken since the landing, images caught in a split second, a breath taken between living and dying.

"It is important," she answered for him, laying a hand on his arm. She stood to leave.

"Take your pictures, so that people do not forget."

They continued the push toward St. Malo. The heavier fighting, they were told, would come in the next two days as they reached the port city. The Germans were heavily fortified at St. Malo. They weren't about to give up the strategic seaport without a long and bloody fight.

Micheleine returned unexpectedly as they traversed the French countryside, and was immediately taken to the Allied commander.

"There's a bit of conversation going on there," Callish said as they were ordered to hold their position. She was in animated conversation with the commander of the American unit, along with a man who wore the robes of a monk.

He was from the Abbey at Mont St. Michel on the coastal island they'd seen earlier that morning. Orders had gone out that the Abbey was off-limits to military personnel. No one was to go out to the ancient island fortress or the village at the base of the island when they made camp that night, and they had continued to skirt the island fortress.

"Something's up." Callish tried to hear what they were saying, translating the rapid-fire conversation that was in French, then English.

"The fellow really has his robes in a knot."

For the past several days, they'd been shadowing German troop movements, pulling farther back into France after the invasion a month earlier. In their wake, the Germans left towns and villages reduced to cinders and ash, inhabitants left homeless, or worse— executed on accusations that they'd cooperated with the Resistance and the Allies.

There was more conversation, then an American lieutenant walked toward them. He motioned to Paul. He exchanged a look with Callish, then followed. He caught a brief glance from Micheleine.

"You're to go with this woman," the commander of the American unit told him. "Choose a man to go with you. You leave immediately."

"What's happened?" he asked her.

"The monk brought word that one of our people is at the Abbey. He's been badly wounded. They received word that the Allies were nearby and sent the monk," she explained. "They are afraid for him to be there with so many Germans still in the area. We have to try and get him out."

"Christ!" Callish whispered, when he told him. "Now we're on a bloody rescue mission? And the village at the base of the island is probably crawling with Germans."

It was a small group that was to go—the boy Nico, who was an expert at sneaking into places unnoticed; Micheleine, who apparently knew the man to be rescued; Callish himself; and four American soldiers.

They were all heavily armed, and against earlier orders they were to get into the Abbey at Mont St. Michel, and bring the injured man out.

"If you have the opportunity," Paul was told, the captain of the American unit tapping his camera, "It would be helpful to have information on just how many Germans there are in the village."

So much for creating a photographic history of the Allied invasion —now he was being sent to spy on the enemy.

There were two ways to access the abbey. When the tide was out, the causeway that linked the island to the mainland was exposed, but anyone crossing it was also exposed to any German soldiers who might be in the village at the base of the island. The second access was by boat when the tide was in, making travel extremely dangerous with unpredictable tides.

The latter choice answered the question about the American soldiers who were sent with them, all trained and experienced in water landings.

The monk had left the island under the pretext of seeing to the spiritual needs of people on the mainland. He was to return the following day by the same means. He had persuaded a local fisherman to leave his small craft anchored in the jetty where other fishermen kept their boats.

With instructions on the location of a sea gate where provisions had been loaded off ships over the centuries, they boarded the fishing boat. The Americans expertly navigated the boat under cover of darkness to the southern tip of the island.

"That's the last time I bloody volunteer," Callish whispered over the chug of the small motor as they slipped around the tip of the island.

Paul didn't bother to remind him that everyone had volunteered, whether they wanted to or not.

They were in luck; the moon wasn't up yet. That advantage also worked against them as the small fishing boat churned through the water. When they were within a few hundred yards of the sea gate, one of the Americans cut the motor while the others slipped over the side.

They waited, waves lapping against the side of the fishing boat.

"Bloody foolish, if you ask me," Callish whispered beside him.

"Is he always like this?" Micheleine asked.

"I try to ignore most of it," Paul replied. Then Micheleine tugged at his sleeve.

"There." She pointed through the darkness to a faint signal light.

The Americans had found the sea gate. Almost as soon as they saw the signal, one of them hoisted himself back over the side of the boat. He started up the motor and they slowly approached the base of the island, heading toward that faint flashing signal.

The sea gate of the island was set back in a small cove with a landing. They tied the boat and climbed the steps up to the landing. The landing extended into the base of the abbey behind thick sea doors that the monk had arranged to leave open at low tide. Inside those sea doors was a massive storage area lined with crates, boxes, lumber for repairs, and a cistern that provided fresh water for the island. Stairs climbed up from the storage chamber into the lower level of the abbey.

"They say it's a thousand steps from the village up to the abbey mount," Callish complained beside him.

"We can always leave you behind," Micheleine informed him.

Callish grumbled, then fell in with them as they started the climb.

It was cool and damp inside the passage that had been carved out of stone centuries earlier. Still, Paul broke out in a sweat that had nothing to do with the climb or the cold, and everything to do with the unknown that awaited when they reached the top of those steps.

What if there were German patrols on the island? What if the monk had been seen leaving and someone had grown suspicious? What if they'd been seen, and a German patrol waited for them at the top of the passage?

The rifle was heavy on his shoulder. He shifted it, grateful for the weight of it.

"It is just here, according to the monk," Micheleine announced as they reached the top step of the next level.

They stepped past her and put their shoulders to the heavy timbered door as the Americans made ready in the event there was anyone on the other side. It creaked and groaned, then slowly opened into a darkened alley. They breathed in cool, fresh night air.

They heard the roar of the ocean on the rocks below. At the opposite end of the alley, light was visible from the street that led into the village.

"This way," Nico called out, and they followed him in the opposite direction, circling around the back side of the island.

He had no idea how long they walked, expecting to find German guards around every turn. Eventually they reached those steps that reached up into the night sky toward the Abbey Church.

"Bloody insane if you ask me," Callish complained. "How are we supposed to get the blighter to the landing if he's injured? And that is if someone doesn't stop us, or kill us?"

Paul caught sight of uniformed guests at one of those outdoor tables. He exchanged a look with Micheleine as she turned and started the climb toward the church.

They stopped several times on that steep climb to catch their breath as wind whipped around the island. Near the top they stopped again, the Americans moving ahead to make certain there were no surprise encounters with Germans who had decided to take a tour of the abbey. A tap on his arm, and they silently moved toward the entrance.

It was quiet inside the church, the silence broken only by the whistle of the wind against those massive doors. Just inside the entrance they were met by one of the monks. He frowned when he saw their weapons.

"This is a house of God."

"And we will defend it in God's name," Micheleine said, pushing past him. "We were told you have one of our people. Please take us to him."

The Abbey at Mont St. Michel was a work of art, going back thirteen hundred years, the different influences that followed—Roman,

Gothic, and the later defensive fortifications of the fourteenth and fifteen centuries—were evident in the chapel, the cloisters, and the narrow window openings at the outer walls.

The monk stopped at another hallway opposite the cloisters.

"Stay here," Micheleine told them. "If there is trouble, get back to the boat as quickly you can." She turned and followed the monk down a dark hallway into another part of the abbey.

They waited, hidden in the shadows beside a massive tapestry mounted at the wall of the cloisters. Paul took a picture of it, but the lighting was poor. It probably wouldn't show much detail.

How long had she been gone, he thought, winding the camera? Ten minutes? More?

Paul checked his watch while two of the Americans stood watch at the entrance. Eventually he heard the sound of footsteps on the stone floor of the sacristy. He laid a hand on Callish's arm against the instinct to raise his weapon, as Micheleine returned.

"Did you find him?"

She nodded. "It is very bad. He has lost a lot of blood. He cannot be moved. I will stay. You must go back with Nico." Before he could ask more questions, she angled her head toward Callish.

"Go on ahead," Paul told him. "Let the others know. I'll be right behind you."

She smiled her gratitude and slipped a folded piece of paper into his hand.

"Stefan is very weak. I wrote down what he told me. There may be more information when he is stronger. You must take this back with you. It is important."

"What about you?"

"We will leave when he is better. The monks will help us." She laid a hand against his cheek.

"You must not worry. God will protect us."

Did she believe that, or was it just something to put his mind at ease about leaving her there.

She glanced at the tapestry on the wall. "Like the story of the tapestry, I entrust you with this." She smiled faintly. "It is called the Raveneau Tapestry. There is a legend about it. Supposedly the lovers were separated." She pointed to the images in the different panels.

"But she rescued him."

He saw the slender figure dressed as a knight, surrounded by other warriors in one of the panels.

"She brought him back to France, here to the abbey," she continued. "He died here, but she was determined to take him home." She indicated another panel.

"To Scotland. You see here, they crossed the channel."

She stared at the images. "It is said there is a secret in the tapestry. Perhaps it is here." She gestured to the next panel.

"She returned alone to the abbey. It is said that she lived the rest of her life here, then joined him. She made this tapestry. It is their story. It is considered a very valuable piece of art, like the Bayeaux Tapestry." She frowned.

"But I fear it will be lost like so many other great pieces of art. I have heard that our people managed to remove paintings from the Louvre before the Germans entered Paris, but other things—statues, paintings, documents, all gone, stolen!" There was passion in her voice now.

"This is what they have taken from us—our history, and the lives of our young men and women, enslaved, murdered." Her voice softened, but the anger was still there.

"I would burn it before I would let them have it."

It was said with such passion that he knew she would do it. She looked at him then, and smiled a sad smile.

"You must go, now. Take your pictures, Paul Bennett. Don't ever stop."

"Isn't there some way to bring your friend with us?"

"You worry for us?"

"What we've seen these past few weeks, the landing, and the countryside..."

She pressed her fingers against his lips.

"It is because of what you have seen that I must stay until he is better." She slipped an arm around his neck and pulled him down for her kiss.

"Go, now!"

CHAPTER
NINETEEN
THE ABBEY CHURCH, MONT ST. MICHEL

"The order of Saint Benedict." James Morgan commented about the mosaic that had been set into the floor as they walked up that last flight of steps to the abbey entrance.

It had been good twenty-minute climb at a steady pace. By the time they reached the top it was almost dark, the walkway lit by lampposts along the way, the sun an orange sliver at the horizon before it slowly sank into the ocean.

Modern lighting had been installed in place of the torches and candles of a thousand years earlier, but Kris still felt the history in the musty coolness of the stones of the passage, in the granite flagstones underfoot, and in the sounds that echoed through an adjacent passageway, in a way she hadn't experienced on that visit years earlier, surrounded by throngs of tourists.

"By the ninth century, the Benedictine order was the standard of monastic life throughout Europe," Kris remembered from those early studies.

They walked up that last flight of steps to the abbey entrance. A directional sign indicated the cloisters were at the end of an adjacent hallway.

"They were called the Black Monks because of the color of their cassocks. Many were scribes while most commoners were rarely educated, except for the very wealthy. Their writings, journals, and translations of scripture flourished between the ninth and twelfth centuries, and abbeys were like libraries for books. Not just scripture, but manuscripts on botany, horticulture, and astrology. Religion spread throughout Europe. It was a way of uniting people, and controlling them."

He gave her a sideways look. "Theology 101 with a little politics thrown in?"

She ignored the cynicism. "I must have been through a dozen abbeys the summer after my second year at college. You get a different perspective when you know the history of things, and how religion was used as a means of controlling people."

"Ah, the summer of enlightenment."

"There was restoration work going on here, and several areas were closed to the public."

"So you settled for a bottle of wine, a young Frenchman, and enlightenment of another sort."

It hadn't been as wonderful as it sounded. There had been a rainstorm. She had missed her train connection back to Paris, and then discovered that the 'young Frenchman' who had offered to guide her and her roommate around had made off with their travelers' checks. She had to call home for money to continue the trip. So much for romantic trips abroad and enlightenment.

"It was two bottles of wine," she confessed, walking on ahead along the passage that led to the Cloisters.

In the muted quiet of stone walls, she could imagine what another young woman might have found in the solitude of the abbey, with only the murmurings of the monks at their prayers, and the distant sounds of the sea measuring out the hours, days, weeks, and years.

That picture was in stark contrast to the image Vilette Moreau had shared of a rebellious, headstrong young woman who had defied both family and possibly the French king, and set off to Spain with a cache of gold and a handful of mercenaries.

Mercenaries—that was the only word for it, in a dangerous land, in dangerous times.

Was it really any different now?

It might have been a trick of the light, her own sense of history, or the story Vilette Moreau had told them. Kris wondered what Isa Raveneau had thought of this remote island sanctuary, far away from family, from everything she had known—a choice made out of anger. Or love?

They crossed another hallway, following the signage and the cloisters opened up in front of them, arched stone columns spanning the massive chamber, leaded glass windows in the outside wall, and the expanse of wall at the end of those rows of columns, modern lighting softly illuminating the massive stone chamber.

She took out the color print of the tapestry that Diana Jodion had printed out for them.

"It was here."

The wall was made of precisely cut granite stones, and matched the wall in the print-out where the tapestry had once hung. It was the same, the corner of one large stone broken off in the fourth row up from the floor; two rows up another stone lighter than the others. It was here when that photograph had been taken.

Voices echoed from the hallway as a group of tourists approached the cloisters. Conversations were a blend of languages and accents as they made their way to the hallway that led from the abbey church.

They retraced their steps to the entrance of the church.

It didn't matter how many churches or cathedrals she'd seen in her travels, there was always that moment first stepping inside that was both amazing and awe-inspiring. Awe at the craftsmanship, the Gothic arches that were like pieces of art, perfectly aligned, identical with a precision that was almost impossible to comprehend, given the era they were built, and amazement at the power of faith that had built them with only hand labor over the centuries.

The abbey church at Mont St. Michel was no different—Norman influence in the base columns, Gothic vaults blending into Romanesque, faith through the centuries.

Rows of benches filled both sides of the church. Candles were set on the walls, while modern lighting drew the eye up to those Gothic arches and the stained-glass dome.

Kris hesitated, then slowly approached the altar.

"Oh, God."

James heard the sound she made, a small sound that echoed in the silence of the church. He saw the expression on her face, colorless, eyes dark. Then he saw the blood where Brother Thomas lay on the church floor.

"No!" He pulled her away, at the same time he scanned the interior of the church, looking for any sign of movement, listening for a sound that they weren't alone.

"We have to help him!" She tried to pull free.

"You can't help him now."

She fought to breathe at the same time it was impossible to breathe, fighting her way past the shock, past what she already knew, had seen in the monk's sightless eyes.

"We have to call someone..."

"Kris." He shook her. "Listen to me! You can't help him, but you can help yourself."

Her gaze snapped to his, still dark, but past that first shock.

"We can't just leave him..."

She had said those exact words once before, staring at Brynn Halliday's twisted body, her sightless eyes. This couldn't be happening!

He shook her. "Whoever did this is out there. We have to get out of here."

"We need to tell someone..."

"Tell them what? That there have already been two deaths, maybe more? And then explain why you came here?"

"What are you saying?" But she knew. There would be questions, with no answers.

What was she doing there? What did she know?

He saw it in the expression on her face.

"We need to leave. Now."

She nodded, fighting back the tears and the anger.

It was ingrained from childhood, an age-old prayer as they left the chapel.

May God keep and protect you.

There was no time to look for another way out. There was only one way down from the abbey church—the same way they'd come from the town below. They had to take their chances that the killer wasn't waiting for them just outside that entrance.

Instinct from a dozen missions in a dozen places with no names kicked in, blocking out everything else—empty streets, a face appearing at a window, a sudden movement at a doorway, adrenaline pumping through.

All he had was the military knife. It was already in his other hand as he slowly opened the church door, scanned the landing, then stepped out. It was empty. He made a sweep in all directions.

A thousand steps down to the town below, with a killer out there somewhere. He motioned for Kris to follow. The cold air outside the church hit both of them, slicing through the shock. The storm that had threatened had finally arrived, rain pelting down.

"Hold onto me," he told her, over the wind that had come up and whipped around the stone walls of the abbey church.

She nodded, jaw tight, teeth clenched as she tried to block out the image of Brother Thomas lying in a pool of blood.

He took her hand and they began the long descent through the driving rain. A hundred steps, two hundred as lightening cracked overhead, then dozens more, the rain blinding them, slipping on wet stones as darkness closed around them.

Thunder cracked overhead, the sky lighting up. Then another sharp crack. The wind whipped at her hair. Her clothes were soaked. She rounded a corner, slipped, and almost went down. James grabbed her, pulled her back to her feet.

Something was wrong. She saw it at his face as lightening lit up the sky. He had bent over, a painful expression at his face. She started back toward him. He waved her off.

"Go!" he shouted over the storm, and hoped he wasn't sending her straight into the killer's path.

"Get to the others!"

Ahead of them, a group of late tourists made their way down those steps. She kept going. She glanced back, saw him briefly as lightening cracked overhead and thunder followed almost on top of them.

At the last turn toward the bottom of the hill, she caught up with the group of tourists, huddled together against the weather, others running down the street below, hoods pulled over the heads, a sea of umbrellas popping open.

James caught up with her, his hand clamped around her upper arm. He saw the question, and shook his head.

"Stay with them." He pushed her ahead into the crowd of tourists —older couples, several families, parents holding hands of younger ones, teenagers running on ahead.

Kris saw the lights of the terminal and the tour office just ahead, then down more steps and they were on the Grand Rue that led back to the tourist center.

The terminal was crowded with tourists boarding the last tram that was departing the island. They followed the other tourists aboard. Both were soaking wet, the other passengers staring as they made their way to two empty seats near the back.

She was shaking from the wet and cold. Another passenger handed her a towel.

James took the aisle seat, his gaze sweeping the faces of the other passengers. Her hands shook as she handed him the towel. He said nothing and took it, shoving it inside the front of his jacket.

"What...?"

He shook his head again, teeth clamped together against the burning pain that set in as the as the cold wore off in the warmth of the tram.

Something was wrong. She saw it in the expression on his face, the way he held himself.

"Tell me!" she whispered, then saw the front of his sweatshirt at the opening of the jacket. It was soaked with blood. He'd been shot!

"Oh, God!" That was the sound she heard over the sound of the storm as they came down from the abbey church.

"You need to hold it together," he whispered.

"How bad?"

The expression on his face told her nothing. There was no expression, no emotion. But the pain was there in that narrow gaze, eyes dark.

His game face? That was what her brother called it, one of the few times he'd opened up about what it was like when they came under attack on one of the missions he had gone out on.

"You leave it behind—the fear, the 'what-if.' You can't take it with you or you risk everyone around you. You learn to shut it off; every emotion, every thought except one—the mission, and survival."

That's what she saw in his eyes now—that dark, cold look, shutting out everything else.

She couldn't shut it out. She started to shake, from the cold, the fear, and anger. Who was doing this? What did they want?

Hold it together..."What can I do?"

He shook his head again. "We need to get out of here."

The causeway was a mile long. It seemed like a hundred miles. Then they were pulling into the car park at the mainland terminal.

James stood slowly, holding onto the back of the seat in front of him, then took her hand, moving along with the other tourists as they departed the tram, watching everyone, each face, pulling her behind him, as others moved ahead with their backpacks, cameras, and souvenir bags. It was then she realized what he was doing—he was shielding her!

They stepped off the tram and she immediately turned toward the row of cars where they'd left the rental. He stopped her.

"Leave it."

"We need to get you to a hospital!"

"No hospital, no contacting the authorities."

There was something in his voice, something she'd heard before, and knew it was useless to argue. He was right.

A clinic, records, a gunshot wound. And it was possible that Brother Thomas's body had been found by now. There was undoubtedly someone who had seen them at the abbey. The French authorities would be called in. There would be questions they had no answers for. And the killer was still out there. A hospital was the last place they could go.

He winced, glancing past her. Safety in numbers. He pulled her toward the tour bus.

They took seats near the rear of the bus, lights overhead turned low as the other passengers took their seats, conversations drifting back—about the tour, someone else's son and daughter-in-law had taken the tour earlier in the year, they really should see it in the spring when the abbey gardens were in bloom. For another couple it had been an item to check off their bucket list as the tour bus reached the roadway. Holiday travelers from a half dozen countries, students, a young couple who'd just gotten married.

And somewhere out there was a killer.

CHAPTER
TWENTY

AUGUST 6, 1944, ST. MALO

The smoke was seen long before they reached the edge of the ancient city fortress.

"It is thought there are fewer than two hundred Germans in the city, but they are strung out between five heavily fortified outposts, and they are destroying everything." Nico whispered the information he had brought back after meeting with local resistance.

"Docks, machinery, at the harbor, and the quay, everything, so that it will not be of use to anyone."

Paul Bennett nodded. "They're destroying the seaport."

It fit with what they'd heard earlier, their goal to take St. Malo, badly needed by Allied forces, and now German determination to prevent that.

"Any word from Micheleine?" he asked, knowing that it was unlikely as they moved south from Mont St. Michel.

Nico shook his head. "She will go north to meet up with others. My work here is finished. The Americans have the information they need." He angled his head toward the resistance fighter who had returned with him, a shadow who slipped into their encampment the night before, and had provided the information they needed about the city.

"You will take my picture, yes?" Nico said with a grin, the boy peeking out from the usually somber expression.

Paul reached for his camera. He'd taken pictures of all of them before, and those candid shots when Nico wasn't aware, a serious expression, those dark eyes, the frown. But he wanted these pictures to remind him of the boy he'd glimpsed. He took several shots.

"You will keep them?" Nico said suddenly serious.

"Yes."

The boy nodded. "We didn't have pictures." He didn't need to explain what he meant—pictures of home, his family.

"There was never enough money, and then the Germans..." He was thoughtful.

"With no pictures, it's as if they never existed. Do you understand?"

Paul gave him the only answer he had. "They exist as long as you remember them," he told him, and wondered what would happen to him, what would happen to all of them.

"I must go," Nico said, suddenly standing. He adjusted the rifle on his shoulder, the boy disappearing once more behind that too-old expression.

"Where will you go next?"

"Where I am needed."

"When you see her..." Paul began, but wasn't certain what the message was. *Be careful* seemed ridiculous. An address where he could write her? Equally ridiculous. When this was over...

"I will tell her that you are well."

Paul nodded.

"We will meet again," Nico said, in that way that people always say things, hoping that it is true.

Paul stood and stuck out his hand. "Bon chance, my young friend."

Nico shook his hand, then tipped his cap in parting and disappeared through the circle of soldiers at the edge of the encampment.

The fight for St. Malo was fierce, and too many times it was uncertain. It was part of the German defense and fortification system from the bay of St. Michel to the mouth of the Fremur river. Names of places, hundreds of years old, were now the center of German resistance, their last hope to hold onto the coast of France.

The city center was surrounded by thick stone walls that had been built to withstand medieval siege by other foreign armies. Reinforced by the German army, it was almost impregnable.

Day by day, seemingly inch by inch, the Allies tried to penetrate those walls, find some opening to the city. A delivery driver attempted to enter the city. They were told he carried food and medicine, but it was rumored he also carried weapons. The truck disappeared inside the gates.

Paul's photographs revealed their frustration in the expressions of soldiers' faces, the American commander as he stared in frustration at the walled fortress through binoculars, and positions that changed daily, sometimes hourly. Then on the third day, determined to take the city and keep the schedule that had been laid out by the Allies, the American commander ordered the shelling of St. Malo.

It was rumored that he sent the Resistance back to tell the people of St. Malo to leave, if at all possible, but there was no certainty that they were able to get to them in time, or that there was even enough time to leave when the shelling finally began at dawn the following day.

It went on for hours, round after round of mortars pummeling the walls and the eighteenth-century buildings of the city beyond. The clouds of smoke were now from the Allied bombardment. When the mortars fell silent, Allied soldiers swarmed through breaks in those medieval walls, and Paul Bennett was witnessing a new and horrific history through the lens of his camera.

"So that others may know," Micheleine had told him, if any of them lived through it.

And then he was pushing into the city with the rest of the Allied forces, moving street by street, house by house through smoldering ruins. He kept moving, kept shooting pictures, his rifle in the crook of his arm, into the next house, the ceiling sagging from damaged timbers, a family huddled in the corner of the kitchen.

Click, click. Then a shout, gunfire, and blood splattered the lens as he shouldered his rifle.

"How will you know what to do?" Callish had asked him over a cold meal two days before.

"What happens if you don't fire your weapon?"

When the German soldier fell at his feet, he couldn't move, was certain he wasn't breathing. Then Callish was in his face, pale as a ghost, shaking him.

"You saved my life! He would have killed me!"

Staring down at the German soldier, somewhere near his own age, probably with a family waiting for him at home, he was struck by the tragedy of it all. He didn't feel like a hero.

"Someone has to tell what happens here..."

He didn't take a picture then. Instead he turned his camera on the family still huddled in the corner of the bombed-out house— the woman, three children, no father.

"American," a soldier said, showing the arm patch of the American flag, as he pushed around them and began to question the woman.

"You, there," he motioned to Callish. "You speak French? Come here."

Paul Bennett walked out of what was left of the house.

They went street by street, the sound of machine gun fire in quick bursts, silent, then more rounds with a brief response of enemy fire. It was a different sound from Allied weapons that they'd come to recognize. Then another burst of Allied gunfire. Then there was no return of gunfire.

The city was in ruins. What the mortar bombardment hadn't destroyed, the fires finished off, smoke billowing from shattered buildings, the bodies of those who had stayed glimpsed through what was left of a wall.

At the edge of the city explosions rocked the docks and the quay out in the harbor, as those Germans who had stayed behind in a last effort to hold the city, destroyed what was left. Then there were the stories from the survivors in the city, mostly women and children. Over the past weeks, the Germans had rounded up all the men and boys, ages sixteen to sixty. They'd been imprisoned on a small island. All had been executed before the Allies reached the city.

He stumbled, caught his footing, and realized that he stumbled over a body. It was a child, a young girl, seven, maybe eight years old. A few feet away was a cloth doll, dropped when she fell. He raised his camera and took the poignant shot, so that people would remember. Then he picked up the doll and tucked it under the girl's hand.

He fought that first instinct to scream at the soldiers around him. Didn't they see what was happening? Innocent people were dead!

"As soon as we secure the city, we're to turn north," a Canadian soldier said, his expression grim.

"Come along, mate."

They all understood. It was in their expressions as they glanced down at the girl, and at him as they passed by. They were all caught in it, one man's madness had brought them all to this.

Click, click, click.

He didn't see the German soldier until afterward, only the movement out the corner of his eye, then that distinctive sound of the German gun. He didn't even feel the pain. There was just the sudden warmth in his shoulder, and he was firing his rifle.

"Bloody Christ!" Callish shouted when it was over. "You've been hit!"

Then the pain set in, fire burning in his shoulder. This was how it happened. It all came down to one last shot against overwhelming odds, one last attempt to hold the line, push back, then die. Someone he'd never met. On any other day in any other place they might have sat down for a pint.

The medic dropped his kit to the ground.

"The bullet went through," he told him, pressing a thick pad of bandage against the wound and tying it off.

"You'll live."

Then the medic gathered his kit and rushed ahead with the advancing Allied soldiers. There were more wounded to tend to.

Callish helped him to his feet. He pushed him away. It took some effort, and the pain was a constant reminder, but he eventually shouldered his rifle on the opposite shoulder, then picked up his camera.

CHAPTER
TWENTY-ONE
PRESENT DAY

t was late as the tour bus reached St. Malo, lights along the stone parapets of the walled city gleaming through the misty rain.

Centuries earlier it had been the home port of pirates, fortified against the Normans and attacks from across the channel. Like so many other places in France, the walled city had been almost completely destroyed during World War II. After the war it had been painstakingly restored including those stone walls.

The rail station was within walking distance of the main street. Passengers departed for hotels, or headed for cars in the car park. Others entered the rail station to wait for the next train returning to Paris.

They hadn't spoken on that long ride from Mont St. Michel. Now, as Kris glanced at him, she saw the effort it took just to keep moving in the tight set of expression on his face.

They'd left the rental car at the car park at Mont St. Michel. They could probably rent another one in St. Malo, but not until morning. It was late, everything was closed for the night, including the car rental counter at the rail station.

"We need to find a hotel..."

James shook his head. He was pale beneath the stubble of two-days growth of beard, and she wondered how much blood he'd lost.

"Check the rail schedule to Paris," he said, keeping his voice low as they entered the station along with several other passengers, including a family with two young children.

"I don't think you're in any condition..."

He cut her off. "Two tickets to Paris. Have you enough for the fare?"

"Credit card."

He nodded as he leaned back against a column, the front of his jacket zipped over the bloodied shirt beneath.

"Stay where I can see you, and don't talk to anyone."

The ticket windows were all closed this time of the night. She purchased two tickets at the automated kiosk.

She glanced around at the other passengers who waited for their rail connection, but had no idea what she was looking for—a face from a crowded airport, glimpsed in those few seconds as someone brushed past her, or an encounter at her hotel in Inverness?

It could be anyone—someone who had followed them from Mont St. Michel, someone who might even have been on the bus.

Watching them even now?

She returned with the tickets. "The next train leaves in thirty minutes."

They sat together on a long bench against the wall in the waiting area of the station with other passengers.

She found herself watching them—older couples, a young family, what appeared to be several older students, bottles of water and rain gear tied to their backpacks. Again she wondered, was Brother Thomas's killer among them?

Then the overhead display lit up with the arrival information for that next train to Paris.

James pushed away from the wall where he'd been standing. He wrapped a hand around her arm and pulled her close as the other passengers made their way to the platform.

"Stay close," he told her as his hand tightened.

They might have been any other couple returning from holiday as they stepped out onto the platform under the covered awning. But she saw the way he checked out everything and everyone as they boarded the sleek silver-and-blue passenger car, quick glances in both directions, equally quick glance back at the rail station and the parking area beyond.

The rail car was only half full, twin rows of double seats lining both sides with baggage racks overhead filled with an assortment of backpacks, overnight bags, a child's stroller, and the usual collection of jackets, coats, and umbrellas.

They took two seats at the rear of the car, and again she was aware of the way he scanned everything as he had at the inn that first night, then again at the abbey.

When she would have taken the second seat next to the window, he shook his head and indicated the aisle seat. She was running on raw nerves and was about to ask what the hell difference it made which seat she took when he leaned over her.

"Take the aisle seat. I'll take the other across the way."

"You're giving orders now?" What the hell difference did it make?

The look he gave her said enough.

"Fine."

She took the aisle seat in the last row. He eased down into the one across from her.

The other passengers settled back into their seats as the train slowly left the station, then gathered speed. Some took out their phones or a book to read, conversations in either French or English over the low hum of the train, and the faint scent of cigarette smoke as someone lit up in spite of the posted signs against smoking.

Others dozed, with over two hours before they reached Paris. As the lights dimmed in the car, James stood and motioned for her to follow. He guided her to the rear of the car.

The bathroom was the size of a closet with a basin, toilet, drop-down changing table, and a narrow bench seat. It was empty. He pulled her inside, slid the pocket door closed and set the lock, then sat down on the narrow bench seat.

He opened the front of his jacket. The lower half of his sweatshirt was soaked with blood. He removed the towel the tour driver had given them, and dropped it into the waste container.

"I'll need your help."

The way he said it—matter of fact—he might have been ordering a coffee or directions to a restaurant. He reached around and pulled the tail of the sweatshirt from the waistband of his jeans.

"The exit wound will be the worst of it."

Her experience with wounds was limited to scrapes and bruises when she'd taken a header off a bicycle as a child, or an occasional cut from a knife in the kitchen at her apartment—not bullet wounds.

He looked up as she hesitated, saw the expression on her face.

"I'll walk you through it. Can you hold it together?"

She nodded.

"You'll need wet paper towels to clean the wound, then more to make a bandage."

She pulled paper towels from the dispenser and soaked them with water at the basin, then wrung them out and handed them to him. He cleaned the wound where the bullet had entered.

"You'll need more for the exit wound."

The wound was low at his side, only a few inches apart from the wound at the front, but almost twice the size, the edges ragged.

She had seen him without a shirt at the apartment in London and that impressive tattoo, but hadn't seen the patchwork of scars—old wounds, at least a dozen of them, all about the same size with several on the back of his shoulder, with that long scar barely healed from recent surgeries.

Shrapnel?

She brushed a finger across the ridge of one of those small scars, and a memory, sharp and painful, swept back over her as if it were yesterday—her brother's casket had been sealed, the wounds horrific from the attack, they were told, and not something they wanted to see.

Her father had insisted, sending her back to the front of the chapel at Arlington. He said nothing when he finally joined her, his face a mask that said everything he refused to tell her.

"Are you all right?"

She forced herself past the memory. "I got it."

A knock at the door of the bathroom brought her back, jarring her back into the world of reality. This was real...the blood was real...

"You'll have to wait!" she called out, not even recognizing her own voice.

"Slow it down," James told her. "Take a deep breath."

She nodded, then wet more paper towels. Her hands shook as she carefully cleaned the wound, wiping away the blood.

"Is it still bleeding?"

"A little."

He heard it in her voice, the same as it was in London after the attack at the nightclub, holding on.

"You'll need to make another bandage. And something to hold both in place." Or he would just keep bleeding and sooner or later someone was going to notice.

She folded a couple more paper towels into a square pad, then pulled the scarf from around her neck.

"Hold this," she told him as she slipped the scarf over the bandage and wrapped it around his waist, then over the bandage low at his back.

"God dammit!" she swore, her fingers clumsy.

"I can take it from here," James told her. He grabbed both ends of the scarf and tied it off, then pulled the tail of his sweatshirt down over it.

She took dragged a hand through her hair as another knock, more persistent this time, came at the door.

"Fuck!" she swore. "Une minute!"

"Fuck?" he said, with what passed for a smile as he tossed the bloodied towel along with the paper towels into the bottom of the trash container, then pulled more from the dispenser and dropped them on top.

It wasn't that he'd never heard the word before. In his line of work it was usually part of any good conversation when things had a way of going sideways, which happened a lot, no matter how much planning had gone into the mission.

He just hadn't expected it from her—the polish, the designer clothes, the high-powered career, cool, always in control...almost always.

There was another knock and something in broken English about others needing the bathroom.

He stood and braced a hand against the wall of the bathroom. "I think you better open the door."

The expression on the face of the woman on the other side of the door said it all—surprise, impatience, and then another comment in French—no translation needed.

He followed Kris from the small compartment, his body brushing hers in the narrow passage as the train swept around a curve. He leaned in.

"That was fantastic, dear," he said, just loud enough for the woman to hear.

Kris looked at him as if he'd taken a hard right past sanity, then caught the look he gave her. She shook her head and would have stepped past him. He caught her against the opposite wall just outside the bathroom. His mouth brushed hers as he leaned in.

"There. Be a good girl now," he said, just loud enough for anyone else to hear and with more far humor than he felt.

"Try to control yourself. This poor woman needs to use the facility."

The poor woman said something that made mention about finding a hotel room, then slammed and latched the restroom door.

"If I wasn't afraid you'd start bleeding again..."

He slowly pushed away from her.

"I love it when you play rough."

He was pale, a sheen of sweat at his forehead and looked as if he might go down at any second. She slipped an arm around his waist.

"Act like you've had too much to drink!" she whispered as she helped him back to his seat. He leaned in against her.

"It wouldn't taste nearly as good as you."

It was after midnight when they pulled into the Gare de Montparnasse station, in Paris. He was awake, face drawn. But those dark eyes were alert.

They were the last to leave the train, stepping down from the car into the noise and chaos of the busy concourse even that late at night.

She was past exhaustion with no idea what the next step was supposed to be. One thing for certain, they couldn't just spend the night in the rail station.

They needed a place to stay. But the hotels she was familiar with were high profile, places she'd stayed with Cate on past book tours that had a way of drawing the media—the last thing they needed.

Marcus Aronson lived in Paris. His name had been on the list of calls Cate had made before the accident. But she had no idea where he lived, and was pretty certain he wouldn't appreciate late night visitors even if he was in the city. He traveled a great deal.

"Where are we going?"

James' hand closed around her upper arm as they walked toward ground transportation. He waived down an Uber driver and gave him an address.

"The friend of a friend."

They passed familiar landmarks and monuments, skirted the river, then into the medieval streets of the Marais with its bars, restaurants, old-fashioned bread shops, and boutiques, an enclave much the same as it was three hundred years before.

He signaled the driver and had him pull in front of one of those old-fashioned bakeries.

La Patisserie sat mid-street among other old buildings, with stone steps just beyond the entrance at the side of the building that led to an upper floor landing.

The entrance was tucked back. There was no overhead light, only the faint glow of a red security light beside the door. There was no sound from inside the building, no ring-tone when he pressed the button, or indication that anyone was there.

A light eventually came on outside the entrance. The heavy steel door slowly opened. Dark eyes peered at them from an equally dark face. A fall of white hair framed delicate features.

"He said you might come here."

"Innis," James whispered as Kris looked over at him.

The door opened further. The girl was slender, wearing jeans, boots, and a turtleneck sweater. A sleek Belgian Malinois stood quietly beside her. But the body language was anything but quiet as the dog glanced up at the young woman.

She spoke to the dog in French and he sat down, not an animal Kris would want to encounter in a dark alley.

"I'm Daenerys." The girl smiled. She glanced past them into the darkened street below, then opened the door further.

"Please, come in."

CHAPTER
TWENTY-TWO
THE MARAIS, PARIS

T he apartment over the bakery had been a private residence in the old section of Paris a few hundred years earlier, with several rooms, including what had once been a grand salon, with more rooms on the third floor at the top of a scarred wood staircase.

The private rooms were typical of the period with high ceilings, arched window casements, stone walls, and wood floors that reminded her of the residence Isabel Raveneau had lived in at Mont St. Michel.

The main salon was empty. An arched doorway led to what appeared to be a kitchen.

"Anthony will be back later," the young woman explained as she turned down a wide hallway.

Like the Raveneau residence, the apartment smelled of old places —stone walls, the dull gleam of wood floors, the pervasive scent of candle wax over the centuries, and a fire in the hearth.

Daenerys stepped to the other side of a doorway at the end of the hallway, and pushed open the door to a bedchamber.

"There are blankets in the wardrobe, and you can turn on the gas in the fireplace. There is food in the kitchen. Do you need anything else?"

"Bandages," Kris replied, shoving her hand back through her hair.

"And something to disinfectant a wound." She was pretty certain the crude bandage she'd made on the train needed to be changed.

There were no questions, not even a flicker of surprise.

Daenerys nodded. "I'll bring what you need."

The door closed behind her.

Kris dropped her shoulder bag into the large wood chair as James eased out of his jacket.

"All the comforts of home."

The furnishings were sparse, along the lines of early street-fare, but the sheets on the bed were clean under a thick comforter. It could have been on the floor and she wouldn't have cared.

"The friend of a friend?" Kris asked.

"Gamers," he replied. "It's a tight community, and for now—safe."

There was a knock at the door. Daenerys let herself in, carrying several items. She set a package of sterile bandages on the table along with surgical tape, disinfectant, and antibacterial salve. The Belgian Malinois waited just outside the doorway.

"Be prepared," Kris recited the motto, at the array of medical supplies.

Daenerys shrugged. "Game nights," she explained. "Things sometimes get, how shall we say...?" She searched for the right words.

"Too real?" Kris guessed.

Daenerys smiled as she turned toward the doorway. She called to Pax in French. He fell into step beside her.

"Let me know if you need anything else. There's ale and wine in the kitchen. The bathroom is down the hall," she added.

"Game night," Kris commented when Daenerys had gone. It was a whole other world.

She went to the basin and turned on the water. Her hands shook as she grabbed a hand towel from the shelf above the sink and soaked it in warm water in the basin. She squeezed water from the towel, and grabbed another dry one.

"Take off your sweatshirt."

"It can wait."

The look in her eyes stopped him. He pulled off the sweatshirt and sat at the edge of the bed.

"You know, sometimes you're a real pain in the ass."

"Back at you on that one," she snapped, in no mood for conversation.

Exhaustion along with everything that had happened since leaving Inverness had taken a toll. She didn't know what time it was, or even what day it was. It didn't matter. The only thing that mattered was that someone wanted them both dead...

She removed the scarf and let it drop to the floor. The blood had dried on the makeshift bandages. The wad of paper towels was stuck to the wound. It had entered low at his side just below his ribs, then exited low in front.

It eventually registered—the sound, that crazy, insane descent from the abbey, the way he held back sending her on ahead. The gunman had been behind them.

She started with the wound low on his back, just above the waist of his jeans. She soaked it, then slowly peeled it away. She tore open a sterile pad and soaked it with disinfectant, then pressed it against the wound.

"Hold this in place."

"You're good at giving orders."

She ignored him as she applied two more thick pads on top in case the wound started to bleed again, then tore off strips of tape and pressed them into place.

"Lean back so that I can get a look at the other wound."

"I can take care of it from here," he told her.

He caught that look again. He winced as he leaned back against the headboard of the bed.

He watched her face as she peeled away the blood-soaked bandage on his side where the bullet had exited—the reaction at the sight of the wound, the deep breath she took, then the way she forced herself past it.

There was a toughness beneath the surface. It came from somewhere, more than a few weeks of wilderness training.

"Tell me about your brother."

She hesitated, then reached for packs of sterile pads and tore them open.

She frowned as she cut several strips of tape, pressing them over the edges of the bandage to hold it in place.

She said nothing, but the pain of that loss was there—in lines that appeared between those slender brows, the set of her mouth—still raw, an open wound that had yet to heal.

"Mark was four years older, a natural athlete—anything, everything."

"Practice every day, all year long—football in the fall, basketball, baseball season. Sometimes they overlapped. He could have gone pro...but there were other things he wanted..."

The frown deepened. Other things that had taken him in another direction. The choices one made. Much like the choices he'd made.

Another memory brought a faint smile. "He coached me in soccer during high school before he left. I always suspected it was probably because of Jennifer Masters."

"Ah," he commented, shifting against the pain of the wound, the warmth in the room reminding him that neither of them had had much sleep the last two days.

"Ah, the real reason."

There was that smile again. Another memory.

"He was such a pain in the ass. He knew all my friends. I couldn't go anywhere that he didn't know about it."

"Looking out for you." But she wouldn't have seen it that way, he thought, as the last twenty-four hours caught up with him.

She pressed several more pieces of tape into place. "When you're sixteen and some place you're not supposed to be, that your parents definitely wouldn't approve of, the last thing you want is your brother showing up and embarrassing the hell out of you." She shook her head.

"We spent a lot of time in one of those all-night waffle houses, and talked about all sorts of things." Her voice softened on another memory.

"He never told them about that." She remembered the conversations, the arguments that had followed.

"Then, 9/11."

He saw that flash of emotion, the slight hesitation, then she pressed another piece of tape into place.

"He was determined to go into the military. He felt it was important, he wanted to make a difference." She smoothed the last strip of tape into place.

She looked up. His eyes were closed, his head slightly back. Asleep.

Was it always like that? she thought. The need to make a difference, to believe in something that was bigger than oneself? And the price some paid?

Seven hundred years ago on a distant plain in Spain, then seventy years ago in another war on the beaches of Normandy? Vietnam? September 11th?

She pulled the comforter over him, and then stood, so tired that she ached. She gathered up the bloodied bandages and threw them into a wastebasket along with her neck scarf, then pressed one of the buttons on the wall switch, the room dark except for the glow of the gas fire in the fireplace.

There was just the one bed, a table and chair, and the basin. That left the floor.

To hell with it, she thought. She kicked off her boots, stepped out of her jeans, and crawled into bed.

She wasn't certain what woke her, or even where she was at first. Then, she felt the movement beside her and heard mumbled sounds, vague at first, then a long arm suddenly thrown across her.

He wasn't awake. His eyes were still closed as he mumbled something, then that name again. A friend? One of the men he'd lost?

She could only guess. But the nightmare tore at her.

It didn't let go. He tossed and turned, lost in that place, fighting the dreams, fighting to hold on.

The comforter had come off. She pulled it back over them as she curled around him. And the tears came as she listened to the pain in his voice, the battle he fought but could never win.

"It's all right," she whispered, not even certain he could hear, holding on. "I've got you."

James sat at the edge of the bed, head buried in his hands as if he could physically push the memories back into the box.

It was still dark. There was only the faint glow that spread across the floor of the room, from the flame of the gas jet in the fireplace.

Something had wakened him, pulling him out of the blood and chaos. He slowly pushed to his feet, the wood floor cold. He glanced back at the bed, and another memory surfaced of slender fingers against his skin, the brush of her hair as she had changed the bandage. Then, another memory—her body warm against his. She stirred, then burrowed deeper into the blankets. He let her sleep.

Innis sat in front of the bank of computers, a gamer's dream for those live-stream marathons.

He had come in a couple of hours earlier, wired for sound, hair standing on end.

"Bloody Christ, I'm glad to see you," he told James. Then, "You look like hell."

"What's happened?" James asked.

"Took my own advice—it seemed like a good time to leave. I've found something."

Several empty cups sat between them now.

James rubbed the ache in his shoulder, the wound below a minor irritation in the scheme of things.

It was still dark outside, except for the streetlight at the corner. After arriving together, Luna had gone to bed in another part of the apartment. Daenerys was stretched out on the couch. Anthony kept them supplied with coffee.

"What else have you got?" James asked.

"Callish," Innis replied, scrolling through the information that he'd downloaded and copied.

"Public records, media stuff about the gallery, that sort of thing. It's all pretty normal stuff. Then I took a look at his financials."

James angled him a look. He probably didn't want to know how he pulled that one off. Innis shrugged.

"It's no different than all those New York financial institutions spying on everyone else trying to get an edge on one another. At first it all looked pretty straight-forward. He opened the London gallery almost ten years ago; big splash, lots of fanfare that included a couple of prominent artists at the time, including..." he scrolled through and found media photos of several live art displays from the opening.

"Some pretty shocking stuff, even for the art world, if you know what I mean."

The photos of actors staged in oversized frames and in various positions that were supposed to mimic modern society were graphic, including two women simulating a sex act that had temporarily shut down the gallery opening. Compared to some of the things that could be found on the internet ten years later it was fairly tame.

Innis scrolled past the pictures of the gallery opening. "There have been other artists featured over the years, more respectable stuff, including some well-known works from the Renaissance, and there was this media piece several months ago about a retrospective of Paul Bennett's photographs from the war for the upcoming anniversary of the war."

There was a photograph of Jonathan Callish with Cate in a media piece about the exhibit that was in the planning stages. There were other media pieces, publicity spreads in several art magazines, show-casing the gallery and the eclectic blend of iconic pieces with the works of newly emerging artists, and a renewed interest in antiquary, relics from Britain's past, obtained on loan, or through connections of the gallery's owner. From everything he saw, it appeared that the gallery was fairly successful.

"I thought that too," Innis agreed. "But I'm a natural-born skeptic. I make my living from make-believe worlds, alternate universes, and people who like to hide in the shadows.

"One thing I've learned, nothing is ever what it seems. So I decided to dig deeper, peel back the layers, so to speak. That's when things got very interesting." He connected a portable hard drive. A stream of information filled the screen, all in code.

"Translation?" James asked, leaning in take a closer look.

"That's just it," Innis said. "You need to be a really sophisticated coder to understand any of this. There are probably only a handful, maybe a dozen people in the world who would be able to crack it."

"Explain."

"They're the sort who work for tech companies building new code, after some time on the other side. They work for government agencies who like to spy on each other, and some private parties who are interested in selling to the highest bidder. It's the sort of thing governments pay a great deal for—with firewalls, detection nets, and trackers.

"I was able to get in," he continued. "But I picked up a tracker; every move I made, the bloody fucker was there. I finally got rid of the bastard. But I couldn't be certain that he hadn't identified me, or at least my location. That's when I decided we should disappear for a while. But I also thought it was important for you to know."

"What else?"

"Follow the money," Innis replied. "It's the one thing you can't hide; it always surfaces somewhere. Someone gets greedy, information gets out, lifestyle changes, sex, drugs, and rock 'n roll." He shrugged at the look James gave him.

"Well, you know what I mean. The point is, it gets out eventually, leaves a trail, if you know what to look for."

"And you know what to look for."

"I've had some experience with this sort of thing," he replied vaguely. "And there's been a lot of money moving around, a whole lot more than shows up on Callish's bank account for the gallery, supposedly business development—a second gallery here in Paris.

That didn't exactly set off alarm bells. From the little he knew about the art world, Paris was a natural location—artists, galleries, and an international clientele for rare artwork.

"You said a lot of money." James reminded him.

"That took a little more digging," Innis replied. "There were three fire walls to get through, dragged my ass all over the globe. No financial institution has that many firewalls." He shrugged. "Makes you feel real secure about your own money, doesn't it?"

"The money," James reminded him.

"Right. Found something in one of the banks in the Caymans. We're talking lots of zeros—a half-million here, a million and a half there, all of it with the same transfer code encryption. That's the only way I found it. It adds up quick over the past twenty-four months."

"How much?"

"Over twenty million U.S."

James sat at the edge of the table. That was a lot of zeros.

"Legal?" he asked.

"Well that's the thing," Innis said. "On the surface it all looks too perfect. Here's something Luna came across when she did some looking around before we left."

James read the internet article on the screen about several pieces of art work, specifically pottery, that Callish handled for a private collector. There were pictures and a description of the rare, pre-Columbian pieces.

"The piece at the table in the background," Innis explained. "It's not from the same period. It's not even from the same continent."

James was running on less than a couple of hours sleep. He ran a hand over the stubble of beard on his chin.

"You'll need to explain that one."

"Luna saw it right off—art history degree from the University of London." Then at the look James gave him, "It's from the Persian empire, around 5th century—B.C."

The background of the photo was grainy, the focus on the pottery displayed for the article. The piece in the background of the photo was a fluted metal bowl with an intricate embossed design.

"It's very rare, according to Luna," he added. "And, since the wars in the Middle East, almost impossible to find. But someone bought it. Then, surprise, the money disappears, never makes it into Callish's business or personal accounts. Like it's been swallowed into a black hole."

James knew well enough that it was illegal to bring any artifacts out of the region, and tightly controlled by local authorities, not to mention his own government. Not that it had stopped terrorist regimes that had systematically looted and destroyed numerous palaces that were also priceless artifacts—the other casualties of a war.

He'd met Callish. It was hard to imagine him involved in smuggling, but not impossible. Nothing was impossible when it came to money. But where had it gone?

Was that what Cate had stumbled onto? A smuggling operation?

The first gray light slipped past the edge of the heavy drapes at the arched windows in the salon. They had been at it for hours.

"He would need a connection, a source to purchase smuggled artifacts."

Innis and Anthony exchanged a look.

"There are people who know these things," Anthony replied.

James tossed down the last of the coffee. He needed to keep the caffeine buzz going.

"I need to talk to them." He needed to know what had gotten Cate killed, and he needed to keep Kris out of it. The night before had been a game changer.

"They don't usually agree to meet with people like you," Anthony replied. "These are not nice people."

James Morgan thought of the places he'd been, the things he'd done.

"Neither am I."

CHAPTER
TWENTY-THREE

Shadows spread across the walls and the faces of those who looked down on the man who knelt before them—the Saints, the Blessed Mother, and the Child.

Flames quivered on the candles at the altar as ancient prayers whispered in the waiting stillness of the Church.

"Eternal rest grant unto Thy servant, and may perpetual light shine upon him."

She took two more steps, then suddenly stopped. His eyes were open, staring, and the blood...

Kris fought her way up out of the nightmare.

The image followed her, slipping out of the box like scattered pieces of a puzzle, other memories:

The freezing cold on the tarmac on a windy day...

A flag-draped casket...

The crumpled wreckage of a car in the French countryside...

She leaned her forehead against bent knees in the shadows of the room and kept breathing, forcing the nightmare back into a box.

She had no idea how long she sat there, eventually aware of the sounds of the house—the hiss and pop of the gas jet in the fireplace, the rain on the arched windows, an automobile in the street below. She glanced over at the bed beside her.

He was gone.

How long had she been asleep? And where was James? Had the bleeding started again?

She pushed back the comforter, and pulled on jeans and the sweater, dark stains—his blood— streaked across both.

She followed the smell of coffee and the sounds of conversation— low, intimate in the way of friends or lovers, another memory coming back from the night before…late, finally reaching the house in the Marais, uncertain what they would find.

Daenerys, with her long platinum-white hair, a flesh-and-blood version out of one of those internet games, the huge dog at her side.

"I have friends in Paris…." Innis had told them.

She reached what had once been the grand salon, and blinked, certain she was still dreaming.

"Innis?"

He sat at the long table that looked like it might be original to the residence— long, dark wood, massive, and the bank of computer screens—in all his colorful, vivid, tattooed glory. He came away from the table, wrapped his arms around her in a bear hug, then held her away from him.

"Bloody Christ! You look like hell!"

She glared back at him. "Your eye shadow is smeared."

He hugged her again. "You're all right, then?"

As all right as anyone could be after the night before.

"Drink this," Daenerys crossed the room and handed her a mug of steaming liquid. Not coffee, but some other fragrant blend.

"Tea?"

"It's good for mornings after," Daenerys explained, not going into detail about what sort of 'mornings after.'

"I blend it myself from leaves I purchase at a shop in Montparnasse, and there are croissants from the bakery."

Eat me. Drink me. It felt like she'd fallen down the rabbit hole.

James had left earlier with Anthony, who owned the apartment and she still hadn't met, after information Innis had brought with him.

"Things got a bit dicey back home," Innis added. "It seemed a good idea to get away for a while."

Dangerous was a better description after he explained what he'd uncovered, digging around in the cyber world.

"When did they leave?" she asked with a frown, thinking about the night before.

"Early. He wanted to meet with someone Anthony knows with connections in the art world." His voice trailed off, the rest left unsaid.

His digging had uncovered the fact that Jonathan Callish was the owner of a second art gallery in Paris, Le Noir, with a staggering amount of money transferred through secure accounts—secure until Innis had hacked into those accounts.

"How much?"

"Over twenty million that I was able to track, maybe more."

Twenty million dollars, U.S.

She knew just enough about gaming and the cyber world, from books Ellison had published, to know that parts of it existed on the fringes of the law. There was that whole murky area that Innis had built his business around, that crossed borders, skirted legal systems, and territorial boundaries.

Twenty million dollars was a lot of money to simply disappear into a black hole.

Welcome to the brave new world, she thought. But just who or what was that at the bottom of that black hole?

It was after noon and there was still no word from either James or Anthony.

The tea Daenerys had provided had worked miracles. Food helped, along with a hot shower and the clean sweatshirt and sweat-pants Daenerys had also provided.

She had retreated to the hot-house garden she kept on the veranda that overlooked the street below. Luna was still asleep in one of the upstairs rooms.

Kris pulled her hair back into a ponytail and leaned over Innis's shoulder.

"Any clue where all that money went?"

"I found a couple of things." He brought up a screen shot that he'd saved.

She looked at him. "Haddon Acquisitions?"

"Right," he replied. "Except there is no Haddon Acquisitions." He brought up more information he'd tracked, along with searches he'd made.

"It's fake, a really good fake, with all sorts of firewalls built in, professional-appearing website, along with a Board of Directors—a reputable-looking group, a list of acquisitions in Dubai, property development, that sort of thing. But it's all fake, a front. These properties don't exist. Those people don't exist."

He had her attention.

"It's that same old thing that's been around for centuries—build a wall and someone will find a way around it—the Romans, the Chinese." He angled a look at her.

"You Yanks should know something about walls..."

Then at the look she gave him, "Any wall that can be built, someone will find a way around it, or in this case through it—brick by brick. The trick with cyber security is to build in a code that continuously changes so that people can't get in. Or at least it cuts down the opportunity."

She was familiar with the theory, just not the exact method.

"Explain, please."

"A hacker can spend weeks or months trying to break a certain code that's written into a program, only to have it change on him, and he has to start over. The whole idea is that it keeps changing and prevents the hacker from gaining access and screwing with things."

"Moving money around?"

"Clever girl. Over the years a lot of tricks have been developed, but not everyone uses them."

Some high-profile hacks in recent history came to mind. Political games. Elections.

"How does it work?"

"Random sequencing—a dozen codes, for example, that change randomly, and your average hacker keeps stumbling around trying to break a code that has already changed."

"Average?" she commented.

"Aye, well, then there are a few who are good enough, and lucky, and they're able to figure out the sequence."

"No longer random," she replied.

"Exactly."

"And you just happen to be very good."

He grinned.

"Were you able to get in?" she asked.

"Aye, that's how I found out Haddon was a shell company. Then all hell broke loose."

"Except that Haddon doesn't exist," she reminded him what he'd told her.

"Exactly. Then this nasty little fucker—sorry—was all over me." At the look she gave him, he translated.

"Think of the guard at the prison gate. A tracker that whoever built the firewall set up on the Haddon site, if anyone without proper authorization tried to gain access. I finally shook him. I don't think he was able to identify me, but I shut everything down. That's when I decided that Luna and I needed to disappear for a while."

Down the rabbit hole with the rest of them.

"There's something else," he added. "Anne called. Your publisher has been trying to contact you."

Not a surprise with everything that had happened.

"They keep leaving messages."

She thought about her cell phone, in hundreds of pieces, but that really wasn't the issue. She could get another cell phone. She could call. But she knew what the conversation would be. Nina would want her back in New York. She couldn't do that. Not yet.

Three people were dead. She had to know why.

Her gaze was drawn to one of the computer screens. A Sky News live feed was being broadcast. There had been an incident at the airport in Paris. Arrests had been made, searches were underway in two districts for those who might be involved. Then the broadcast segued into a segment from the previous evening.

"Authorities still have no leads in the brutal murder of a Benedictine monk who had just concluded evening services at the Abbey Church at Mont St. Michel. Church authorities have issued no statements at this time, but there is concern that this may be a repeat of the brutal attack by insurgents on a priest in London several months ago. The abbey will remain closed until local authorities have completed their investigation."

Paris was a city on edge and under siege, and James was out there somewhere.

"That whole scene at the abbey must have been pretty intense," Innis said, glancing over at her.

Intense—there was a word. There were other words—horrible,

terrifying—and then no words that could describe finding Brother Thomas lying in a pool of his own blood, their escape from the abbey church, the train trip from St. Malo...

She rubbed her arms against a sudden chill in the room that found its way into the pit of her stomach.

What was keeping them? What information was James hoping to find?

"You said that Anthony has a cell phone?"

Daenerys nodded. "He would call if anything happened."

He would call. Cate had called, and she didn't receive her message until it was too late.

"I'm going to fix something to eat," Daenerys announced. "They will be hungry when they return."

"Anthony was born here," Innis said, watching her. "He knows his way around the city, the safe places, and the ones to stay away from."

That was what she was afraid of. She looked at the antique clock on the large mantel. Late afternoon. It was getting dark out on the street, clouds lowering over the city skyline.

"I've sent you something..."

She forced herself to concentrate on something that had bothered her the night before, when she and James had found the wall in the Cloister where the Raveneau Tapestry had once hung.

"Do you still have access to Cate's files?"

Innis nodded. "I downloaded everything from the cloud before we left. I didn't want to leave anything that anyone else might find."

"I want to take another look at the photographs Cate gave you for her father's exhibit."

She spent the next several hours looking at those old images, taken in another time and place, over seventy years ago, faces of war-weary soldiers, the wounded, stark images of another war.

Similarities to the present day weren't lost on her, images of soldiers returning from Afghanistan and Iraq, flag-draped coffins, the faces of loved ones waiting. Most of the soldiers in those old photographs couldn't have been more than eighteen or nineteen years old. But they were already old men because of what they'd seen and experienced.

Paul Bennett hadn't been much older then, but he had an eye for capturing just the right moment, the right emotion that would reach across generations years later in those iconic images that stared back at her now.

Did it ever change? she thought. Or was Man doomed to keep repeating the mistakes of the past?

Poland, Czechoslovakia, Normandy, or Iraq, Yemen, Syria, Afghanistan decades later. Other times, other places, the same conflicts, people dying.

She pushed past those images, trying to find the reason Cate had sent that photograph—something important enough that she had left that last manuscript unfinished. She had Innis bring up the photograph of the tapestry.

What was she looking at? What did Cate want her to see?

The tapestry in Paul Bennett's photograph was a series of black-and-white images, while the images in the color plate that Diana Jodion had made for them were lighter, brighter, taken with the advantage of additional lighting at the abbey years earlier. Other than that, they were almost identical.

Not quite identical.

"Can you enlarge and enhance this photo?"

She had spent hundreds of hours studying color images for book covers, bent over a light table with the art director and the layout for the next advertising campaign for the next bestseller at Ellison Publishing, looking for that visual hook that captured the reader's attention and translated into sales. Romance book covers, thrillers, murder mysteries, the next DaVinci novel where the image could make or break a sales ranking. In Cate's case, a simple cover with subtle images shaded into the background that told a story of their own had been the perfect hook to millions of sales.

She had him continue to scroll through other photographs that Paul Bennett had taken in the sequence with the photograph of the tapestry. There was a photograph of a young Paul Bennett in uniform, then a group shot in the next photograph.

"That one," she pointed to the four young people, including Paul Bennett, and a younger version of Jonathan Callish. The other two people in the photograph, a woman, and a young man, were dressed in civilian clothes.

The woman was slender about the same height as the young man who appeared to be around fourteen or fifteen years old. He had that gawky appearance and thin, rangy build of adolescence, but by the look in his eyes as he stared into the camera, boyhood had been left behind long ago.

The woman appeared to be around twenty years old, although it was difficult to tell from the black-and-white image. She was dressed in oversized men's pants, gathered, and belted at a slender waist, with laced boots, her shirt buttoned up and tucked into the waist of those pants, and the too-large wool jacket with a rifle over one shoulder. The boy was dressed almost the same, right down to the rifle.

French partisans? Or possibly French Resistance?

Both had been heavily involved with the Allies during the war, and in the weeks and days leading up to the Normandy invasion. By the expressions on their faces, there was a camaraderie among the four young people from different parts of the world, caught up in a war.

Paul Bennett's photographs had been carried in all the prominent magazines after the war—Life, Time, the Saturday Evening Post. He had given only one interview over the years, on one of the anniversaries of the Normandy invasion.

She finally found the interview after a long search. There were several paragraphs about the invasion, along with a half-dozen of those iconic war-time photographs.

Paul Bennett had returned to France after the war the article went on to explain, in an attempt to find members of the Resistance he had come into contact with.

"We owed our lives to them," he was quoted as saying in that article, with photographs that juxtaposed the destruction of the war alongside other photographs of the slow rebuilding of towns and cities throughout France.

"Without the information they provided, often at the risk of their own lives, there might have been a different outcome to the war."

There was a poignancy to the article and those black-and-white photographs, without the usual opinion and sensationalism found in modern journalism pieces. It provided a glimpse into a young man's view of that horrible time. It also explained who Catherine Bennett Ross was, the person behind the story, what drove her to take on dangerous assignments—the Six-Day war, Vietnam, the Falklands,

Beirut, Iraq. That straight-forward perspective, but with a deeply human insight into world events. Like father, like daughter.

"I keep my boots by the door," Cate once said of the next assignment. "And my head down."

She had received her share of wounds on those dangerous assignments, a grazed head wound from a stray bullet, a broken ankle that she walked on for three days because she had just one opportunity to get the story, along with other assorted bruises and close encounters, and one brief marriage.

"He was nice enough," she said once. "But he had some strange idea about me staying home and raising a half-dozen kids. I thought about that for about three minutes, then packed my bags and left. Although," she added, "he was pretty good in bed."

And according to rumors, there had been more than one affair over the years. A few moments grabbed in some war zone, several days at some remote location, then off on the next assignment.

Kris thought of Marcus Aronson. He had been in and out of Cate's life over the years, both correspondents after they first met on assignment covering the Six-Day War for the BBC. He had left journalism after the war, then a professor of European history at the University of Paris. He had been a consultant on two of Cate's books.

Kris had spoken with him several times during the editorial process on both books, fact-checking, verifying information Cate had included. They met at the London book launch for Cate's first book. The last she knew he still lived in the Montparnasse.

"You need to see something," Innis told her. "Luna found this."

"More digging around?" Kris commented.

"You might say that. It took quite a bit of searching, considering the source. The Vatican isn't well-known for sharing. But she wanted to take a look around."

"The Vatican?" She knew from her studies years earlier that the Vatican had vast archives that went back centuries—kept under lock and seal. Not just anyone got into the Vatican archives—scholars from time to time, theologians, seminaries, but even that was restricted.

"You hacked into the Vatican archives?"

"Luna hacked into the archives," he clarified. "She's doesn't care much for the Church." He shrugged and gave her a smile.

"She's a bit of a heathen."

"A very talented heathen," Kris commented as she sat in the chair beside him and watched as he scrolled through files.

"Aye, she loved the challenge. The Vatican has an impressive security system. It took some time, but we got in." He opened another file and brought up several black-and-white images. He enlarged them one by one.

It took her a minute before she realized what she was looking at— a black-and-white photographic archive of the Raveneau Tapestry.

"These photographs were taken at the abbey in 1912."

Kris stared at frame after frame, scene after scene. The photographs weren't the best quality, but it was possible to see most of the detail in the scenes. There were almost two dozen photographs, many the same as the ones in the copies of the color photographs Diana Jodion had provided, and several that she didn't have.

The tapestry, like others that had been created during the Medieval period, was like a pictograph made of linen and dyed yarn, a montage of people and events, scene after scene painstakingly hand-stitched over decades, each panel a story in itself, like the Bayeaux Tapestry. But this story was deeply personal.

He magnified the images that showed the events of a young woman's life: hunt scenes, other scenes with a young man, then a panel that showed a knight and several warriors riding into battle.

"According to what we were told, he was sent to Spain," she pointed out, barely able to control her excitement.

The next panel showed the battle.

According to Vilette, James and the others had been overrun at Teba, most of the Crusaders slaughtered, with a handful taken prisoner, James of Montrose among them.

The next scene showed a messenger arriving at the chateau, and the young woman was then seen astride a horse wearing the armor of a warrior. In the next scene, they had arrived at a fortress on a coastal shore.

"Here." She pointed out the next scene as the messenger in the earlier panel could be seen delivering something to the figure outside the gate of the fortress.

Gold for James of Montrose's ransom?

In the following panel, the small band led by that warrior in knight's armor are seen surrounding a cart as they leave the fortress.

"According to what Vilette Moreau told us, James was badly wounded at Teba."

From the images of the sun and moon, rising then falling, it appeared they traveled for several days to the western coast of Spain. She pointed to an object in the cart.

"What is that?"

Innis brought up another image. Possibly more gold coins to pay for their passage back to France?

He enlarged then sharpened the image.

"It looks like some sort of box."

The image lost detail as he enlarged it, but it did look like a box of some kind, possibly a coffer. They were common to the period, often used for storage of documents, money, anything of value. In the next scene, the group was seen boarding a ship, followed by a sea voyage with a familiar image in the distance—the Abbey at Mont St. Michel.

Vilette told them that Isa and James were given sanctuary at the abbey by the Benedictine monks. The following scene showed the young man in a bed, the young woman standing beside him, their hands joined as one of the Benedictine monks stood with them.

The last rites? Kris wondered. Not according to the expression on Isabel Raveneau's face. She was smiling as the monk seemed to give his blessing.

In the next scene Isabelle Raveneau could be seen weeping. The young man was dying, his hand resting in hers. Then in the next scene he had been dressed in armor, and a ship was seen leaving the island.

"She was taking him home."

"Where?" Innis asked.

She pointed out the image in the next scene, those iconic white cliffs. It would have been a long journey—England, then north to Scotland, if what Vilette had told them was true.

The following scenes showed a long journey overland by horse cart, the changing seasons shown in leaves that fell from the trees, then patches of snow. The next scene showed a solemn ceremony with only Isabel and the man who had accompanied her to Spain as they stood beside a gravesite next to a stone wall in a small churchyard.

"What's this little piece?" Innis pointed out an image. He enhanced the image as much as possible.

"It's in every scene, along the border."

"Can you bring up the scan of the photograph Cate sent me?"

The magic of computers. With a few keystrokes, Innis brought back up the scan of the black-and-white photograph Paul Bennett had taken. He split the screen image and brought the two photographs up side by side.

"They're the same," Innis said. "Here, and here. All along the edge."

A tiny symbol that appeared throughout the tapestry, that hadn't been obvious in the photograph Diana Jodion had provided. But it was there in those photographs taken in 1912, and again in the photograph Paul Bennett had taken during the war, a symbol that must have held great meaning for the young woman who had painstakingly stitched it over and over into the fabric of the tapestry.

Kris sat back in the chair. She stared at image after image that he brought up, the same from one scene to the next, some of the images smaller than others, but it was there along the bottom of each panel.

Innis scrolled through several more scenes.

"Whoever stitched the bloody thing was either a glutton for punishment, or had nothing better to do. Or possibly on drugs. What the bloody hell is it?"

"It's a trinity knot and thistle."

CHAPTER
TWENTY-FOUR
AUGUST 12, 1944, NORMANDY, FRANCE

St. Lo, then Caen.

They'd been on the move for days, pushing north, then joining up with another British unit, the 3rd. They slept in foxholes, ate cold rations, and kept moving.

Town after town had been reduced to ruin as Allied forces swept inland from those beach landings pursuing an enemy who left a trail of scorched earth. Convoy after convoy followed, supporting the advance with more infantry, food, and fuel. And there were the staggering losses where the fighting had been fierce—a determined Allied offensive pursuing an equally determined, lethal German army.

His photographs told their own story—the contrast of the invasion force with average people who had lived under German occupation the past four years.

It was rumored that in Paris, little had changed with the Nazi occupation. For the most part, life went on as usual in the City of Light. Local citizenry mingled with their German occupiers. Restaurants, museums, art galleries remained open. But in the countryside, it was different.

In small villages and hamlets, resentment ran deep toward the occupiers. There were food shortages. Young men had gone off to join the Resistance, aligning with the free-French, and other Resistance fighters that slipped into the Allied encampments, and provided information at the risk of their own lives.

How many had paid that price was unknown. But in each town, each village, each encounter with the Resistance, he asked about the young woman who had become almost a folk hero for her daring escapades behind enemy lines, hoping to see her again.

"We're moving out in the morning," Callish told him, returning from a trip to the latrine, the improvised comfort station at the edge of the encampment.

"We're to join up with the 49th."

Paul shook his head. "I've been assigned to the press corps."

"How is the wound?" Callish asked.

He didn't consider it a serious wound, after seeing other wounds, body parts.

"Just a scratch. I've had worse hunting in the Highlands." That was a bit of an exaggeration but the only one he was going to make. There had been that penicillin shot that hurt like bloody blazes, a fresh bandage by a passing corpsman, and he was back at it.

He'd received the news earlier, about the re-assignment when he'd turned in the latest rolls of film to be sent off to London in the next dispatch.

Callish nodded. "I heard one of the journalists was taken prisoner at Verdun. They executed the poor blighter."

Paul had heard the same.

"We leave in the morning. They say the Germans are planning a big offensive, a last stand if you will, in the north," Callish said, lighting up a cigarette.

"The Yanks are pushing after them, and the 49th has joined up for support. Bloody Christ! I didn't sign up for a trip to Germany."

Had any of them?

But after the bombings in London, U-boats in the North Sea, and the past four years of bombing raids from their airfields, few were naive enough to think it was all just going to go away—bloody lessons from the first World War.

"Keep your head down," he told Callish. The man was always complaining about something—the weather, cold rations, the lack of toilet paper—they were rationed three squares a day, while the Yanks had it to spare.

They were all in this bloody mess together and they usually got along, talking about familiar places they both knew in London, Callish's studies at university that had been put on hold with the war, and the girl he hoped to marry.

Paul had his position at the Mirror waiting when he returned—if he returned.

The thought of taking photographs of babies and newly wedded couples wasn't his life's ambition. There was more to be seen through the lens of a camera. Stories to be told in those black-and-white images. Hundreds of stories in the expressions of the soldiers who had seen too much, in the stark images of a battlefield barren of every last tree and shrub, the earth scarred by a violent struggle, and the heart-wrenching images in a small town one had never heard of but was somehow like every town where women wept and children begged for food.

All stories needed to be told.

They made their farewells in that way. The words weren't said, but it was there, along with the usual 'I'll be seeing you' and the agreement to meet at Leicester Square after it was all over, with no notion that they would see each other again.

The press corps was a composite of Yanks, Canadians, and Brits, some who had landed with the Allies, others that had been flown in days after the invasion. They all met in a correspondents' meeting with military command.

There were certain messages that were to be put out, for distribution to radio stations and newspapers, after approval in London. Photographs were to be carefully screened before they were released. They didn't want people back home to be seeing corpses loaded on transports, the wounded in field hospitals, or bodies floating in the surf on those beaches.

"That doesn't mean we won't see it or know about it," Robert Dunnett of the BBC said, standing beside him in that briefing. "Or write about it later, eh? And who's to say," he added, "that you send all those rolls of film back to the desk in London?"

Paul had read Dunnett's pieces that appeared from time to time in the London Times, and knew of his work for the BBC. He liked him immediately. Dunnett stuck out his hand.

"My photographer got lost in the shuffle," he explained, which was a polite way of not saying that the man had either lost his way or ended up a casualty.

"What say we team up? I'll write the articles and you take the pictures."

An opportunity to work with Dunnett would probably never have happened under any other circumstances. But these weren't other circumstances. He shook Dunnett's hand.

That handshake set him on a difference course, one that took him to the front of the march that was headed north, and an encounter with someone he thought he might never see again from those first desperate days after the Allied landing.

They had reached Lisieux the day before, troop transports churning the dirt roads into seas of mud after days of rain. Ahead of them, the German army was in retreat, laying down mines to slow the armored onslaught, tanks setting up defense perimeters in what was rumored to be the build-up for a brutal offensive near the Belgium border—the Bulge, they called it.

Dunnett had been kept busy, fingers flying over the typewriter he packed along, looking up through a haze of cigarette smoke, only to swallow back more coffee in a frenzy to make the latest dispatch back to London.

Paul's work with the camera had been limited to the encampment, hundreds of soldiers burrowed in just beyond the village, waiting.

"You still taking your pictures with your little camera?"

Micheleine smiled at him from across the fire that struggled against the misty rain, the first campfire they'd been allowed in the last few days. She had been among the civilian Resistance that had joined up with them, reporting back on advanced enemy positions.

Paul smiled. "Someone once told me that I need to take them so that people will know what happened here."

The smile deepened as she ducked under the overhead canopy that protected against the rain and joined him beside the fire.

"Someone should teach you to build a fire."

"Aye, well, everything is wet, and command doesn't want us giving away our position."

She leaned in closer, as if sharing a secret. "The Germans know your position, but they are too busy trying to figure out theirs."

They talked, ironically of things old friends talk about when they haven't seen each other in a long time. War had a way of doing that, compressing everything into small pieces of time—months ago became yesterday, yesterday became today.

She motioned to the small table where Dunnett had been pounding out his story for the BBC, then had run off to meet the dispatch. A can of rations sat beside the typewriter.

"That is supper?" she asked, her dark eyes wide with disapproval.

"A gourmet meal when you're allowed to heat it up," he replied.

She made a sound that could only be interpreted as disgust and shook her head.

"Come." Her hand wrapped around his. "The French people are poor after these past years, but the least we can do is share a warm supper that is not found in a can."

Her idea of a supper that wasn't in a can came compliments of one of the residents in Lisieux. He and his wife were supporters of the Resistance.

The food was simple, roast chicken and summer vegetables in a thick wine sauce, with the rest of the wine in their glasses at the table. A fire burned in the fireplace that heated the rest of the two-story house that had been in the owner's family for a few hundred years.

After weeks of rations, usually eaten while on the march, a hot, home-cooked meal was like a feast, and the wine was smooth, warming through him with a faint glow.

"Their son is somewhere in the south of France," Micheleine explained, taking a sip of the wine.

"He went before the occupation. They have not heard from him in some time." The rest went unspoken.

"But now, with the Allies in France and General de Gaulle gathering the free French into an army, they hope it is almost at an end."

Hope. There were times it was the only thing that was left.

"What about you?' he asked.

She shrugged. "I will be going north with the others. There is still work to do. The snake has not yet let go of my people."

North, toward Belgium and that offensive that was building up.

"What about you, Paul Bennett?"

He smiled at the way she said his name. "The word is that we'll be going to Paris."

She took another sip of wine. "We will take back our city," she said, with a sudden fierceness.

"And crush the snake."

The fire had burned low.

"What will you do after the war?" she asked.

What would he do? Not weddings and birth announcements. The war had changed that.

"I would like to see the Highlands again." Didn't everyone want to see home again?

For him, the Highlands would always be home, no matter how far or how long he was away. It had a way of imprinting itself on you— the jagged peaks, misty glens, with rainbows forcing their way through the clouds. And the smell of it.

It was there even over the smell of that home-cooked meal and the haze from the wine, the memory strong.

"It is like the forest, I think," she said. "Different from the city. It reaches inside you and won't let you go. I remember the smell of the grass in summer when the sun is hot."

"You're from the country?"

She'd told him little about herself in that way that people protected that part of themselves, especially in war.

"Oui!" she said with an impassioned laugh. "My father's farm at the edge of the forest, very much like this. He raised sheep. We had a garden. It was my mother's home, from her family many generations back. Very quaint, you would say. Provincial. I hated it growing up, so far from everything. But we explored everything, all the old places. Now, I miss it very much."

Growing up? She was all of nineteen, yet years older in experience he knew. They all were.

"Tell me about the Highlands."

Where to begin, he thought.

"It is a wild place," he said, remembering the last time he and friends took a motorcar far into the north, past the Cairngorms, into those wild places.

"There is a certain smell of it—the land, mountains green in the summer, snow in the winter, and the sky changes from one moment to the next—so blue it makes your eyes hurt, then the clouds come rolling in and the water churns with magical creatures in deep pools —water horses," he said with a mock serious expression.

"Water horses?"

"Of course, they're magic. And then there is the heather, the hills full of it in spring. But the winters, they are my favorite, fierce, powerful, storms crashing down from the mountains and you can hear the spirits crying on the wind."

"Spirits crying on the wind?" she asked with an amused expression.

"Well, that's the way the old folks tell it. And the finest whisky in all the world, made from the water that comes down out of the mountains with the smoky taste of peat and just a wee bit of spice. Very different from your wine."

The wine was gone.

"There is a room at the back of the house, an old storeroom with an outside entrance."

She stood and held out her hand, that smile and a question in her dark eyes.

"What about the owner and his wife?"

Her hand tightened around his.

"They will not bother."

The room was small. Shelves against one wall held spices, canned foods, powdered milk, and fresh food—baskets of carrots, potatoes, shallots, and several bottles of wine.

"I see that they have enough food when I am here," she explained. "In exchange, they report on things they hear and see, and hide our people." She set her backpack on the chair.

A bed sat against the other wall, with a worn but clean coverlet. Extra clothes, simple garments one might find among the people in the French countryside, hung on hooks. A basin with a pitcher sat on the washstand. There was a small cast-iron stove for heat. She lit it, carefully setting the wood, then closing the door.

Did she know what those simple things meant? Simple things that weren't a cot or bedroll on the ground, a porcelain basin that wasn't a helmet that he'd shaved and bathed from, a roof overhead that wasn't a tarp or lean-to after weeks sleeping out in the open.

"Micheleine...?"

She pressed her fingers against his lips.

"No questions, Paul Bennett."

The heat in the room, the wine, the touch of her hands as she unbuttoned his shirt answered the only question that mattered.

In the shadows of that small room with only the glow of the fire from the cast-iron stove, they undressed each other. Beneath the sound of the rain on the roof, they came together, skin against skin, their breaths mingling, his hands in her hair, her legs wrapping around his.

Whispers, words that made no sense, or needed to. Touches, as old as time, as new as that moment. Then flesh against flesh, a silent question in the stillness of that room, and then he was moving inside her.

"Now I know," she whispered afterward, sprawled across him, their bodies slick in the warm cocoon of that room.

"What do you know?" he asked.

"What lies beneath the kilt," she replied, making him smile.

"Are you certain?" he asked, opening one eye to look at her.

She reached beneath the blanket, her hand closing over him.

"You must show me again," she whispered huskily, her mouth moving over his, even as she moved over him, her breasts brushing his chest as his head went back at the things she was doing.

"Micheleine!" he whispered, different this time, not a question, his fist closing around her hair. Her answer was in the heat of her body as she took him inside her.

"When will it finally be over?" she asked, as they lay together that next morning.

"The build-up will take weeks," he replied, what he had heard from Dunnett, not exactly a secret any longer.

"That will take us into winter." He looked over at her. The comfort of a fire, a bed, and four walls. Not a cold cot or soggy blankets.

They should have slept well the night before. Except that they hadn't slept at all. They'd made love, hands reaching, needing the contact, needing those moments when they came together. Human touch, the assurance that the world as they knew it wasn't completely gone. Hope.

"Will you be safe?" He had tried not to ask it, knowing full well they were both headed into uncertain places. But after the past hours...

She shook her head as she came to him then, pulling him down for her kiss, her body opening to him, and all he wanted was this.

"No questions," she whispered.

CHAPTER
TWENTY-FIVE
PRESENT DAY, LE NOIR, PARIS

The rain had let up.

The streets filled with people in spite of the cold—tourists, locals, and those who lived in the shadows—Paris by night, the gleam of the Eiffel Tower over the skyline, that gleaming glass pyramid outside the Louvre museum, admired for its architectural simplicity, loathed by Parisians of all generations, an insult in the midst of historical French culture, the Seine, a river with two identities—the right bank lined with exclusive shops, and the iconic left bank with its Bohemian history that included world famous artists and writers, and the Rue St. Denis with its prostitutes and junkies.

Two hundred years earlier, Paris had collected them all—misfits, anarchists, revolutionaries. Now there was a new generation of misfits, anarchists, and revolutionaries. They were called terrorists, and they left their mark on the city.

The call finally came as they sat outside the all-night Café. The message was brief. Anthony tucked the phone back into his jacket pocket.

"He'll meet with us. But he won't be at the club until around midnight."

James nodded. "I want to make another stop first."

The Eiffel Tower loomed to the east as Anthony eased the motorcycle around a corner a half block away, and cut the motor.

Farther down the boulevard, the gallery occupied the ground floor of one of those iconic 17th-century buildings spread throughout Paris, with an alley along the back. They left the motorbike in the alcove of a building and walked that short distance.

The front entrance was locked with the faint glow from the alarm system keypad in the reception area of the gallery. The hours for the gallery were stenciled in gold lettering on the glass beside the door with a number to call for an appointment.

The gallery was dark, making it impossible to see anything inside. James motioned for Anthony to follow him to the alley at the back of the building.

They waited.

"Perhaps no one will come tonight," Anthony suggested.

"They'll come," James replied.

Regular as clockwork, according to the information Innis had found, shipments twice a week, at night. The question was, what was in those shipments?

They rounded the corner of the building, then stopped as head-lights flashed from the opposite end of the alley. A signal?

James held up a warning hand and they retreated back around the corner of the building. When those headlights didn't appear as the truck rolled toward them and out onto the street, he eased back around the corner keeping to the shadows at the wall of the building.

The truck had stopped midway down the alley and turned in, headlights gleaming off large roll-up doors.

He left Anthony at the street, then continued down the alley. The driver of the truck cut the motor, followed by a brief conversation in French as he slipped inside the opening of the bay, at the off-side of the truck.

He glimpsed two people, one tall, the other shorter, slender, their features hidden by shadows inside the loading bay. It was only a momentary glimpse, but there was something about the shorter figure as he fell into step behind the taller man, the way he moved, then the slamming of a door as they entered the back of the gallery.

There were steps at the far end of the loading area that led up to a landing with a light over the back entrance of the gallery. He glanced at the overhead security system, then edged around the back of the truck. It was enclosed with high sides and a lift gate, the type used for transporting cargo or furniture.

He kept to the shadows and moved silently along the side of the truck. When he reached the driver's door, he peered inside the window. The cab was empty, except for the weapon—automatic, short barrel with a long magazine, tucked into the backpack that lay on the other seat.

France had some of the strictest gun laws in the world. It wasn't the sort of weapon found in your local sporting shop. He slipped around to the back of the truck.

What sort of shipments were usually found in the warehouse at the back of an art gallery?

Art was the natural answer—statuary, vases, paintings, valuable pieces, consignments for customers who wanted to remain anonymous, while other clients wanted to add to their private collections. And what might be worth the amount of money Innis had found in those financial records Innis had hacked into?

With a glance at the doors where the driver and his partner had disappeared, he carefully eased open the latch on the back gate of the truck. He ran the beam from the small flashlight over one crate, then another, then the part of the cargo that wasn't in a crate.

Bloody Christ! There were enough weapons in the back of that truck to start a war, or supply one that was already going on. The question was, where were they being taken? What third-world country where people were dying in the jungles, mountains, and deserts? What the hell was Callish into?

He eased the door shut, then moved around to the other side of the truck, careful to keep out of the range of that security camera. He suddenly stopped. Another automobile, that had been blocked from view by the larger truck, was parked several feet away at the far side of the loading bay.

It was a late model white van, the sort used for service businesses and found all over the UK and Europe. There was absolutely nothing distinctive about it—no decals, no company logos, no phone numbers to call for the plumber or repairman— except the crumpled bumper and the cracked windscreen.

There was no sign, no marquee, only the glow of the number 417 on the landing, with steps descending from the street level down to the abandoned metro line and station below.

James hesitated for the same reason he'd refused to take the cross-channel tunnel from Dover. Anthony stopped halfway down the steps.

"You do still want to meet le Angel?"

Angel—the name was no small irony considering the reputation of the man who went with it, a shadowy figure who conducted business in the shadows, rarely seen, a contact who often came across information that was valuable to both the authorities and criminals, supposedly a legitimate nightclub owner, and someone who might have information about the Paris gallery.

Still, he hesitated. He knew places like this, hidden places, dangerous places. He rolled his shoulder against the tightness that had little to do with old wounds and everything to do with gut instinct. He rubbed his palms down over the pockets of his jeans and wished for something more than the knife he carried.

Dark places, hidden places. Hidden people.

"You're certain t he'll be here?"

It was after midnight, and after what he'd seen at the gallery, that instinct had sharpened. These were dangerous people. Somehow Cate had stumbled into something, and now they were in the middle of it. But just exactly was *it*? And what did all of it have to do with a photograph Cate's father had taken during the war?

"It's Friday night," Anthony replied. "He'll be here."

James silently swore to himself then followed him down, pushing back the uneasy feeling that tightened the back of his neck in places like this, where you couldn't see things in front of you until you were almost on top of them. Or they were on top of you.

The tunnel was dark except for ambient lighting and what appeared to be old-fashioned street lamps along the sides of the tunnel.

He'd heard of these places, reclaimed beneath the streets of Paris, reusing spaces that had been abandoned.

"Tell me about him."

"He's a businessman," Anthony replied, his voice echoing off the stone and concrete walls as the tunnel loomed like a black hole in front of them. He suddenly stopped and climbed several steps in a recessed area in the wall and a door.

Over the doorway was that same number, 417. Anthony seized a handle and opened the door.

"He's a gamer. He won three hundred thousand at our last tournament. He has a lot of business enterprises all over the city, and no love for your gallery owner. When I mentioned the gallery, he was most interested to meet you."

They walked down a well-lit hallway. He saw the glow of other lights before they ever reached the entrance to the club, then through an arched opening where they were met by two men dressed in black turtlenecks, black suit jackets, and jeans. Every nerve went on alert at the slight bulge beneath both men's jacket fronts. Anthony briefly spoke with one and they were allowed to move ahead.

He had been in caves in Afghanistan, from the simple hollowed-out spaces to intricate webs of tunnels carved deep into the mountainsides, but it didn't prepare him for the huge space that opened up before them.

Paris was well-known for its underground catacombs, areas that had been carved out underground over the centuries. There were chambers that had been used to hide from the Nazis during the occupation of World War II. But this was no crudely carved hiding place from a couple of centuries earlier.

It was not quite midnight, but the nightlife of Paris had slipped underground, tables that lined both sides of the club filling up, couples of every mix and description out on the dance floor, while a disc jockey put out a stream of rap, funk, and dance pieces that pumped into the cool air blended with the scent of marijuana and a vague undercurrent of incense and perfumes of choice.

The glow of strobes and under-floor lighting was a blend of hot pink, bright blue, and purple, a rainbow that changed to the beat of the latest piece from giant speakers, while waiters in tight, ball-hugging shorts delivered fruit-embellished drinks, shots, and other alcohol of choice. Club 417 was open for business.

As soon as they entered the club, he looked for more guards, and other exits. Beneath the glitz and glitter, the booze and entertainment, the club was no different than any off-the-map night spot.

A slow scan of the club and he knew the locations of several guards, no doubt with the polite, disguised titles of 'hosts,' strategically positioned throughout the club. Whoever Anthony's contact was, he was a careful man. He also saw the women, some of them no more than girls, who worked the tables and the customers. The younger the girl, the higher the price. When she got older, she would disappear, probably out on the streets to survive in the oldest trade. And that was if she was lucky.

The raised platform was in the far corner of the club with a view of everything, an arched doorway in the back wall behind the platform—an exit, no doubt in case the crowed got out of control, the club was raided by some rival, or there was a surprise guest that made an unexpected appearance. He thought of the club in Paris that had been the target of terrorists, along with another in Florida. The unexpected had become all too common.

The platform was tucked back behind a wrought-iron half wall, the man behind it unlike the other guests or the guards posted at either side, an empty shot glass before him, dark eyes watchful in the way of someone who is always looking over his shoulder and always has bodyguards. Just your usual underground businessman.

One of the guards came forward. The tension tightened along every nerve ending at the anticipated pat-down, the knife extricated from his back pocket and laid on the table. The smile from across the table was unexpected as James exchanged a warning glance with the guard. Anthony made the introductions.

"This is the man I spoke to you about. Captain Jack, this is Captain Morgan."

James angled a glance at Anthony. He was a friend of Innis's but James had learned a long time ago not to trust a friend of a friend. There was an old saying, the enemy of my enemy is my friend. He preferred his own version, the enemy of my enemy might also be my enemy.

"Captain Morgan," their host replied. "A fellow pirate, perhaps." He chuckled. "And I see that you came armed. I expected no less, of course. It is the nature of business." He ran a finger along the blade of the knife.

"A fine weapon and it has seen some use." That dark gaze met his.

"Some," James replied.

"It will be returned when you leave."

It was almost comical, James thought. The man across from him could have been that iconic pirate from several recent films, an alter-ego and undoubtedly not his real name, right down to the dreadlocks and braided goatee. The only thing missing was a gold tooth.

"Please," their host indicated the chairs across from him. "Be seated, a drink, and you must tell me about your interest in le Noir."

It was subtle, but there was a definite undercurrent, an edge in the way he said it. Rules learned long ago—meet the other's gaze directly, allow him to speak first, and never trust a man who stands at your back. He gave the guard a steady look. At a nod from his employer, he stepped to the side and seemed to melt into the wall.

"Yes, I think we understand each other very well," their host commented.

"A drink, then." Their host raised a hand and one of those scantily clad servers appeared.

James shook his head. "I don't drink." Not in strange places, he thought, but didn't say it, where any beverage might contain a few extra drops that worked in just a few seconds.

Captain Jack smiled, revealing not one but several gold teeth. "You are a careful man. And you come for information. What are you willing to provide in return?"

Quid pro quo, whether it was several million US, stolen weapons, or a solution. There was always an exchange.

But what did he have?

Information—twenty million dollars funneled through an obscure art gallery, in a way that had taken an expert hacker several attempts to find it. He'd bet the man sitting across from him had no idea it existed, and for someone who probably had a piece of everything that went on within his district, a percentage-take on twenty million, just for the privilege of doing business in Paris, came to a healthy sum.

It was a lesson he'd learned embedded in the Middle East—everyone always got their piece. It was just a matter of getting what you wanted or needed, in return.

And then there were the weapons. Did Captain Jack know about them? Was he part of it? Follow the money.

From what Anthony had told him, Captain Jack, whoever the hell he really was, controlled the underground of Paris—goods, services, some legal, many not. And the French authorities looked the other way because his enterprises generated capital, and he also controlled a vast army of enforcers whose job description was to protect his business interests. And business interests such as his had undoubtedly suffered terrorist activity that had hit the city. No one liked to lose money, no matter which side they were on.

"Information for information," he replied.

Captain Jack exchanged an amused look with one of his guards. "What can you tell me that I do not already know about my city?"

"Twenty million US, possibly more, being moved through a local business."

It was possible that Captain Jack already knew about the amount of money moving through the gallery. Then again maybe not. But it was a safe bet he didn't know about the weapons. Beside him, Anthony took a slow deep breath.

It was a dangerous game, trading information for information, or the promise of a great deal of money for information. He'd learned that in Afghanistan, working with local tribal leaders.

The enemy of my enemy...

Captain Jack's eyes narrowed. It was the only physical reaction, but from experience it told him what he needed to know, and what Captain Jack didn't know.

"How would you have such information?" Captain Jack casually replied, fingers drumming on the table top.

"I know people."

Captain Jack leaned forward in his chair. His gaze met James' in slow appraisal.

"You are not from Paris. What people do you know?" He reached out and grabbed James' wrist. He stared at the tattoo of the sword that ran the length of his arm.

"The blade— a symbol of power and strength. Tell me, what are you a captain of?"

James sensed rather than saw Anthony's sudden uneasy movement.

He thought of the others with that identical mark, three of them, a team, a brotherhood, and that long weekend leave before that next mission when they had all gotten that identical tattoo.

On the teams there was no rank. It disappeared when you went out. There was only the man next to you, and the man next to him, a brotherhood. And then that last mission, and of the four he was the only one to come back alive.

"Myself," he replied, holding onto the memory.

Again there was that quiet appraisal. Captain Jack released him.

"This is my city," he explained. "I was born here, my parents before, and several generations before that. But there is an evil in Paris today, people murdered in the streets." He made a sweeping gesture of the nightclub.

"In nightclubs, concert halls, sports arenas. There are those who bleed my city, and I don't like it. When my city suffers, the people suffer, and I don't like that. Now, tell me about twenty million dollars."

Information for information.

He told Captain Jack what he knew, that someone was moving high numbers in his city, possibly in stolen artifacts. It seemed a natural connection—the gallery and stolen art, remembering the collection of looted artifacts they'd come across in the desert mountains on an early mission. He was dangling the carrot, a carrot that Captain Jack might profit from. It was a long shot, but it was all he had.

"There are large transfers of money," he explained. "Several million at a time, twenty million over the past twelve months, all of it into an untraceable account."

Captain Jack snorted. "And you just happen to have this information about these untraceable accounts."

"I know someone."

People like Captain Jack, who made their living in the shadows, relied on information. If someone lied, they were probably found in some back alley with their throat cut, or floating in the river.

The Captain nodded. "Twenty million. That is a great deal of money for someone who never has gallery showings in a gallery that is rarely open except to receive shipments. I know this, because I also know someone."

He sat back. That narrowed gaze wandered out over the dance floor and the scores of people who paid well to get into his club. Then Captain Jack angled a look over at him.

"An oversight perhaps on the part of the gallery owner. He will need protection for his business interests."

And a percentage off twenty million US, to start off, would go a long way toward building a lucrative business relationship.

"I appreciate the information. Now," Captain Jack leaned back in his chair, his gaze meeting James' once again.

"How may I help you?"

"The name of the gallery owner."

Captain Jack sat back at his chair. Several moments passed. It was possible his gamble had failed. People like the captain certainly weren't bound by any code of honor. He might just as well tell him to fuck off. He finally relaxed, and smiled. It was all in the body language.

"He goes by the name of Faridani. Adnan Faridani." There was an edge in the way he said it.

"He is not French. He holds Belgium citizenship, and there is a woman who has been seen several times at the gallery."

No name for the woman. It was obvious that was all the informa-tion they were going to get. But it was enough for someone with a particular expertise, like Innis.

Captain Jack rose from the table. "It has been most interesting, meeting you, Captain Morgan." He held out his hand.

Shake hands with the devil, James thought. It wasn't the first time.

"You should also know that there is a truck full of weapons in his warehouse, enough to set the city of fire."

That dark gaze hardened. "I don't like it when someone hurts my city."

James nodded. They understood each other. Meeting over.

"Please stay," the captain told them. "Enjoy yourselves, as my guests. The night is just getting started.

James shook his head. He'd been in too many places, seen and done too many things not to understand that being a guest could be dangerous.

They had what they'd come for, a name, and more—the fact that Captain Jack hadn't known about the weapons or the amount of money being laundered through the gallery, and that the gallery was a front for a smuggling operation.

It was after two in the morning. The club scene had amped up for the night. Every table was full and the dance floor was jammed with bodies as they were escorted to the front of the club. His knife was returned to him as they reached the exit.

The street scene they found above ground was different than the one they'd left earlier. Sirens filled the night air across the city, and a military helicopter swooped low overhead.

Anthony stopped two men on their way into the club. The exchange was in French, but their expressions were guarded, their body language nervous. They headed down those stairs to the club below.

Anthony's expression was grim.

"There's been another attack in the City."

That was bad for business.

CHAPTER
TWENTY-SIX

I t was a diversion, something to keep her mind occupied.

In college, it had been an amusement, one of her roommates into spirituality, the cards, crystals, that sort of thing. Luna looked at her across the table.

"All right." Kris finally gave in and sat down. "What do the cards say?"

Luna shuffled and then did a full spread.

"Hold a question in your thoughts," she told her. "Something you want an answer to, something that is important, then pick three cards."

When Kris had picked the cards, Luna nodded thoughtfully.

"Interesting. Now, pick three more."

Kris chose three more cards, turning them over one at a time.

"There has been loss. These two cards indicate something very painful. But that is now ended."

That was no secret. Cate's death had been a painful loss.

"There will be challenges. These two cards show an obstacle, but it is temporary. You will go through a period of confusion, then you will need to make a choice."

Great, Kris thought. Confusion and choices. What about the outcome? That was the question she held in her thoughts.

"Pick two more cards."

She got as far as turning over one.

"The moon," Luna commented with a frown. "Mystery, the subconscious, and dreams. Turn over the second card."

As she reached for the second card a sound from Daenerys had them both looking up.

"It's across the city," she said, turning up on the audio on the latest newscast.

Images filled the video screen—emergency vehicles, armed police, streets blockaded as bodies were carried out of the open-air market, a scene that had become all too familiar.

People on the sidewalks huddled together, clinging to one another, several bloodied from flying glass and debris, others waiting with expressions of pain, fear, hope, waiting for word of survivors.

There had been two attacks, the second one unfolding blocks away as an automobile plunged into the front of a crowded restaurant; the horror of the market scene replayed, guests trapped inside as the vehicle caught fire.

Kris stared at the screen, those scenes eerily familiar—the shock and disbelief, the bloodied bodies, and another image…sightless eyes staring back at her.

No one said a word as the footage from the attack played over, updates flashed across the bottom of the screen—a dozen dead, countless others taken to hospital. Men, women, old, young, couples out for late supper, possibly a night of celebration, everything changed in those moments as the truck plunged through the front of the exclusive restaurant.

"That whole scene in London must have been horrible," Innis said, glancing over at her.

Kris nodded. She hadn't spoken about it. But it was there, every time there was another incident—London, Paris, Madrid, New York.

Was it ever going to end?

It was a question she'd asked her brother. There had been no answer then, or now. She pushed away from the table, unable to watch any more of it.

Innis watched as she went into the kitchen, poured a glass of wine, then simply stared at it.

"What was the last card?" he asked.

Luna turned it over, her dark gaze meeting his.

"Death."

It was after two in the morning, and there was still no word from either James or Anthony. She poured a cup of coffee, fighting the fatigue and raw nerves.

What the hell was Cate doing in France? What was she after? What did that last text message mean? What did any of it mean? It was like a giant puzzle, the pieces swirling around in her head.

She had finally reached Marcus Aronson earlier that evening, another piece of the puzzle. Cate had contacted him twice when she was there.

What had they talked about? What did he know about her reason for being in France? Where she was going? Whom she had met with?

"Dear girl," he said when he had answered the phone. "Where are you? Are you all right? The media reports..." And more questions.

"Yes, yes, I understand," he replied. "Of course, we must meet. There may be something that Cate mentioned that will help," he had continued when she explained the reason she was there.

"My dear Kris," he had said again. "We live in dangerous times— what is one to do? Still, I can't imagine what you've been through. Are you safe? Where are you?"

The sound of his voice—a friend who had known Cate for so many years, a consultant on her books, possibly a lover, and someone who understood the close friendship they had shared.

Her throat tightened. After everything that had happened, it would be good to meet with him. Still she had hesitated giving him their location.

Innis had assured her that it was impossible for anyone to trace her call on the cell phone he had provided. He and Anthony used other phones like it, all throwaways, to communicate with clients, some who had rather questionable business activities but participated regularly in the online gaming tournaments they had put together, all part of the underground cyber world they lived in.

"We're staying with friends," she finally replied. "I can meet you somewhere in the city."

"Nonsense, you must come to my apartment in the Montparnasse. You have the address, of course. We can talk, and hopefully I can provide something that will explain the reason Cate sent you that message." He had paused then.

"My dear friend, Cate. So sad. After all the places she traveled throughout her career, for it to end like this. I shall miss her so very much."

There was a sound over the telecast on the widescreen, the rumble of a motorcycle from the street below.

They were back.

It was just nerves, she told herself, her hands tightening over the mug of coffee, the uncertainty after everything that had happened the past few days, the news about another attack.

Just nerves, she thought, as she hung back in the kitchen, refusing to give into them as Daenerys left the kitchen and crossed the living area to the entrance of the residence. She took a slow, deep breath as Daenerys threw back the iron latch and opened the door. And another deep breath as Anthony appeared, then James, both soaking wet.

"Bloody Christ!" Innis exclaimed, before anyone else said it. "The least you could have done was send a text message. You don't write, you don't call. What does it say about our relationship?"

"If you kiss me, I'm going to break both your legs," James replied, with a glance around the grand salon of the old residence as everyone gathered about them— except one.

"Aye, well then, a hug," Innis replied, wrapping both arms around him, then high-fiving Anthony as the telecast replayed on the screen behind them.

"It's been on since the first broadcast came through," Innis explained. "You're all right, then?"

Anthony nodded. "It took us a while to get back. A lot of streets are blocked off; we had to take the long way round," he shrugged.

"Have you had anything to eat?" Daenerys asked.

"One of your herbal snack bars that I found in my backpack," Anthony made a face. "From our trip to Cannes last summer."

"I made a stew," she told them. "There's enough for everyone."

Kris heard the back-and-forth conversations, Innis's attempt to disguise the concern they had all felt, and Daenerys' common-sense solution—once a crisis was over, serve food.

Everything had been set out, the giant cookpot put back on to simmer, bowls and plates, a basket of fresh French bread, and wine set out.

She caught James' glance as she came out of the kitchen. She was fighting her own emotions—relief with a healthy dose of anger. She returned to the table with the bank of computer screens, various segments of the news with the latest details playing in the background. She gathered up notes she'd made, along with copies of those photographs of the tapestry that Innis had discovered.

When Anthony would have said something, Daenerys pushed him toward the kitchen.

"Come along. You can help me get everything ready."

They disappeared amid the sound of dishware being set out, the popping of a cork, and whispered conversation.

Luna gathered up the deck of Tarot cards and shoved Innis toward the kitchen.

"You can help," she informed him, with a glance over at Kris.

"Innis found some additional information about the tapestry," Kris explained matter-of-factly. She concentrated on the notes she'd made, gathering everything that they'd made copies of.

"Photographs taken earlier than the ones Diana showed us. There are several of all of the panels. There might be something in them that can tell us what Cate was after."

"Kris..."

"And I had him enlarge the photographs Paul Bennett took," she continued, needing the distance of conversation.

"About this evening..." He needed her to understand.

"I made notes," she added.

He heard it in her voice, knew her well enough now that he recognized it, that way she had of retreating into details—calm, everything under control, emotions carefully hidden. Like the morning after the attack in London.

He saw it as she reached for another piece of note paper, the way her hand shook, and she almost knocked over the bottled water. She made a grab for the bottle. His hand closed over hers just as it was about to topple over.

"We need to talk."

She did look at him then, eyes as cool as ice.

"You should have called."

It was that simple, but nothing simple about it.

"There wasn't time," he explained. Or the opportunity, he thought, at the club or in the alley behind the gallery, and then with the latest attack, the city was like an armed fortress. But there were things she needed to know. She pulled back, glanced at him again.

"It's late."

She shoved the piece of paper on top of the pile she'd gathered and pushed past him. She needed space, thankful that he was there, and at the same time needed him to not be there.

He followed her. He needed her to listen, to apply some of that logic, and to understand. This wasn't a game. It wasn't some holiday weekend with a side-trip to Paris. People had been killed, and she was in the middle of it.

She laid the paperwork on the table beside the bed.

"Those bandages probably need changing."

He'd taken off his jacket, wet from the ride through the rain back to the apartments. There were damp spots on his sweatshirt, and some other stain that hadn't been there before. Her stomach tightened at the thought his wound might have started bleeding again. She gathered gauze pads and tape that Daenerys had provided earlier.

"You'll have to take off your shirt."

"It can wait."

She gave him that look and tossed the bandages onto the side table.

"Fine."

She wasn't prepared for how fast he moved. He pulled her around and pinned her against the wall, a hand flattened on the wall at each side of her head.

"Enough!"

Her head came up—surprise, then anger and some other emotion she wasn't prepared for. She went with the anger and tried to push past him. He blocked her.

"Supper is ready..."

Innis had followed from the salon and stood in the open doorway. He glanced uneasily from one to the other.

"Get out," James told him. "Now!"

"Right. No problem." He was already gone.

They stood there like two combatants, each unwilling to budge, unwilling to step away.

"It's late," she said, trying not to give into raw nerves, the fear over the past several hours, the possibility that he might not come back, and the cold fury that he had.

He refused to let her off that easily.

"Look at me."

She was angrier than he'd ever seen her. Not the incident at the airport, anything that had followed, not even her meeting with Inspector '*Dickless*' with the Inverness police had made her this angry.

"You could have called."

Even as she said it, she realized how it sounded. As if he needed to check in. But she needed him to understand. If something had happened...

"Not with the people we went to see," he fired back at her, trying to control his own temper.

"Where we met, not even the French authorities go there. These people operate in the shadows. They make their own rules, and they don't trust anyone. They would have been suspicious of a phone call."

"I should have been there," she threw back at him.

"You had no business there," he added, his voice suddenly quiet.

Too quiet. A warning? She ignored it.

"No business?" She couldn't believe what she was hearing.

"That's right. These aren't nice people. They run underground businesses, and buy and sell just about everything, including drugs and women, some of them very young." Children, too, was his guess, a hot commodity in the underworld that people like Captain Jack operated in.

"The young ones bring an especially high price, lots of profit. But they're not young for very long once they get passed around." He didn't spare the details. "You might bring a couple thousand dollars."

The anger boiled over. "If you're trying to scare me..."

"You need to be scared! These are the sort of people Cate would have interviewed in some village or remote compound with an armed escort, and the sort of place where everything, anything can be bought or sold for a price, and human life is the cheapest commodity of all. We were on their home ground tonight. There were guards and they were armed. I didn't want you there. I won't take that chance."

She knew what he was doing, and it only made her angrier.

"That's not your decision to make, and I don't need your permission."

She was on dangerous ground and she knew it. She'd seen his reaction before, at the roadside tavern on the road to Inverness, the quiet before the storm, the way he had looked at those young men. It was there now in the expression on his face.

"It's not about permission! If something happened out there...!" He'd needed to get through to her, to make her understand what they were dealing with.

It was that simple. And anything but simple, her body pinned against his.

"Bloody Christ!" he swore, hands fisted on the wall.

He wanted to drag her back to that bed, or the floor, or up against the wall. He wanted to strip away that cool composure, to feel that long body naked against his, to tear down the barriers until he found the heat that he knew was there, then lose himself in her.

He swore again, and pushed away from the wall. He didn't look at her, didn't trust himself to leave the room if he did.

The door slammed behind him.

CHAPTER
TWENTY-SEVEN

he apartments were unusually quiet.

Her first thought was that it was early, no one was up yet. But the light that slanted in at the edge of the drapes was that hazy gray of Paris in winter, the sun angling over the rooftops mid-morning as she pulled back the heavy drapes.

James hadn't come back to the room, not that she expected it. There had been too much anger. They both needed some distance, some time to cool off. Still, they needed to talk.

She pulled on sweatshirt and sweatpants and went in search of coffee, badly needed with only a few hours' sleep. She heard voices as she approached the salon, then discovered those voices were the latest newscast on the widescreen.

The broadcast was in English from a French news affiliate. Images from the attack at the restaurant the night before flashed across the screen—armored vehicles, emergency personnel, soldiers in camouflage with masks pulled up over their faces so that only their eyes were visible. Like actors in some macabre horror film, with weapons that had become almost commonplace on the streets of Paris, and the bodies of people who had been inside enjoying an evening out—couples, young, middle-age, and a child whose lifeless hand spilled over the edge of a stretcher.

"The latest attack in an increasingly long list of attacks over the past three years, even as authorities and military have a heightened presence across the city of Paris. Three people are known dead, with several more taken to area hospitals. No word on their condition. We will have more information at the midday."

"It has been on all the news channels this morning."

She didn't hear Luna come into the salon, wasn't even aware she was there until she spoke. She stood a few feet away, a long braid over one shoulder, the images that flashed across the screen reflected in her eyes.

"It is not the city that I remember," she said with a trace of sadness. Then she looked over at Kris.

"My mother was French. I was born here. I was nine when I went to live with my father."

Old enough to remember, or old enough to forget. She didn't explain and Kris didn't ask.

"Where is everyone this morning?"

"Innis went with Anthony and Daenerys to the warehouse," Luna replied. "There is a tournament tonight. There is always a lot of work to do to set up," she explained.

"They need to check the game stations to make certain they are working properly. Food will be delivered this afternoon, and Innis wanted to check the internet connections one more time.

"We usually link up from the café, but with everything that's happened…" She didn't need to explain. "We'll host the games from Paris."

Game night.

Kris had heard them talking about it the day before—high stakes, with players expected to participate from across the globe. Tournaments in the past went on for hours, sometimes days, and with a buy-in of five thousand dollars per player, a great deal of money was at stake for the winner, and the hosts.

She went into the kitchen. Some of Daenerys's special-blend coffee was in the brewer. She poured a cup, the caffeine and cinnamon blend pushing back the lack of sleep.

"He didn't go with them." Luna poured a cup for herself, as if she read her mind.

"He said something about a rental car, and wanted to check out an address. He had Innis pull up information before he left." She hesitated. "You might want to take a look."

Had she heard their argument the night before? In spite of thick walls in the old building, with six people living in close quarters, there wasn't much opportunity for privacy.

She followed Luna back into the salon, and pulled up a chair beside her in front of the wide-screen.

"It had to do with information they got last night." Luna keyed in a link. Images came up on the screen, and she scrolled through them.

It took her a moment to figure out what she was looking at—video from a security camera. The date and time came up across the bottom of each frame.

"It is from the gallery," Luna explained, "le Noir."

The 'how' Innis had come by the footage wasn't a mystery. He'd obviously hacked into the gallery security system, a man of many talents.

"They went there before their meeting last night," Luna explained.

He and Anthony had gone to the gallery the night before—something he hadn't bothered to mention at the time. Not that she'd given him much chance.

There'd been too much anger when there was no call from either of them after the attack at the restaurant, not knowing where either of them was, not knowing if something had happened to them.

Was that the address he had gone back to check that morning?

She studied frame after frame as Luna scrolled through—a shot from an outside camera as a large enclosed van approached down a darkened alley. Then another shot from another camera as bay doors slowly opened and the van entered what appeared to be a large garage. Another camera picked up interior shots as the van slowly pulled inside. There were several more frames as the driver and a passenger got out of the van.

It was the passenger who caught her attention—the slender build, dressed in a dark turtleneck shirt, dark cargo pants, and boots. Then the profile beneath the edge of a ball cap as the passenger turned to say something to the driver. It was only a glimpse, features hidden by shadows.

That was all it was days before, at the airport in Edinburgh, someone seen in a matter of seconds, the fight over her bag, then gone.

"Go back," she told Luna. "Replay that last part, then stop."

She stared at the still frame image. It was an impression more than anything, that sense of seeing something—or someone—that she'd seen before.

It took a moment for it to sink in, for her to wrap her head around what she was seeing. She sat back. She felt as if she'd taken a blow to the stomach. It was the same person from the airport.

She looked at the rest of the footage, concentrating on that slender figure as the two people rounded the front of the van, then crossed the garage and climbed the half dozen steps into the back of the gallery. She sat for several moments trying to absorb what she had seen.

If the person was the same one she'd had that encounter with at the airport, then it was connected to everything else that had happened—not a random thief, but someone after something.

What? Obviously not the usual ID, cash, credit card theft, but something that had to do with Cate's accident. And had been trying to stop her since.

The photograph?

"Innis pulled up messages from your cell account." Luna brought up another screen.

"James wanted to know if anyone had attempted to hack into it."

Something else he didn't bother to tell her.

"What did he find?" If someone had hacked into her phone, they would have access to all her information, including calls she made.

"Nothing that seemed obvious. It depends on their expertise." Luna gave her a faint smile.

"There are some people who can access an account and leave no trace."

One guess on who 'some people' might be.

"There were several voicemail messages."

She wasn't surprised. She'd been out of communication since leaving London. She turned on her phone.

There were three messages from Alec.

"Where the bloody hell are you? The media is all over the attack in London, and there is security footage from that attack at Mont St. Michel! Call me before the old man has a bloody coronary!"

Her publisher had called a half dozen times, the message the same, and Nina had left two messages.

"Ellison is meeting with our legal department over everything, but he needs you here. You need to call in so we can discuss everything that's happened."

Then the last message.

"My dear Kris." The accent was familiar from dozens of calls in the past, and meetings in both London and Paris when he had joined them for Cate's latest book launch—Marcus Aronson.

"Such sad news about our friend Cate. I cannot believe it. You must call me."

The sound of his voice, that slight accent—French, that she'd come to recognize and that had become more pronounced the longer he lived in Paris. It brought back memories of those earlier trips to promote Cate's latest book, late-night discussions at their hotel after the media had left, a cigarette usually in his hand, although not the last couple of times as the major hotels set up smoking venues, the rest of the hotel off limits.

He was tall, handsome, and seemed to have a perpetual tan, courtesy of a distant ancestor, he had once joked, and with those startling blue eyes. He had more gray in his hair than the last time she saw him, which only contrasted the tan and those blue eyes. And he had an amazing knowledge of European history, particularly military history. He'd made a career of it. And there had been two books that had been published about prominent battles, including the Middle Ages.

Only once he'd spoken about that earlier career as a field correspondent, when he and Cate had worked together.

"We were both up for the same assignment," he had explained. "I had more experience, more time in the field, but the assignment went to Cate."

He had sat back then, watching Cate across the table. He smiled that charming, some would call it sexy smile, that had a way of pulling you in.

"I have always suspected she may have slept with the bureau chief to get that assignment." He had winked at Kris across the table.

It was said with humor, but Kris had the distinct impression he was the only one amused.

"Only because I refused to tell you the name of my source for that assignment." Cate had fired back at him. "The bureau chief wasn't interested in me. You missed out all the way around."

It was pure 'Cate,' the way she had of slipping something in when no one was expecting it, and then not certain how to take it.

"He knew exactly how to take it," Cate assured her when they went to their rooms later that night.

"And he knew it was true. Everyone did who worked out of London in those days. He just didn't want to acknowledge that the man might have had his sights set on him. Too much male ego. It's the reason things didn't last between us. That and distance. It's a killer. But he was pretty good in bed." She had laughed then.

"Maybe too much ego in bed."

She was the last person Kris would have described having a big ego. It was about experience, things she'd seen, people she'd known—good and bad. It was always about the story, and it was the closest Cate ever came to admitting she once had an affair with Marcus. The friendship had somehow managed to survive.

"But he was pretty good."

On a scale from one to ten, Kris had asked. Cate had thought about that.

"Probably an eleven." She had laughed again at Kris's expression. "Alright, a twelve."

Right up there with an American colonel stationed in Germany, who had been with the OSS during World War II. The little information Cate had shared about him, his background, and military exploits, had become the basis for the main character in her first book.

After that conversation, Cate had referred to Marcus as 'Twelve,' more than once. That way that something stuck, she found it difficult to maintain that professional relationship when she spoke with him as a source on one of Cate's books.

The physical part of their relationship aside, though, he was obviously deeply saddened by Cate's death. It was there in his voice, and that message.

She thought about waiting until James returned, then decided against it. She had no idea what Marcus's schedule was and wanted to talk to him as soon as possible to find out what Cate might have told him. She reached him as he was leaving for a late morning class at the university.

"I've been worried about you!" Marcus was saying. "Yes, yes, the incident in London has been all over the media, and after what happened to my dear friend...Of course, we must meet. I have just the one class, and then we could meet afterward."

They agreed to meet as his apartment in the Montparnasse. She had been there before with Cate. His apartment was across from a small park surrounded by Cafés, art studios, and shops.

"Of course," he assured her. "I will help whatever way I can."

She brushed aside Luna's concern and her suggestion that she wait for James to return. She had just enough time to shower and dress.

CHAPTER
TWENTY-EIGHT

"Where?" James demanded.

"She was gone when we got back from the warehouse," Innis explained.

"She went out," Luna explained. "She made a call, and made arrangements to meet someone.

He recognized the name. Marcus Aronson, who had once worked with Cate and was a resource on two of her books. His number had been on the list of numbers Cate had called when she was there.

"I tried to talk her out of it, to wait until you got back," Luna told him.

He swore under his breath. She'd been angry the night before, resented that he'd gone alone with Anthony. Stubborn!

"Did she say where?"

"She left this." Luna handed him the note Kris had left.

"She spoke with him this morning and they arranged to meet."

The note was brief, that she'd gone to meet Aronson, and would be back later.

"How long ago?"

"Thirty, maybe forty minutes," Luna replied. "She took the metro."

He swore again, that tight feeling turned into a knot at his gut.

The Anthonys' apartments in the Marais were safe. There'd been no indication that they'd been followed there—he'd checked. But out on the street was different. And she'd taken a borrowed phone. It could be traced if she left it on.

He pushed past Innis and went to that bank of computers at the table. Legal or not, whatever it took to find it, he needed an address and he needed it now.

"Number sixty-five, Rue du Chambord in the Montparnasse," Anthony announced a few minutes later as he hit the print function for after hacking into the university records that had provided Aronson's home address.

James grabbed the printout. She had a forty-minute start, and according to Anthony she needed to make two changes on the metro to make the connection in the Montparnasse. He was already out the door. His only chance was to beat her to that address.

The streets were a nightmare; congested with midday traffic and roadblocks that weren't shown on the map display on the phone Innis had given him. After the third roadblock, he tossed the phone into the passenger seat and followed last-minute directions Anthony had given him.

He crossed the river, dodging through traffic, saw the street marker he was looking for and cut off another driver as he shot around the corner. He pulled to the curb and cut the motor.

According to the street directions he was only a couple of blocks from that address on the Rue du Chambord. He pulled the phone from his jacket pocket. Anthony came on at the first ring. There'd been no call from her. He shoved the phone back into his jacket pocket and hit the street.

According to the information Anthony provided, the first metro train from the Marais District had been delayed, long enough that she had probably missed her first connection, and possibly the next one after that. With any luck she might only just be arriving for that meeting with Aronson, and the route she would most likely have taken would put her on the same street as he cut across traffic and turned down the Rue du Chambord.

He had a description of the jacket, and ball cap she was wearing with the logo of Innis's favorite football team on the front of the cap, and looked for it among tourists and day travelers bundled up in jackets and ball caps, and sidewalk artists who braved the early winter cold, their easels set up in a perimeter around open-air Cafés and coffeehouses.

He darted through ambling tourists and pedestrians who stopped to admire an artist's work or join the line outside one of the cafés amid the aroma of coffee and food.

It was just a glimpse—a flash of blue among hooded sweatshirts and a variety of other head coverings—crossing the street ahead, but it was enough to have him pushing through the crowd at the sidewalk with a new urgency. Then he saw her.

That athletic, long-legged stride, the way she stopped for cross traffic with the confidence of someone who navigated the streets of New York, and the way she checked the sidewalk ahead, glanced back in his direction briefly, then scanned the street before stepping off the sidewalk.

He followed her from down the street, instinctively scanned the sidewalk, then crossed over after her. Aronson's apartment was in the building at the end of the block.

Among the street noises, automobiles, motorbikes, and delivery trucks, a distant rumble that rolled under his feet. It was the sort of sound that was felt rather than heard, a long rumble, once experienced never forgotten.

He had felt it before, and knew it in that way that something imprinted itself in the brain...if one lived through it.

Eight years before. Falluja. People in the streets, at the market, and that deadly sound. He pushed through people on the sidewalk and shouted a warning at her on the run.

Kris stopped, certain she heard her name over the street noise in the street. She heard it again, surprise followed by anger, as she saw him dodging through people on the sidewalk.

He saw the expression on her face—surprise, then the anger that was still there from the night before. He had no time for either as he shouted and made an arm motion for her to get down.

There was something in the way he came at her—urgent, his expression something she'd seen before, not the anger of the night before, but glimpsed that night in London just before the van hurtled across the patio of the Blue Oyster, then the chaos that had followed, the crash of tables and chairs, the screams, bodies thrown around like dolls.

"Get down!" he shouted again, that deep rumble rolling beneath the pavement at the street, beneath his feet, then the explosion that tore through the apartment building at Number sixty-five Rue du Chambord.

She heard it but like others around her had no idea what it was. It was as if movement was suddenly suspended, time slowing, everything around her seen in slow motion, the expressions on the faces of people on the street, a young woman with a child, an old man smoking a cigarette, traffic on the street.

Then she felt it, like a large truck rumbling through the street, rolling toward her. Then it exploded at the apartment building only yards away and she was slammed down onto the sidewalk.

The blast threw him to the ground. Fragments of plaster, wood, and rock showered down on the street and sidewalk. He pushed back to his feet as a thick cloud of smoke and dust rolled out of the front of the building.

She had been only a dozen yards away when she had turned, surprised, then the anger that gave way to something in those last seconds before the explosion.

He found the old man and helped him up. The young woman seemed to be all right. She was stunned, but reached for the child who seemed to have escaped unharmed. The bodies of others lay about like scattered dolls.

He found her beneath the plaster half-wall of the flower shop where she had been standing when the apartment building exploded.

He shifted pieces of the crumbled wall off of her, tossing other pieces of brick and plaster until he felt the fabric of the jacket.

Kris fought her way up out of the dust and debris. When his hand closed around hers, she held on. She'd lost the baseball cap, and dust from the broken plaster was in her hair and on her face.

He looked for blood, but didn't see any.

"Are you hurt?"

She was dazed, coughing, trying to push him away.

He held on. It was instinctive, that first shock, then as it began to wear off, the instinct to survive, to fight her way out of it.

"Are you hurt?" he asked again, but even as he asked it, his hands went back through her hair, feeling for any indication that she'd taken a blow to the head, then down her neck, across her shoulders.

"Can you stand?"

Numb, disoriented, she finally nodded. He pulled her to her feet.

"We need to go. Can you walk?"

She nodded again, holding onto him.

"Oh, God," she whispered, at the sight of the shattered apartment building. "Marcus..."

She was in shock. He saw it in the expression on her face, her eyes wide and dark. She fought it, then fought him as she turned back toward the apartment building. He pulled her back.

"You can't help him now."

"No!"

He held onto her.

"It might not be over!"

He scanned the street, cars that had been caught in the explosion of debris, people dazed, coming out of a Café across the street as clouds of smoke and dust billowed into the air.

There was no time to explain or try to convince her of the danger she was in out in the open. His arm tightened around her, pulling her with him, away from the shattered ruins of the apartment and the carnage, as the too-familiar sound of sirens filled the air.

CHAPTER
TWENTY-NINE

Everything was a blur as they sped through the streets of Paris —people on the street, traffic as he cut from one lane to the next, a closed street, the startled expressions of pedestrians as he cut down a sidewalk, then sped through an intersection and down another street, his gaze constantly going back to the rear-view mirror.

She had no idea where they were.

He downshifted, rounded another corner, cut through an alley, then out onto another street. And still had no idea where they were as traffic gradually thinned, and the rental car picked up speed.

Shock. She knew the signs and fought it as she caught pieces of his conversation with Anthony on the cell phone, the lights of the city fading behind them.

"I've got her," James said into the phone; then, "I know. We're not coming back. It's too dangerous. "

There was a pause; then, "It's best you don't know."

Hell, he didn't know. He only knew he had to get her out of Paris. They needed to disappear.

"Bon chance, my friend," Anthony said as the call ended.

She had no idea where they were going, and then it didn't matter as heat churned out the vents, wipers skimmed rain from the windscreen, and darkness closed in.

. . .

He glanced into the rear-view mirror, making certain no one had followed from the roadway, then took the turnoff, slowly rolling past the inn with a small tour bus and several other automobiles in the car park.

On the street, tourists were still out in spite of the rain, walking along the sidewalk, entering a nearby restaurant.

The inn had easy access to the roadway, with a market, shops, and a church, typical of small, rural villages.

He glanced over at her. She hadn't said a word, and after first leaving the city, he thought she had dozed off. Then he saw her eyes, fixed on the roadway as they drove north, her expression pale, emotionless.

He knew only too well that it was an illusion. She was in shock, then the numbness when that first shock wore off. Another glimpse. She had been holding herself in, holding on, arms wrapped around herself.

"Where are we?" she asked, barely a whisper.

"Just outside of Amiens." He pulled into the car park. "We need a place to stay for the night."

Until he could convince her that they needed to go to the authorities. She stayed in the car while he went inside.

Kris's hand shook as she pushed back her hair. She hurt everywhere. She was covered in dust from the explosion, and there was a tear in the knee of her jeans. At least she was fashionable, she thought, in that absurd way after something happened and nothing made sense.

"Number twenty-four, over the street," James said when he returned.

He locked the rental car, a hand on her arm as they went inside.

The inn was in the typical style of old houses in Normandy, with heavy beams and white-washed walls, shown in travel brochures.

A warm fire blazed in the main room. It was empty except for an older couple who sat in front of the rock fireplace with glasses of wine.

Their room was decorated in a French country theme, the comforter on the bed in a floral pattern and trimmed in blue and white stripes. The area rug was dark blue and gold, with a mahogany wardrobe, table, and two side chairs.

A plastic display stand with brochures on the table advertised local tours of World War II battlefield cemeteries and war memorials in both French and English, with black-and-white photographs on the front that looked as if they might have been taken just after the war.

"Step back in time and visit these hallowed sites where brave men died," was printed across the top of the brochure above a black-and-white photograph of soldiers that reminded her of Paul Bennett's photographs, their expressions exhausted with that same expression she'd seen in other photographs, of too many places seen, too many deaths. How many, she wondered, never made it home.

"I'll find us something to eat," James said as he made a quick check of the room and the adjoining bathroom.

"It's better if you stay here. It's not a good idea to be out and about. Kris?"

She turned and looked at him, pale, eyes dark. He'd seen that same expression too many times in other places.

"A hot shower will help."

She still said nothing.

"I won't be gone long. Bolt the door after I leave, and don't open it for anyone."

He waited in the hallway outside the room, then finally heard the bolt slide into place.

Kris sat on the edge of the bed, the past hours pushing their way through the shock and exhaustion, playing back in that cruel way when the brain refused to shut down.

She closed her eyes, but the images followed her there, like photos someone sent on her cell phone—the Montparnasse with its Bohemian blend of shops and restaurants, the apartment building at the end of the street, the smell of rain that morning, sounds on the street, a young woman, and her child, then that other sound, someone shouting her name...

The tears came then, streaming down her cheeks.

No sound came from inside the room. He inserted the key and slowly pushed the door open.

She sat on the edge of the bed, arms wrapped around her as if she was physically trying to hold herself together.

He locked the dead bolt and set the chain. She didn't look up, didn't move, didn't give the slightest indication that she knew he was there.

This was different than the attack in London. She'd been scared, there had been that first shock, but she'd fought her way through it. This time, it was as if she'd shut down, barely holding on, holding herself in.

"Kris?"

There were all kinds of pain. He knew that well enough—the pain of physical wounds that eventually healed, and the other, deeper wounds that never healed, never went away—the pain of losing someone, and the worst pain, the loss that came afterward that you were alive and they were gone, a loneliness of pain and regret, and guilt that was always there just beneath the surface, waiting for that moment in the middle of the night.

She looked up at him then, and the wound was there, open, raw, in the expression on her face.

She was shaking even though it was warm in the room. He went into the adjoining bathroom and ran hot water. She still hadn't moved when he returned.

He pushed the jacket off her shoulders and knelt on the floor in front of her. He wiped the dust and grime from her hands and arms, gentle where the skin was raw and bruised from the fall she'd taken when that half wall collapsed.

"Tell me if this hurts," he said as his hands moved up her arms, gently probing the smoothness of bones, then her shoulders, collarbone, the back of her neck.

He took his time, taking care if he should find swelling, a cut, dried blood, smoothing back the hair on her forehead, gently wiping away more grime from her cheek, the tears, the bruise from the London attack just starting to turn a pale shade of green. Battle wounds.

She made a sound. Not physical pain, but that other sound that came from deep inside, that different pain.

His touch, the simplest contact, pulled her back from that dark place. She looked up at him as fresh tears slipped down her cheek.

"If I hadn't contacted him..."

Guilt.

He brushed strands of hair back from her cheek where they had fallen forward. He knew more about that sort of thing than he could ever explain.

According to her phone log, Aronson was apparently the last person Cate met with before the accident. It made sense to meet with him, as much sense as any of it. He just wished he'd been there to talk her out of going there. But he knew how that would have gone over.

His fault. The argument after he'd gone with Anthony the night before without telling her. That bloody damned stubbornness. If he could change it, he would, to keep her from that pain. But he couldn't.

"That's not a place you want to go," he said gently. "Cate contacted him. After what happened, he knew the risk. It was his choice to meet."

"When I close my eyes..." The words caught in her throat. "Does it ever go away?"

He wanted to tell her that it would be all right, that in time she would forget what had happened that day, what she'd seen. But it was a lie. Those were the things you carried with you. They hadn't invented a pill yet to make you forget certain things. Until they did, you had to live with it. She had to live with it.

"You need to get some sleep."

She nodded, but made no move to undress. He helped with her sweater, then jeans, and tucked the comforter in around those long legs. If she was lucky, very lucky, she was too exhausted to dream about what had happened. God knows that would come later.

Hours later, the inn was quiet.

The gas heater churned out heat that fogged the edges of the glass as he watched the street below. There was an occasional car that passed by, then disappeared onto the roadway. Tourists.

A sound reached through the shadows in the room, faint at first as she moved, restless on the bed. The edge of the drape eased back into place as he crossed the room.

She'd lost the comforter and curled into herself with the cold and the nightmare dream. It finally let go. He pulled the comforter back up over her shoulders.

He should have stepped away, left her alone. But he knew all about alone, the cold, dark places, that hollow ache deep inside, and the fear that you might never feel anything else again. He felt it in the slender hand that reached out through the shadows in the room and wrapped around his.

"Don't go," she whispered.

She pulled him down next to her, her head on his shoulder as he slipped an arm around her.

"Marcus...?"

He knew the question. She already knew the answer.

"Go back to sleep," he whispered, smoothing back the hair on her cheek.

It would be morning in a few hours, and there was a conversation they needed to have about continuing on with this. She had to accept now that it was too dangerous, too many people had been killed.

But not now.

He felt the movement on his shoulder, eyes that looked back at him through the shadows.

"You need to get some sleep."

"When I close my eyes..."

"I know."

He did know, she realized. The places he'd been, things he'd seen. Anne had spoken about it, and Cate.

"Hold me."

Simple contact, the need to feel anything but the pain, to be able to block out everything else, for just a little while, a few hours. It was there in her voice, and anything but simple, in the heat of her body beside him, in the way her breath caught at her throat as the words whispered between them.

He should leave. She would be all right, she was strong, at the same time, she moved closer.

"James..." She needed more...she needed him.

Didn't she know what this was all about? he thought. Didn't he?

Anger, the raw pain that filled her voice, her fingers as she touched him.

It didn't matter.

His hand went back through her hair, thick strands running though his fingers, and another sound, a different sound as her mouth found his. The tears were there, and something else that had been there from the beginning—anger, sadness, and strength. He tasted all of it, and swore again as her hand stroked low at his belly then moved beneath the waist of his jeans.

He touched her, edging the lace down at her shoulder, her breast filling his hand, then tasted her again as her back arched and she pulled him closer. He watched her eyes, that dark place that he knew too well, then the way her breathing changed. Her teeth grazed his shoulder, then a different sound as her hands moved low at his back and she pulled him inside her.

———

Four a.m.

A record for someone who rarely slept.

She moved without waking in the bed beside him. He pulled the comforter over her and tucked it in.

Bloody fucking hell!

That was the only word for it, and with more than a little sarcasm, he realized that is exactly what they'd done. More than once. Something close to insane, as if they could both drive away painful memories with the physical need to feel something, anything, except the pain.

He pulled on his jeans then reached for his jacket and took out the pack of cigarettes. He tapped one out of the pack and lit it, going to the window.

Bad for his health. Another irony everything considered.

"Do you ever think about ending it?" the psychiatrist had asked during one of those counseling sessions to determine if he was mentally fit to return to duty.

Only every single bloody fucking day, he thought at the time; sometimes several times a day.

It was Cate who had brought him back from the edge. No psychobabble, no suggestions from someone who'd never been in-country, who had no idea what it was like to lose men in combat, to see their bodies blown apart, only pieces left. It was all just notes in an I-pad, fingers tapping away, a report filed somewhere later, and not a clue about any of it. It wasn't in any text book, or endless case studies. It was inside him, like a cancer.

"You have to find your safe place," Cate once told him from behind that scarred bar at the Tavern.

"Sometimes it's a place...sometimes," she said, in that way she had of hitting the mark, "it's a person."

Her safe place had been the Highlands where her father was born, out at the Tavern on the outskirts of Inverness, and those solitary hikes she made into the mountains.

"The trick is to find your way back," she had added then. "Something worth coming back for."

The books had been her reason to keep coming back, the stories she wanted to tell, needed to tell, people she'd met and known, friendships she'd made over the years—truth in a world that seldom wanted to hear the truth.

He glanced back at the bed. Kris had been part of that, as Cate's editor, then as a friend. Loyalties, a handful of people you could trust. The others were just faces, people who passed through your life, strangers.

He scrubbed his hand back through his hair. It came back again in the shadows of the room staring down at the street below, the inn quiet that time of the night. Something in the back of his head—an impression, a word, that instinct.

"We can give you something to help you sleep," the psychiatrist had told him.

Drugs. But not something that could take away the nightmares. He glanced over at the bed, listening to the sound of her breathing.

"After a while it's not the first thing you remember, or the second," Cate once told him, understanding far better than most people, including the psychiatrists and therapists.

"Then you realize that other things matter more."

CHAPTER
THIRTY

She was alone.

That was the first thing she was aware of. Then the next, as she remembered other things.

She tried to block everything out, an arm flung across her forehead. But it was there, pushing out of the box, images, memories from the day before, and a sound in the room—the sob that climbed out of her throat. The tears followed.

Hard truths.

She'd never been one to run away from them. There were times there was no running away, because when you were alone, they were still there impossible to escape, waiting for you in something that someone said, in something you saw, in the middle of the night.

She had hoped that Marcus might be able to provide some insight into all of it. He was an expert on European history, he'd made a career of it after stepping away from his stint as a field reporter. And Cate had spoken to him several times over the past month leading up to the accident. She might have shared something with him that she'd discovered—something that might make sense out of all of this. As it was, they'd never know what she might have told him.

The hard truth now was that they were at a dead end. She didn't know where any of this led or what the next step was. Maybe James was right, they should just go to the French authorities and tell them everything.

Her throat tightened. She felt that same helplessness that she'd felt when her brother died, the same anger that she should have been able to do something; at the same time, deep down inside, there was nothing she could have done. Mark had made his own choices and decisions. The problem was, she had to find a way to live with those choices and decisions.

She pushed back the comforter and headed for the bathroom.

The water beat down, easing sore muscles from the day before, filling the small bathroom with steam, and probably violating some environmental laws about how much water she used.

Screw it. She'd take her chances with the water authorities, if there was such a thing in the French countryside. When she stepped out of the shower a half-hour later, she felt almost human again. Almost.

The room was quiet as she wrapped a towel around herself and stepped out of the bathroom.

Choices.

So much for the 'morning after,' that conversation, and the part where one of them felt the need to say 'This was a mistake.'

She took a deep breath and pushed it into the box.

"My wife is French, you know," the innkeeper explained, in that clipped English accent.

"Her family has been here for generations," he said with a smile, when he showed her the closet that opened up under the stairs that contained a small workstation complete with computer and printer, for the tech-connected traveler that couldn't stand to be disconnected from the digital world.

"She's quite good, you know. She put together the website for the inn, and she orders almost everything online, from local merchants, of course," he added with a smile.

The tour group had left earlier, on their way to one of those well-known local battlefields, and James still hadn't returned. She needed that now, needed the space.

"American?" he asked as she glanced past him to the wide-screen on the wall of the main room, and the mid-morning broadcast from Paris. Video of the explosion the day before played across the screen.

"Yes," she replied, pulling her attention away as the broadcast continued with other news of the day.

"New York."

"Ah, we've had several groups through this season from the U.S. with the anniversary of the war and all, although business has slowed somewhat with the winter season, the weather you know," he commented as he provided the login for the computer at the workstation.

"And your husband?"

She hesitated, then let him assume what was easiest.

"He's from the U.K.," she replied, side-stepping a direct answer.

"Ah, yes. I thought I heard a bit of accent there. Scots, is it?"

He had a good ear. As she had discovered, most of the time the accent disappeared, and James Morgan could have been from anywhere in the English-speaking part of the world. She only picked it up a few times when they were in Scotland, the way most people had of slipping back into the local accent when they were home for a while.

"I'll leave you to it, then, pastry and coffee at the courtesy bar," he was saying.

"Just ask if you have any questions. We're familiar with all the local sites from the war, and with low season it's a good time to get out and about to see things. Not quite so crowded."

Coffee and pastry could wait.

"I was hoping to find information about the French underground during the war, and those who belonged to the Resistance."

"Ah." He lit up with new interest. "My dear wife might be able to help you there. Her uncle was quite active in the Resistance during the war. He was the only man in the family. Poor chap never returned. Sophie has done a great deal of research on that part of the war—letters, journals, that sort of thing, quite a collection and people send her things all the time. She's quite an authority on the resistance, with her uncle one of them and all. She's at the museum, across the way, this morning."

"Across the way?"

"Just there," he indicated the building across the street through the paned window at the great room. It was one of those picturesque, white-washed Norman-style buildings, with heavy timbers that had probably stood there for the past three hundred years, give or take a few decades, and were found throughout the French countryside.

"She opens up for the museum people when she's finished here for the morning. Quite a collection they've acquired over the years. It's a passion for her. You might drop by. Most interesting..." He looked around.

"Very well then. I'll keep the coffee hot," he said to the empty room.

The street was quiet except for an occasional car, a Café owner next door rolling out the awning over tables in the patio, the smell of coffee thick in the air, damp from rain the night before.

A flat, polished piece of granite at the entrance was etched in both French and English—'*Dedicated to those who bought freedom with their blood.*'

Inside, the museum smelled of old wood, the sort of mustiness found in hundreds of old stone houses, churches, and public buildings throughout Britain and France, with dark wood floors and glass cases that contained an amazing amount of artifacts—photographs, a canteen, several firearms, a bloodstained scarf, a silver chain and cross, letters, fabric insignias, all carefully documented, a few with the simple, sobering words—*Found in the forest in an unmarked grave.*

The museum was cool and dimly lit, with lamps set at intervals at a long, low table, much like a library. Photographs of those who had belonged to the Resistance, lined a wall—some portrait-style from before the war, family photographs, but most were random black-and-white shots, an expression caught unexpectedly by the camera.

One had been enlarged, life-size, and mounted onto a wall. She recognized it immediately. It was an enlargement of a photograph taken by Paul Bennett!

As with all of his war-time photographs, it was a black-and-white photo. But there was something haunting about it, shades of gray in the shadows on the man's face.

He had no name, at least not one that was provided in the brief narrative that went along with the mural. It wasn't necessary. That image watched her, even as she walked past, the man's gaze fastened on her, a nameless man willing to risk everything to protect his family, neighbors, strangers against overwhelming odds.

What was it that made a person willing to risk everything? That made people like James Morgan, her brother, Cate, willing to risk their lives, for something greater than themselves? Something they believed in? The story?

Time had a texture that could be felt. She had discovered that years before when she first traveled to Europe, that summer break from college. Old pebbled glass, the cool patina of old wood, stones worn smooth from generations of footsteps, the scent of wood and stone that someone else had breathed two hundred years ago, that she could almost imagine a voice whispering, "I'm still here. Don't forget me."

There were newspapers in wood-framed cases in English, French, and German, that told stories of bombings and lists of the dead from a nearby city, carefully preserved, along with other photographs, letters, and personal diaries from ordinary French citizens — men, women, boys, school girls, farmers, clerks, teachers, and a priest. Several had been enlarged and covered the walls, so that other generations later might remember. The words pulled at something deep inside her:

"1942, October 7: Remy was caught by the Gestapo yesterday. We attempted to learn where he was taken; only fourteen years old, a child, and many are never heard from again. There is no word yet..."

"1943, April 11: We have heard that life is much the same as always in Paris. So it is in a city with Cafés and the theatre. The Germans do not want to destroy what they enjoy. So easy to look the other way and pretend nothing has changed. But here, the people do not have enough to eat, and always there is the fear of the knock on the door in the middle of the night, and the execution squads..."

"1943, October 19: N. (initial only) was nearly run over by a German convoy as she returned from the village yesterday on her bicycle. She must be more careful. She is fourteen years old and there are stories about what they do to young women. But she will not listen. She insists what she does is important. My greatest fear is that the Germans will discover the messages she carries."

Of thousands who had joined the Resistance, their names printed on lists displayed on another wall, many were killed or imprisoned.

Others were simply never heard from after the war, including Sophie Martin's uncle. After the war, families had provided pictures with names, stories, mementoes, to make certain they weren't forgotten. Their faces looked down at her from the walls of the museum.

This had been Vilette Moreau's world, a dangerous world of young partisans like Nico Simonescu, and a young woman named Micheleine, from a photograph Paul Bennett had taken.

"Their faces tell a story, no?"

Sophie Martin was tall and slender, dressed in a long black skirt with a brilliant, multi-colored sweater in shades of red, green, and blue against a black background. Her silver hair was closely cropped, molding her head, and framing warm brown eyes and pretty features.

She smiled softly. "You can almost hear their voices, the pain, the loss, the determination, yes?"

Like the woman who stood beside her? That defiance reaching down through the decades into another generation, with determination that those names and faces would not be forgotten.

"They come here for many reasons, the tourists," Sophie Martin continued. "The younger ones have no understanding of what this was all about, except what they have read." She made a sweeping gesture of the museum.

"But there are a few, descendants of one of those," she gestured to the wall. "Historians, someone writing a book. There are others who would like to forget. This is our way of keeping their memory alive, perhaps more important in the times we live in when things are too easily cast aside and forgotten, but the world is still a very dangerous place."

A very dangerous place.

Kris nodded. It reminded her of something Cate wrote in the front of one of her books, a quote borrowed from Winston Churchill— "Those who do not understand history are doomed to repeat it."

There were some—Cate—who would argue that they were repeating the past now—in political battles around the globe, the financial collapse of third world countries, wars in the Middle East, terrorists in the streets of New York, London, Paris.

"Are you perhaps writing a book?" Sophie Martin asked. "There are many stories here."

The next book. Was that what Cate was chasing when she sent that photograph?

Kris had never met Paul Bennett. He died several years before Cate's first book was published. But she felt as if she knew him through the stories Cate had shared, and his photographs.

She had read somewhere that looking through the lens of a camera was like looking into someone's soul. Paul Bennett had that gift, the ability to wait for that moment and then capture it in some of the most iconic photographs of the twentieth century, including a photograph of a seven-hundred-year-old tapestry.

She had hoped Marcus might be able to fill in the blank spaces, answer some of the questions. They had spoken about it before she went to meet with him. She rubbed her wrist and the raw bruise there, another reminder of the world they lived in.

"I'm looking for information about a young woman who was with the Resistance during the war."

She took out that photograph that Paul Bennett had taken at the abbey in those days, just after the Normandy invasion, that included a small group of Resistance fighters and a beautiful young woman with a defiant expression. She showed it to Sophie Martin.

"Ah," she said softly. "The one they called Jehanne."

CHAPTER
THIRTY-ONE
AUGUST, 1944, AMIENS, FRANCE

The press vehicle, a military truck that had been requisitioned for their use, lurched, bottomed out in the rutted road, then lumbered forward at the head of a long line of military transports that wound through the French countryside.

They'd been on the move for days, passing villages, small towns, the burned-out hulks of vehicles, transports, and tanks, following the enemy.

Each morning there were the briefing meetings with the members of the press, overseen by an officer who was the official liaison between the military and the journalists and photographers traveling with the combined Allied forces.

Refugees displaced when their homes were ravaged, old men, women, children carried belongings they could take with them or packed on the back of a horse or mule, young boys, too young to fight with the Free French, armed with pitchforks and knives, a priest whose church had burned—they all became the story of the war.

Bob Dunnett scribbled in his notebook, and Paul took photographs.

They told the story that others would see in the London newspapers, the toll of humanity caught in the midst of a brutal war, the resilience of the human spirit, the defiance of those who refused defeat.

By night, he held a flashlight between his teeth, hastily scribbling off a letter to his mother and sister, another one to his editor at the newspaper with descriptions to go along with the rolls of film that he was sending back, and a letter to Micheleine, with no place to send it, no idea where she was, or if...

"I think of that small room often, a place apart from all of this, and wonder where you are. I am taking my photographs, the ones that I'm required to take for the newspaper, then there are the others that I take for myself, of this place, the people, your country, with no idea if anyone will ever see them.

"You said, the pictures will tell the story. I remember the look on your face, the expression in your eyes. It is your story. I can only hope that I have told it the way you would want.

"I met an old man who told me a story of a young woman, who left her family and joined the Resistance. He did not know her real name. She is called Jehanne, the people's Joan of Arc, their hero, their hope...you are their hope.

"I have no idea where you might be. I can only hope that I will see you again."

Other men wrote letters to wives, sweethearts, families, then posted them with the next dispatch. They had been told that all correspondence was put on a flight back to London—if the flight made it out and wasn't lost somewhere over the channel. There were almost daily reports of those that didn't make it back.

He turned out the flashlight and tucked the letter to Micheleine into his pocket. A letter with no place to send it.

Amiens had been heavily bombed during the winter by the RAF and bore the scars in burned-out buildings, whole sections of the city leveled next to others that had survived almost unscathed, in one of those ironies of war.

It was rumored that the prison, held by the Germans, with hundreds of prisoners who belonged to the Resistance, had been the target. Many prisoners had died during the bombings. Many of those who had escaped were rumored to have been recaptured and executed.

The bombing mission months earlier had been considered a success, but it was difficult to understand how successful with so many dead. What was left of the German occupation forces had retreated in the weeks since the Allied landing, while the people of Amiens attempted to reclaim their lives.

Against the leavings of war, women hung out laundry to dry from second story windows. A nun escorted a group of school children past the tumbled ruins of houses. With fuel shortages, horse-drawn carts delivered a load of reclaimed bricks to a hotel that was being rebuilt.

Street after street, block after block, Amiens rose from the ashes. And he took his photographs while Robert Dunnett sat back at the command post that had been set up, typing away on his typewriter, pushing the deadline for the post back to London. In a matter of days, possibly tomorrow, they would be pushing north toward Belgium, joining up with the Americans.

Among the buildings that had escaped relatively unscathed was the thirteenth century Cathedral of Notre Dame. The peaceful silence inside the cathedral was deceptive, the war just outside those massive doors. But here, he could almost believe none of it existed—the bombings, the suffering, the blood, and death.

He took a photo of the transept piled high with sandbags, the center aisle left with chairs for worshippers. At the high altar, the statue of the weeping angel stared down at his camera, the image caught just as the light fell across the angel's face.

Tears. For the suffering, for the dead, for man's inhumanity to man.

He'd attended mass regularly as a child. His mother had insisted on it. But after arriving in London, working long hours, then the war...he didn't remember the last time he attended services.

A sound had him turning around, that reflexive instinct since the landing at Normandy, the way things changed you.

"I did not mean to startle you." The priest stepped out of the shadows. "We get so few visitors. Those who come, now that they can, come in the morning before starting their day."

Now that they could—with the Germans gone.

"I'm with the Allied army that arrived last night."

"Yes," the priest nodded. "We received word several days ago, praise God." He glanced at the Leica camera.

"I meant no disrespect, Father."

The priest shook his head. "Among all the horrible things you must have seen, I think that neither God nor I will object to your photographs in His house, a house of peace. You are a believer?" he asked.

Paul smiled. "I was raised on it. My mother insisted."

"Ah, yes, mothers are like that. And school perhaps?"

He nodded. "Several years of it."

"But not recently?"

"I was in London."

"Yes, the bombings." The priest gazed skyward toward that magnificent, vaulted ceiling.

"But the people still managed, even in the underground rail stations," Paul replied.

The priest smiled. "The church is God's house," he commented, making a sweeping gesture of the cavernous nave with its stained-glass windows.

"But in truth, God will find us, wherever we are, even in an underground rail station."

Paul smiled. His mother had said something very similar.

"So," the priest said, "this is your journey."

A journey?

He'd never thought of it that way before. But he supposed that it was a journey. The photographs were his journey, of places like Amiens and the people, like the good father.

"I pray you will have a safe journey. If you would like to confess your sins before leaving..."

Confession. He'd never thought himself as a sinful person, but all men sin, someone once wrote, and when he thought of the past weeks, the bodies in the surf, more bodies—the enemy, in the bunkers, at St. Malo, and a half dozen other places...

He'd never believed in the confessional—confess your sins and God will forgive you. Just say it and all is forgiven?

The last weeks had taught him that it wasn't that simple. There were things that were never forgotten that you carried with you, images like the photographs he took.

"Some other time."

"I understand. Our doors are always open. But tell me, how will you return to your unit? It is late and the Allied camp is at the other end of the city."

He'd caught a ride earlier on one of the command vehicles, with the thought of walking back. The past weeks there had been a lot of walking, everywhere in London before that, and frequent hikes in the Highlands.

"I'll be all right, Father."

"Come," the priest said, heading for a side door off the nave. It opened onto a small courtyard. In the corner was a bicycle leaning against the wall.

"Take it."

"I can't do that," Paul told him.

In a city that had been occupied, then bombed, transportation was highly valued, especially with the lack of motor fuel. In the towns they'd passed through, most people walked, rode bicycles, or rode in horse carts. Trains sat abandoned in rail stations for lack of coal or oil. They had provided as much fuel as they could spare for ambulances for the hospitals.

"Of course you can," the priest insisted. "God provided it when it was much needed. Now as you see, it sits in the corner. Perhaps you will be able to take more photographs of our city before you lose the light. Yes?"

"Thank you, Father."

He took several more pictures with the priest's blessing, a place of God in the middle of war, a place of God that survived in spite of war. His mother, deeply devout, would have simply smiled and said, "Of course, dear."

It was almost dark as he cut across the town square, through the Allied check point, then walked through the camp to the tent for the press corps. He leaned the bicycle against the front of a vehicle.

Dunnett looked up from his typewriter. His glasses were pushed back on his forehead, his thinning hair twisted in that way that meant he'd been hard at it. He tapped in a final sentence, then grabbed the paper from the typewriter and added it to the stack on the table.

"I've got to get this over to dispatch. They have one last pouch going out tonight. Where are my glasses?"

Paul gestured to his own head. Usually they were beneath

Dunnett's helmet. He'd already misplaced one pair that had never turned up.

"Right you are. By the way, there's a lad been asking for you. He came in with a group earlier. They're over at the command unit."

A lad? Nico?

He headed for the command post, a sprawling tent that had been set up for the joint Allied command, and he couldn't help wondering if they'd yet figured out who was supposed to be in charge.

His head came up at the sound of his name, and he grinned. There was no mistaking that lanky frame that looked as if he'd added at least two inches, that shock of dark hair that spilled across his forehead, or those dark eyes that had seen too much. Fourteen going on forty. But the flash of that grin was all boy.

A handshake would probably have been more appropriate, but Paul wrapped his arms around that bony frame, and hugged him like he would any of the mates back home.

"When did you arrive?"

"Just a couple of hours ago," Nico replied. He brushed back the hair on his forehead. "We've been on the move the last four days, trailing a company of Germans." His expression tightened.

"We ran into one of your patrols and thought your people should have the information."

Paul nodded. "When was the last time you had a hot meal."

A shrug of that thin shoulder. He shook his head. "A week, maybe longer. It's not a good idea to build a fire when you're in enemy territory."

"Aye, well come along. I'm with the press corps. They eat a bit better than the others." He glanced past Nico, but no one was with him.

"She's not here," he said. "I haven't seen her since Bouville."

The food was mostly tasteless, but hot as promised. The coffee was better.

"Is she well?" It seemed a foolish question, all things considered, when what he wanted to ask was if she had mentioned him, passed any messages along in case they met up.

Nico nodded. "The last I saw her. Then she left with another group."

"Do you know where?" A question he had no idea if Nico would answer.

He'd learned more about her in the weeks since they were together, a shrugged shoulder when he asked a question of one of the French Resistance when their unit crossed paths, no answer at all when he mentioned the name he'd learned, Jehanne.

Or a grudging nod, "That one is fearless. The Germans have a price on her head."

"Paris, maybe?" Nico answered in that way that might mean something, or nothing at all.

Paris. Dangerous, still held by the Germans. They weren't about to give it up without a fight.

According to Dunnett, they were headed north as well—Belgium, and it was going to be bad. Dunnett couldn't wait.

He flicked a cigarette into the fire beyond the table. Would he ever see her again? Did she want to?

Nico scraped his plate clean, then stood. "Merci." He thanked him for the meal, then reached inside his jacket.

"She said I was to give you this, if I saw you again." Nico handed him an envelope.

"She said to tell you that she didn't burn it."

Paul tore open the envelope that contained a folded note, and a photograph.

Dear Paul,

We are moving again, there is still much to do. I think of that night and your funny smile when I said that I knew what was beneath the kilt.

I pray you are safe—you and your camera. Do not think too harshly of my camera skills. I borrowed it from a friend.

You must continue to take your photographs, so the world will know.

It was signed with just her initial, "M."

He took out the photograph. It was a black-and-white shot, poor lighting, the hand less than steady as if quickly taken, but it was enough that he recognized the tapestry and remembered what she had said at the abbey.

"I would burn it before I would let the Germans have it!"

There had been reports of raids across the whole of France after the Allied landing, including the rumor of a raid at the abbey and other places they passed through, valuable artwork and priceless artifacts stolen in a last, defiant, humiliating act by the German army.

The tapestry had meant a great deal to her, an important symbol of so much that had been lost, and her refusal to see it confiscated to decorate some high-ranking German official's bungalow or tent. Her people's history, she had called it, with that fierce passion.

The tapestry was safe. Somewhere.

CHAPTER
THIRTY-TWO

Where the hell was Innis?

James marked the time on his watch: ten seconds, fifteen, twenty.

Pick up the fuckin' call!

He scanned the electronics store as customers came and went—an older couple, the young man who had arrived just after he walked in, with tattoos that would have impressed Innis, and a couple of girls, teenagers checking out the latest in cell phones.

The signal at the inn had been weak at best. The signal was stronger inside the store, through the rooftop dish he'd spotted earlier and no doubt a signal booster somewhere in the back of the store.

It was almost noon. Gamers that were in for the full tournament in Paris would still be at it. Those who dropped by to watch had gone home hours ago, or zoned out on their substance of choice.

Thirty seconds—the minimum amount of time needed to track a call, if someone was scanning for a hit, and if they were capable of it.

After everything that had happened, after Cate's phone log had been hacked, he wasn't into taking chances.

The voice that eventually came on was hoarse—too much to drink, or too much recreational substance—but recognizable.

"I need information." James stepped to the back of the store where no one would overhear the conversation.

"Do you fucking know what time it is?" Innis croaked irritably on the other end of the call.

Did he? James wondered.

"Most people call it the 'next day,'" he replied, no patience for attitude or conversations about the time. "I need information."

He ignored the crude response on the other end of the call.

"I need to know about Marcus Aronson," he replied. "Everything you can find on him—interviews, his early career as a field correspondent, then at the university, known associates, wives, lovers, children. Everything," he said again.

Forty seconds. He was running out of time, out of that safety zone.

"He's probably among the dead." Innis replied the obvious. "They're still sifting through the rubble. It was all over the news."

But why was he dead?

In the wrong place at the wrong time? A coincidence? He didn't believe in coincidences.

"And I need you to work your magic on that image from the security film. It's important. I need a face and an identity to go with it."

"Anything else?" Innis sarcastically replied.

"I'll let you know."

Fifty seconds. The muscles at the back of his neck tightened.

"Call me as soon as you have something." He ended the call, cutting Innis off mid-complaint. He tapped in another number and left a message.

"Aye, Danny, I need your help. That friend of yours. It's important." He gave the name of the person at the gallery that the Captain had given him.

"It's important."

He didn't leave a name but ended with something Danny would recognize.

"Running on empty, my friend."

Both calls had been brief, short enough that they might not have been picked up.

Call it paranoia, call it that extra sense that woke him in the middle of the night, that had saved his ass more than once. He liked to think of it as insurance.

Watch, listen, be aware of your surroundings. He scanned the shop—Mr. Tattoo in a long conversation with the clerk, no doubt something philosophical considering the words inked down one arm under an elaborate skull—'brotherhood, love, peace;' the older couple, staring at Mr. Tattoo and whispering back and forth; the careful glances between the two girls, then the quick grab of the display phone that would have made a street thief envious, and in a few years they would be mothers of the future generation, or supporting a habit with whatever could be stolen and sold on the street.

He pocketed the throw-away phone and headed for the exit, passing the girls on his way out.

"Put it back," he told them. "They've got you on camera." He angled a glance toward the camera scanning the store. The risk of hanging out in such places, but he had to take it.

There was that deer-in-the-headlights look from both of them, then a quick exchange of conversation. The phone was placed back on the counter.

Out on the street, he marked the time again. Danny was a creature of habit and a connoisseur of all things female. He checked his voice-mail regularly to connect with the latest 'love of his life.'

If he was still in the country, it was only a matter of hours before he checked his voicemail and got his message.

———

The museum archives were a labor of love and determination, that those who had been part of the French Underground were never forgotten.

There were hundreds of documents that had been scanned, hundreds of personal stories in letters, journals, notes scribbled at the edge of an old newspaper, a message passed from someone to someone else with dates, times, and numbers that Sophie Martin explained were troop numbers, strengths, numbers of vehicles, all in coded messages.

Some of the records contained an index that then sent her to a particular page within the document. But for most there was no such thing as 'word search.'

Kris eventually found an entry under the name of a young boy who had fled Czechoslovakia after his family was murdered. He had joined the resistance in France. He looked back at her from a black-

and-white photograph taken over seventy years before by Paul Bennett.

Nico Simonescu.

There were three entries about Nico, from those who had either met him, or worked with him. He was nicknamed the Sewer Rat, from stories of how he had escaped from Prague by crawling through the sewers until he reached the edge of the city and met up with a group of gypsies fleeing the Nazis. He was small for his age, possibly from poor diet in the months after his country was invaded, but his eyes told a different story, of anger and fierce determination.

She'd read other accounts of survival, often unable to comprehend how people lived through such horrible times. Nico survived, and had made his way to France where he joined the Resistance, no longer a child from what he'd experienced.

From the journal of a Resistance fighter, translated into English:

"The boy slipped into the town, past the roadblock, and was able to bring out four of our brothers who most certainly would have been caught and executed. He is called the Sewer Rat, and for good reason."

Then another entry, scanned from a letter Sophie had been sent to be included in the archive, written by a young woman in the photograph of the tapestry taken over seventy years earlier:

"He is young, but not when you look into his eyes. He reminds me of my brothers, who I pray are safe. But I have seen that same look in his eyes— reckless, unafraid, so young." It was signed simply with the letter 'J.'

And then an entry from a faded letter dated December 9, 1944:

"We cannot know if we will succeed. It is ridiculous, preposterous, and yet we must try. Too much has been lost, stolen by the Germans. It must not fall into their hands. I would burn it before I would let them have it. Tomorrow we go to the hospital. If I do not return, I know it will be safe. J."

Then what appeared to be a prayer. *"God will protect from the godless."* It was signed with just the initial 'J.'

"Jehanne," Sophie Martin explained. "It was the name the people gave her. She was much like the Maid of Orleans."

"Joan of Arc?"

Sophie nodded. "She was their heroine in a very dark time, the things she did, the lives she saved. She was someone for them to believe in, she gave them hope. Her real name was Micheleine Robillard."

Kris stared at the scanned copy of the wrinkled letter.

"What are these?" she asked, pointing to a series of images that had been drawn in the margin of the note.

Sophie shrugged. "Perhaps something that reminded her of home. It is hard to know."

"And this?" She pointed out the mark, a cross with two bars hastily drawn in pencil, made at the bottom of the last page beneath the initial the young woman had signed.

"It is the Cross of Lorraine. It was carried by Saint Joan. It is said that she believed that as long as the cross never touched the ground she would be protected by God. It became the sign of the Resistance."

Another religious myth? The things people believed in that crossed cultures and centuries.

"You do not believe in such things?" Sophie asked.

Kris had believed, once. She had studied religion, then she had walked away from it.

"It didn't protect her," she pointed out.

"It protected the people, the promise of God in a young woman, and centuries later, a small, poorly armed Resistance that also carried the cross and helped turn back evil."

Messages, ancient symbols, a young woman the people of war-torn France had called Jehanne. It was all very entertaining, but it didn't explain what Cate was after, or the reason she was dead.

James found her in at the back of the of the museum sitting in front of a computer screen.

Reckless! Stubborn!

She shouldn't have left the inn. Didn't anything that had happened mean anything to her? The attack in London, at the abbey, the day before?

"Kris..."

"I found the woman in the photograph that Cate sent."

CHAPTER
THIRTY-THREE

"Her name was Micheleine Robillard. She was fifteen when the Germans invaded France. She lost her father and two brothers during the war. She joined the Resistance, carrying messages across enemy lines, once inside a fake cast on her arm. She guided people out of France who were on watch lists, sabotaged communications, and was rumored to have killed a high-ranking German officer."

"Go on," he told her. They needed to talk, but it was clear certain things were off limits. For now.

"They put a price on her head," Kris continued. "That didn't stop her."

Like someone he knew.

"She went behind enemy lines, disguising herself, and managed to smuggle weapons into a hotel where several Resistance fighters who were to be executed the following morning were being held."

She'd tried to imagine the courage it had taken. But there were always stories of people who did incredible things in horrible times.

"She was caught by the Germans in the last months of the war, sometime after that picture was taken, as they retreated towards Belgium.

The Battle of the Bulge. He had studied it—that last bloody battle where the Germans had almost turned the Allies back. Almost. But fate, divine intervention, sheer blind luck, whatever you wanted to call it, they had succeeded. Strategists, military scholars, and historians still analyzed the series of battles that eventually led to the liberation of France and the end of the war.

He could guess how it had ended for a young French girl who joined the Resistance. An army making a last stand didn't have time or manpower to guard prisoners. Every soldier was needed for that last offensive, prisoners were expendable.

Kris's voice softened. "She was tortured and then shot, her body burned in the forest as the Germans retreated. According to another resistance fighter who escaped and survived the war, she never gave them the information they wanted. A letter was found after the war in a cellar where she and others hid from the Germans. It was probably the last letter she wrote to her mother."

She skipped over the personal part of the letter, and read the last part.

"Too much has been lost. It must not fall into enemy hands. Tomorrow we will go the hospital."

"You think she was referring to the tapestry?"

She heard the doubt in his voice, the skepticism that a young girl referred to a lost artifact that had been hidden from the Germans to keep it safe.

"She knew where the tapestry was at the time of the Allied invasion—the photograph Paul Bennett took at the abbey proves that," Kris pointed out. "After everything that had happened during the war, it makes sense she didn't want it to fall into the hands of the Germans."

According to everything they'd learned about it, the tapestry was considered an important piece of art, even if it wasn't as well known as the Bayeaux tapestry. And it was no secret that the Germans had looted thousands of pieces of art and other valuables during the war —paintings, sculptures, gold, jewelry.

"And she left this letter, hoping someone would find it."

"What hospital?" James replied. "Where?"

She folded the papers and put them in her bag. She didn't know, but she had found something else—where Micheleine lived before the war.

The next step. She'd just found it.

"Her family had a farm near Arras before the war," she explained as they left the museum. "It's possible someone still lives there."

He knew where she was going with this. He pulled the phone out of his jacket pocket.

"You need to see this."

The text message from Innis had come in just after he got back, with a link to a site that contained those images he'd asked him to have a go at. He enlarged the photo when it came up. Even with the limitations of the size of the screen on the phone, the details were sharp, picking up the background in the warehouse at the back of the Paris gallery, enhanced so that there were no shadows, no blurry details in the image of the young woman that emerged.

Even with her hair tucked under the cap, the bill pulled low, it was the same—a brief glimpse at the airport in Edinburgh, a certain way of moving that came up in the next shot, the profile shot. That shadowy figure had a name.

Alyia Malik. The artist they'd met briefly at the London gallery, and Jonathan Callish's wife.

Kris stared at the images, one after the other, her brain slowly catching up with what she was seeing.

How? Why?

"Think!" James told her. "It's what you're good at."

He laid it all out, every encounter, each incident, information Innis had hacked along with what they'd learned from Diana Jodion about the tapestry and their meeting with Vilette Moreau.

"Cate took those photographs to Callish. He knew about the tapestry."

Kris knew it was a short step, that Alyia Malik had also known about it.

"Right after we met with him, you go to meet with Brynn Halliday."

And it was just another small step that his wife had known about it.

"The van from the attack was at the Paris warehouse." He wasn't going to let her off this time.

"And we know someone hacked into Cate's phone account, following all her calls, everyone she was in contact with."

They'd also been following her phone list, along with the text message and the scanned photograph Cate had sent her.

And someone had been following them, from the beginning.

"Someone was looking for something at the Tavern," he went on. "My guess? The photograph of the tapestry. And they're trying to stop you. They've already proved they're willing to do whatever it takes."

He caught up with her out on the street.

He was trying to scare her. She was way past scared. She was terrified. What was Cate after? What was the story?

A lost artifact?

Diana Jodion said it was uncertain that the tapestry was worth anything, depending on its condition, even if it was found. There were tapestries in museums all over Europe, nice to look at, but the value was in the historical importance, what it told about the Medieval period, the hand work that had created it.

The Bayeaux tapestry was important as an archive of events in a time period when there were few written historical archives. But another tapestry from the Medieval period even if it could be found?

Was there a secret in the tapestry? Something woven into the fabric?

Vilette had been certain of it. But was that nothing more than the colorful imagination of a woman who had led a very colorful life? Looking for the spotlight one last time with a story that no one could prove?

Then why were four people now dead?

"You've done more than anyone could," James reasoned with her. "With everything that's happened, now the explosion in Paris, we need to turn everything over to the French authorities."

The next step.

Earlier that morning she would have agreed with him. She didn't know what the next step was. That was then. Now she knew who the young woman was in that photograph, possibly the last person who had seen the tapestry before it disappeared. And that letter, hidden in a niche in that cellar, that found its way into a museum decades later. She might have walked away from all of it, if not for that letter.

"Kris."

She heard it in the change in his voice, and the hand that closed around her arm.

"Last night..."

No, Kris thought. She couldn't do this. Not now.

"You're right," she told him. "About everything."

It was too easy, he thought. After everything that had happened, after every excuse, every argument, and that cool logic that she'd thrown at him.

Too easy.

He followed her to the upstairs room they'd shared the night before, and that bed.

She ignored it, and him.

The sweater was dry where she had hung it earlier over a chair in front of the furnace. She folded it and put it in her shoulder bag, along with food he'd brought back the night before. The curse followed her down the stairs to the lobby.

Monsieur Martin frowned, then handed her one of the brochures for the car rental agency that he kept for guests. She thanked him, then paid the bill for the room.

"Goddamn!"

She heard it as she left the inn.

"Wait!"

She didn't—she knew what the conversation would be.

It had started to rain as she crossed the street and followed the directions Monsieur Martin gave her. She ducked under the canopy of a restaurant awning, then started across the next street. Her head came up as a car swept around the corner and braked to a stop, blocking her.

James shoved open the passenger door. The anger was still there, in the expression on his face, in the way he refused to look at her, at his hand wrapped around the gear lever.

"Get into the fuckin' car!"

CHAPTER
THIRTY-FOUR
NOVEMBER 9, 1944, NORTHERN FRANCE,

Françoise went ahead, slipping into the darkness, the misty rain closing around him so that he might not have been there at all, like a ghost. They had all learned to be ghosts.

He was from this area and knew it well, every farmhouse, each stream, and low-lying area, even a series of caves where they'd hidden two days before. He'd made it his business to know it all and it had served them well, allowing them to remain hidden as the German forces moved around them, moving steadily toward the Ardennes forest.

But why? Why subject men and equipment to the worst of the coming winter? Winters in the north could be brutal.

Already there was snow on the ground, making movement slow and exhausting as they pushed their way over muddied roads and then no roads at all. It had snowed that morning and they had been grateful, the four of them, for it had covered their escape.

Three days earlier, they had followed enemy movements, alerted by their contact in the south. Something was happening, something the Allies were not aware of, and it was critical to get information.

They'd been playing cat-and-mouse with them for months, ever since the Allied landing, the German infantry scattered by the unexpected numbers of the Allied forces.

Cat and mouse. She liked the image it brought, but she had refused long ago to be the mouse.

A sound, almost impossible to hear, brought her head up. When you lived by the sound of a footfall, the shift of a weapon, or a sudden drawn breath, you heard everything. Even a familiar footfall, as Françoise reappeared, silently waving them on.

Once they had the information they were after, they had a name that meant safe haven—a widowed woman and her young son. Lucia was her name. Her farm was across the river. When they reached it, emerging one by one on a hand signal from tree cover at the river's edge, they stopped and surveyed the flow of the river in both directions. It was higher than anticipated.

Françoise waved them down along the embankment and they followed single file, ghosts grateful that it was a moonless night in spite of the snow that muffled their footsteps and filled in their tracks. They had walked no more than a couple hundred yards when Francois held up a hand in a signal to stop.

It was invisible to the naked eye, submerged just beneath the surface of the water, connecting one side of the river to the other, and she breathed a small prayer of thanks. No doubt the woman's son was responsible for the 'life line,' a rope that had been carefully hidden.

They crossed one by one, hand over hand, rifles carefully secured across their shoulders to keep them dry, the rope drawn taught to prevent them being pulled under and swept away. By the time the last man crossed behind her, they were all soaked to the skin and freezing, but they had made it across.

The farmhouse wasn't far, Françoise promised, as they all fell into line behind him, silently shaking, teeth clenched together to keep them from chattering, and always, always, an eye and an ear to the path behind them and the forest surrounding them.

There was blood on her hands, not the first time. But this had been different, not at a distance with a shot taken, but almost intimate and terrifying. Then the anger that came after.

She didn't want to think about that now. There was only one thing that mattered—getting the information to the Allies.

Her hands and feet were numb. It took every ounce of strength to continue, when Françoise slowed his pace, then cut off the path to the edge of the forest. The dark shape of a farmhouse was barely visible through the falling snow.

He went first, as they had long ago established—count to thirty, then the next one follows, until all were across that open space.

There was no light from the windows or door, nothing that indicated anyone even lived there, until they were all inside and the warmth of the fire in the stone hearth stung their faces and hands.

The boy, no more than nine or ten, greeted them, motioned for the door to be closed and the blanket dropped back into place that prevented any light escaping.

No names were asked, or given. It was necessary to protect the boy and his mother. They were each handed blankets, then followed the boy to a storeroom off the kitchen. A candle lit their way, flickering as the boy crossed the storeroom, then almost extinguished as he removed a plank of wood in the floor.

Françoise dropped down beside him, lifting one board after another, exposing an opening with a wooden stepladder that descended deep into the ground. One by one they went down the ladder into the darkness.

The subfloor chamber was damp, but warmer than outside the farmhouse. Along the walls were shelves, almost barren now, but had no doubt once held food put up for the winter, before the war. There were other signs of war, more blankets carefully folded and set aside on a bench by others who had no doubt made their way to the widow's farmhouse, with two cots in addition to the bench, a small cook stove, and a crystal radio set.

The walls were made of stone, angling back, until they disappeared into the shadows as the boy lit an oil lamp.

They were cold, exhausted, and one of the other men, Phillipe, who had been with Françoise, was badly injured as they made their escape.

She asked for bandages and something to disinfect the wound. The boy returned with cognac, a sheet torn into strips, and hot soup his mother had prepared. They all shared the cognac, then while the others ate soup with warm bread, she bandaged Phillipe's wounds. The one in his shoulder was the worst of it—a gunshot wound as he pulled her from the German captain's tent.

He was a small, wiry man, agile like one of those circus performers, capable of sneaking into small places which was probably the only reason she was alive.

"Merci," he whispered. "It is much better now. You have done this before."

She gave him a faint smile, along with more cognac against the pain.

There was no physical resemblance, but it was there in the kindness of his eyes—an encounter months before, and someone she would always remember.

"A few times," she replied, and finished tying off the bandage. "You will live," she told him, and prayed it was true, for all of them.

France was going to need people like Phillipe—small, but with a big heart—when all of this was over. Françoise was another matter—big, rough, cold, with a hatred of the Germans that was never explained but that she could only guess at. Didn't they all have their reasons?

And then there was the young man, a thief in a former life, according to the little they knew about him. More than once he had 'acquired' something badly needed, with a shrug of the shoulders and a too-handsome smile that she was certain could acquire just about anything from the girls.

She wasn't interested, not that he hadn't tried. It had ended with a knife at his throat, but it hadn't dimmed that smile. Afterward he accepted that whatever he intended with her would probably get him killed. In that strange way of things, afterward, they became friends who knew they could rely on one another.

They all came from different places—Françoise from the northern district near the border with Belgium, her wiry friend from Calvados before the war, Phillipe from a dozen different places.

They had been laborers, a postal clerk, a thief, simple people like herself who worked on the farm near the old quarries. But all of that changed with the war. They were all the same now.

They took turns drying their clothes over the small cook stove, the smell of damp wool thick in the cold of the cellar. Then while the others took turns sleeping, she sat in a corner, wrapped in two of the blankets, and thought about the information she had learned.

The Germans were planning a massive offensive against the Allies. They had been coordinating infantry, tanks, and air cover along the border with Belgium.

They called it the Ardennes Offensive, and according to the infor-

mation she had been able to obtain, the high command was determined to split the Allied forces, creating a wedge that would divide
them, then bring defeat.

But that information had come at a cost. Even now, she could still
feel the German officer's hands on her, smell him on her skin, the
blood. The cast she had worn on her arm, part of her disguise as a
young girl working at a local inn under German control had not
deterred him. He liked young girls.

She had always been slender. In school she was teased because of
her flat body, until she wasn't. The simple, straight dress, thick stock-
ings, and worn shoes, with no make-up and her hair pulled back with
a ribbon completed her disguise as she worked among the tables,
delivering food and wine to the German officers in spite of the cast on
her arm.

It was a word, then a phrase, spoken in German, in between crude
remarks in halting French that they prided themselves on. But among
those phrases spoken in their own language was enough to tell her
that something big was going to happen.

The officers were to stay the night, a warm bath and a bed. With a
word to the innkeeper, she arranged for him to offer to send cognac to
the Major. He would send the girl.

She knew what she was doing, it was no more dangerous than
dozens of things she'd done before. But she knew from the Major's
touch on her hand that he was looking forward to more than the
cognac.

The cognac was plentiful, she saw to it. The fire in the captain's
room built high, his intentions equally high. He was surprisingly
gentle, but that may have been the cognac. Afterward, she could not
say that it was what she expected, only that he had not used her
badly.

She would never know exactly what gave her away, possibly that
she was not the virginal girl that he had hoped for. But by the time he
discovered the truth, the cognac had worked its way through his
bloodstream. Or so she hoped. He wakened to find her lifting the
small leather journal from his jacket.

The cast that had been her disguise possibly saved her life. It all
happened so quickly, in seconds, yet seemed to last forever. When he

came at her, she swung her arm to protect herself, catching him along the side of the head. The blow stunned him but also sobered him when he came at her the next time.

The knife lay on the table beside what was left of the wheel of cheese the innkeeper had sent up with the cognac. It was not the training with the Resistance or even being raised on a farm where the slaughter of chickens or a pig was commonplace. It was survival instinct, that absolute certainty that if she didn't pick up that knife and use it that she was going to die. And that same instinct as she thrust the knife high up under the major's ribs.

She saw the surprise in the expression at his face followed by disbelief, then that brief flicker of rage before he collapsed against her.

They both went to the floor, the major sprawled across her. She fully expected his fellow officers to come charging through the door, and she would never be able to get the information in that journal to the Allies. Instead, it was her small, wiry friend, who popped through the narrow second-story window.

He was surprisingly strong, and dragged the dead German officer to the bed. He covered him with blankets as if he were only sleeping, then returned to where she sat on the floor. He stripped the bloodied slip from her and handed her the dress she'd worn as part of her disguise. Her hands shook but she managed to pull it on. Then the boy took off his coat and wrapped it around her.

He pulled her toward the window. She had recovered enough, and crossed the room to the chair with the major's coat thrown over the back. She retrieved that small black journal and together they slipped out of the inn, across the roof, then down a drainpipe and slipped into the forest, where Françoise and Phillipe were waiting for them.

Now she leaned back against the wall of the cellar and closed her eyes for just a few minutes. She smiled faintly at a memory…months earlier, a night stolen in the middle of war, so very different from the hours past.

He had been gentle, her Scot, with his photographs, and for just a few hours nothing else matter, nothing else existed.

Where was he now? she wondered. Still taking his photographs? Was he still alive?

He would never know what those few hours had meant to her. It was like coming alive again, to be able to feel something when she thought she would never feel anything again.

The pencil in the coat pocket had been sharpened with a knife so many times that only a stub remained, but it was enough. She began to put thoughts to paper, addressing the note to her mother—"Maman," small drawings in the margins as the words filled the page.

When she was finished, she carefully folded the paper and then tucked it into a niche in the wall.

Paul Bennett buttoned the collar of the field coat against the cold. They'd finally made camp after moving north with the Allied command for weeks. The weather had set in at Neufchateau, halting their advance amid rumors that the Germans were mounting an offensive near the Ardennes.

Dunnett had been at the morning briefing and then made for his typewriter, while the Allied high command had set up their command post in an old church at the edge of town. He had been allowed to take staged photographs—the Allied officers deep in meetings, planning their strategies, while Dunnett provided the script that would be read in the newspapers in London and New York. But after the briefing and after the photo session, he had slipped out and made his way through the enlisted encampments that surrounded Neufchateau.

A word here, a word there, and he learned that the Resistance had made contact with the high command just the day before. They had brought important information, and as soon as the weather cleared enough, they were on their way again.

"Micheleine Robillard?" he asked one man, who shook his head, then another, aware that this tight-knit group might not tell him anything, even if they knew. Discretion, silence, often meant the difference between life or death.

"Why do you ask?" a young man replied.

He was lean and handsome with the sort of looks he supposed a woman would be drawn to, and the smile would pull them in.

"She's a friend." He finally settled on the word, because she had been that, even briefly, and more.

"I was wondering if you knew her, possibly could tell me if you've seen her."

The young man smiled, pushing his cap back. It was the sort of smile that might mean anything.

"Jehanne; I know her."

"Is she well?" he asked with sudden hope.

He nodded. "The last time I saw her." The young man's eyes widened. "The woman is fearless," and made a slicing gesture across this throat. "I would not want her for an enemy."

"Where? Can you tell me where you saw her?" Paul demanded.

There was a gesture that could only mean one thing. Paul pulled the pack of cigarettes from the front of his jacket and offered him one.

"How long ago?" he asked, the flame of the match flaring at the tip of the cigarette.

A stream of smoke filled the air. The young man smiled. "I am Phillipe. You will remember, yes?"

"Yes, of course."

If he didn't wipe that grin off his face, Paul was going to wipe it off for him.

"How long ago did you see her?"

"Several days." That shrug again. "A few weeks. It's difficult to remember."

Paul grabbed him by the front of his coat.

"Was it several days, or a few weeks?"

The cigarette dangled from Phillipe's lips.

"Three weeks."

"Where?"

"North."

That told him very little. They were all north of somewhere.

"Eh! What is this? Phillipe?"

A large man appeared, a thick, bushy beard covering half his face, equally bushy brows over his eyes like feelers on a giant bug.

"This one was asking about Jehanne," Phillipe replied as he adjusted his coat and cap.

"Eh? How do you know Jehanne?" the taller man demanded.

"We're friends. I was hoping for some word about her, where she might be."

A long stare, the flat expression.

"She is gone," the man finally replied, and then motioned to the one called Phillipe.

CHAPTER
THIRTY-FIVE
DECEMBER 4, 1944

I t was coming soon.

They'd been hearing about it for weeks—an Allied offensive to push the Germans out of France and back to Germany. But the bloody weather had stalled everyone off, with storm after storm and mud that bogged down both man and machine. And then there were the fuel shortages. But here in Arras, at the edge of the offensive, the calendar meant the Christmas holiday was close, with a new year right behind it. And hope.

Paul Bennett caught a ride on an armored troop vehicle from their base camp into the city now occupied by Allied forces. The vehicle slipped around a corner, passing boarded-up businesses. But lights glowed near the city center and farther out across the city, in spite of the mandatory blackout.

He'd heard that several of the high command were there in the city hall. Others were encamped in other buildings against the latest storm, while a perimeter had been set up with heavily armed guards controlling traffic in and out of the city.

He'd entered the city earlier with Dunnett. Command wanted photographs for those back home on the evening dispatch, a political move that showed the progress that was being made with war-weary people back in London. Nothing that revealed their location; all photographs were carefully screened before they were let out to the press. But the sort of photographs that showed locals welcoming the

Allied forces—happy faces, grateful wives, and children waving—with other photographs of burned-out buildings, carefully screened to match headlines:

"This is what we're fighting for! The liberation of France...the liberation of Europe!"

Arras had been liberated in September, but the signs of German occupation were everywhere. They passed more buildings, windows blackened, military vehicles sweeping through the rain-slickened streets from the latest storm that had blown in from the channel. Then the spires of the Cathedral of Notre Dame appeared through the swirling rain.

"Just here," he told the driver, then swung down as the driver made a rolling stop, then down-shifted and waved him off. He pulled up the collar of his field jacket and climbed the steps to the entrance of the cathedral.

A sign board near the entrance gave the hours of Sunday services. In the center of Arras, with the war all around them, occupied by yet another foreign army, the people of France went about their lives.

It was quiet inside the cathedral, several candles on the high altar. The war seemed far away, beyond those ancient medieval walls with Gothic vaults looming in the shadows. It was here he hoped to learn something about Micheleine's family, something Nico had mentioned the last time Paul saw him.

"She never spoke of her family, you see," the young man told him. "To protect them, I think. But more than once, I heard her ask about Arras, in the north."

Arras. At the center of two world wars. A medieval city that had withstood bombing, invasion, and occupation. Yet it survived.

How long it had been since he had been in a church, the quiet stillness of it wrapping around him, reminding him of Sunday mass as a child, the certainty of faith a constant in his life, the world beyond far away. And then the typical questions of youth—was it real? The stories, the teachings, the absolute faith in a world that seemed to rapidly spin out of control, the rumored atrocities, foreign-sounding names and places.

He'd wandered, to London, university, then the war exploded at their doorstep, and he took his photographs. He left the university. Between assignments he drove ambulance, while the world exploded at their doorstep. Raised on it, he attended mass only sporadically, then not at all.

Did God exist is a world that seemed determined to destroy itself?

"There is no service this evening."

He spun around, instincts sharpened over the past months, his hands closed over his rifle. The priest held his hands up.

"We have little of value, my son. The Germans have seen to that."

Paul shook his head, hands relaxing. "Forgive me, Father, I meant no disrespect."

"We live in uncertain times," the priest smiled gently. "You are welcome of course. Please, come. Stay for a while." He indicated the rows of pews in the main chapel.

"The church is always open." He walked with him, his cassock frayed at the edges but immaculate.

"It has been a while since you were in a church," he speculated.

"A while."

"Your accent," the priest speculated. "Not English. Scottish perhaps?"

Paul nodded. "My mother is Scottish. My father was English."

"Ah, and family?"

"My mother and sister are in the north."

"They are safe, then?"

"Yes, far from the cities."

"And you are far from your faith?"

"It has been a while."

There in the chapel, he felt the pull, that deeply ingrained sense of awe as a child that had wavered as he became an adult.

"God is always here, waiting, patient, and now you have found your way here."

"I'm looking for someone," he began. He realized how that sounded. Millions of people had been displaced across the whole of Europe. If rumors were true, hundreds of thousands had simply disappeared, loaded onto trains that disappeared—men, women, children, whole families. And he was looking for someone.

"Her family may be in Arras. I had hoped there might be some records here at the church; the city hall has few records."

He'd been there the day before and learned the German occupation army had destroyed all official records—records of births, marriages, deaths, as if the people whose names were on those records and documents never existed.

"I know the Church keeps records of its parishioners. I was hoping you might be able to find them. Robillard was her family name."

The priest shook his head. "Sadly, I cannot help you. When the Germans came, they destroyed the records in the cathedral—hundreds of years of history, the names of families, records of births, deaths, everything. As if they could wipe out the past of the church. The few things that have survived were books and some of the older archives that are centuries old that we were able to hide from them. Everything else was lost. They burned everything they found." He shook his head sadly.

"Do you remember the family?" Paul asked. "Husband, wife, two sons, and three daughters. One of the daughters was named Micheleine. She would have been fifteen when the war started. Her father and brother were with the Resistance. They were killed."

Again, the priest shook his head. "Robillard is not an unusual name. There are parish churches beyond the city, in the smaller towns and villages. Perhaps they belonged to one of them." He laid a hand on Paul's shoulder.

"I will ask about the family. Someone may know of them." He started to ask where he could contact him, then stopped.

"But you will be moving on when the weather clears."

"I'll come back."

Paul took out a pencil and tore a piece of paper from the notepad he carried to keep a log of the photographs he took. He wrote down his name and the address of the newspaper in London.

"If you should hear of them, please send a letter to this address." If they were still alive. He handed the paper to the priest, then turned to leave.

"Stay for a while," the priest told him. "The storm has not yet passed. It is dry inside, and you are welcome. God does not require that you pray. He asks only that you are here."

How long had it been since he had been in a church? Four years? Longer?

In London, with the bombs and the city burning around them, there were times when the only thing that mattered was survival.

There had been no time for church. There had only been the warning sirens, and the mad dash for one of the underground shelters.

There, once, with the bombs raining down overhead, the explosions felt through the stone walls and underfoot, a deacon and several parishioners had also sought shelter. There in the smothering darkness his voice reached out through the fear and uncertainty.

"Yea, though I walk through the valley of the shadow of death, I shall fear no evil for though art with me..."

The 23rd Psalm, and a voice in the wilderness of death and destruction.

He had walked away then, just as he walked away now, unable to reconcile the death and destruction he'd seen, in London and on those beaches months earlier, and in villages and towns since.

"I will pray for you," he heard the priest say as he left the chapel.

He caught a ride back to the apartment over a market where he and Dunnett had been encamped the past several days. It was one of the few buildings the Germans hadn't occupied. It was small and the water service was often non-existent, but it was dry and near the city center where the high command was housed. The owner of the market had only the barest of canned supplies on the shelves, but had greeted them with much enthusiasm.

"Take my photograph," he said in heavily accented English when they arrived and he saw Paul's camera.

"So the world will know that we are at last liberated."

Dunnett had just returned from a meeting of the handful of fellow correspondents who made up the press corps.

A cigarette hung from his mouth as he pulled his latest dispatch from the typewriter and stuffed it inside the leather portfolio.

"What is it?" Paul Bennett asked, eyeing the open duffel bag on the narrow cot behind Dunnett.

"We're moving out, part of the forward advance." There was an excitement in Dunnett's voice—the hound on the scent of prey; in this case the prey was the next story to be written.

"We have to report to base camp in thirty minutes. A driver will pick us up. But I need to get this over to communications to make the next flight out to London."

Thirty minutes. There wasn't enough time to get back to the cathedral and leave a message if Micheleine's family should be found.

Dunnett returned just as the driver was pulling up to the front of the market. His typewriter had already been packed into the case. He tossed his duffle bag into the back of the Morris military vehicle.

"That was good timing," he commented, as Paul crawled into the cab of the Morris beside him.

"Did you find the person you were looking for?"

Paul shook his head.

"Too bad, that," Dunnett commented. "Now it appears we're off on the final push against the Germans. No telling when we might get back this way."

Paul glanced back over his shoulder at the spires of the cathedral reaching into the skyline as the Morris sped through the rain-slicked streets, swerving around other vehicles, toward the edge of the city.

If any of them made it back alive.

CHAPTER
THIRTY-SIX
PRESENT DAY

A century earlier Arras stood at the edge of the western front during World War I, and was reduced to little more than rubble. The infamous trenches became death traps for many and could still be seen a hundred years later, some filled in with sign posts to mark their location, others grown over in that way that nature reclaimed what was abandoned after the smoke of battle cleared.

In some remote locations, the barbed wire that had marked the narrow fields of battle that were all that separated Allied and German forces, and where so many had died, could still be found—rusted, broken in places, a reminder.

The war to end all wars.

Then in World War II, Arras had been occupied by the German army as part of the occupation forces determined to take France, eventually liberated by the British weeks before the Allied push against the Germans.

The scars remained. Buildings that had been razed either by bombing or fire in the first war had been rebuilt on the shell of centuries-old foundations, faint lines of newer construction seen in the stones and bricks on the walls of Flemish Baroque buildings in the town center.

The original Cathedral of Notre Dame had been built somewhere between the eleventh and fourteenth centuries. Once the most beautiful cathedral in northern France, it had been destroyed during the French Revolution, rebuilt, then destroyed again by shelling during World War I.

After the war it was rebuilt in that previous Gothic design, and rose majestically into the skyline as they drove past the town square.

"Where?" James asked.

A single word, the first he'd spoken after the drive north in silence, anger between them like a wall. He didn't agree with her decision to continue, but he didn't try to talk her out of it again.

Where to search? Where to begin? Where to find records of a young woman who had once lived there and then gone off to fight the Germans in World War II?

The manager of the tourist office directed them to the public library.

"They have many books about the war," he explained.

The library was one of the few buildings that had survived the war, a massive complex of baroque colonnaded buildings that had been updated through the years with new technology. There were reading rooms, computer kiosks, and political banners on the walls, along with life-sized photographs of famous authors of the twentieth century—Jean Paul Sartre, Camus, and Georges Simenon, juxtaposed with photographs of young twenty-first century authors.

She gave the young clerk at the main desk her business card and explained that she was interested in information about local history during World War II.

He provided directions to an area of the library with an extensive collection of books and periodicals about both world wars including an extensive computer archive.

Kris felt like they were starting over, searching for a needle in a haystack, one file after another, pages of information that only went back to the years after the war, other information that pre-dated the war. James sat across from her in front of another monitor, scrolling through archives of daily newspapers from the same period.

It was time-consuming, complicated by the language barrier. Hours later, she rubbed the headache that had begun from staring at the computer screen. Another file, and more documents. Then, an entry caught her attention. It was a reference to a newspaper announcement, from May 18, 1954.

"Where can I find this?" she asked the young student clerk at the desk in the department, and showed her the reference number she'd written down.

"That is a micro-filmed document," the young woman explained. "Older documents that were archived many years ago. We have a microfilm reader over here."

It had been years since she'd used a microfilm reader at Columbia, studying ancient texts that had been recorded on microfilm before computers, a system rarely used any longer with libraries updated with scanned and cross-referenced information capable of being accessed by hundreds of users at the touch of a computer screen.

She leaned over James' shoulder as he scrolled through dozens of archived newspaper pages from May 1954, then slowed on the 18th.

"There." She pointed to the entry that came up. It was typewritten in French, a marriage announcement. One of the names leapt off the screen at her—Angeline Robillard.

1954. Almost ten years after the war. Was it possible they had found a member of Micheleine's family?

From what she already knew, Micheleine's father and two older brothers had died during the war, leaving behind her mother and a younger sister. If she was alive, her younger sister could have been in her early twenties in 1954.

"What about the other name—Marchand?"

In a time before cell phones, websites, and dating services, young men and women often married people they'd grown up with, people their families knew from the same community, like Arras, made up of farmers, shopkeepers, and tradesmen where their children all attended the local Catholic school together. It was possible that Angeline Robillard had known Albert Marchand all of her life. It was also possible it was just another rabbit hole.

Apparently Marchand was a common name. There were records for three with that name, but only one for M. Marchand, b. 2Apr 1991. Too young to be the Albert Marchand who had married Angeline Robillard. A relative?

"What about local census records?" she asked the clerk.

"Only for taxes and the military."

James entered the name in the file record for those who had served in the military.

"Nothing."

"What about local property owners?"

They were told that information could be found at the Land Registry.

It was late afternoon when they found the office.

"Our records only go back to just after World War II," the woman at the counter informed them.

"Everything before that was destroyed. The only records we have from that time period are those that were kept by the property owners themselves, or in the case of property transfers such as death."

"Or marriage?" Kris asked.

"Possibly," the clerk replied.

"This would be from 1954," she told the clerk. "Under either the name Robillard or Marchand."

"What are you thinking?" James asked.

"The Tavern," Kris replied. "When Cate wanted to buy it and restore it there were no records of ownership. The only thing anyone knew about it was that a man by the name of Brian was the last person who lived there." She tried to remember the name Cate had mentioned.

"Brian McCallan." James knew the story; he'd grown up on it with road trips out to the tavern with his mates and a case of ale.

"The only problem was," Kris continued with what Cate had told her at the time, "there was no record he ever legally owned the Tavern. Apparently he just moved in. But there was a record of ownership by a woman who inherited the property after her husband died a century earlier. All anyone knew was that Brian McCallan moved in somewhere around 1920." She remembered several conversations while Cate was trying to buy the Tavern.

"Everything was tied up for almost a year while Cate's solicitors worked through all the legal obstacles. A description of the property was found in the woman's records under her family name, but there were no surviving heirs, so it was declared an abandoned property, and Cate purchased it at auction. Her bill from the solicitors was more than what she paid for the property."

The clerk had returned and provided copies of what she had found.

"We have a record from June 1954, in the name Marchand, a property registration with a copy of a marriage certificate." The clerk handed her a printout of the record, including the certificate.

It was in French, but she immediately recognized the names at the bottom of the marriage certificate.

Albert Marchand and Angeline Robillard.

They'd just found that needle in the haystack, including an address where the original property transfer had been sent after it was recorded—Rue Chauvel, Montigny, France.

"North of the city," the clerk told them.

Kris gathered the copies the clerk had made for them and put them in her shoulder bag. She hesitated as she turned to leave.

On a sudden thought, she asked, "Where is the hospital located?"

"Hospital?" the woman replied with a frown. "There is no hospital here. The nearest hospital is the university hospital at Amiens."

No hospital. What then had Micheleine meant by that message hidden decades earlier?

It was early afternoon when they left the library, lights gleaming beneath a leaden sky along the colonnaded buildings as they returned to the rental car. She slid into the passenger seat. James slipped behind the wheel.

"This old property map lies along a single-track road twenty kilometers north past this village."

She looked up when he made no comment, didn't even seem to be listening as he stared into the rear-view mirror.

"What is it?"

He saw it as they came out of the library, just a glimpse. He might have been wrong, but it was that other sense that had him watching out the side mirror, through the flow of late afternoon traffic, the glare of lights, and the rain that had begun.

A silver-gray car, late model, European, with the windows blacked out, at the curb on the adjacent street. When he looked again, it had pulled away and disappeared in traffic.

"Nothing," he replied, tucking it away.

CHAPTER
THIRTY-SEVEN

Twenty kilometers was like stepping back in time as the road wound north through rolling countryside in shades of gold, amber, and brown with the season, dotted with cows with dark circular marks around their eyes, slipping through stands of ancient oaks, then emerging past orchards that spread to the edge of the forest.

Signs from another time marked the way for modern day tourists, scholars, the curious.

World War I trenches—2 km; Somme Battlefield—40 km; Dunkirk —just over 200 km.

Taking the traveler back in time, to battlefields, that desperate struggle, the age-old conflict of good against evil, the ghosts of the dead in fields with rows of white crosses.

The village of Montigny had no strategic importance, that distance from the larger city to the south, perched on the edge of that conflict, the whitewashed houses with slate roofs, sandstone foundations, the spire of the small stone church, picturesque in its quaintness, stark contrast to one of the bloodiest wars in human history.

Beyond the village, men had fought and died on both sides, the scars of World War I covered over by the forest for a hundred years, in that way that nature reclaimed its own. And then another war that had claimed the sons and daughters of the village—simple people, farmers, idealistic young men and women like Micheleine Robillard

—Jehanne, as she became known to the people of France. Their very own Joan of Arc.

What was your secret? Kris thought, that note written on that slip of paper, then tucked away in a niche in a wall, hidden for almost four decades before it was found in that cellar almost by accident, a footnote from another time and place in a small museum in Normandy.

She thought of that fifteen-year-old girl when the war began. She'd lost her father and two brothers to the war, left alone in a world gone mad.

When Kris was fifteen, the most important thing in her world had been passing the college-level courses she took, beating out her school's rival in girls' soccer and going on to the regional competition, that first serious flirtation with one of her brother's friends home from college at the time. It was serious on her part, excited when Patrick Brady promised to come down and watch one of her games.

He didn't make it to the game. No surprise now, looking back on it, but it had been important to her. One of those early infatuations that had been so unimportant in the scheme of things, but part of being fifteen years old and making that painful transition from adolescence.

"What was it like when you were fifteen?" she asked as James turned on the wipers, clearing the icy rain that had begun to pelt the windscreen.

She caught the quick sideways glance, the frown, and half expected some off-hand remark that her brother might have made about hanging out with friends, places he shouldn't have been, pushing back on that Catholic upbringing and other rules that most teenagers pushed back on, testing the limits, without a care in the world except whose parents were gone and where the next Friday night party was; certainly not living day-to-day with the enemy in every town, at your door.

He continued to stare down the roadway and she almost thought he hadn't heard or chose to ignore her.

"Bread-and-jam sandwiches," he finally replied, then thoughtful again.

He'd thought about how to answer that—about the craziness, the wildness, the things he hoped Anne didn't know about but suspected she did, a comment here, a sideways look and a word dropped years later.

He thought he was so smart at fifteen. Didn't all adolescents? But there had been other things too, things that came with growing up without a father, suddenly aware how his mother struggled to make ends meet, living on welfare while going to school at night, with a pain-in-the-ass kid who thought only of himself until the day there was nothing in the small apartment to fix a sandwich for lunch, and he had complained that there was only bread and jam.

"Bread and jam make a fine sandwich," Anne told him at the time, as she spread two slices of bread, then folded them together. She had hugged him then, and wiped a tear from her cheek that she thought at the time he hadn't noticed.

She'd started work with a management company—administrative assistant was the name of the position. More classes, more experience, and then her own business in property management, and no more jam sandwiches. Years later there were other things that had called, tapped into who he was and who he wanted to be.

And years after that, he stood across the kitchen in her townhouse on one of those trips back home and made himself a jam-and-bread sandwich. It was there in the expression on her face, the way her eyes softened.

"Aye," she said at the time, almost a whisper. "It makes a fine sandwich."

He'd forgotten that until now. But it had mattered at the time.

Things that mattered.

The glow from the instrument panel of the rental car reflected in his eyes.

"And work, turning wrenches for Will's father—good, hard labor, grease on your hands, the smell of petrol, and the rumble of a motorbike. He was like a surrogate father. Will and I earned just enough to keep ourselves out of trouble—most of the time," he added with another sideways glance and almost a smile.

"He spent his earnings on cheap ale. Whatever I earned went into the bank account to help out."

"Jam sandwiches," she commented. "And Julie Hennessey?"

He shrugged. "A diversion, for a while. Then we were both on to other things."

"Dickie Simson," she replied. His had been college and then the military.

"It seemed that she might have regretted that one. They hit a bad patch."

"Tried to get back together with you? A brief encounter when you were home on leave?"

"Aye, well, there were a few pints to take the edge off, then she went into how unhappy she was. It never went any further. We'd both changed."

"Regret?"

God knows she had own—about her marriage, about things that she should have told her brother instead of the things she'd said.

"Regret is a cruel taskmaster." His voice had gone low. "For things that never were, and never will be." That shrug again.

"We'd both changed. We were in different places."

"She didn't have that youthful glow any longer?" she teased.

"She had the glow, and some extra baggage—three little ones at the time. I wasn't into taking that on, and Anne was just getting her business off the ground. I took out a loan at the bank to help her get started."

It explained the closeness between mother and son, the struggle of early years that she'd never experienced in her own family, never even thought about. Things that made a person who they were, that had shaped him, along with that trip to Lochaber—the protector, the guardian.

"It was best she and Dickie worked things out. They were meant to be together."

Fate—things that happen for a reason.

She had that conversation once with Cate, who had experienced so much, seen so much, cheated death more than once chasing the story, and lived to tell about it and then write about it.

"Maybe there is some divine reason to all of it," Cate had said late one night after the last stop on her latest book tour.

"Maybe I was supposed to experience all those things so that I could write the books. Why do some people die, and some live in situations against all odds?"

The conversation had turned philosophical then, in the way that a very fine whisky will do.

"Why is a young soldier sitting next to me in an armored vehicle killed, and I escape uninjured?" she continued. "I never really believed in God until that assignment, never gave it much thought. Maybe I was too busy, or too wrapped up in other things.

"But when that young man was dying and I held him in my arms and tried to stop the bleeding, he kept telling me not to worry. He wasn't afraid. With the vehicle disabled, gunfire all around us. And right there in the middle of all that blood and death, he smiled. Not at me, but at something else. I don't know how else to explain it, except that in that moment, I knew he was completely at peace."

It had been one of her last assignments before she left the business —things that happened for a reason. Vilette would have said it was the path she was supposed to follow.

"Do you think Anne will marry Tom Jeffries?" Kris asked, remembering the conversation between mother and son when they were in Inverness.

"She should," he replied. "She deserves to be happy, and Tom's a good man." That sideways glance again, and that faint smile.

"But God help him if she says yes."

CHAPTER
THIRTY-EIGHT

EARLY DECEMBER, 1944, NORMANDY, FRANCE,

First, it was the German occupation, trucks and automobiles rumbling on the roadway, a juggernaut of metal and iron that followed weeks of persistent rumors, and then finally the news over the scratchy broadcast from the radio that Paris had fallen almost without a single shot fired. At least none that anyone would talk about.

Afterward, there were pictures in the newspaper of centuries-old monuments in the city, draped with the German flag, the swastika like a black skeleton against blood-red and white, street signs replaced with signs printed in German, the city and a thousand years of history disappearing beneath the black boots of Adolph Hitler's army.

Then word that came down that the French people were now required to cover the expenses of the occupying army with the franc reduced to one-fifth the value against the German mark. When they could not pay, food, animals, anything of value was confiscated, "to pay your share," they were told. Until people were reduced to starving.

Next there were rumors of people who disappeared from towns and villages around the countryside, loaded onto rail cars, requisitioned, and transported to Germany under the Service du Travail Obligatoire, forced labor in German factories to feed the war machine. Others were taken, leaflets distributed in town centers and villages, declaring that, "After each incident of resistance, a number, reflecting the seriousness of the crime, shall be shot".

It was then her father and brothers left their farm, to join the Resistance, with the Vichy government powerless to stop the atrocities, complicit, some said, in the brutality against the French people, lining their own pockets, playing the game against the time when the war would be over.

Micheleine Robillard stood in the doorway of the kitchen in that small house on their farm, her sister Angeline leaning in and staring up at her with the innocence of seven years of age, unable to understand their mother's weeping, the words whispered across the wood kitchen table.

"There is enough food in the cellar to keep you and the girls," she caught the conversation, glancing back and forth between her mother and father with far greater understanding.

"But do not squander what you have."

"When will you return?" her mother had asked. A question that had no answer.

Her father had covered her mother's hand then, in that way she had seen hundreds of times, a gesture meant to comfort, now with far more meaning.

Her brothers stood behind him, dressed in their woolen field coats and hats, hunting rifles hung over their shoulders—Stephen and Robert, seventeen and twenty years of age. Earlier, Robert had crossed the orchard separating their farm from their neighbors under cover of darkness—the fox, their father called him—and said goodbye to Anne Marie Lechance. They had grown up together and planned to wed. But all of that had changed. Now there would be no wedding, even though Anne Marie carried his child.

Micheleine's father turned then and motioned her to the table.

"You must help your mother," he told her. "Gather as much of the crop as you can. Think of our friends and neighbors, save the rest of the crop for yourselves. Dried apples will stay a long while in the cellar. When there is no more money, you will need food for barter."

"Yes, Papa," she had replied, with the maturity of someone far older.

"I am counting on you to take care of things. If you need help, go to Lechance. He is old, but he is strong as a bull and will help you and your mother."

Then the three of them were slipping out the back door of the farmhouse under cover of darkness, food sacks over their shoulders, hasty kisses for her mother, her father's callused hand gentle against her cheek.

"If you need to leave, you know the safe place."

Micheleine nodded, blinking back tears in spite of her determination not to cry. He had showed it to her brother's years before. She had followed in spite of his instructions to stay home, only discovering that the shadow that had followed them through the forest was no fox or deer, but his wayward daughter.

"What am I to do with you, Micheleine?" he had said that day, fighting his way between anger that she had tracked them, and the same pride as when he taught his sons to track and hunt in the forest.

"I want to go with you," she replied, what seemed perfectly logical at the time.

In the days and weeks after her father and brothers left to join the Resistance, those tracking and hunting skills had proven invaluable after their chickens and pigs were seized under the new confiscation ordinance. From her hunting in the forest after the apple crop was in, she often brought back rabbit or grouse that her mother prepared for their meal, until it became too dangerous to wander into the forest with Germans constantly moving along the roadway, encamped in the forest, or occupying the village.

It was her mother who decided that she must leave.

"It is not safe for you to stay," her mother said, returning from the village where she went weekly to take mended clothing to friends, messages hidden in her sewing basket.

"A young girl was found." The rest of the story had become a familiar one.

"She was raped and beaten. Monsieur Cousteau does not think she will live."

The doctor had passed messages to the outlying farms. They were all aware of the danger, and for that reason she had curtailed her trips into the forest, never taking the same trail twice, often taking no trail at all. She wore her hair tucked into her camp and dressed in some of her brothers' clothes. She was an excellent shot, and she'd also learned to use the knife.

"You must go," her mother announced. Cousteau's son, it seemed, was leaving to join the Resistance.

"What about you and Angeline?"

"We will stay as long as we can. If we must leave, so be it."

It a matter of hours, everything had changed. Talk of joining the Resistance was talk no more. Preparations were made. Her mother washed and dried clothes she would need, the rifle her father had left behind was cleaned once more and secured in a leather scabbard he had made. Her hair was braided and then tucked under her cap. Then it was time to go, young Cousteau's knock at the back door of the farmhouse.

Contrary to her mother's stoic announcement and all the preparations that had followed, Simone Robillard had pulled her into her arms and hugged her fiercely.

"If you see your father and brothers..."

"I will tell them you are safe and well," Micheleine finished the thought, her mother's brave smile unable to hide the tears.

"And you..."

"I will stay safe," she promised, brushing a kiss against her mother's cheek.

Cousteau was waiting for her at the corner of the house. No words were exchanged, he simply nodded, then started off through the orchard to the forest beyond.

She would have been a liar if she said she wasn't scared, as she glanced one last time at the single light from the oil lamp on the farmhouse that had seen several generations of Robillards.

The farm itself was nothing special, a small wood and stone structure with a loft, that had once been a barn before it was converted into a home for her grandfather and his family, the loft divided between sleeping areas for the Robillard sons and daughters who had followed.

The orchards and the gardens had sustained them three hundred years before, and now with the cellar that her father had the foresight to dig and then line with stones left behind at the quarry.

Thinking back on that now, the memory of the last sight of the farmhouse was as strong as ever. Special. It kept her going, kept her fighting.

Her mother and sister were safe, according to the last word she had before leaving. They had survived the disaster of Dunkirk, occupation by the German army, and now they had received word through their sources that the Allied Invasion was on.

She remembered going through the mental checklist her father always insisted on. The rifle, she knew, was loud and drew too much attention, only to be used as a last resort. The knife she had carried that day, was the preferred weapon, silent if messy, but not if one used it correctly. And who would suspect a young girl to have such a knife, much less use it?

That long-ago day, she and Cousteau had met up with another man who led them to still another, a careful arrangement to protect those involved. They were masked, then taken to an encampment. There they trained over the next few weeks. Missions were planned, then they were sent out, with one objective—to disrupt communications, gather intelligence on German defenses, provide first-hand intelligence information, and if possible, get back alive.

Some made it back, many were lost. The fight went on, hiding by day in the loft of a barn, or the cellar of a house by night, sleeping in shelled-out buildings, caves, the hollow of a fallen tree, or the burned-out hulk of a tank that had been abandoned.

She dreamed of the sun filtering down through the branches of the trees in her father's orchards, the way it was before the war with the taste of an apple as she bit into it, juice running down her chin, and the warmth of the soil pushing up between her toes as she ran barefoot through the fields with her brothers.

Of their friend Anne Marie and her new baby, her mother and father, and the faces and names of those who were lost. They were always followed by dreams of blood and death, nightmares that wakened her suddenly in a cold sweat, and haunted her for hours after.

She wasn't an innocent young girl any more. She had lied, stolen, and killed. Time condensed into just the next moment, the next mission, a few stolen hours, a stranger's gentle touch against all the days, months, and seasons that might never come again.

CHAPTER
THIRTY-NINE
PRESENT DAY

The village of Montigny lay between rolling hills that spread toward the forest in the north and rows of orchards to the west.

Once a medieval town, an agricultural center, then almost forgotten in the centuries since as the larger, more prosperous city, with its cathedral and commerce, grew to the south with major roadways that connected it to other French cities to the east and coastal ports to the southwest. And this small village, all that remained of the medieval town with its typical slate-roof houses and ancient church, was where Micheleine Robillard had once lived.

Kris imagined it was little changed since those medieval times, the sun poking through clouds as the road wound north, orchards with trees covered in the last months of fall with yellow leaves, the fall harvest over.

Had Micheleine run barefoot through her father's orchards, she wondered, picking low-hanging fruit, munching on an apple as she day-dreamed, time moving slowly as summer drifted into fall?

What where her dreams? Were they any different from other young girls, safe, the outside world and the looming war distant, not even a reality yet?

That would have been before the war, before her father and brothers joined the Resistance, before a girl of fifteen followed them and became a symbol of hope to the people of France in a dangerous time; not unlike another girl centuries earlier. A girl of fifteen who became known as Jehanne.

When she was fifteen, the world was safe and secure, and the most important thing was keeping her grades up so that she could qualify for the girls' soccer league. Her brother had coached her that last summer, before his first tour.

"Keep your eyes down field!"

How many times had she heard that?

"Keep moving! Drive! Go to your cut-off!" Strategy from his own soccer experience.

"Make the other girl anticipate you! Then do what she doesn't expect. Control the ball! Find the opening, then pass. Trust your teammate!"

It drove her crazy. He drove her crazy. And she was a better player for it, good enough to make the college team. And he was there to see them win that last game and the championship.

The sign was at the roadside, then the rooftops came into view.

The village was like a picture from a calendar or a brochure promoting places to visit on the next vacation, the main street winding through a cluster of plaster cottages with slate roofs, the center of the village closed to automobiles, with vendor stalls lining the street. Market day.

Weekly markets were found all over France, where people gathered to purchase local produce, crafts, food prepared by local chefs, the sounds of vendors, tourists, and farmers, mingling with the smell of fresh baked bread, meat prepared over an open fire, and an insane variety of cheeses.

James parked the car and turned off the motor.

"It's a place to start," he said, hitting the remote lock on the rental. "Small towns, everyone knows everyone for miles around."

He watched her as they left the car. He would give her this much. If nothing turned up, then he would take the next step. He had to, to protect her. Then they needed to have that talk after what had happened at the inn in Amiens.

They were both adults. God knows they were capable of making their own choices and decisions. And mistakes.

It should have been easy to simply call it for what it was—sex, that survival instinct after what had happened, basic human need, a mistake, pure and simple.

It should have been.

She walked ahead, entering the closed street, joining people afoot, cyclists in their tight shorts and helmets who took advantage of the food and wine, locals with baskets hooked over their arms who meandered from stall to stall, the women picking up a piece of fruit followed by the usual chatting away that was inherent in small villages, people who appeared to be from the larger city purchasing fresh produce, eggs, an assortment of late-season berries, squash, and baskets of red and gold apples from those orchards.

It reminded her of street fairs in New York, that blend of cultures, accents, home-made crafts, and food. They were fewer now.

Thousands of miles away from New York, the smell of food from one of those stalls filled the air, along with conversations in French and English along with a blend of Dutch and German, the way it had for hundreds of years.

She spoke with the vendor, a short, portly man with an immaculate apron tied around his substantial waist, a balding head, and hand gestures typical of a man who appreciates food, and asked about a family that a friend had told her lived in the area and gave him the name—Marchand. He shrugged, filling a bag with his specialties—she must try this and some of this...

She thanked him, no doubt paying more than the food was worth. No answer, but the small beef wrapped pastries were delicious.

"What did you expect?" James commented. "Your French is so bad, he was probably propositioning you."

She shrugged in answer. "A man who cooks like that? I could be persuaded."

There were other food stalls offering olives in seasoned oil; truffles from the forest that she would have paid a small fortune for, back in New York; cinnamon pastry from the local patisserie, the scent thick in the fall air; and then there was food grown locally—roasted nuts, squash, persimmons, pears, apples, and honey, gleaming like liquid amber in jars.

It was possible that neither family lived in the area any longer. The war had changed things. People were scattered or left after the war, unable to make a living on farms the way they had before the war.

Others moved to the cities where there were jobs as cities were rebuilt after the war.

Small villages were now picturesque stops that found other ways to survive, where people rode bicycles through the countryside, escaping the cities for a weekend or holiday. Others escaped permanently, leaving the cities behind for a simpler way of life, possibly like the young woman in the next to the last stall. She was slender, with dark hair and green eyes, a long braid hanging over one shoulder.

She was younger than the other vendors, pretty, with little makeup except for lip gloss, and freckles across her nose. Typical college student, Kris guessed.

She wore jeans, a flannel shirt buttoned over a thermal shirt, sleeves rolled back at the cuffs, hiking boots, and the usual array of tattoos that circled her wrists. There was a tattoo of a lotus blossom at one side of her neck, and another symbol inked on the opposite side —the Cross of Lorraine! The symbol the French Resistance had adopted during the war.

Coincidence?

It was late afternoon and the girl was stacking empty trays. A few apples were displayed on her table. By the number of empty baskets spread across the front counter, it had apparently been a good day.

"Those are not so good," the girl told her as she picked up an apple. "These are better." She pointed out another tray with a half-dozen apples.

"These were picked earlier in the fall, sweeter."

She was packing up for the day as customers thinned. Others were also closing, packing up what was left of jars of honey, olives, wine, the food vendor closing down his grill.

The girl spoke to the vendor in the next stall with animated conversation in that way of people who know one another. He laughed and gave her a jar of almonds with something in that conversation about sharing it with someone.

It might be nothing—that particular tattoo—a popular design that had caught the girl's attention in some local tattoo parlor. She thought of Innis and Luna with tattoos covering both arms, most of which meant nothing to anyone else, but had particular meaning for them.

What were the odds, she thought, at the same time she handed several Euros over to the girl for the apples.

"Do you live near the village?"

There was that cool expression again and a shrug of the shoulders in that vague way that might mean anything.

"Not far," the girl replied. Then a polite, "Merci." She said something to the vendor and they shared a laugh. Then she ducked under the canvas at the back of the stall.

A coincidence? Possibly.

Kris stepped over to the next stall where the vendor the girl had been speaking with was packing up what was left of the assorted packages of smoked and roasted almonds he had been selling. She picked up a jar of cinnamon-roasted almonds.

"Do you know the girl who was in this stall?" she asked him.

"Eh?" he looked up. She hoped his English was better than her French.

"Do you know where she went?"

He smiled. "Valentine? You have some of her apples. Qui," he gestured toward the village.

"She was late for work," he chuckled. "But Sevier will forgive her. She is his best worker."

"Work?"

He nodded. "The café, La Maison Ondine. Everyone knows it. Good food."

"Thank you." She looked around for James.

He was at the far end of the row of stalls talking with the woman. As customers, a couple in biking gear, and others pushed around her, it was impossible to get his attention. She glanced back the direction the girl had gone.

The café was crowded. It took her a moment to find Valentine as she grabbed two platters of food and navigated through the tables to the customers who had placed the order.

An apron was tied around a slender waist and she moved with the energy of an athlete. Considering the crowded tables, she needed that energy to keep up with the flow of orders that were placed and food that came from the kitchen, with only one other person, an older man, possibly the owner, who poured wine by the glass, and chatted with the guests, while passing orders through to the kitchen.

She finally wedged between guests and caught the girl's attention.

"Oui?" the girl said, efficiently juggling two armfuls of plates.

. . .

Bloody hell! One minute she was there, then she was gone.

James scanned the line of vendor stalls, cyclists who had stopped for the evening before continuing on in the morning, couples who meandered along the line of vendors, those who were already packing up their merchandise.

"The woman who was just here," he asked the startled vendor, the last place he had seen her.

"American, pretty, shoulder-length reddish brown hair?"

A shrug of the shoulders and that vague expression.

"We had an argument," he told the man. More truth to that than not.

The old man's expression changed to one of sympathy.

"Ah, lovers' quarrel." He gestured toward the village. "La Maison Ondine," he replied with an amused expression.

Lights had come on throughout the village, glittering through the misty rain. Most shops were closed—a small pharmacy, an antique shop, the local butcher, the small medieval church at the center of the village, surrounded by stone houses, one that had been turned into a bed-and-breakfast, the local feed and grain store in a centuries-old barn, a flower shop where the young clerk finally gave directions.

The House of Ondine, that a few centuries earlier had been the local brothel, unless he missed his guess, another local business establishment.

He scanned the street, the automobiles and bicycles stretched along the main thoroughfare, the lights that glowed from the crowded Café, tourists and cyclists spilling out onto a patio under a striped canopy, others gathered around a stone fire pit.

He pushed through the crowd that had gathered at the entrance, the sting of warmth and the smell of food hitting as his gaze swept the café.

Kris saw the anger in the set of his jaw, the way his mouth tightened as he cut through the crowd that had gathered at the bar.

"This is Valentine Marchand." She introduced them before he had a chance to say anything.

Valentine handed the scanned photograph back to her. "We will talk later, when it is not so busy."

She gave him an openly interested look, then picked up her tray as the owner called out in French.

"She recognized the photograph of Micheleine Robillard," Kris explained, as Valentine picked up an order and crossed the café to a far table.

"Albert Marchand is her grandfather."

The fire had burned low at the stone hearth at the café. It was only just after eight in the evening but most of the guests had eaten and then either traveled on, wanting to get to the next destination before it was too late, or headed for accommodations in the village at a handful of quaint French countryside homes that owners rented out during holidays and the summer season.

Valentine had taken off her apron, laying it over the back of the chair as she joined them.

"My grandfather has told me about her, Micheleine, my grand-mother's sister." She gestured to the scanned photograph that Kris had showed her earlier.

"He has another photograph of their family taken a long time ago, with their brothers when they were all very young, before the war. Micheleine was very beautiful. She used that, the stories I've been told, when she was with the Resistance to get information from the Germans that she passed on to others."

There was no judgment or criticism in her voice, only pride.

"She would have done anything to help the people of France. The more I learn about her from my grandfather, she seemed real, not just someone who died and was forgotten."

"From what we've been able to find out about her, she was not forgotten," Kris assured her.

"Oui," Valentine nodded. "They called her Jehanne—Joan of Arc. I have heard this before." She explained what they already knew.

"It was very difficult then, so many died." She glanced around at the few remaining guests. "My grandfather does not like to talk about it, about what he did during the war. I think most people don't under-stand what it was like, or they don't want to," she added, taking a sip of wine.

"I chose the Cross of Lorraine to honor her memory, and my grandfather." Her expression was sad.

"He will want very much to meet you. To tell you about Micheleine." She looked down at the photograph.

"I am very sorry about your friend," she told Kris. "It was on all the news channels. CB Ross was very well known in France for the books she wrote. I know my grandfather will want to help any way he can."

Until then, James had listened, occasionally glancing around the café, watching the other guests. His expression, one that Kris had seen dozens of times, was unreadable, like his thoughts, but not the warning.

"You need to know that it could be very dangerous. "

He told her about the incident in London and at the abbey. He didn't want to frighten her, but she was entitled to know the risk.

"We were to meet with a friend of Cate's, who I was hoping might be able to tell us something," Kris explained.

"We were able to track her calls and we know that she met with him just before the accident. They worked together a long time ago, a very good friend. He lived in Paris...the Montparnasse."

Valentine's eyes widened. "The explosion in Paris?"

Kris nodded.

"The authorities are saying it was another terrorist attack."

Kris and James exchanged looks.

"Kris was supposed to have met with him. The explosion happened just before she got there."

Valentine nodded, dark brows drawn together in a thoughtful expression.

"I understand. One of my friends..." She looked down at her hands wrapped around the wine glass.

"He was at the concert hall. He was such a good, kind person, so intelligent." She looked up. There was sadness there, but also anger.

"In many ways it is the same as it was for my grandfather—the terror, the deaths. No different, I think." She took a sip of wine and looked over at them.

"You have experienced this too, in your cities." She was thoughtful again, as if the answers might be found in her wine glass.

"In the midst of terror, we find hope. It is all we have, it is enough." She smiled softly.

"My grandfather told me, that they use to say this to keep themselves going during that horrible time. And they found it—hope—so many times in the people who hid them at great danger to themselves, in someone who sacrificed himself so that they could escape, in the work that Micheleine did." She stared down at the photograph.

"Your friend found something that was perhaps very important. My grandfather would tell you that after what they all went through during that time, there is nothing anyone could do that would frighten him." She looked up then.

"He will want to help you if he can, for her, for all of them."

"Eh, Valentine," the owner called out. "The weather is not good. You should go."

The last of the customers had left.

Valentine smiled. "Sometimes, it is as if I have two grandfathers, yes?" She handed the photograph back to Kris.

"Where are you staying?"

Kris tucked the photograph into the notebook that contained the print-outs and copies she'd made. She exchanged another look with James.

"We didn't make arrangements. Under the circumstances..." She left the rest unsaid.

"We'll find a place for the night," James told her.

Valentine frowned. "Most of the houses are rented for the holidays. You will not find a place to stay in the village. There is more than enough room at my grandfather's house, and he would not be pleased with me if I let you return to Amiens."

"We can't do that..." Kris couldn't bear the thought that they might be bringing down something on Valentine and her grandfather. Especially after everything that had happened over the last several days.

"My grandfather would be very angry with me if I didn't bring you home with me. It is the way he is, yes? He is eighty-five years old, and I do not think he will change." A smile at that.

"I will help Monsieur Sevier close for the evening, then we will leave."

"Shouldn't you at least call your grandfather and tell him?"

Valentine shook her head. "I tried to call him earlier, but the line was out."

Monsieur Sevier made a sound as he came out of the kitchen.

"Ju-Ju again," he muttered. "He is worthless!"

Kris exchanged a look with James. Ju-Ju?

"He scares the crows from the orchards," Valentine replied, with an eye roll at what appeared to be a long-standing discussion.

"You will see," she told them. She shook her head. "And the cell coverage is poor. It does not matter. My grandfather hates cell phones." She grabbed her apron.

"I will only be a few minutes. My car is in the back. I will meet you there and you can follow me." She disappeared into the kitchen, Monsieur Sevier making several comments in French.

He was obviously acquainted with Ju-Ju, and didn't hesitate to offer an opinion from the animated conversation Kris was able to pick up. Valentine appeared briefly in the doorway of the kitchen as she helped close for the evening and made a hand gesture, no translation needed.

"Ju-Ju seems to have quite a reputation."

James nodded. Ju-Ju, whoever or whatever he was, wasn't the concern.

No bloody cell phone coverage at the farmhouse. They would be cut off. He didn't like it. She would call it paranoia, but that sixth sense had saved the lives of him and his teammates more than once.

But not that last time.

Nothing he could have done, the unit commander told him when he was debriefed, repeated by the 'head' doctor in Germany and again in London. There was no way he could have known the number of insurgents waiting for them or that they'd been given bad intel in the first place—until it was too late.

Too late. And his team had paid the price, four men dead. He glanced down at the tattoo of the sword on the inside of his wrist—a bond shared, and a promise he hadn't been able to keep. He pushed back the chair.

"I want to make a call before we leave."

He left the café and headed for the rental car. The street that ran through the village was empty, except for the rental. It did little to ease that tightness at the back of his neck, as if someone had taken hold of him, that persistent warning that had followed from London.

He hit the remote, the light coming on inside the rental. He slid inside as icy rain pelted down.

The truth was, he hoped they wouldn't find any of the Marchand or Robillard family still alive after all these years. With no other contacts, no other calls that Cate had made to follow up, that would have been the end of it and she would have had no choice but go back to New York.

He lit a cigarette and turned on the phone, the nicotine burning through the uneasiness and that nagging feeling.

The screen lit up.

Good old Danny, he thought, as the text message came through.

"Adnan Faridani, bit time money, import export business, educated in London; rumor he's been radicalized and connected to bombings in London, Berlin, Paris. BTW Faridani is his mother's family; real name Malik. Slippery, dangerous, has connections. If you have more info???"

He had information, all right, from Captain Jack, not exactly what you would call a reliable source. Still, he'd learned to use whatever source he could find when he was in-country.

Malik. The name brought up the image from the video footage. There were common names. In-country, it seemed every other man or boy was named Hasan. Bogus, part of the disguise. That was obvious. And it kept alive the ones who helped them with information if he or his men were caught and interrogated. But the name Malik wasn't nearly as common.

Was there a connection to the artist? Then the next thought, was Jonathan Callish involved?

Ancient artifacts? Smuggling? Twenty million dollars' worth? Especially if his gallery wasn't doing well?

It was no secret, terrorist groups needed financing for weapons. Over the past several years, the goal had been to cut off the funding for these groups—sever the head of the snake. But as soon as one group had their funding cut off, they found another source—oil, legitimate business enterprises, a web of money sources, and from the beginning, ancient artifacts had disappeared from the Middle East, only to be rumored to have been 'acquired' through a private source.

Was it possible Malik, or Faridani, or whatever the hell he was calling himself, might be that source?

Then, the next question: What might a seven-hundred-year-old tapestry be worth to a private collector with almost unlimited resources, depending on its condition?

Millions? Tens of millions? Possibly more?

It was risky to stay on the phone, but he needed more information. The call was picked up on the third time around.

"Jesus!" Innis said over the background noise. "Where are you?'

"No questions," James told him, then explained what he needed.

"I don't know," Innis replied. "It's like a war zone after what happened yesterday, military on the streets, raids in a couple of the districts, everything shut down. This will take some time."

"No," James fired back at him. "We don't have time. I need you to find Adnan Faridani, possibly under the name Malik. I need to know where he is, and I need it now. Get back to me when you have something." He shut the phone down and started the rental car.

CHAPTER
FORTY

M ist curled over the roadway, swirling over the hood of the car, then rolling back as the road slipped around the next bend. Then, several kilometers past the village of Montigny, the tail lights of Valentine's car, an ancient Volvo, angled sharply then disappeared down a dirt track. He made the turn-off, then stopped the car just off the roadway. A light snow had started to fall, the flakes landing on the windscreen.

He stared through the darkness down the dirt driveway where the Volvo had disappeared. He said nothing at first, that same silence since leaving the village.

"I put a call into Danny," he finally said, still staring down the driveway that cut back through the orchard of the Marchand property.

"I had him check with some people he's worked with." Fingers drummed the steering wheel. He still didn't look at her.

"The man at the gallery in Paris goes by the name of Faridani."

The name meant nothing to her.

"The Paris gallery is a front," he continued. "Faridani funnels money from the sale of stolen artifacts to a terrorist group that has claimed responsibility for several attacks and bombings throughout Europe, and the UK.

"He came on the art scene two years ago," he went on to explain. "He popped up occasionally prior to that—at university in London, well-educated, but always on the fringe of things, rumored to have been seen with some of the bad characters over the last few years. He turned up again as an authority on Middle Eastern art, acquiring pieces for private parties."

There was more, she could tell by the expression on his face in the glow from the instrument panel, the way he stared down that dirt track. He was someone else now, someone she'd only glimpsed the past few days. He didn't put the car in gear, but instead kept staring down the road that cut through the Robillard orchards.

"Faridani is the name he goes by. His real name is Hasan Malik."

Malik. The same name as Jonathan Callish's wife!

Her thoughts reeled.

Did Callish know? He had to. Was he somehow involved? She took that next step.

It made sense. Cate had worked with Callish on the collection of her father's photographs for the gallery showing. It was possible he already knew about the photograph of the tapestry when they went to see him that day in London. That meant that his wife probably also knew about it.

Had he or someone else—his wife?—then followed to the Blue Anchor? And after that?

She felt almost physically sick at the possibility that Jonathan Callish was involved in this, that he might have had something to do with Cate's death.

He saw the expression on her face, the disbelief, then the struggle against other emotions. Betrayal was a bitter pill.

He put the car in gear and eased down the dirt track that angled back alongside the orchard, the lights of the farmhouse gleaming in the distance.

The Robillard farmhouse was typical of old farmhouses in the French countryside, with white plaster walls, low-hanging eaves, and the half-door that had once been painted red but had faded over the years to a pale salmon color, and like the café in Montigny, looked as if it had stood for centuries, except for Valentine's car parked in the side yard, and an old tractor that sat between rows of barren trees in the glare of lights from the rental car.

A black-and-white dog shot out the door and ran straight at them. Valentine immediately called him back—the notorious Ju-Ju. He stopped, looked back, then ignored her and did the typical dog thing and anointed a tire on the rental car, then shot back for the house.

"My grandfather's dog," Valentine said, meeting them at the door. "He is good at chasing the crows from the orchards."

"We met," Kris replied as Ju-Ju sat on the floor, tail thumping.

A large country table sat in the middle of the kitchen, with four chairs that had once been painted blue but were now faded. Shelves lined the wall on either side of the window above the porcelain sink. Blue-and-white plates and an odd assortment of bowls and cups lined the shelves. The slate stones on the floor were worn smooth.

This, Kris thought, was where a young girl who became known as Jehanne had lived as a child. This was where two brothers had lived and gone off with their father to fight the war and never returned. And it was where young Albert Marchand had returned after the war almost eighty years ago, and married Micheleine's younger sister.

Time. It was etched into the surface of the table, on the chipped bowl with the apples in the middle, and the worn stones of the floor.

"My grandfather is in the other room. It's warmer in there." Valentine led them into the adjacent room.

Albert Marchand, twelve years old at the end of the war, was now an old man. He sat in the chair before the fire, dressed in a heavy sweater and work pants, wisps of white hair molding his head. Heavily veined hands lay over a book he'd been reading. They were the hands of someone who had worked hard all of his life, and now sat before a warm fire in the woodstove.

What did he know? Kris thought. What would he remember?

"I have brought friends," Valentine announced, crossing the room, and laying a hand on his shoulder.

The eyes that looked over at them were old eyes, eyes that had seen too much in eighty-five years, but still sharp, curious.

"Eh? Friends?" he asked.

Conversation in French followed, most which Kris couldn't follow. She heard both their names as introductions were made, then Cate's name was mentioned, and that sharp blue gaze fastened on her.

"Come closer so that I may see you." Valentine translated for them, then told him something in French. She exchanged a look with Kris and nodded.

Kris sat in the chair on the other side of the small table between them. Ju-Ju lay at his feet. Those sharp eyes watched her with keen interest.

"My granddaughter tells me that you have asked about Micheleine," Valentine again translated for him.

"That was all a very long time ago." He made a dismissive gesture. "Why do you want to know about her?"

"A friend of mine sent me this." She showed him the black-and-white photograph of the tapestry that Cate had scanned to her as Valentine continued to translate, and explained the reason they were there. He glanced at the photograph.

"There have been others," he replied with an indifferent shrug. "They came wanting to know about her, then left. They want to know for their stories in the magazines and on the internet, on the anniversaries of the war." He made another gesture and she saw the amused expression on James' face.

"Then, they leave. They do not care about what happened, they do not understand."

He sat back in the over-stuffed chair.

"I don't like talking about the war." He snapped his mouth shut. "We need more wood for the fire."

Kris exchanged a look with Valentine as he pushed out of the chair, stepped over Ju-Ju with surprising agility for someone of his age, then made his way to the woodstove.

James picked up several pieces of wood, neatly stacked in the basket beside the woodstove, and handed them to him. A heavily veined hand locked around his wrist.

Albert Marchand stared down at the tattoo of the sword with the number of James' unit at his wrist.

"Military," Albert said in surprisingly perfect English, and Kris exchanged another look with Valentine. Apparently he could speak it when he chose to. That sharp blue gaze was fastened on James.

"I think perhaps you have seen war," Albert said, with a knowing look.

James nodded. "Some."

"And death?"

James nodded and Albert patted his wrist, his expression shifting again. He put several pieces of wood on the fire, then latched the door. He returned to his chair.

"Different times, different wars," he said, easing back into the chair. "And now again, different enemies. We understand these things, you and I."

"Aye," James replied.

Albert turned that blue gaze on her.

"What do you want to know about Micheleine?"

And so it began, an unexpected connection between two men, one old, one young, who had both seen too much, experienced too much, and carried the scars.

Over the next two hours, she told him everything, beginning with the photograph Cate had sent, that last text message, and everything that had happened since.

"You believe she spoke of the tapestry." Albert gestured to the copy of that photograph. "And you have come here to learn what I know."

Kris nodded. "We need your help. I need to know why my friend died."

He nodded, then looked over at Valentine.

"We must have coffee for our guests."

"Behave yourself," she told him with mock seriousness. She leaned past him and took the old shotgun propped against the chair beside him. She set it against the wall beside the hearth.

"He says it is to chase the crows from the orchards." She explained. "I'm afraid he will shoot himself."

"If I chose to do that, it would already be done," Albert grumbled, but his eyes twinkled at what was obviously a frequent argument between them. Valentine kissed him on the forehead then went to the kitchen.

"She is bossy, but she has a good heart," he told them. "She works very hard and she takes good care of me. This will be hers one day. She is the only one of our family left."

He gestured across the room to the long table that sat against the wall beside the woodstove.

"There are pictures, before the war; Micheleine, her mother and father, brothers and sister, and my Angeline."

Kris picked up the framed black-and-white photograph of the young family that had obviously been taken before the war. Both parents were seated, with a boy standing at either side—Micheleine's brothers who had died in the war—a toddler on her mother's lap, obviously Angeline, and a young girl seated on the floor in front, the hem of her dress tucked under her knees. There was no mistaking the young Micheleine.

The dark hair was the same, the eyes, her features, strength in the stubborn set of her chin—strength enough to protect her family when her father and brothers had gone off to join the Resistance, strength when they were killed and she took their place fighting the Germans, possibly hiding a priceless work of art from them.

The coffee was dark and strong as Albert told them about the young woman who became known as Jehanne, and the last time he had seen her when she returned to the farm in those last days of the war.

"She had been wounded. I tried to convince her to stay, there was hope that the war was almost over. But she could be very stubborn." He paused, passed a hand over his mouth at the memory, then went on.

"She was afraid her presence would endanger others. The Germans were still everywhere, moving ahead of the Allies. Danger-ous, no one was safe." He paused again, remembering, old anger in the expression on his face.

"No one," he repeated, his mouth working with other words that wouldn't come. He cleared his throat.

"She said there was still work to be done." He was thoughtful at the memory. "We all had work to do." He frowned, a slight tremor on the hand that wiped his eyes.

"I did not see her again. There were rumors of things that happened," he said in that sad voice, as Valentine brought more coffee.

"Her mother cried and cried afterward. First her sons, then her husband. All gone." He looked over at James.

"You know what it is to lose those you love, family, friends," he said.

"I know," James replied.

Albert nodded, in that unspoken way she had seen more than

once with her brother Mark, that silent communication between those who have been in dark places where no words are necessary.

"Did Micheleine ever mention anything to you about the tapestry in this photograph? It was called the Raveneau Tapestry."

He stared at the printout. He shrugged and shook his head. "I would remember if she said anything about it."

Then she handed him the copy Sophie Martin had made of the letter Micheleine wrote and hid in that cellar.

"This letter was found after the war. It was written to her mother."

He studied the copy of the letter, the perfect neat letters and those unusual marks that had been made at the edge of the paper. The lettering and those marks had faded over time. The copy was barely legible.

"It was found in a cellar at a house outside Amiens after the war," Kris explained. "It mentions a hospital, but we were told there was no hospital here during the war."

Albert stared down at the printed copy of that last letter Micheleine had written. Over seventy years ago.

What did he see? What did he remember?

His hand trembled slightly as he rubbed it across his forehead as if he could physically pull the memories out of his thoughts. He slowly shook his head.

Kris tried to hide her disappointment.

"I am sorry," Valentine apologized. "I know this was important to you...because of your friend."

"Souviens..." Albert said in French, something he hadn't thought about in a very long time, since he was a boy, before the war.

"Je me souviens."

"Qu'est-ce que c'est?" Valentine asked him.

"Le carrierre," Albert replied.

Valentine looked over at them.

"The quarry."

CHAPTER
FORTY-ONE

was very young, before the war," Albert explained. "Micheleine's brothers, they were older. They didn't want me with them, a nuisance they said." A smile at the memory in spite of the late hour of the night.

"But I followed them anyway." Ju-Ju lay curled at his feet as he continued to reminisce.

"No one was supposed to go near the quarry—too dangerous they said." He winked at them.

"I threatened to tell their father if they didn't take me with them."

A boy on an adventure, like most boys, before the war, Kris thought. Over seventy years ago.

Vilette, Micheleine, and Albert Marchand, their lives divided into two time frames—before the war and after. An event that had changed the lives of so many, and ended so many others.

As he described that day long ago, two teenagers and a young tagalong on an adventure, Kris thought of pictures she had seen of quarries around the world in online articles about changing ecosystems, natural resources that had either played out or were shut down because of environmental hazards. Places that were huge open wounds carved out of the earth, enormous earth movers scraping away layer after layer, leaving scars on the landscape, with photographs of mine workers from places like South Africa, in search of diamonds or other precious metals, squinting as they emerged from dark holes in the ground.

"It was closed for many years," Albert continued. "Since before the first war, too dangerous to go there, the old ones who once worked there said—explosives left behind, cave-ins, tunnels where one could get lost. But we were determined to go, perhaps because it was forbidden." That boyish smile appeared.

She could imagine the young boy he had once been, as the memory took hold and he told them about the long ride in the farm wagon, almost bounced off more than once on the dusty road on that long-ago summer day. When they could drive no farther, the road blocked by enormous boulders that had been rolled into place to block others from continuing on, they had all piled out of the wagon and continued on foot, down through the heavily wooded forest that eventually opened at the edge of the limestone quarry.

"It was like a building carved out of the stone. There were windows, some of them broken, and steel doors that rolled back," he continued.

"Etienne and Edouard finally pushed one door open, and we went inside. A tree had grown from the floor through the ceiling over the years," Albert continued.

"Dirt and debris covered everything. "We walked down a long tunnel. It was dark, but they had brought lanterns. There were marks carved into the walls. I tried to remember them so that we could find our way back."

Clever boy, Kris thought. And years later, clever enough to elude the Germans during the war.

"The tunnel went in many directions. Etienne decided that we should each go a different way to see what we could find then meet back at the entrance. I went with Edouard. We followed a rail track into another part of the quarry.

"There were several rooms cut into the stone walls, one with a table, another larger one with cots lined up along a wall, more cots in another room, rolls of old cloth, utensils, and a long wood table.

"It was said that the English had taken their wounded there during the first war. We found marks on the walls, days marked off, carvings, and crosses."

A place where the English had taken their wounded during World

War I, the tunnels and walls of the quarry mine, refuge in the midst of slaughter and dying. Cots lined up against a wall, tables, rolls of cloth. A hospital?

Was that what Micheleine had meant in that letter?

She looked at the copy of the letter, then handed it to Albert.

"Did you see anything that looked like these marks?"

"I remember a carving of a woman with a scarf tied around her head, and she wore an apron. I remember thinking she was so beautiful in such an ugly place."

A carving of a woman wearing an apron.

If the quarry had been used a as a hospital, with wounded soldiers on those cots, was it possible what he had seen was a carving of a nurse made all those years ago by some young soldier recovering from his wounds?

"There was talk many years ago about reopening the quarry," he continued. "But nothing came of it."

A forgotten place from another century. Forgotten, and possibly the perfect place to hide something that someone didn't want found.

But places like that didn't just disappear, Kris thought. Over the years, using modern technology, satellite images from outer space, infrared equipment, numerous old temples and artifacts hidden or buried, had been discovered that decades earlier would have been impossible.

"Do you think you could find the entrance again?"

She avoided the look James gave her but she could feel it, and the anger that this was to be the end of it, that it had gotten too dangerous to continue. Four people were dead, and with the information Danny had provided, that danger might be close, too close. And what about Valentine and her grandfather?

"I could take you there," Valentine spoke up.

Her grandfather frowned at her, and said something that could only be disapproval.

"You are not the only one who has been there," she told him.

"It was the last summer before I went to university. Several of us decided to go there. It was grown over, but it wasn't caved in. We had no flashlights and decided against going inside." Again there was that shrug, typical of her grandfather.

"So I never said anything to you about it," she explained to Albert. She looked over at Kris. There was excitement in her voice.

"We could go tomorrow. Perhaps you will find one of those marks," she gestured to the letter that Micheleine had hidden decades earlier.

"Then you will know if that is the place she wrote about."

"No," Albert said quietly. "It is too dangerous."

Valentine knelt in front of her grandfather's chair. "How many times have I listened to you say that no one today wants to know what happened then, no one understands, and soon no one will remember." She took his hand in hers.

"If we can find one of those marks, if the tapestry is there, it would be a way of remembering what happened, the sacrifice that was made to keep it safe."

"And if there is nothing?" he asked her.

"Then there is nothing," she replied. "But we have to try, we have to hope."

Kris saw the way his expression changed on that one word. Hope.

"Stubborn," he told his granddaughter. "You use my words against me."

"Like someone I know very well," she told him.

Albert looked over at James.

"You will go with them." When James would have objected, Albert shook his head.

"You must go, you must keep them safe."

"You don't understand."

"I understand very well, my young friend." It was there in the expression on his face, in his eyes. The same expression when he had seen the tattoo of the sword and recognized a kindred spirit.

Kris saw the anger, the conflict, his eyes dark when James finally looked at her. Nothing was said. It wasn't necessary.

"It was my grandmother's room when she was a little girl," Valentine said as she retrieved wool blankets from the chest that sat against the wall and laid them on the bed.

And Micheleine's, Kris thought.

The metal frame bed sat against the end wall in the second-floor room, tucked under the eaves of the farmhouse. A tall, old-fashioned dresser with hand-painted flowers that sat against the wall beside the door, like the table and chairs in the kitchen, had faded over time. A straight-backed chair and small writing desk sat under the window. A half dozen wooden pegs lined the wall adjacent to the door, a woolen neck scarf thrown over the one at the far end. Wood frame windows covered with chintz curtains were closed against the storm, icy rain pelting the glass.

This was where a young girl had spent her childhood and watched the signs of war that eventually took her father and both her brothers. And then her.

She imagined generations of children over two hundred years earlier who lay on cots or blankets beneath those same eaves, whispering in the dark when they should have been sleeping, planning their next adventure. Then another generation, listening for other sounds, of an automobile on that dirt road, voices in an unfamiliar language, boot steps on the wood floors below.

Micheleine Robillard had returned that last time, Albert told them, wounded but alive, hiding from enemy patrols after the Allied invasion. They had spoken in that very same kitchen and he had shared a piece of bread with her, all he had for a meal. She had asked about friends, neighbors, people from the village, then about her mother and sister.

"Tell them I am well, and give them my love," she said as they parted that last time.

"And you will come back when this is over," young Albert had replied. Then they parted, and he took the secret of that last meeting with him.

It had been cold, snowing hard, he said, the weather much the same as now. And it had grown dark. He learned later that she had she stayed the night, waiting for morning, and the weather to clear.

Had she slept one last time in that same bed that she had once shared with her sister? What were her thoughts? What were her dreams? Were they filled with things that haunted her, things she'd seen and done? Or was there someone special who filled those dreams? Did she sense that she would never see her mother and sister again?

"There are times, when I am up here, it's almost as if..." Valentine softly smiled.

"You will think it is foolish." She hesitated again. "But there are times it's as if she is still here. That if I turned around suddenly, I would see her standing there. Foolish, yes?"

Not foolish, Kris thought. It was part of who Valentine was.

"There are extra blankets in the chest," the girl said as she plugged in the oil heater on the wall.

"It gets cold up here during the winter."

"I didn't mean to take your room," Kris replied, when it suddenly occurred to her that was probably what she had done.

Valentine shook her head. "My room is downstairs at the back of the house, if my grandfather should need me in the middle of the night. He sleeps in his chair most nights, but usually not more than a couple of hours at a time. He is restless, and has dreams. But tonight, your friend will keep him company."

Ghosts of the past, something else James Morgan had in common with Albert Marchand. He hadn't spoken when she left with Valentine, but had instead retrieved the chess board Albert had pointed to on that long table.

"Do you play?" the wily old man had asked. "We will see," he added with a smile as James set the board on the table between them.

"There is more room here," Valentine pointed out. That smile again. "Private for you and your friend."

Kris almost laughed. She doubted James considered her a friend at the moment. And when they left the room downstairs there wasn't even a glance away from that board and the game, another glimpse of James Morgan.

Where, she thought, had a young man who grew up with no father, then went off to war and saw too much, lost too much, learned to play chess? In some remote corner of the world with friends who were gone? Their memory in a tattoo on his wrist?

"The bathroom is downstairs," Valentine went on to explain, pulling her back from her thoughts.

"You have to turn the heat on the boiler for the shower. It is electric but takes a little while to warm up. There are towels on the shelf." She hesitated at the door, a thoughtful expression at her face.

"Thank you," Valentine said, surprising her.

"We should be thanking you," Kris replied. "It isn't everyday two strangers show up on your doorstep with a story most people wouldn't believe."

Valentine shook her head. "You don't understand." She was thoughtful again, trying to find the words to explain.

"There are times when I see a look on my grandfather's face as if he has gone far away. It is a sadness for things I cannot understand. But tonight, these past hours, I have seen a change in him. It is because you are here, and James Morgan who has seen some of the same things and understands what my grandfather has carried with him all these years." She took a deep breath.

"He is the only family I have left. It is the reason I came back. I know that he will be gone one day. So, I say thank you. Please understand that meeting you both has meant a great deal to both of us. Even if the tapestry is not there."

Things that mattered, Kris thought when she had gone, and she pulled the blankets over herself.

CHAPTER
FORTY-TWO
DECEMBER 24, 1944

Micheleine knew every turn in the path, the place where the three large rocks sat at the edge of the stream, the water slowing as it pushed past, then gathered speed as it tumbled over the spillway that had been built centuries earlier, falling into the pool below.

Even beneath the mantle of snow that blanketed everything, she knew it.

She had grown up here, chasing imaginary creatures through the forest that stood at the edge of the orchard, like giants gathering at the edge of the apple and pear trees in their neat, perfect rows.

Now, in the gray shadows from the moon, they were like skeletons, their limbs stripped bare of the last of summer leaves, the crop of apples and pears withered on the ground with no one to gather them. Food for the crows, a bitter thought. There had been no one to harvest the apples.

She glanced toward the farmhouse that had stood there since her mother's grandfather's time, and before—stone walls, the slate roof. It was almost Christmas. The house had stood through two hundred Christmases—her grandparents, their grandparents before them, and theirs before them.

It would stand a hundred more years, her father had said, proud of the farm with its abundant crops, good water, far from the city, a place he had earned through his marriage to her mother and years of hard work, often coming in from the orchards, his strong hands covered with dirt, knuckles cracked and bleeding from the cold.

He and her brothers always washed in the outside basin her mother insisted they wash in—a towel hung on a hook waiting for them at the end of the day, lights from the lanterns gleaming in misty welcome in the windows, smoke curling from the pipe on the cook stove.

"Where is your coat, ma petite?" her mother scolded, suddenly reminding her that she'd left it over a low-hanging branch before scaling the ancient oak at the edge of the orchard. A stern look, then a soft smile.

"You must find it in the morning. Come, wash. Supper is ready." The damp fall air, ripe with the smell of roast meat, potatoes, and apples simmering in butter and sugar, her mouth watering with childhood innocence that only asks, "Is there more?"

Gone now. All of it was gone.

No lights burned in the windows, no fire in the cook stove. No welcoming smells greeted her in the shadows at the edge of the house.

It was almost Christmas. She'd forgotten that, forgotten it each of the past four years. Once there were the smells of Christmas from the kitchen—a bird roasting in the oven, the pastries from earlier in the afternoon laid out on the sideboard, the roast potatoes and squash. And apples simmering in the iron skillet on the cook top, the smell of cinnamon and brown sugar pungent in the air.

After supper her mother would pour melted butter over the apples and her father would be the first to taste them. The suspense would build as he savored the first taste, like a winemaker testing that first sip of wine. Then he would look over at her mother.

"Superb. Magnifique!" he would declare and they would all taste their own simmered apples covered with buttery sugar sauce.

They all knew it was their father's prized apples that allowed them such a feast, but he always gave the credit to her mother.

Afterward, her father would retire to his chair before the fire in the small adjacent living room and take out the Christmas book. Even though they had all heard the story since they were babies, they all gathered round—her brothers Emile and Henri, who were fifteen and sixteen that last Christmas, her younger sister who was a toddler, and herself, after helping Mama wash and put away the blue dishes.

They listened, her sister dozing off in her mother's lap, her brothers eager to be off with their friends on the neighboring farm, her father's deep voice wrapping around the words, the fire glowing in the hearth. Then he would read from the Bible with all their names entered in the first pages, right after the date her parents had married.

She squeezed her eyes shut. Those memories, the smells, the sounds, the voices of those who were now gone moved over her in the frosty air like a warm, comforting shawl wrapped around her shoulder.

She slowly opened her eyes, the memories, sounds of laughter, her brother's teasing, their mother's reminder that they must go to bed if they wanted the Christmas spirit to visit their farmhouse. Otherwise he would pass them by. But there were only the shadows and an ominous darkness that stared back at her from the windows of the farmhouse. No candles glowed, waiting. No voices were heard over the rustling of the wind through the barren branches of the trees.

Maman? Angeline? Fear sharpened. Where were they? Had something happened? Had the Germans come in that final sweep toward the north?

Only an eerie silence whispered back at her on the wind, sighing around the corners of the old house, scattering leaves against the stone walls. Not this too!

Beside the kitchen door, the wash basin stood on the shelf, as it had every day of her memory, empty now, waiting for hands that would not return home. Her hand shook on the metal latch. The kitchen door opened easily, leaves swirling across the threshold before her.

Familiar shadows loomed out of the darkness—the hulking cast-iron cook stove, the sharp angles of the kitchen table, six chairs neatly tucked at the edges, the gleam from a copper pot on top of the stove as if it waited for her mother's hand. Then, a sound behind her.

She spun around, the pistol that she'd taken off a dead German soldier in her hand, her hip bumping the edge of the table, staring at the figure in the doorway.

"Belle," she exclaimed with relief at the gray-and-white tabby cat that sat in the opened doorway, named for the elegant and beautiful

French actress her mother had seen once at the cinema on a day trip to the city before the war. It had always seemed a mistake, with little resemblance between the actress Annabelle Gadot and the cat named for her, with long hair sticking out all over as if she had been caught in a storm.

She laid the pistol on the table and scooped Madame La Belle into her arms.

"You are not starving," she said into the soft fur over the stout body. But where were her mother and sister?

Belle provided no answers, only the loud rumble of purring, kneading her claws into the shoulder of her wool coat.

"Where have they gone, ma petite," she rubbed her cheek against the soft fur, using the name her mother had called her as a child, taking some small comfort in the warm body that burrowed against her in greeting, in spite of the unsettling feeling in her stomach that something was wrong, very wrong. If the Germans had been there, surely they wouldn't have left everything just so—clean pots, the chairs tucked at the table.

A movement in the window caught her eye. She set Belle down and retrieved the pistol. In the shadows of the kitchen she held her breath and waited, hands wrapped around the butt of the pistol. A slender hand wrapped around the edge of the door, then pushed it farther open.

"J-J-J-Jehanne!?"

A familiar voice, the familiar stutter. Heart pounding, she lowered the pistol.

"You should not go sneaking about, Albert. It is dangerous," she scolded. "You never know who you will run into."

"I knew it was you. I followed you from the edge of the orchard."

Albert Marchand, with more courage than sense. Clever lad, she hadn't known he was there.

"What are you doing here?"

It was no place for a boy, so far from the safety of his father's farm, with the rumor of enemy patrols throughout the countryside.

His voice hardened. "Keeping watch for Germans. We have heard they were spotted not far from here."

The Allied landing weeks ago, her people guiding them through occupied France. Soon, she prayed, wincing slightly.

Soon they would take Paris and push the enemy back into Germany. She had delivered the last dispatch three days ago. The timetable was set, even now as the German army swept across northern France, burning everything in their path. Towns, cities, rail depots bombed. It was winter, and their only objective as they retreated was to inflict as much pain as possible, starving an already starving people, murdering prisoners, their bodies discovered in forest clearings or merely dumped along the roadways.

How many of her people? Fifty, a hundred, more? Her people.

They had fought in the shadows these past years, living off the land or food others risked their lives to give them, setting up a network of safe houses, striking by day, disappearing by night, leaving families far behind—of those who were not herded out into the streets and executed, an example to those who helped anyone against the Third Reich.

There would be those who said it never happened. Time would erase the truth of what happened, except for the few who wrote about, and those who took pictures; photographs too horrible to look at, too horrible to ignore.

She thought of Paul Bennett, older in years, no longer young in what he had seen, and for just those few moments she held the memory close against the dark shadows of the night.

"Where have they gone?" she asked Albert, afraid of the answer yet needed to know.

"Grandmere, your mother, Angeline, they have gone to Ondine's house in the village. They are safe."

La Maison d'Ondine!

Father in heaven, she thought, the old house used to be a brothel and a way-station on the old road from Amiens to the coast.

She smiled in spite of the pain. He was right. No one would find them, no one would think to look there, or know of the old escape tunnel beneath the house.

She heard the way his voice softened around her younger sister's name. They had played together and gone to the local school together before the war. Angeline had always looked up to Albert in spite of his stuttering and the way his ears stuck out.

His hair had grown long now for lack of a decent cut, and the stutter eventually disappeared unless with a stranger. Lost youth, like so many other things.

A handsome young man, but old too soon. He was a true son. Like that other one, Albert was no longer a child but a young man who had seen too much, yet he was brave with a true heart, like another son centuries earlier, the story about the tapestry and a young man who had given up his life for others, and protected a secret.

"And you," she said. "You will be careful."

"They will not c-c-c-catch me," he replied, the words tripping over themselves. "I am too fast."

So young, she thought again. And yet Albert was only a handful of years younger than herself. A handful, yet she was decades older in experience. She could hardly remember when she was twelve years old. She laid the pistol within easy reach.

"You are hurt!" Albert exclaimed, eyes widening at the dark stain beneath her other hand as she leaned against the table. He laid the rifle down and reached for a lantern.

"No!" she told him. "No light. Someone might see."

He stood over her. "What can I do?"

"Water from the pump and a towel if you can find one."

"It's too dark, I can't see anything."

She retrieved a flashlight from inside the coat and pushed it across the table. "Close the shutters and keep the beam low."

He went about the kitchen, closing the shutters over the windows at the sink that had once looked out on her mother's garden. There was the sound of water from the pump, and he returned to the table. Then silently watched in the beam of that light as she opened the front of the coat and pressed the towel against the wound.

"How b-b-b-bad...?" he whispered.

"Not so very bad," she lied.

It could have been worse—the bullet had passed through, a narrow escape, but there had been much blood. They had separated then, she and the others. If one was caught, the others might get away and join with their fellow partisans in one of the safe places.

They had encountered a patrol, left behind as the German division moved to the north ahead of the Allied army. They had come upon the patrol, outnumbered, but they had the advantage of knowing the countryside. They had left the bodies for the crows, just as the

Germans had left so many of her own people. Then, splitting up, the decision to come home had been a simple one. It was close by, and the one they called Jehanne would be far away, moving with the Allies, if they believed the rumors.

She had been on the move for three days after sending the others off, refusing to slow them down. She couldn't remember when she last slept.

"What will you do?" Albert asked, his breath creating a faint cloud in the wintry cold of the darkened kitchen.

"I will find others and join them. There is still work to do." she replied, glancing across the kitchen table at the boy who was no longer a boy. The war had done that to all of them—a whole generation.

"We have heard the Allies are very near Paris," he whispered through the darkness. "It will be over soon." Then, his voice wistful, "It is almost Christmas."

Christmas. How many had come and gone since she was last there?

There was a time she had thought it would never be over, that it would all go on—the shortages of food, then no food; the gaunt faces of the people in the countryside; the ever-present enemy tanks, a reminder that they were not their own people any longer but part of the Reich; and the arrests, the bodies of those who were made an example, then those who simply disappeared, their bodies discovered later in a forest clearing, riddled with bullets, left for the crows.

"I must go." She moved stiffly, the towel tucked into the waist of the too-large pants. She'd stayed too long—she needed to be on the move.

"Come to the village," Albert replied. "You will be safe there."

She wanted to. She wanted to see her mother and sister, to sleep without thinking she might waken with a gun at her head, but she was not so naive to not know what would happen if she was caught.

The Germans had a price on her head. They would execute her on site along with everyone else found with her. It was the stark reality of the reputation she had earned, and she wouldn't have changed any of it. She shook her head.

"I will stay the night here," she decided. She had not seen anyone else nearby.

It was cold. There would be no fire, but at least she would have a roof over her head that night, and she would be gone before the sun rose.

"You will tell them that I am well? And give them my love?"

He nodded. "What about food? You must eat."

Did she look that pathetic, she thought, that even a twelve-year-old boy noticed?

No sleep, and no food these past days. It was how they all lived, on the run. He shoved an end-slice of bread into her hand.

"What about you?" she asked. It was a long walk to the village through thick forest and snow, and he'd obviously brought the crust of bread with him for a reason.

He shrugged a thin shoulder. "There are apples beneath the trees. One has only to dig beneath the snow. They are not so bad."

Her father's prized apples that had once supported their family, before the war.

She nodded and tucked the bread into her pocket. "You will be careful."

"And you, Jehanne," he said with a solemn expression. "You will come back when this is over."

She watched through the glass in the window as he made his way past the garden, then darted into the cover of trees at the edge of the orchard, keeping to the shadows.

Sneaky little devil, she thought with a weary smile, as he disappeared completely.

Oh, how she would have liked to go with him, but it was too dangerous. If she was caught with them...but she wouldn't put him or anyone else at risk.

The kitchen was as she remembered it: the chairs painted blue, the table where her mother had served meals, the porcelain sink where they had peeled apples for one of her mother's apple pies, the crust so flaky that it fell apart, her father complimenting her mother on another fine meal, her brothers arguing with one another.

Gone.

She pushed away from the kitchen counter. Her side ached, but at least the bleeding had stopped for now, and she was so very tired. Perhaps now that the Allies pushed toward Paris it would end soon.

She was tempted to sleep downstairs on the overstuffed sofa her father had purchased for her mother, before the war. It wasn't new, but her mother acted as if it was the most beautiful thing she had ever seen. There was also the old rocking chair where Grandmere used to sit before the fire when she was very old, before the war.

Everything, every happy memory, was before the war.

But in spite of the fact that it would have been wiser to remain downstairs where it would be easier to escape if necessary, she climbed the stairs to the upstairs bedroom under the eaves that she had shared with Angeline.

Here too was exactly as she remembered it, the narrow bed they had shared, the boys in their room across the way. Her parents had slept downstairs in the room her father had made behind the kitchen. More private for them, and she smiled at that memory, as if all of them were not aware of the nights he and their mother closed that door and made love.

As children she and Angeline had lain under the covers and listened to the sounds from the room below, then giggled at the silence. They lived on a farm, they had animals, they were not naive to what passed between a man and a woman; still the thought that Mama and Papa did those things made them laugh.

All these years later, she did not laugh at the thought, but smiled softly with her own memories, the ones she chose to remember, the young photographer who had been so gentle, even shy with her, then the passion they had found in one another for just one night.

Memories.

She held onto them, as she'd held onto them the past years, at times the only things that kept her going, kept her fighting, even after her father and brothers were gone.

There was no heat, and her breath clouded in the shadows of the room with only the light from the flashlight.

She took a book from the book case—Aventures d'Alice au pays des merveilles.

Her father had brought it back for them from a trip to Amiens, before the war. She loved the story, stepping into that make-believe world, like Alice through the looking glass. She glanced at the mirror over the dressing table. She had convinced Angeline that the magical world was just beyond the glass, she needed only to look for it.

But the evil queen had transformed, she thought, into another evil these past years. And like Alice, she was so very tired.

She didn't undress, too dangerous if a German patrol should find its way to the farm, but instead lay on top of the bed and pulled thick wool blankets over herself.

Dozens of memories swept back over her as she lay in the darkness, listening to the wind as it came up and rattled a branch against the window—her brothers whispering in the next room, plotting their next escape from work with their father the next day in the orchards; their mother's gentle scolding that the morning would come soon enough and they must be quiet and get to sleep; her sister burrowed against her like a squirrel, until she lay at the edge of the bed and shoved her back; their father's loud snoring that seemed to shake the walls of the old farmhouse, even from that room downstairs.

And dreamed of another room in another house, and the feel of a man's body as they came together.

She wakened hours later at first light.

Everything gradually came back—Albert, the news that Angeline and their mother were safe for now, the memories, the nightmare of the past four years. She sat up and winced at the pain in her side.

She found the hairbrush on top of the dresser, and slowly pulled it through her hair.

Whom did she see looking back at her now from the mirror? Was she Alice, once very tall, now very small? Where was the rabbit?

There were no answers, only the cold and the silence, reminders that it was dangerous to hold onto fairy tales when the real world waited just beyond the window.

It had been foolish to come there, she thought, with a sudden catch in her throat. Dangerous. But it was almost over, she was certain of that now after the past months following the Allied invasion. But she had needed to make sure her mother and sister were safe. And dear Albert.

She remembered him with his pile of straw for hair, ears that framed his head like squash from the garden, and the stutter when he spoke. The stutter was still there, but less than before. He had changed. Twelve years old now. She still thought of him as the boy she had known. He was no longer a boy.

It was there in the expression in his eyes, the gauntness of his cheeks, and eyes that had seen too much. She remembered the child who laughed so easily, words tripping over themselves. No more. There was no laughter on Albert Marchand's young face.

Mon dieu, they had all changed. The war had done that, and the Germans taking what they wanted, people imprisoned, shipped off to camps, and worse.

She could hardly remember what it was like before the war—no fighting, no more deaths—her father and brothers stomping through the house, her mother in the kitchen...to be able to sleep and not be afraid of waking.

Sights and sounds filled every corner of the old farmhouse, along with photographs of her grandparents, her parents when they were married, the sight of her father's hound stretched out on the rug in front of the woodstove.

"Quit daydreaming, Micheleine. Help your sister set the table."

She could hear her mother's gentle voice admonishing her—the sights and sounds of home, before the war, as she went downstairs.

She slowly crossed the kitchen, those memories strong as if only a moment ago. Only the pain was different. She pressed her hand against the bandage on her side that she'd made from one of her mother's towels cut from a flour sack.

The bleeding had stopped. The bullet had passed through. She shivered with the fever that had set in. Mama would scold her.

"Micheleine, how many times must your father tell you not to go to the quarry. It is too dangerous, and you've torn your dress. Now I will have to mend it again."

But she was no longer that girl. That girl had died a long time ago. Who was she now?

Jehanne, the name the partisans had given her? A simple farm girl who wanted only to go home?

But as she looked around the kitchen one last time with its scarred counter, porcelain metal sink, and the emptiness that looked back at her from every corner, she realized that what she remembered no longer existed. It was gone, just as Etienne and Edouard were gone, their father, and so many others.

A light snow had started to fall as she left the farmhouse. She hesitated just outside the door at the thought that she should lock it, then laughed to herself.

There was no lock, only the latch that her father always set in place. And the reality that no lock would stop the Germans if they chose to come there. They would kick down the door, then not finding whatever they were after, they would torch the house as they had burned so many in other towns and villages she had seen. But the tapestry was safe. They would not have that.

She pulled the field coat more tightly about her as she entered the orchard. She found half-frozen apples the crows had left behind beneath the layer of snow, and smiled faintly. Albert was right. They were not so bad once she brushed off the snow and dirt.

She looked back as she made her way deeper into the orchard, almost certain that she heard her mother calling her as she had when she was a child.

But it was only the sound of the crows.

CHAPTER
FORTY-THREE
PRESENT DAY, PARIS, THE MARAIS DISTRICT

The display lit up, the small icon pulsing across the darkened apartment.

Innis rolled over, his feet hitting the bare floor, swearing as cold air hit his bare ass.

"What is it?" Luna asked, sleep thick in her voice.

"Go back to sleep." He tucked the comforter around her, then grabbed his jeans and left the room, hopping barefoot from the floor to the frayed area rug, then over to the table with the computer screen.

Bloody Christ, it was cold.

He slid into the chair, goose bumps in the cold apartment playing across a vivid tattoo of Khal Drogo that glared back from Innis's chest as if he had sprung from his flesh.

Hugging Khal Drogo with arms wrapped around himself against the cold, he opened the message from the gamer in Turkey who had taken on the persona of 'Warlord,' and claimed to have sources into a large Islamic group.

Warlord was hard to pin down, more so than other gamers he communicated with, maybe because of that connection—gamer by night, local terrorist by night?

"No go," the message opened. "The one you asked about was last seen riding into the woods, two winters past."

'Riding into the woods'—gamer-speak for disappeared—two

winters past needed no explanation. The wanker hadn't been seen in two years. He could be anywhere.

Innis signed off, then attempted to access a rogue server he'd used in the past; a new player in cyberspace that was there one day, gone the next, like disappearing into a black hole.

He knew the logic—limited time at any one location, pass on information, contacts, or redirect funds from point A to point B, possibly to point C. Then disappear. No trace, as if it never existed. These blighters were sophisticated and experienced at hiding out—disappearing into the forest.

He swore when the access failed—not just denied, but came back with the message that it didn't exist. At least for now. Over the past twenty-four hours, most of them trolling around cyberspace, he'd come across the same thing, his screen lighting up with the contact, then cutting off.

A little cyber sleuthing, and he'd discovered a pattern, a sequence in the information string that changed, then changed again. But there was a pattern if you knew what to look for. And he did.

Whoever was driving this engine had programmed it to randomly connect to other rogue servers, then move on after a certain amount of time, signals bouncing from one to the other like ping-pong balls. But it was done almost seamlessly, so that anyone using the server probably didn't even notice the hand-off.

Hiding in the forest. Lions, tigers, and bears, oh my, he thought. Security at its best, or worst, depending on how you looked at it, and depending on who was using it. And what they were using it for. Brave new world.

He loved that book and had read it several times. He shook his head, talk about being ahead of your time, clued in to things that other people hadn't even thought of yet. Before he and his mates were even born!

He caught the alert from downstairs, the feed from the security camera appearing on the little screen in the lower corner. Anthony returned and entered the apartment, then the faint click of the door a few seconds later.

"You look like shit!"

"Va te faire!" Anthony replied, crushing out the stub of a cigarette, then throwing his jacket across the back of a chair.

Innis's French was limited, but the tone and the hand gesture that went with it, needed no translation.

"What have you got?" he asked.

Anthony scrubbed a hand back through his hair, then slipped into the chair beside him.

"I went to the club first. The captain has friends. He also has a financial planner who knows people in banking. They have connections all over." He made a sweeping gesture.

"He's pissed. Twenty million dollars gone, right under his nose. He was willing to help. After all, he is a businessman. He went to some of his friends." Anthony rubbed the fatigue from his face.

"The money didn't pass through the usual channels."

No bloody fucking kidding, Innis thought. He was the one who had found that out.

"Where did it go?"

"Crypto currency; a broker out of the Caymans, not exactly sophisticated, but all in small transactions with fake accounts, then passed into another offshore account under an individual name."

"Not the gallery?"

Anthony shook his head. "Under the name of Gold Star Holding."

"Gold Star." At least he had that to work with. He needed to find out who the players were.

"Anything else?" Innis asked.

"I went by the gallery. Gone."

"What do you mean gone?"

"Stripped bare, no displays, no framed paintings, no priceless piss urns, gone. Nothing left behind."

Not good, Innis thought.

Who walked away from a successful black-market operation? That was the question. The answer—no one, unless they were afraid of being caught. Or simply moved on, to set up in another location. Or?

He spent the next several hours checking all his sources, all the back channels, all those places that supposedly didn't exist.

He finally found it. A coincidence?

"Bloody fucking ironic."

"What is it?" Luna asked, leaning over his shoulder as she set a plate of food in front of him later that morning.

"Gold Star Holding."

"Gold Star?"

He sat back, thinking. Being a fairly good gamer, he'd acquired a good imagination. He particularly liked war games.

"The gold star is a symbol of the ultimate sacrifice of a family member. But it has other meanings."

"What other meanings?"

He scrolled through several images until he found what he was looking for."

"Oh," she said softly. Then, "It could be just a coincidence." He gave her a look.

"I don't believe in coincidences."

The morning newscast had come on, video shown in a small box that opened on the widescreen display. He hated news. It was never good.

When he went to block it out, Luna stopped him.

"Wait. Turn up the audio."

Bloody Christ! Innis thought. Luna's startled gaze met his, at the latest news update.

"Do you think they know?" she whispered.

He had no idea. Communication had been fucked at best. He had sent a text message earlier but had no idea if they had picked it up.

"I've got work to do," he replied.

He needed to find James Morgan.

CHAPTER
FORTY-FOUR

James stepped out of the farmhouse into the cold morning air, the sky just beginning to soften through the bare branches of the trees in the orchard.

Sleep was a cruel bitch, he thought. It teased, then disappeared, leaving him like so much garbage that had been tossed out.

He glanced up at the second story window of the farmhouse. Had she slept at all?

He had thought about going up to that room...Valentine had mentioned it in that way that assumed the obvious. He wanted to. No questions, no arguments, just the heat that had been there between them from the beginning.

A temporary thing? The heat of battle? Whatever you wanted to call it.

He wanted the feel of her skin against his, he wanted the sounds she made when they came together, he needed the way her breath caught when she came, the way she held on and then gave back.

Bloody fucking hell! He cursed as he went to the rental and punched in the remote code.

Too much coffee—Valentine had made the last post somewhere around three in the morning.

It was still there, the caffeine buzz that made him edgy as he scanned the dirt track, then the orchard beyond.

The door of the rental car was already iced over. He forced it open then slid inside. The icy interior was only marginally better as he took a chance and powered up the cell phone.

There was a brief connection, then the signal dropped. He swore again. If he had a laptop, he could have linked up to a military satellite using an old code and connected to Innis. They never did away with the old ones, just added new ones.

Would it have made a difference that last time, that last mission? He wondered. Up-to-date intel that might have told them about the trap they were walking into? Was it possible their position, all their movements had been hacked? He'd never know. No one would ever know. That's the way it worked, just another 'unfortunate situation,' and casualties of war.

No service.

Kris wakened—restless, the sounds of strange places as she lay in the darkness of that room, the hum of the oil heater, the storm, the rattle of a tree branch on the window. She finally gave up the possibility of any more sleep.

The wood floor was cold beneath her feet in spite of the heat the oil heater cranked out. She pulled on her jeans and sweatshirt, and went downstairs. Ju-Ju greeted her at the bottom of stairs, thrusting a wet nose into her hand. She scratched his neck, then went into the kitchen. She discovered that she wasn't the only one unable to sleep.

A fire burned in the woodstove in the main room, Albert in his chair. Valentine stood in front of the ancient cook stove. She looked up as Kris came into the kitchen.

"Fresh coffee is ready." She wrapped a potholder around the handle of the metal coffee pot and grabbed two mugs from the shelf.

"What about your grandfather?"

"I made a pot earlier. He has had enough. The doctor only allows him one cup a day—too much caffeine. Last night, oo-la-la, too much coffee," she whispered.

"They were up all night playing chess. I do not think my grandfather won so many games."

Games? More than one. That explained the empty bed this morning.

"He has gone to the village. The cell coverage is better there," Valentine explained.

More messages? Kris thought.

"He will be back soon."

Albert made a sound from the adjoining room. He'd obviously heard everything Valentine said.

"If I want coffee, I will drink coffee—strong, black, as I always have. What do the doctors know? I am eighty-five years old. I will die someday. They will die someday. Now, bring me more coffee!"

They exchanged looks. "Eighty-five years old, but sometimes I think he is no more than ten years old."

"Are you going to make me come into the kitchen?" he called out.

Valentine sighed. "You see what it is like." She took down another mug from the shelf.

"I'll take it to him," Kris volunteered.

"Set it there," Albert said without looking up. He made a gesture with a wave of his hand. His other hand rubbed his bearded chin as he concentrated on the board in front of him. He reached for a piece, the game obviously left unfinished.

Kris frowned as she studied the chessboard.

"That move will leave your pawn unprotected."

Albert slowly looked up at her.

"And a counter-move will open up your queen and you won't have any defense," she added.

He looked back down at the board, and frowned.

"Do you play?"

"Some. My brother taught me," she added, her voice softening at the memory.

"Then sit. We will play until James returns and see how well your brother taught you."

She set the mug down beside his and slipped into the chair across from his. At a glance, she picked up several moves that had been made earlier. James Morgan was a formidable opponent.

"Your friend is a good player," Albert commented, seeing the way she studied the board. "The last move was mine."

"They played most of the night," Valentine explained. "Neither of them slept!" The last was aimed at her grandfather.

"Bah!" he replied. "I can sleep when I am dead."

Valentine shook her head and threw up her hands. "Now you see what I must deal with," she said, in a way that suggested she wouldn't have it any other way.

Several comments in French flowed back and forth between her and her grandfather. Kris couldn't keep up. Instead she studied the moves James had made earlier before leaving for the village, then made a move of her own. It was a classic defensive move, but it also set up the next one.

"Qu'est-ce que c'est!" Albert exclaimed, his gaze suddenly drawn back to the board.

"What is this?" he demanded.

"Your move," Kris replied. Valentine smothered back a sound very much like laughter, then covered it with a cough.

"I think you have met your match," she told her grandfather.

"We will see," he replied. "We will see."

Albert Marchand might be eighty-five years old, but he was a sharp, cunning old fox. But almost two hours later and several moves, and she had almost had him.

She concentrated on the board. The move was clear, but she hesitated, then moved a different piece. He made his move and easily took her bishop. He eyed her across the board, taking a pull on his pipe.

"Your brother is a good teacher."

She pushed back from the table.

"Yes, he was."

She stretched against sitting the past two hours as she went into the kitchen and joined Valentine, who leaned against the edge of the porcelain sink.

"I saw that last move," Valentine commented. "You let him win."

Kris shrugged. "It's only a game."

"Not to him. He plays to win. There are times I think he considers me the enemy when we play. He does not like to lose."

Kris glanced back into the main room, at the old man with thinning white hair who sat hunched over the chess board, studying it as if he would find something there, a ring of tobacco smoke circling his head.

What did she see? An old man, time etched in the lines on his face, with a trace of the boy peeking out at her every once in a while, suddenly looked up, that expression in his eyes.

Did he guess that she'd thrown the match?

"What is this?" Valentine said, staring out the kitchen window.

Kris glanced over her shoulder, down the dirt track that led through the main orchard to the roadway.

A white service van had pulled onto the dirt track. It stopped, then slowly backed out. Ju-Ju shot across the yard toward the end of the track, barking furiously.

Valentine shrugged and turned away from the window. "It is probably turning around after discovering they are lost. Tourists, the weather," she shrugged again. "They probably missed the turn-off to the village."

Kris only had a glimpse before the van backed out, but it triggered a memory of the van that had plunged across the patio of the Blue Oyster in London, scattering tables, chairs, and bodies...the same white van, the same crumpled right front fender!

The roadway was icy, the rental car breaking loose as he took the turn too fast, eased off, turned into the slide then brought it back, and pressed the pedal down again.

His fist tightened over the steering wheel. Over two hours! But he had what he needed.

Faridani was gone, cleared out of Paris sometime over the past two days, right after the explosion, right after he and Kris had left the city. But where?

That was the question; a question that had several possible answers, or only one answer, an answer he didn't want.

He eased off the pedal as he approached the familiar roadway sign that advertised fresh apples in season. He slowed the rental car, then stopped just short of the dirt track. Tire tracks carved through snow that had fallen overnight, over the ones he had made earlier when he left the farmhouse. He got out and examined the tracks. The newer ones were wide and deeper, made by a vehicle heavier than the rental car, and cut down the length of the track toward the farmhouse.

At that distance everything looked the same, like it was when he left earlier; smoke curling from the pipe on the roof, the ancient Volvo parked in the side yard. Except for those new tracks.

The muscles tightened at the back of his neck. The only weapon he had was his knife. He slipped the blade from the sheath on his belt. He left the car and slipped into the orchard beside that dirt track, then made his way to the farmhouse.

The deeper tire marks led all the way to the farmhouse, then stopped just behind Valentine's car. There was a light at the kitchen, but no sounds came from inside, no conversation, no Ju-Ju barking as he approached. Only silence, the sort of silence that made his gut tighten. As he approached the door to the kitchen, Ju-Ju shot around the corner of the farmhouse.

The dog went straight to the door and started pawing at it, barking frantically. James quieted him with a hand on his head, then tried the latch on the kitchen door. It swung open freely. Ju-Ju shot past him.

He followed slowly, cautiously, easing the door open farther, then stepping inside the kitchen. It was quiet, too quiet, except for Ju-Ju. The dog whimpered from the adjoining room, then a voice in French, weak, then heavily accented English.

He found Albert on the floor in front of the woodstove in the big room. James gently turned him over while Ju-Ju pawed at the old man's shoulder.

"Tout est bien, viell ami," Albert whispered to the dog. "C'est bien, old friend," he told Ju-Ju. He been struck alongside the head, the wound bleeding badly.

"They were through the door quickly. I tried to stop them," he said in English as James helped him to the chair. He grabbed hold of James' sleeve.

"Valentine and your friend...they took them."

"How many?" James asked.

"Four, they wore masks. One of them was a woman, I am certain of it. "

A woman. Alyia Malik? James thought.

"Did they say anything?"

Albert shook his head. "It happened very fast; they said they would kill them if anyone followed. They wanted Valentine to take them to the quarry." His hand tightened and the expression in the old man's eyes was that of a young boy who had once fought against the Germans.

James checked him over. He didn't seem to have any other injuries, and a cold compress and a bandage stopped the bleeding on his head. But still, he couldn't be certain there weren't other injuries that could be especially dangerous for an old man, no matter how tough he had once been.

"You need to see a physician."

"Bah!" Albert made a gesture as if knocking on wood. "What is a little blood? I have had worse." His gaze sharpened.

"I know people like this. They care nothing about human life. They will kill Valentine and your friend when they have what they want." Then he added. "We must find them."

"You're not going anywhere."

"You think that because I am old that I cannot keep up, that I will hold you back. I know the countryside and the forest since I was a child able to walk. And I know the inside of the quarry. You do not."

He knew Albert was right. Still he hesitated. He didn't have the right to risk another person's life.

"You think I do not know the risk? That I am afraid?" He pointed to a wood box at the mantel over the woodstove.

"Bring me the box."

It was old, the shape of a shoe box, and scarred.

"Open it," Albert told him.

The pistol was old, vintage World War II, 9mm, wrapped in a wool cloth.

"I was nine when the Germans first came to the village. They took everything—food, any weapons that could be found, men from their farms, my father and older brother. I never saw them again. It was a warning to the rest of us." He stopped then and gathered himself before continuing.

"Micheleine's brothers and father were gone by then, and she had joined the Resistance. I went to someone I knew and told him I wanted to join the Resistance too. Too young, they said. But they could not stop me." He pointed to the pistol.

"I took that off a German officer after I killed him. I was eleven years old. Not too young. Not too old, now."

"All right," James conceded. He took a look around. "We'll need a few things."

"This." Albert held up the pistol. And the shotgun.

The old man's expression was hard, stubborn, and he had the impression he was glimpsing the young boy he had once been, who had fought in another war, childhood lost too soon.

"Dieu nous choisit," Albert said, in that quiet determined voice. "God chooses us, my friend."

CHAPTER
FORTY-FIVE

The cell phone was useless. Montigny was almost twenty kilometers in the opposite direction. It would take too much time to return and contact the authorities. By then Kris and Valentine would be dead.

James turned the rental car around and headed away from the farmhouse. Following Albert's directions, they found the cut-off road Valentine had spoken of the night before, deep tire marks in the snow that matched the ones at the farmhouse. They followed those tracks, stopping short of the end of the road as they rounded a curve and spotted the van, the same white van he had seen at the gallery warehouse. And the same van that had been used to run Kris down in London.

Faridani.

It was all there, the last pieces falling into place in the message he was finally able to pick up from Innis earlier when he'd drive to the village.

Captain Jack's people had been watching the gallery, watching for the next shipment of artifacts that never came. Everything had been cleared. Faridani was gone. But there was more. It had been all over the news in the aftermath of the explosion in Paris two days earlier.

Cross, double-cross, and Kris was right in the middle of it.

He got out of the car and slowly approached the van, the old 9mm pistol held in front of him. He stopped and listened several times, but there was only the sound of the forest. He picked up a small branch sticking up out of the snow and tossed it at the van.

It hit the rear window with a loud crack. Nothing. No sudden movement inside the van, no movement outside the van or from the perimeter. He slowly circled the van.

A quick glance inside the front passenger window confirmed it was empty. He reached for the handle to the rear compartment. It moved freely. He swept the cargo door open. The cargo area was also empty, except for several empty water bottles, a knit ski mask that had been thrown aside, a couple of wadded-up rags, and blood on the floor of the cargo area. He sensed rather than heard Albert come up behind him.

"Blood," Albert said, and his thoughts mirrored James.

"Not a lot," James commented, making a sweep of the inside of the van.

He made a quick search under the driver's side instrument panel and he found what he was looking for. He took out the knife and severed the wires to the van's electrical system. Then he made a thorough search of the cargo area.

Something caught his attention. He picked up one of those wadded rags. He recognized the chemical smell. They'd been drugged to make everything easier. He handed it to Albert.

"They're still alive," the old man said.

At least until Faridani had what he wanted, James thought.

Valentine knew the way to the quarry, but Kris knew the rest of it, from what Sophie Martin had told them, and that letter with the pictures and symbols on the edge.

He returned to the rental car, retrieved the backpack, and slung it over his shoulder.

"This way," Albert motioned from the dense tree cover. "Less chance that we will be seen."

James hesitated. It had been in his mind to have the old man wait at the car, then if he needed to leave quickly, at least one of them would get out.

Albert settled the argument by removing the shotgun from the scabbard on his back. He set off through the forest at a steady pace, the loaded shotgun held in the crook of his arm. Any doubt he had about Albert Marchand disappeared as he pushed to catch up.

The taste was metallic, slightly sweet, nausea backing up into her throat.

She'd been drugged, everything slowly coming back in bits and pieces—the white van at the end of the road, the desperate attempt to bolt the kitchen door, Ju-Ju barking frantically as she tossed the printout of that letter into the woodstove, the look of fear on Valentine's face as they came through the door.

Albert had been struck as he confronted them. Valentine screamed as he went down and went after his attacker. Kris raised the shotgun but never had the chance to fire it. The blow caught her on the back of her head. Dazed, slipping in and out of consciousness, she was hauled to her feet, and then dragged from the farmhouse.

She caught a brief glance of Valentine as they were both pulled into the van. The rest of it was a blur—her wrists bound, then that sickly sweet smell as the cloth was pressed against her face and a hood was pulled over her head. There were four of them, she thought, as she sank into darkness and the van lurched out of the driveway. Then another voice from the front of the van and something familiar.

"Be careful. We need them alive to help us find the tapestry once we reach the mine."

She had no idea how long they rode in the van, she was only aware when it stopped. She was dragged from the van, then heard a muffled sound certain it was Valentine. At least they were still together. Then she was shoved forward, stumbling through the snow, the cold seeping through her jeans. A tree branch whipped at her face. She stumbled and sank up to her knees in the snow. She was dragged back to her feet.

"Keep walking!" the warning, a woman's voice, hissed at her. "Or I will kill you myself."

"A quelle distance?" one of their captors shouted in French.

How far?

Valentine cried out as she was struck.

Tell them! she wanted to shout. Nothing was worth dying for. But nothing came out, that metallic taste dry in the back of her throat.

Someone shouted the question again. She finally heard Valentine's muffled reply. There were other sounds, and then she was being pushed forward again.

She had no idea how much farther they had gone, her jeans soaked, dragging at her with every step.

Was Valentine somewhere behind her? What had she told them? Then they suddenly stopped.

There was discussion, but she couldn't hear what was said. She tried to see through the fabric of the hood. She could only make out when one of them moved, a dark shadow against the white glare of snow. Then she heard the sound of metal scraping over metal. The entrance to the quarry that Albert had described?

She was dragged forward, stumbled, then the cold was different. There was no wind, no glare of snow, only the echo of voices. She was shoved down onto a hard surface.

She listened for sounds, but heard only the distant sound of air moving in hollow places. She struggled to sit up, levering herself up until she fell back against another hard surface at her back. A wall somewhere inside the mine?

Nausea rolled in her stomach, that sweet taste still at the back of her throat. She took slow deep breaths, trying to clear her head, trying to think past the panic and fear that would have been so easy.

Unable to see, she focused on sounds. Where was Valentine? Had they taken her some other place? Was she alright?

She worked her hands against the cord that was tied around them, trying to loosen it, then stopped at a new sound and listened. Someone cursed in French, a man's voice, followed by a muffled moan.

"Put her there." That same voice close now. "She may still be of use to us."

Valentine?

Oh, God, she thought. What had they done to her?

Fear returned, along with James' warning.

"You don't know these people; what they do to women, children, anyone who gets in their way!"

Then the hood was suddenly yanked from her head. It took a few seconds for her eyes to adjust to the shadows.

Light spilled in through a gaping hole in the ceiling where a tree had fallen, taking the reinforcing timbers with it. She made out the shapes of at least a dozen cots, some sagging with decay, others crushed beneath limbs that had fallen with the tree, just as Albert had described.

Then she saw Valentine, slumped against the wall across from her. Her hood had been removed, her face bloodied and bruised, her head slumped forward.

"Unfortunate, but necessary."

That voice, the sense of familiarity from the van.

Kris stared at the doorway and the man outlined there in light that spilled through from the passage. He was tall and slender, with silver white hair and light blue eyes.

CHAPTER
FORTY-SIX

M arcus Aronson slowly crossed the chamber. He pulled a chair from the shadows and sat across from her. It took several more seconds more for her brain to catch up.

Marcus? He was alive?

"You have questions," he said. "It is understandable."

Questions? At the moment all she could do was stare at the man seated across from her. She was still struggling with the fact that he was obviously part of all of this.

"Why, you ask," he finished the thought for her. "The same question she asked."

Whom was he talking about?

"She knew," he replied. "She even spoke of it when she came to Paris and asked for my help. After all those years, after Sinai, then Beirut, Berlin, then Afghanistan. She wrote about it, thinly disguised, of course, in her first book."

He was talking about Cate.

Kris pushed past the drugged haze. She thought back to that first book Cate had brought to her, that had skyrocketed onto the bestseller lists, that glimpse behind the events when the Six-Day war blew up in the Middle East; people behind the scenes who could have prevented it; the powerful people; political gamesmanship; and someone who had uncovered a deception that ignited everything, but was persuaded against speaking out about it; a burned-out journalist who ended up hiding out in a Paris hotel as people died; and the other one, a one-time lover, who exposed it all, but too late. All of it disguised by fictional names, dates, and places, to protect the innocent.

And the not-so-innocent, Kris thought, including the one who sat across from her now.

But why? What was the motive?

It had to be there, she told her assistants and the handful of authors she worked with. What was it that drove someone to kill?

Envy? The career he lost with that one decision, if that fictionalized story was only a thin disguise of real events? Something that had been rumored from the moment the book was released, but that Cate had always cleverly refused to discuss.

Greed?

What had he received in exchange for the story? A bigger story? Something that might have surpassed Cate's career at the time, and then never materialized?

Or had he simply taken a payoff to hold back his part of the story. After all, it was only supposed to be a small, regional conflict. Except that it had blown up into all-out war, and someone else found out what he had uncovered, too late to stop what was happening.

Revenge?

It was possible that it was always there, simmering beneath the surface—revenge for the career that abruptly ended as Cate's only continued to grow; the accolades and awards she received that he felt should have been his when the story that started it all hit the bestseller lists. Then the teaching position in England that quickly ended, followed by the position in Paris, and two books about Medieval military history…an authority in his own right, who received only brief attention, and then those books quickly ended up on dusty library shelves.

And Cate's part in it? The former lover who tried to help him all those years later, who used him as a source in each of her books with whole paragraphs written about his brilliant expertise and the value of his friendship.

Had he carried that envy and hatred all those years? Then Cate had gone to him with that photograph taken at the end of World War II, something she was trying to track down, possibly another book, and the tapestry. In a twisted, horrible way it was about the story.

"After the accident, I needed to find out what you knew," Marcus explained. "How much Cate had told you."

The last he almost spit out, anger and resentment. She was part of it too, Kris realized, probably from that first book. How had she missed it? The cool conversations that hid the resentment, the tone that she now realized had been condescending, resentful.

"The airport in Edinburgh," she whispered, hoarse from the dryness of gag and that chemical.

He shrugged. "It should have been so simple—grab your bag, and find out what information you had, what Cate had sent you. But you refused to let go, refused to let it all go. Just like her."

That's where Alyia Malik came into it. It was there in that video from the gallery, that sense of familiarity, then earlier in the van. But she had failed that day at the airport. By then they'd already ransacked the Tavern.

"What about the Blue Oyster in London?"

Was that meant to kill her? What was one more murder?

"That was unfortunate," he said, again with a shrug of the shoulders, as if it was no more important than a missed call or appointment.

"Again, it was an attempt to frighten you, stop you. But you had a friend that night and unfortunately that reporter got in the way."

There was that word again. *Unfortunate*—dismissive, like a piece of lint he brushed away. And the friend had been James Morgan, who saved her life that night.

And others?

Callish knew she would go to see Diana Jodion. She was an authority on medieval tapestries, but could tell them little about the Raveneau tapestry. If she knew where it was, she would have made that known herself. Cate had spoken to her. At that point, it was all they had—Cate's cell phone log. Something that Marcus didn't have. Not at first. Later?

"Brother Thomas?" she asked, the horrible scene at the abbey church flashing back, the blood on the stones, almost as if it was a ritual killing.

"An authority on the history of the abbey," Marcus replied. "I had spoken with him in the past, very knowledgeable." He smiled faintly before continuing.

"He contacted me. Cate had been to see him. I knew it was only a matter of time before you and your friend went to the abbey, that same curiosity, like her. He knew things about the tapestry from the abbey archive. His death was regrettable but necessary," he explained. "But you didn't stop, even when your friend was injured."

Regrettable? Murder?

"What about Faridani."

He looked at her then. "Faridani, yes. He knew about the photograph."

"From Jonathan Callish," she replied. It was obvious now. Alyia Malik would have told him.

"Hmmm," he replied, thoughtful.

What was her part in all of this? Hardly the starving artist. A terrorist? Like her brother?

She thought back to that first encounter at the London gallery, the showing Alyia Malik was preparing with those themes of blood and death. And Jonathan Callish, the adoring, proud husband.

"She knew people," Marcus replied. "Others who were also interested in ancient artifacts."

Of course, Kris thought.

"Callish's partner in the Paris gallery."

A cold hollow feeling settled in her stomach. It was no secret that priceless pieces of artwork had been disappearing from the Middle East since the first Gulf War, the funds used to fund terrorist activities that included the slaughter of innocent men, women, and children from countless villages and towns, child abductions, girls paired-off with terrorist fighters, boys drafted into paramilitary groups, and weapons used against coalition forces, people like James Morgan...like her brother. And countless others who had paid the ultimate price.

It all came together—Faridani or Malik, his real name, and someone with connections to the Middle East and stolen artifacts. He didn't bother to deny it. And he needed an expert who could authenticate ancient art for prospective clients—black market artifacts stolen out of the Middle East and other places, then sold to the highest bidder, priceless pieces of artwork hidden away in private galleries, that funded terrorist activities. And people died.

Not unlike the Germans during World War II. They even had a name for the agency created by the Nazis. The ERR—Einsatzstab Reichsleiter. Just a different time and place, but the crimes and brutality were the same.

"The explosion in Paris?" she asked, still struggling with the fact that he was alive. Very much alive, and dangerous.

He shrugged. "You were late that morning."

Someone else in the wrong place at the wrong time, she thought, like London, like a Paris nightclub, and other unfortunate casualties. That was what he intended to happen, except, as he had already told her, she was late that morning and would have been just another casualty in the war on terror.

It was all about greed and revenge, about choices and decisions Marcus Aronson had made decades earlier. He'd lived his life since hating Cate and everything she had achieved—the career he felt should have been his, the bestselling novels she wrote that were a reminder of what he might have had and what he had thrown away, the former lover who tried to help him, had protected him all those years, and had gone to him with that photograph and an incredible story.

Envy, greed, revenge, with one more thrown in. Betrayal.

"What's in this for you?"

He half turned. "Recognition, possibly a book, with the names changed to protect the innocent, of course."

"You betrayed a friend for a few minutes of fame? You son-of-a-bitch!" She kicked out with her feet in a futile effort to reach him, to knock him out of the chair, to wipe that self-satisfied, cold expression off his face.

He shook his head. "So brave, so reckless, and so futile." He stood then as two others entered the chamber and joined him—Alyia Malik, and a man who bore a striking resemblance and had to be her brother, Hasan Malik.

They were both dressed in black pants, turtleneck shirts, and boots —the shadows she had glimpsed in the van before the hood was pulled over her face.

Valentine moaned softly as she was dragged to her feet. Malik struck her.

"Let her go." Kris told Aronson. "She doesn't know anything."

"Oh no, my dear," he replied in that professorial tone as if delivering a lecture to a student.

"You are going to help us find the tapestry, and she is going to be...shall we say, motivation?"

They didn't have the copy of Micheleine's letter! She realized it now. They hadn't found it. It was smoldering in the ashes of the woodstove in the farmhouse. They hadn't found it!

And when they found the tapestry? If it was there?

She knew the answer. Neither she or Valentine would be left alive to tell about it.

They would simply be left there, like so many others who had died a century earlier, who had carved their names and symbols into the walls, and on lists etched into memorials in London, Paris, and at Lochaber, Scotland. The tapestry would find its way into some collector's hands at an exorbitant price that would be used to fund more terrorism, more deaths.

She was dragged to her feet. Then both she and Valentine were pulled through the opening of the chamber out into the passage that connected countless tunnels and rooms.

The prayer whispered through her thoughts, something she'd convinced herself she didn't believe in or needed.

Please God...

CHAPTER
FORTY-SEVEN

"There is a guard," Albert said, handing James the vintage field glasses, from another time, another war.

He focused in, the guard coming into view, an AK47 snugged in the crook of his arm. He scanned past the guard, taking in the entire perimeter, then the slope of the wall at the mine, then back to the entrance.

Albert had been certain there were four of them at the farmhouse. That meant that three more were inside. And Kris and Valentine were somewhere in there with them.

He crouched low, hidden by the cover of low branches and scrub. He glanced along the ridge of the hillside that was in fact the mine itself. Albert had spoken about a fallen tree that had collapsed through the roof and then grown inside the entrance.

He stood and felt the hand on his shoulder. He nodded to Albert then silently slipped through the cover of oak and pine, working his way toward the entrance of the mine, then slipped behind a boulder and waited. Eventually the guard came into view, making his sweep around the front of the mine.

James took in everything, it was second nature after too many missions—the guard's height, approximate weight, anything else strapped to his body, the flak jacket, the way he moved then shifted the weapon.

God chooses us. Did he believe it? Did he believe in anything?

It slipped out of the box and moved along every nerve ending, the way it had from the beginning, that first sight of dark, shoulder-length hair with red burning through it, the way she had looked at him, the stubbornness...

They would kill her. He knew that, and it would be easy to just leave the bodies there in the mine where no one would ever find them.

It swept back over him. The sound of automatic weapons' fire, the smoke, taking him back as the adrenaline pumped.

Eric on his right, Case behind him, three out in front, Mikey screaming over the handset, yelling coordinates as everything exploded around them; then Eric was down, shadows swarming at them through the smoke and fire, the handset on the ground...He tried to grab it, but his arm was numb at his side, pain tearing through his shoulder; somewhere overhead the drone of a helicopter; he saw Case go down, the blood, then it was over...

'Captain Morgan? Can you hear me? Hold on, Captain!

Then a hand on his shoulder, pulling him back, holding on, someone who knew, who understood...

"Let it go, my friend," Albert said gently.

James took a deep breath, then another. Albert held out a hand to him. He nodded in understanding.

"It is always there," the old man said. "The dark beast, the things we have seen and done, that comes in the night, but it will not take us. We cannot let it take us. There are still things we must do."

In Albert's face he saw himself—the things that both had seen and done; different wars, decades apart, the same. The wounds were the same, carried inside. But there were things that had to be done.

"Merci, my friend," he told him.

He slowed his breathing. His heart rate followed. Everything around him slowed—the next step the guard took, a step closer, then another, one more step, and then turned back toward the entrance.

Any gunfire would alert those inside. He couldn't risk it. He pulled items from his pocket that he'd purchased—two pull-cords for a chain saw, knotted together, with a handle at each end.

He slipped out from behind the tree cover and closed the distance to the quarry entrance. He waited, then as the guard approached then turned back, he stepped from behind a large boulder. In one quick motion, the cord was around the guard's neck and he pulled it taut.

There was that instinctive struggle, the guard kicking out as he fought the cord on his neck. The automatic rifle fell into the snow as the guard clawed at the cord with both hands. He tightened it. The guard kicked out once more, then ceased to struggle. He slowly eased him to the ground.

"You said there were four," he whispered as Albert came up behind him. The old man nodded.

James handed him the automatic rifle, then checked the guard and pulled the 9mm from the guard's shoulder holster. The clip was full, the 9mm better at close range and in tight places.

Albert nodded. "Four."

That meant three more were inside, including Faridani, and the woman Albert was certain had been with them. Alyia Malik.

He remembered that brief introduction, the paintings she was preparing for a show at the London gallery—War and Aftermath.

"Come," Albert said, cradling his shotgun and the automatic rifle in one arm with surprising agility.

"In case one of them should return."

Together they dragged the guard's body out of sight of the entrance to the mine.

James crouched low, eyes narrowed on the entrance.

"I don't know what I'll find inside."

Albert nodded. He patted the shotgun, the rifle propped against a tree trunk.

"No one will get past."

James didn't try to persuade him against it or suggest he hide in thick cover where it was safer. He knew what the reply would have been. Albert laid a hand on his arm as he rose and started toward the mine entrance.

"Bring them back safe," he said, his expression slipping, a thought that went unspoken. Then it was gone, but they both understood his meaning.

James made his way slowly toward the entrance of the mine, moving from the cover of one large rock to another, at the same time watching for any sign that one of the others had been positioned inside.

Logic told him no. They wouldn't be expecting anyone. Not yet. And the guard had been placed at the entrance to prevent anyone going inside who might show up.

There was that point when there was no more cover to hide behind, the last half-dozen yards to those steel doors, when he would be fully exposed. He bent low and ran the last several yards. He reached the entrance and flattened himself against the outside of one of the doors.

The other door stood ajar. A quick glance, and he was inside.

It was just as Albert had described. The roof had caved in long ago. Debris, rocks, large cut-limestone rocks that had formed the roof were scattered everywhere, and a tree stretched up through the opening in the roof where it had grown over the years.

He glimpsed a wood sign on a stake that had been driven into the ground and then rotted over time and collapsed, the faded warning in both English and French.

DANGER!

He stepped past it, stopped, and listened.

There was only the faint movement of air from the gaping hole in the ceiling and the opening at the door. There was no other sound, no movement.

Where would Faridani have taken them?

A sweep of the entrance revealed what Albert had told him from that earlier visit with Micheleine's brothers, before the war.

The entrance led to a passage that ran in two directions, parallel to the entrance. Tracks embedded in the floor ran in both directions, no doubt where rail cars loaded with limestone had once been brought to the surface and then loaded onto wagons at the entrance.

One passage was blocked by rock and debris that had caved in long ago, just as Albert had described it. That left only one possibility in the opposite direction.

Light from the entrance disappeared after the first dozen yards, but there was light intermittently from other sections of roof that had fallen in over the years. He followed the passage to a room that opened along one wall, then another, stopping, listening, then continuing on, deeper into the passage, then another room.

Row after row of cots filled the room. Most had rotted and collapsed, but several were intact, even a century later. A metal table with shelves stood against one wall. Several glass bottles and vials were scattered across the dirt floor where they had either fallen or animals had gotten to them looking for food. Another table sat against the wall with a chair pushed back as if someone had only just left, to return in a few minutes.

The hospital.

How many men had been taken there? English? French? The wounded? Dying? Those cots told the story.

Another war, in another place. Always the same.

The next room was smaller, only half the size of the first one. A dozen cots lined one wall. Was this where the more critically injured were taken?

A couple of threadbare woolen blankets had rotted. There was a pair of boots that sat at one end of a stretcher. An old oil lamp sat against a wall, and piles of old rags had been tossed into a corner.

Bandages for the wounded? They were soiled and stained with dirt and grime. Except for the one that had been tossed onto the top of the pile. It was relatively clean. There were no stains, only that faintly sweet smell, the same smell he'd picked up in the van.

At least one of them had been there, he thought, and not long ago. Then, taken some place else? But where?

If they meant to kill Kris and Valentine, they would already be dead. That meant they wanted them alive, at least a little longer, needed them alive to find what they were after.

There was only one direction they could have gone. The light was thin, then faded altogether as he returned to the tunnel passage.

"Where?" Marcus demanded as they came to the end of the passage where it opened in two directions.

"Where?" he demanded again, walking back to her, Alyia Malik with a firm hold on her arm.

"Tell me!" he demanded.

They needed time, Kris thought. James would have returned to the farm by now and Albert would have told him what happened.

Albert. Was he all right? Or had he become just another casualty in Marcus's glory game?

He jerked her head up, his fingers bruising her chin as he forced her to look at him.

"You will tell me."

When she refused, he nodded past her, where Faridani stood with Valentine. So brave, so angry. It was there in the expression on Valentine's face. There had been no time to tell her she was sorry for dragging her and her grandfather into this.

Marcus looked back at her. Someone she thought she knew, had respected for his knowledge and his friendship with Cate.

"Your silence is wasted, my dear." He nodded again at Faridani.

He yanked Valentine's head back, the blade of a knife gleamed in the light of the lantern they'd brought with them. He pressed the tip against her throat. Blood appeared.

"Do you know how long it takes for someone to bleed to death?" Marcus asked her.

"No!" Valentine cried out, even as blood ran down the length of that blade. "Tell them nothing!"

The Cross of Lorraine, the tattoo she had gotten in memory of Micheleine, was covered with blood.

"You don't know these people—you don't know what they do..."

James had warned her, tried to stop her. He knew, and she had seen it—Brynn Halliday, murdered in London, Brother Thomas in a pool of his own blood, James shot as they fled from the abbey. And Cate.

"There were drawings," she told Marcus. "In a letter Micheleine left behind before she died."

"No!" Valentine screamed, then gasped as a hand closed around her throat.

"What drawings?" Marcus demanded.

"At the hospital."

"Where?"

"Somewhere in the mine."

He grabbed her by the arm and pulled her forward.

"You will show me."

"I don't know!" she insisted.

"What sort of drawings?"

"There was a figure of a woman, carved into stone."

"Bring her," he snapped, pulling her into the open space where those half tunnels intersected along that narrow track.

"Here!" Alyia announced. "The figure of a woman."

An angel, Kris thought. Albert had described her, the way he had seen her as a child. The image etched in stone at the wall. She wore a headscarf and an apron. No angel, but possibly the image of a nurse, carved decades earlier by some soldier who had been taken there?

"Tell me!" he demanded.

She caught a glance from Valentine. A tear slipped down her cheek. She furiously shook her head.

"A military insignia with words in French."

"What words?"

"Never give up."

He repeated the words, then in French as he searched down the side next passage the beam of the flashlight playing across the walls.

"It is here!" He shouted. "Bring them."

Faridani grabbed hold of her arm, and pushed her down the passage. She caught a glimpse of the insignia on the wall.

"The next one," Marcus demanded.

"The year 1918," she thought back over that list of symbols even as she looked around at the floor of the passage for something she could grab.

"And the word paix."

"Peace?"

They continued down the passage as Marcus scanned the beam of the flashlight along the wall.

"It is here," he called out when he found it. "The next one!"

"Rows of crosses."

They passed other rooms, some with cots, others completely bare, then a large room that opened onto another, those marks on the wall, tiny crosses cut in stone, that matched the drawing in the letter.

She stumbled in the shadows. Faridani cursed and dragged her back to her feet. The words were broken English, but the message was clear.

"Cut the rope," Marcus ordered. "It does no good if we have to keep picking her up."

Faridani hesitated, then cut the rope on her wrists.

She rubbed both hands, massaging the blood back into her numb fingers.

"The next image," Marcus demanded.

And the last one, Kris remembered. Was the tapestry there, in a room inside the mine where she believed Micheleine had hidden it from the Germans decades earlier?

She thought of the photograph Cate had sent, a black-and-white photograph of a medieval tapestry that had disappeared over eighty years ago. Is that what Micheleine meant in that last letter?

"I pray it will be safe in the hospital..."

"Tell me!" Marcus shouted at her.

"A lion standing over a dragon."

He nodded. "Just so, the English lion and the German dragon."

Marcus moved ahead, playing the beam across the walls at each turn. She was pushed after him. Alyia was behind them with Valentine.

Was the tapestry there?

Fear knotted her stomach. Once Marcus had what he wanted, they would be killed. She was certain of it.

What was it like to die? She had thought of that so many times after Mark was killed. Did he know before it happened? What were his last thoughts? Was he scared?

She had thought about that so many times, her strong brother with that quirky sense of humor. Would he have been angry? Or some other emotion? Fear?

Not that, she thought. He had never been afraid of anything, and he had believed that death wasn't an end. He even told her that once, strong in the faith they had been raised on.

"I've seen too many things that had no other explanation," he once said. "Friends..."

Brad Morris, she thought at the time. He had been killed in a car accident their first year of college. He had known Brad since kindergarten. They had shared everything, and went off to college together. Brad didn't agree with her brother's decision to go into the military, but he supported his right to make that decision because that's what real friends did. Then the accident.

"There are times," Mark said afterward, when he was home on leave from one of those first missions he'd been sent out on.

"I know he's there, right beside me, just like when we were in high school. We don't lose them, kiddo. Their spirit is always with us."

The information that came back after Mark was killed, the official version and the other versions from men he served with, never said anything about that last time, what his thoughts might have been. There was just the formal letter...

"We regret to inform you..."

But knowing her brother, she was certain about one thing. He would have tried to fight his way out; he wouldn't have given up. He didn't quit...

Which way had they gone?

James asked himself again. And again there was no answer in the shadows of the passage or the stagnate cold air. Nothing, then a sound.

Was it his imagination? The way the simplest sound—the drip of water or the movement of bats seemed to come from one direction, then another, the way it echoed off stones and rock walls.

Not bats, the sound of water, or the wind through the broken roof of the mine?

Voices!

He heard it again, and moved quickly. He followed the passage until it opened into that large cavernous room. Another passage with rooms along both sides, then the passage ended, splitting off in two directions. But which one?

It was crude, but he recognized the image Albert had mentioned, the figure of a woman with a scarf and apron, the same as one drawn on the edge of the letter Micheleine had left behind.

It came again, another sound, and he was already heading down the passage. The sound faded, slipped away. He searched the walls of the passage. The military insignia carved in stone almost leapt off the wall at him. He followed the passage, stopped, listened, then kept going.

The drawings in the margin of that letter were directions in the mine. He heard another sound, almost turned back uncertain the direction it had come from, then saw the year, 1918, etched in stone.

He turned, moved down the passage, then saw them—rows of crosses, someone had carved into the limestone wall.

A lion and dragon was the last drawing Micheleine had made. He heard it again. He was close and cut the beam of the flashlight. He ran and followed that sound, someone shouting.

Please, God. Let them both still be alive...

CHAPTER
FORTY-EIGHT

The room was filled with shovels, picks, lanterns, and other mining equipment from a century earlier—benches that had rotted and collapsed, helmets on a shelf that had partially collapsed.

They were inside the part of the mine that had been abandoned when it was closed down, before World War I when the English and French had brought their wounded and dying to the mine from nearby trenches and battlefields.

Marcus swept the beam of the flashlight across the walls, then over again, running back and forth in the room like a madman, kicking aside a shovel, then back again.

"Where is it?" he demanded, turning on her. "There is more. There has to be more! You will tell me!" he demanded.

"That was all that was in the letter," Kris told him. "Just those drawings."

"I don't believe you."

He struck her. The blow sent her sprawling to the hard stone floor.

"There has to be more. Tell me!" he threatened, standing over her.

She slowly picked herself up off the floor.

"I told you, I don't know!"

Alyia's brother stepped between them. Articulate, educated, a brutal terrorist who constantly eluded coalition forces, according to the information James had, a purveyor of fine art and antiquities to finance terrorist activities.

How much did Jonathan Callish know about his brother-in-law's activities? Was he part of it? Or simply another victim?

She found it hard to believe that he was part of anything so complicated, illegal, or dangerous, with his polished nails, expensive Saville Row suits, and an equally expensive address in Mayfair.

His father had served with Cate's father during the war. After the war they had remained friends, bonded by that wartime experience. Years later, Cate considered Jonathan a good friend, trusting his expertise. She had worked with him on a collection of her father's photographs, planning that gallery showing.

But the London gallery had apparently not been doing well. They had seen it for themselves the day they went there looking for information about that photograph Cate had sent—the limited pieces that were offered, a cancelled showing, Jonathan's vagueness about the photograph at the same time he was planning a showing of his wife's works.

War and Aftermath—the images had been stark and brutal. They made one look away, trying to absorb what the brain was seeing as it tapped into something deep inside, the artist's form of expression.

Kris had seen it in gallery showings in New York over the years. There were pieces that drew you in, others that tapped into something inside you, still others that left a person confused about the message the artist was trying to convey.

There was no confusion about the message Alyia Malik conveyed on those canvases. And the Paris gallery was apparently a façade, a funnel for funding terrorist activities.

How much had Cate uncovered? Did she know the Paris gallery was merely a conduit for stolen artifacts used to fund terrorist activities? Or was the accident as simple as professional rivalry and revenge?

Faridani dragged Valentine in front of her. That slick, polished veneer was stripped away, in its place, a cold, dispassionate expression. It was like staring into the eyes of a snake.

"You will tell us," he said, his voice low, dangerous with promise. "Or you little friend will die slowly, right here, before your eyes."

He would kill her. Kris knew it. It came from the terror in London, then the abbey. And she saw it in his eyes.

Valentine's life, her life, meant nothing to him. Videos of beheadings, bodies dragged through the streets of some foreign city. One more death meant nothing.

Is this what her brother had felt? What he had experienced in those last moments? What James Morgan had experienced on that last mission that had gone so terribly wrong? That awareness of things all narrowed down to a single, fine point? And then death.

The look in Valentine's eyes told her that she also knew.

Please help me, God.

It came from some place deep inside, a place she had closed the door on after Mark's death, a need to believe in something more, even as she had pushed it away. Faith. Not for herself, but for Valentine... so young, she didn't deserve this, there was still so much life ahead of her.

Valentine shook her head. She understood. She accepted what was about to happen. It was there in the expression on her face, in her belief in the things Micheleine had stood for—that passion and conviction against the evil in the world. She wore it in the tattoo of that ancient symbol a young French girl had taken centuries earlier.

Afterward, there were things that she would remember, sharp, crystal clear—Valentine's smile even as the tears slipped down her cheek, the peacefulness in those last moments, a calmness that surprised her and oddly enough reassured her.

It came slowly, in that way of things that seem to move out of time, slow motion, an awareness and an image that she'd seen on the wood door across that room inside the quarry mine. A symbol Micheleine Robillard had given her life for. And the last symbol found in the letter. She almost laughed out loud. It was so obvious, but only those who understood Micheleine and what she had fought for would have known.

Jehanne, the people of France called her during that dark time, their own Joan of Arc, who lost both brothers and her father to the war, then went off to fight in her own way. She had done things, and the cost had been high—in the end she paid with her life. But she had never given up the one thing she vowed the Germans would never get their hands on. A symbol to the French people, something to believe in. The Cross of Lorraine.

Things that mattered.

"Wait!" Marcus shouted at Faridani. He followed the direction she stared beside the door.

The professor who had spent the last thirty years teaching Medieval history, writing about it, the symbol of a martyr centuries earlier, and the symbol of the French Resistance during the war.

"Of course," he whispered.

"What is it?" Faridani demanded as Marcus crossed the room. He traced the symbol that had been carved into the door, sealed years earlier, the long line with two lines across, one shorter than the other.

He slowly smiled.

Faridani let go of Valentine and crossed the room. He stared at the marks that had been cut into the door.

"Open it," he ordered Marcus.

She stood beside Valentine, Alyia Malik holding a gun on them, and watched as they tried the latch.

The latch moved freely but the door remained sealed, nailed shut decades earlier. Faridani retrieved a shovel from the other side of the room. He hacked away at the door, wood splintering with each blow. Several more blows and the door gave way. Marcus pushed him aside and pulled the door open. He grabbed a flashlight and entered the room. Faridani followed, and Kris felt Alyia's hand on her shoulder, shoving her forward.

The room was approximately the size of the outer room, the air musty in that way of places that have been closed for years.

Wood boxes lined one wall, a warning in French painted on the sides—Explosives!

A canvas cloth was draped over more wood boxes against the other wall. But it was the large rolled canvas that lay against the far wall that had Marcus pushing past Faridani.

"Help me lift it," he ordered.

Faridani crossed the room and seized the other end of the thick rolled canvas. Both struggled to lift it.

Kris exchanged a glance with Valentine. Was it possible they'd found the tapestry?

They carried the rolled canvas to the center of the room, then slowly unrolled it. One image after another gradually emerged in the glow of flashlights—a pastoral scene, then a hunting scene, typical of Medieval artwork, then another image of a young man and woman beneath an arch covered with greenery and flowers, intricate handwork with words stitched into the massive linen panel that had been rolled inside the canvas and hidden away for over seventy years.

The words were in Latin, and along the bottom of the panel and scattered throughout, another symbol—the thistle and trinity knot, the same as the pendant Vilette had given her.

It was everywhere throughout the panels, painstakingly stitched one at a time. Then another panel emerged—a knight astride a horse and a young woman with an outstretched hand.

Isabel Raveneau and James of Montfort.

The story Vilette claimed had been handed down through her family, the medallion, those images in a letter tucked away centuries later.

"It is the same as the photograph!" Marcus exclaimed with excitement. He was like a child at Christmas, unwrapping presents under the tree.

"You are certain?" Faridani asked. "There is no doubt?"

"The colors of the yarns, the fabric as it was in the fourteenth century. The images. And to find it here after all these years. Yes, yes! "Marcus excitedly exclaimed.

"Incredible!"

Marcus couldn't contain his excitement as he studied one image after the other. He reached out as if to touch it then pulled his hand back.

"No," he said more to himself. "Too fragile. We must be very careful. After all these years, centuries, we don't want to risk any damage. My God, it is beautiful..."

He was like a kid, mesmerized by a video game, oblivious to anything or anyone else as he bent over the tapestry.

"Burn it," Faridani replied.

Like Marcus she was certain she hadn't heard him right. When Marcus didn't respond but continued to stare at the tapestry, he said it again, much louder and with unmistakable authority.

"We will need to get help to remove it," Marcus went on, lost in his own thoughts.

"No!" Faridani replied. He nodded at Alyia Malik.

"Burn it! It must be destroyed."

Kris saw the stunned expression on Marcus's face, the brief smile as if it were some joke.

"What are you saying?" Marcus asked, incredulous. He did laugh then. "You cannot be serious! It is a priceless work of art. These scenes are an important part of history."

"Your history!" Faridani told him. "Not mine! It is a blaspheme against God and it must be destroyed. It must never see the light of day."

"You have a buyer, you told me," Marcus exclaimed, still trying to understand. "To find it, after all these years...it is priceless! Why would you want to destroy it?"

But he knew. Kris saw it on his face, that moment when the stunned expression shifted and became anger. And she knew.

The secret, Vilette had told them about. If it was there, something to be feared, and destroyed? Something powerful?

She had studied religion, briefly, theology and faith handed down through the ages and across cultures, the true meaning of faith and how it had influenced civilizations. It was only her first two years of college, before changing her major to journalism after Mark died, when she questioned everything she had believed before, and had turned her back on things that seemed to have no place, no reality in the modern world.

But there were those who still believed in the power of faith, who were willing to kill and die in the name of their God, and would destroy anything that got in their way, including a seven-hundred-year-old artifact that might hold a secret that challenged everything?

Was it there? The secret that Vilette Moreau was so certain her ancestor had stitched into the threads of the tapestry after closing herself away in the abbey at Mont St. Michel? Or was it just another myth that had been passed down from one century to the next, then lost in obscurity until their search began?

It didn't matter.

It only mattered that Faridani, or Malik, or whoever he called himself, was determined to destroy it.

Alyia Malik pushed past them. She knelt at one corner of the tapestry a long handled lighter in her hand.

"No!" Marcus lunged at her and struck the lighter out of her hand. Gunfire exploded and Marcus staggered back. He stared down at the dark stain that spread across the front of his shirt. He made a sound, part gasp, all anger, and lunged toward Faridani. Another shot and his head snapped back. He fell to the floor of the chamber.

Kris pushed Valentine toward the doorway.

"Run!"

The blow came from behind, pain exploding as she was thrown against the wall, then another pain, sharp on her arm as she went down, Alyia Malik standing over her.

She would be next, she thought, even as she saw Faridani turn toward her. He shouted something, but she couldn't hear over the sudden explosion of gunfire from the entrance of the chamber.

James was through the doorway. He made a quick sweep of the room in the light of Faridani's flashlight and stepped over a body—Aronson by the white hair that was all that was left of his skull. Then a movement to his right, he spun back around aiming chest high at that shadow. Three rounds and Faridani's body spasmed. Then another, and he was down.

Faridani's flashlight hit the stone floor as he went down, the beam spinning crazily. A woman screamed, and someone came out of the shadows at him, dressed in black cargo pants and turtleneck—Alyia Malik. Eyes wide, expressionless, like he'd seen dozens of times in Afghanistan, she lunged at him. The knife grazed his arm, throwing the shot off. A wounded sound and she fell into the shadows.

He swept the far wall, the beam from the flashlight exposing letters painted across the ends of boxes, the warning clear in any language, then a large rolled canvas. He scanned past, the beam playing across dark hair, pale features, eyes wide and dark with the edge of shock.

Kris heard her name over the ringing in her ears. Then a hand on her shoulder.

"Stay down," he told her.

He swept the room again and nudged the bodies. Alyia Malik wasn't one of them. He bent down and pulled Kris against him.

Her arm went around his neck as she held on, her face buried in his shoulder, a hand fisted on his back.

"He killed Marcus...He tried to destroy the tapestry."

She was losing it—that part that came after, when the adrenaline was gone. Like that night in London, when everything had fallen apart, and he was there.

"I've got you." He held on to her. She was alive. He closed his eyes against the doubts, the raw fear that had him running through the passages like a madman.

"Can you walk?"

She nodded, clenching her teeth against the shaking in her legs. She winced.

"I think it's broken," she said, holding her arm.

"Tuck your hand inside the waist of your jeans to keep it steady until we get out of here."

She glanced past him to the bodies, outlined in the light from Malik's flashlight, Marcus's shattered skull all that remained.

"Valentine?"

"Here," the girl called out. She crawled out of the shadows where Kris had shoved her. She stood, bruised, shaken, but alive. She swore in French.

"I tried to stop her, but the bitch got away."

"She won't get far," James assured them. "Are you all right?"

Her face was a mass of bruises, and blood was smeared on her neck where Faridani had cut her. She nodded. She tried to smile, then the tears came. She cursed again, then looked past them to the bodies on the floor.

"They wanted to destroy it," Valentine whispered.

She crossed the room and knelt beside the tapestry that Micheleine had fought to protect so long ago.

"She was here." She touched the edge of the tapestry. "In this place, and it was important to her to keep it safe." She took a deep breath.

"We need to go," James told them both. They needed to find Albert, then contact the French authorities.

Had Alyia Malik gotten past Albert? Or had she escaped through one of the other tunnels?

There were dozens of them spread throughout the quarry. She

would have needed to find one of those rooms with the roof caved in, and she would be gone.

They retraced their steps, following those images that Micheleine had drawn on the edge of that letter in the last days and weeks of the war, and finally reached the main passage that led to the entrance.

A loud explosion echoed off the walls of the passage.

"Stay here," James ordered. He ran ahead, disappearing into the looming darkness.

"Grandfather?" Valentine whispered, and ran after him.

They reached the entrance to the mine, coming up behind him. Albert looked up, the old shotgun he used to scare the crows from his apple trees in the crook of his arm.

Alyia Malik lay sprawled across the limestone floor near the entrance, the pistol under her hand where it had fallen.

Albert patted the stock of the shotgun and shrugged.

"She tried to escape."

CHAPTER
FORTY-NINE
LONDON

K ris grabbed the remote and turned up the audio on the midday news feed from the BBC.

The broadcast was live from Paris, outside the office of the Directeur Centrale de la Police Judiciare. A reporter from CNN thrust a microphone at the white-haired man who had just emerged from the building.

Albert appeared on screen, in his field coat, work pants, the white hair tucked beneath the beret, his favorite shotgun in the curve of his arm—for shooting the crows that invaded his orchards. Valentine stood beside him.

"There are reports circulating that you were instrumental in stopping a recent terrorist attack, and responsible for the deaths of several terrorists. Can you comment on that now that the official investigation has been closed?"

She smiled at the correspondent's persistence, thinking of someone else who had a reputation for being equally persistent.

"We got them, Cate," she whispered.

They had all given statements to both the French and British authorities, along with everything they had uncovered about the connection to the terrorists, playing up Albert's role in tracking them down. Shortly afterward, James was called back to London. There had been phone conversations, checking up on her after surgery on her arm and she was released from hospital. Then she returned to London and work.

In the investigation that followed, there had been the usual skepticism over the weapons found at the quarry, along with Albert's age. Then his role with the French Resistance during World War II and his relation to Micheleine Robillard, who was still revered as a hero of the war, made it into the media.

In that curious, often bizarre way that a family connection creates momentum, often outright notoriety, the small village of Montigny and Albert's apple farm had been inundated by the curious, reporters, and historians.

There had been no questions about Alyia Malik's death. During the investigation, Albert had simply stated that he was afraid for his life, she came at him with a gun, and he fired to protect himself. And then there was the connection to her brother, a known terrorist. Anything else was lost in the media frenzy about the death of one of the most notorious terrorists in recent history, who had terrorized the people of Paris and other cities around the world in the past with a series of fatal attacks.

"Eh?" Albert replied with a hand cupped behind his ear. "Je ne vous comprends pas."

He didn't understand the questions being asked?

Wily old fox, Kris thought with a smile as Albert continued to toy with the journalist, and wished Cate was there to see it.

"Please," Valentine played her part. "All of this has been very difficult. He is an old man who saw his responsibility and wishes now only to return to his farm."

She slipped her arm through Albert's and appeared to offer physical support as they were escorted by an officer of the court that had conducted the investigation into the incident at the quarry mine, and had concluded it that day with no charges to be brought against the elderly hero of France, who had once fought with the Resistance.

Her smile deepened as the elderly man bent his head toward his granddaughter to catch something she said as the reporter continued with his segment completely. They both smiled. Checkmate, Kris thought.

"An incredible story from Normandy during World War II," the reporter continued. "A priceless work of art, known as the Raveneau Tapestry, hidden from the Germans for over seventy years, found in an underground hospital from World War I.

"It was recovered and is currently in the possession of the Louvre Museum at an undisclosed location in collaboration with UNESCO. The Louvre, with the assistance of Ms. Diana Jodion, an expert in Medieval tapestries who is curator at the Bayeaux Museum, will be overseeing the restoration. It is anticipated that restoration will begin immediately, now that the investigation into recent events has concluded."

Kris looked at the scans Diana had sent her. Contrary to the reporter's statement, restoration had begun just after the tapestry was recovered from that room in the quarry not quite a month ago, by representatives of the Louvre under supervision by Diana, and with special permission by the Ministry of France.

It was critical, Diana had argued, to avoid damage and possibly theft by fortune seekers or others, after the story first hit the media. In the weeks since, with her team assembled and hard at work, Diana had sent those first photographs.

The tapestry was in surprisingly good condition, considering its age and conditions inside the quarry filled with debris, explosives, many areas caved in, and exposed to the elements. Micheleine Robillard had chosen its hiding place well.

Those first images were now spread across her office wall at Brighton House Publishers, a work in progress, along with Cate's last book.

Kris had been given the monumental task of seeing that unfinished project completed. Just the week before, she'd finished negotiations between Cate's estate, her publisher, and Trevor Allen, a well-known author in his own right, who had agreed to co-author the book and finish the manuscript.

After the negotiations, she had taken a few days off to deliver the contract to Cate's legal team, and take a meeting with Dickie Simson, Inspector of the Inverness Police, after it was determined that Cate's death was no accident, but a homicide.

It was Candlemas, and after everything that had happened, and with James still in London, Anne Morgan had suggested a holiday getaway to the Shetland Islands. The locals who claimed Viking blood were celebrating Up Helly Aa.

There were traditional feasts, a lot of single-malt whisky, and a full-sized Viking galley with dragon's head, complete with shields and oars, and a processional with participants dressed as Viking warriors that looked as if they could have stepped off a television soundstage for the series.

The last night of their stay, the galley was pulled by a torch-bearing procession to the beach. After a traditional blast from a ram's horn, the galley was set ablaze by hundreds of torches, then cast adrift in true Viking tradition.

She had returned to London with an extensive file of Cate's notes and had been knee-deep in work ever since. There were daily Skype meetings with Nina and David, roundtable discussions with the marketing department in New York and Trevor Allen, not to mention coordination with distributors in the US as well as the European market. It was possible they might be able to make the Frankfurt Book Fair for prelaunch.

And there had been regular calls with James Morgan as he handled inquiries by the military about his involvement in hunting down Faridani. Anything else he was involved with, he couldn't talk about. She had hoped they could get together for dinner, but that hadn't happened.

There was a light knock, and Jewel poked her head inside. So much for do not disturb, Kris thought.

"There's a gentleman to see you," she explained. "From the telly," she whispered.

Kris groaned. She'd made only one brief statement to the media after returning to London; any further comments were handled by their legal team out of the New York office. She pulled the latest draft from Trevor out of the printer. She'd be burning the midnight oil the next few nights, then get back to him with any changes, and they just might stay on schedule.

"Tell them 'no comment,'" she said, adjusting her glasses.

"He said you would say that."

Kris shoved her reading glasses back on her head as Jewel pushed the door open.

James Morgan stood just outside the door to the office.

"He didn't look the sort to say 'no' to." Jewel grinned, gave him an openly admiring glance from her five-feet-two-inches, then made an excuse about work that needed to be done.

Kris hadn't seen him since first returning from France, a quick trip that ironically ended as it had begun, at an airport. He'd been required to report in right away after everything came out in the media.

"He's down to Taunton, I think," Anne Morgan had explained on that earlier holiday trip. "He wouldn't say more than that. All official, you see."

But there had been something in her voice, something hesitant, a pause, then a too-quick smile at something she didn't want to think about.

Now he stood in the doorway of her office—jeans, sweater, and leather jacket, but different—clean shaven, hair cut short.

How many times had she seen that same expression—the way one dark brow lifted slightly, that direct look, one corner of his mouth angled up, that thin scar from some teenage mishap, at the airport in Edinburgh, at Danny's flat in London.

How long did it take to know a person? Months? Years? Or only a few days?

She had known her ex-husband for almost eight years, two of the years married to him, but she had never really known him, what was important to him, things that mattered.

She had known James Morgan only a few weeks by comparison, yet she knew him—someone who had saved her life and risked his own, someone with his own pain, the losses, someone who held her when the nightmares slipped out of the box.

She rounded the desk, then leaned back against it, arms folded. She knew him, just as she knew the jeans, the sweatshirt, and leather jacket were deceptive. It was there in the expression in his eyes, and the haircut. High and tight, her brother called it.

"Back at it," she said, forcing the words past the sudden tightness in her throat. This was what Anne Morgan hadn't mentioned.

He nodded. "I've been cleared to return to active duty."

Keep it light, she told herself.

"Bullet hole and all? How did you pull that off?"

There was that half smile again. He rubbed the bridge of his nose in that way she had come to know meant something that vaguely resembled the truth was next.

"Aye, well, I explained that it was just a cat scratch while on leave."

"Blaming poor Robbie, are you now?" Robbie, Cate's resident cat at the tavern, that was now living with Anne Morgan.

He nodded. "Sneaky beast, that one."

She laughed in spite of the tightness in her throat. He gestured to the desk, barely visible beneath stacks of print-outs, memos—that whole "less paperwork with computers," that only seemed to add to paperwork.

"You're back at it as well."

"There's a lot to do. We're hoping to have Cate's last book out by next Christmas."

"How's the arm?"

She held her cast aloft. "Two more weeks, and it comes off. Then I just have to remember not to swing at anyone for a while."

And he would be gone, she saw it in the way he looked over at the windows and the dark sky beyond, icy rain hitting the glass.

"When we left France, there was something I should have told you." He did look at her then.

As in, 'I'm in a relationship,' or 'that was an incredible night, see you around,' or some sort of bullshit comment that people said to each other to ease their way out?

She'd heard it all before from her ex. She wasn't into explanations.

"I have a lot of work to do..." she said, not quite meeting that dark gaze. "Maybe a drink later?" Keep it light, no explanations, no expectations.

"Kris..."

There was something in the way he said her name, something he wanted to say. "That night..."

He reached out and tugged at her hair, dark, with those red highlights, silky in his hand.

"You need to know..." He hesitated. That accent thickened, slipped through the way it had when he told stories about his misspent youth, about pranks he pulled on the nuns at school, or that field trip to a monument in the Scottish Highlands.

He leaned in with that half-smile, as if sharing a secret.

"You need to know that I don't usually kiss a girl on the first date," he whispered.

She couldn't help it. She burst out laughing, the first time in a long time. Oh God, she needed that, she thought. Laughter.

First date?

It had been a long time since anyone had used that phrase, at least since she was in high school and that first date had been to the movies with her brother and his girlfriend as chaperones.

They hadn't been to the movies, but it had been a helluva first date. Still, she couldn't resist.

"What about Julie Hennessey?" Old conversations, safe territory.

He shook his head. "Ah, Julie Hennessey. She was a forward lass, a good second date."

"Had her way with you, did she?"

"Before I knew what happened."

"That quick?" It hadn't been quick between them, Kris remembered. So much for youthful inexperience. She'd take the longer version.

"Aye, youthful lust."

"Back seat of Anne's car?"

He frowned and shook his head. "The back room at Will's father's shop.

"The smell of grease and burning rubber, a sure way to a girl's heart. What about Dickie Simson?"

"She claimed that she never told him about it. But I suspect he knew. That would explain some of the citations he wrote me up over the years—revenge."

"And five children later," she added.

"As I said, she was a very forward lass. There was a bit of a hurry-up to their wedding."

She gave him that look. He shook his head.

"I had been gone for over a year."

"Threw you aside, did she? Heartless wench."

He shrugged. "We took different paths. Hers was with Dickie."

Her loss, Kris thought.

Then he had been off to university, then the military. Ironically, the same path James of Montrose had followed centuries earlier, according to what Vilette had told them and the little that was known about a young boy from Scotland taken in by Isabelle's family.

"You're going back." The laughter was gone now.

Her eyes were that dark color, deep blue, filled with shadows.

"Aye," he said, his voice low, the teasing gone. "I need to do this." And he needed her to understand.

"There are things that were left unfinished."

She nodded, staring out the window again. She remembered something Anne Morgan said—that if he had the courage to make the decision to go into those dangerous places, she needed to have the courage to accept it.

"How long do you have before you leave?"

"Three days."

"So soon?" She tried to keep the emotion from her voice, but even then, time was slipping away.

"They've already processed me through. I leave out of Taunton at the end of the week."

She didn't ask where he was going. She didn't need to. Back where it all happened, back where he had lost some of the men on his team. Things that were unfinished...things that mattered. She took a deep breath, trying to hold everything in—three days, airport farewells, then go on with her life, work, Cate's last book.

"There's Skype," he added. "When we're not out in the field, and text messages."

Skype and text messages, and thousands of miles away from anywhere safe. She nodded, trying to be brave, trying not to think about the what-ifs.

He smiled. "Danny's back for a while. He's a bit rough around the edges. But you'll like him. He'll keep you in touch. And then we'll go out when I get back, a drink, supper."

When...if he came back.

"A date?" She fought to keep her voice steady, calm.

"Well, the nuns at St. Anselm's would probably approve of a proper date."

If they only knew, Kris thought. Then again, they probably wouldn't be too surprised.

He pulled her against him, his hand in her hair.

"I'll be back," he whispered. "I promise." His lips brushed hers. Then he was gone.

She made her way to the executive bathroom. She turned the faucets on full and hit the auto hand-dryer, the noise drowning out her sobs until there was nothing left, and all she could do was hold on.

'Please, God...'

CHAPTER
FIFTY
INVERESK, SCOTLAND

t was in all the media. In spite of the on-going war in the Middle East, in spite of the upheaval in the wake of Brexit, and scandals that had rocked the American political system.

The search had brought them there—archeologists with infrared equipment capable of seeing deep underground, representatives from the National Trust, historians from the University of Edinburgh, the BBC with their cameras, Diana Jodion from the Bayeaux Museum, and the parish priest of Inveresk,

Weeks and months of work, painstaking research, and Diana's analysis of the tapestry along with stories handed down through Vilette Moreau's family, the reconstruction of the Montfort-Raveneau family history, had brought them to the small parish church, with its crumbling stone walls and the stone fence that surrounded the burial grounds that dated back hundreds of years.

The tapestry was like an archive of the lives of two people—Isabel Raveneau, raised in privilege and affluence, a beautiful young woman, if the images in the tapestry were an accurate likeness, and James, adopted into the Montfort family, a young man of uncertain birth, indebted to Simon de Montfort, educated at the Universitee de Notre Dame, given a military commission; then that ill-fated campaign to Teba in Spain, the last Crusade to the Holy Land, where he was taken prisoner, the dangerous journey to free him, and the last months at the Abbey Mont St. Michel when he lay dying, then the last voyage Isa made—James of Montfort, a true son of Scotland, taking him home.

According to Vilette and stories that had been handed down through her family, his true family refused to allow him to be buried in the family plot. Instead, depending on what they found, he was buried in the kirkyard of that small crumbling church.

It was all there in over a dozen beautiful, stunning panels, painfully hand-stitched by Isa Raveneau at the abbey after James' death, an archive of love and death, and faith, a secret woven into that last panel. That secret, hinted at in the kneeling figure of a young woman, kept safe by another young woman centuries later during one of the most horrific conflicts of modern history.

And Vilette's claim that Isa had given birth to James' child after his death? There was no absolute proof of it after seven centuries. Except for the pendant with that same image—the thistle and trinity knot.

It had brought them all here, Kris thought, as she stepped off the flight in Edinburgh, coming full circle to that first trip after she had received that text message from Cate, almost a year ago. Her last message.

"We need to talk..."

And the story.

There was that déjà vu moment as they made their way through baggage claim to transportation, where her publisher had arranged for a driver to meet them, a memory from a year ago, and someone else waiting for her. James Morgan.

They'd exchanged text messages and there had been those Skype calls, linked up by satellite from some place he couldn't talk about. Then weeks when there was neither.

"I'll call when we get back."

Back, from those secret places, back from things he couldn't tell her about.

She lived in that gray area, limbo, the dead zone, some called it, where she'd been before, when her brother was over there—that place between anger and that raw, naked fear, praying there would be that next call and fear at what it might bring. Holding on.

Prayer.

When had she said that first one again? When had she started to believe in it again? Needed to believe in it?

That horrific night in London over a year ago? At the abbey? Paris? At the quarry? When everything else was stripped away, and people had died?

She often thought of Micheleine Robillard the past year.

What were her hopes and dreams? What had she believed in? The tapestry and the secret woven in it? Or was it something more than that? What had sustained her? Faith as Albert once said? That sent her off to join the Resistance? Faith through horrifying losses? And then faith to face her own death?

The medallion Vilette had given her was warm between her fingers where it hung from the chain around her neck.

Vilette had lived long enough for her claim to be traced back as far as possible, and there had been an article in the French newspapers and on the internet about her claim to be related to Isabelle Raveneau.

Kris smiled, one last time in the spotlight.

"Too bad about the old girl," Alec Cameron said as the driver made their way through late-morning traffic from the airport. "Since she claimed to be a descendent of Isabel Raveneau."

He had accompanied her up from London. She'd been coordinating the marketing strategy for Cate's book with him from New York, then working directly with him in the London office as the release date drew closer. There were conferences to book, marketing meetings for the European release, and press meetings.

He had become a good friend, even though that was all it was. He'd accepted it with typical British stoicism.

"You can't blame a lad for trying."

Now he looked out the window of the limo at the gray sky that hung over the countryside like a soggy layer of cotton.

"Bloody, fucking cold, I say," he complained. "And wet. Bloody rain!"

"As opposed to London?" She couldn't resist, remembering her last trip over to visit Albert and Valentine.

It had still been warm then. The apple crop that fall had been especially good, and Valentine had launched her website with the apple recipes handed down from her grandmother, with help from Innis in Paris, before he and Luna decided they needed to take a long vacay—some place warm and tropical, as the investigation continued with questions about internet hacking, rogue operators, and Anthony was forced to move his gaming operation from the apartment in the Marais.

Albert chose to remain at the farm in Montigny as the hunt for James of Montfort's final resting place continued through the winter months. The tapestry had been found and Micheleine's role in keeping it safe from the Nazis decades earlier had been recognized throughout France, a country that had suffered much at the hands of terrorists the past several years, and in need of heroes, even if it was a nineteen-year-old girl who had been dead for decades. Like another girl, centuries earlier she had been compared to.

Micheleine.

You can rest easy now, Kris thought, *wherever you are*, her fingers wrapped around the pendant.

There was no documentation where she was actually buried. There was no stone in the abbey graveyard. A marker had been placed in the churchyard at Montigny, but she wasn't there either, one of those lost during the war.

Kris had worn the pendant since Vilette gave it to her, a reminder of Vilette's faith in her ancestor, the faith of friendship, faith that she had once thrown away, and now needed to hold onto more than ever.

"This is probably another snipe hunt," Alec grumbled. "This will make the fourth gravesite they've searched."

"Speaking of snipes..." She glanced out the window as the driver wound their way out of traffic toward Inveresk, and that old parish church where the search had narrowed.

"Have you ever actually seen one?" A long-necked bird with a sprout of feathers on its head, she thought, angling a look at his long frame and red hair spiked up all over his head. Not far off.

"Don't start," he fired back at her "or I will hand over the dog book author who keeps sending in re-writes.

"Fluffy Does France?"

"Fluffy Goes to France," he corrected her. Then, grumbling as he stared out the window, "Fuck Fluffy, disgusting little mongrel!

"The little beggar hiked a leg on my desk the last time the author came in for a meet. It's an Eames desk, for God's sake! And she's coming to the office again Wednesday next. On second thought," he said with particular delight. "I'll hand her over to Leonard."

The new junior editor who had been angling for his own projects.

Not nice, Kris thought, but she remembered the author she had first been given. Trial by fire.

"Or possibly adopt a Staffordshire," he added. "Bring it into the office, comfort dog and all that? See how Fluffy likes to play."

He really had his red up, Kris thought. She probably needed to arrange to be away from the office that day.

The village of Inveresk dated back to the time of the Romans. The road to the village was a single track off the main roadway, winding along an ancient stone wall. The village was a cluster of white-washed buildings with slate roofs and stone walls that dated back a mere three hundred years. St. Thomas church dominated the center of the village with its spire reaching over two stories into the leaden sky.

After Diana's analysis of the symbols and Latin words stitched in that last panel of the tapestry, countless church archives had been researched, along with the records of the burial grounds. From those hand-stitched words, the search had brought them to Inveresk.

Long abandoned, the older church at the far end of town with its stone wall surrounding the graveyard had deteriorated and crumbled to ruins. The grave stones in the kirkyard had been worn by time and the elements.

The abandoned church dated back to the twelfth century, at a time when Christianity was expanding throughout Britain. It was there, in that ancient kirk yard, the archeologists and historians from Edinburgh and France had narrowed their search. If the clues Isabel Raveneau had sewn into the tapestry were correct, then there was a good possibility this was where Isa had brought James to be buried.

Four days ago, after weeks of searching, carefully archiving each gravestone, each ancient grave, their infrared equipment found something unusual for a small, remote village graveyard—an intact grave slab more than a meter beneath the surface, in a place where those buried had been simply placed in the ground with a simple marker, or none at all.

Careful examination of the site had begun by archeologists, a representative from the National Trust, and the parish priest from the newer St. Thomas church at the town center. Diana had texted her the day before from the site.

"You must come. They have found something!"

The weather had been typical for Scottish winter—rain with more rain. And cold.

Pictures from Diana's cell phone had followed, as the excavation was approved and carefully continued, even through a light snowfall.

After weeks, months, and centuries, was it possible they'd found James of Montfort's grave?

The rain had stopped, the sun struggling through a heavy cloud bank as they arrived at the inn where Diana was staying. It was old, with stone walls, two wings that extended out around the car park, that typical slate roof, and a spiral of smoke from the second-story chimney. The research team had taken over the more modern inn built at the edge of the village to accommodate tourists during the high season.

She gave the clerk her credit card, then sent a text to Diana to let her know they'd arrived.

"The old parish church?" she asked the clerk.

"You'd be with them at the kirkyard, then?" the young woman asked. "Down the road, past the car park for the buses, on a bit of a rise."

Her accent was thick, the word 'down' sounding more like 'doon,' and reminded her of James Morgan in that way that a turn of a word or a phrase slipped out and brought back a memory of those days in France.

She thanked the clerk, and grabbed her umbrella.

"Not even a wee dram first to warm the blood?" Alec suggested. Then something about 'hard-hearted wench,' as he caught up and fell into step with her.

"You know, there are times you can be very stubborn."

It wasn't hard to find the parish church and the kirkyard. It had been turned into a village of its own—automobiles, trucks, vans, film crews, people hovered about in thick coats, while others brought in lighting on long poles, cameras to document everything, and Diana standing at the edge of the circle of archeologists and historians who had gathered around that corner of the graveyard.

She looked up and waived a gloved hand, then hooked her arm through Kris's arm as they joined her.

"They've cleaned off the grave slab and documented everything," Diana explained.

"Dr. Melrose from the university has dated it to the fourteenth century."

Fourteenth century. Was it possible? Kris thought.

The kirkyard was a beehive of activity and anticipation as ropes were carefully secured around the grave slab that was etched with letters and images.

"See…" Diana pulled her over to a computer that had been set up against the weather under a canvas canopy. Cables snaked back to the van, images displayed on the screen as the archeological team worked.

"God chooses us," Vilette once said.

Had God chosen this path for her?

She thought about that as the months slipped past, the investigations played out, and she struggled with the loss of someone who had been a good friend. It played out in the media, on the internet, and across the headlines in both France and the UK.

Jonathan Callish was possibly the most pathetic player in all this. Like a pawn on Albert's chessboard, he was used by other people, a much younger, beautiful wife with a secret agenda and connections, then her brother, a dangerous terrorist. As the London gallery failed to draw well-known artists and wealthy patrons, Alyia connected him to a source for rare antiquities for those wealthy patrons that frequented other galleries and auction houses—her brother.

Hasan Malik, or Faridani, the name he was known by in art circles, had access to rare artifacts according to the investigation that eventually exposed the depth of his connections throughout the Middle East that included smuggling and human trafficking. Those connections provided a source of rare artwork that found its way into private collections, not unlike the artwork and priceless artifacts that disappeared during World War II. But the sale of these artifacts funded terrorism.

It might all have gone on, if Cate hadn't gone to Jonathan about that photograph of the tapestry and asked his expertise on it. Whether he told Alyia about the photograph, or she might have seen it, would never be known now. What was known was that Faridani found out about the photograph, and Cate's questions about it—an ancient artifact that supposedly held a secret, a secret only rumored about, that he was determined would never see the light of day.

Connected with ample resources and the ability to track every place Cate went and the calls she made, Faridani also knew about the text message to Kris the day Cate died in that car accident.

The more they learned about where Cate had been and whom she had spoken with, thanks to Innis, Faridani also knew.

She knew now that it was Alyia she had encountered at the airport in Edinburgh, that slender, hooded figure so familiar on the Paris gallery security footage, and Alyia who had searched and ransacked the Tavern, and then again at her hotel.

Faridani had driven the van that night at the Blue Anchor, the incident that killed four people, including Brynn Halliday. No surprise, that Kris had been the target. Faridani was determined to stop her. James saw the van later at the warehouse behind the Paris gallery, the front fender damaged. It was the same white van at the farmhouse in Montigny. Shell casings found at the abbey, also tied Faridani to the shooting at the Abbey Mont St. Michel. A simple DNA test from the knife that was found on him by French authorities, also tied him to Brother Thomas's murder.

So much loss, so much pain. So many lives lost.

Was the secret Vilette Moreau spoke of there, beneath that ancient grave slab?

Diana's hand closed over hers. "Look," she said with growing excitement. "See what they have found!"

Across from them, the parish priest whispered a silent prayer as stone grated against stone and the grave slab was slowly lifted away from the stone burial box.

Diana's hand tightened over hers.

"The slab is intact. This was a person of importance. And see the markings carved there!"

An expectant quiet spread over the site as the slab was slowly hoisted from the crypt and then gently lowered onto a wood platform. Cameras recorded everything, then turned back to the crypt. A thick cloth lay over the body with an image stitched onto it.

"The House of Raveneau!" Diana whispered. "Her mother's family."

The shroud was made of linen that had deteriorated over time. The remains of a woman's body, dressed in fine garments, were still intact.

"Mon dieu!" Diana exclaimed. "Can it be?"

As cameras continued to record everything, the body was carefully removed. Precautions were taken against damage as it was taken to another platform shielded from the rain by the canopy overhead.

The shroud had covered the woman's face when she was buried, and her hands or what was left of them were barely visible from the sleeves of the gown she wore that was made of what appeared to be fine satin. A crucifix was clutched in the slender bones of her hands. And on one finger was a silver ring with a simple crest on it.

Kris had seen pictures of ancient graves and burial sites in her early studies. There had never been that sense of horror or revulsion, but a sense of how one had lived their life and what that life might have meant. This was so much more than any of them had hoped for.

"It is the same as the tapestry."

Diana had sent the latest pictures. She had studied them, fascinated with the intricate details that had taken a lifetime to create. And one panel that showed Isabel Raveneau as an older woman, her hand closed around the crucifix that still hung about her neck, and a simple ring on her hand.

She was here. Isabelle Raveneau had returned to be buried with James of Montfort. There was no doubt now that the archeological team had found his grave.

"Are you all right?" Alec asked. "You look as if you've seen a ghost."

Not a ghost, Kris thought with a smile, but a woman, who had loved someone, had held onto her faith that he would come back to her, shared that small window of time with him at Mont St. Michel, and had then brought him home. A true son.

"I'm fine."

The path she was meant to follow, as Vilette once told her when she gave her the pendant?

Excitement spread as the team members worked against time and the elements, taking photographs, cataloging everything.

Isabel's body was carefully wrapped to preserve it, then lifted into one of the large vans to be taken to the university, to be photographed and analyzed before being returned to the gravesite. Then the team began the work of removing a second body from the grave site.

In spite of deterioration over the centuries, dark hair could be seen along with the knight's garments and shield he had been buried with.

"You see," Diana pointed out. "His shield. The story in the tapestry is true. The commission of knighthood."

The image on the shield was the House of Montfort. But it was the simple shroud and the hand-stitched image that revealed far more—a trinity knot and thistle, symbol of the land of James' birth and faith—Scotland.

There were artifacts in the crypt that were carefully catalogued and then removed—the knight's sword, a mace, and a smaller knife, along with other tokens from those who had known him, Diana explained—a small glass vial, still intact, its contents remarkably preserved. But it was the last item in the crypt that caused the buzz of conversation and anticipation—a stone coffer that lay at his feet.

Was this the secret James had brought back with him from Teba in Spain? A secret shared with him by another knight in that fortress prison where he was taken after that failed battle? The secret James and Isabel had brought back to France? And painstakingly stitched into that last panel, along with the image of that short voyage from the abbey to Scotland?

The stone coffer was slowly lifted from the crypt into the light of day for the first time in almost seven centuries. Letters were carved in the stone at the front of the coffer and a design encircled the box.

"It is not Latin," Diana whispered, as cameras continued to record everything along with the historians' commentary about what they had found.

Not Latin, that they might have expected to find, the same as written on so many ancient grave slabs from the same time period. But a much older text that the archeologists remarked with surprise.

"It's ancient Hebrew," Kris replied. It was a name, recognized from her early studies at college.

"Yeshua."

Beside her, Diana made the sign of the cross.

"What can it mean?" she whispered.

What was inside the coffer? Artifacts? Possibly an ancient text? Nothing after all these years?

Whatever was or might have been inside, was something that

Hasan Malik had been determined to keep the world from knowing when he tried to destroy the tapestry.

A blaspheme against the one true God, as he had told Marcus when he told his sister to burn it?

The crypt was closed and the contents removed to the university at Edinburgh for further study and analysis before the coffer was officially opened.

Scientists, theologians from around the world and a dozen faiths, historians, lay people, set the internet on fire after that single name in old Hebrew was leaked to the media. Whatever might be in that stone coffer had upended both the modern and ancient world.

Over the next several months it was a story that slipped from the world of archeology onto the opening page of every newspaper and media outlet. And finally, state of the art, high tech equipment allowed them to look within the coffer without opening it out of concern that exposure might cause the contents to deteriorate.

What had they found at that remote Scottish village? What did it mean? The faint image that had emerged on their screens was startling – the vague outline of a goblet that had been hidden for centuries. And with that name, Yeshua?

Had they found the cup of Christ?

Diana Jodion had been bombarded with requests for an interview. From her office at the university, she simply informed the media that she was concentrating on the restoration of the tapestry.

The University of Edinburgh had gone into information lockdown, leaving the media with only those early videos from Cate's career, her accident, and speculation about what archeologists had discovered at that gravesite.

In New York, David Ellison had his legal team working overtime on negotiations for exclusive book rights, and Kris, along with others who had been at the site, had been sworn to silence until further notice, and the London publisher had to employ full-time security while meetings went on, for exclusive world rights.

It had all started with that black-and-white photograph Paul Bennett had taken during the war.

Cate would have loved it.

CHAPTER
FIFTY-ONE

Kris scanned the floor of the bookstore that was a London landmark, the rows of books, and the center table where Trevor Allen sat with copies of the book he had co-authored with CB Ross. The line was backed out the door in spite of the cold weather. They had made the Christmas holiday launch.

SEVEN DAYS, an inside look at the first Gulf War, from someone who had been embedded with the military, ate, slept, and moved with them, with Cate's inimitable style of story-telling that took readers into the lives of those who were there, along with a searing look at decisions that were made through the eyes of the main character.

The collaboration with Trevor had been one of those rare moments in life, an opportunity for someone who ironically had served with coalition forces during that time and had experienced many of those same moments.

The book was on the bestseller lists on presale numbers even before it was released, then launched in New York two weeks before. Several signings had been set up, coordinated through their New York publicist. Trevor had returned just in time for the launch in the UK and Europe.

"The van just arrived," Jewel announced, her face flushed as she reached Kris.

"They'll bring more books in straight away."

Just one of the glitches that sometimes went with a book-signing, those behind-the-scenes details that sometimes fell through the cracks. This time it was a delayed delivery from the distributor. But in that unflappable way he had, that reminded her so much of Cate, Trevor had soldiered on, chatting with people who had come to buy that last release from a favorite author, deftly handling questions about the collaboration, listening to customers' stories about a son, a daughter, a husband, or brother who had served during that time, and others who still served.

The investigation into Cate's death had been closed two months earlier, and Diana Jodion was hard at work on the final restoration of the tapestry. Negotiations for a book about the search for the Raveneau Tapestry, had just finished. It was on the preliminary schedule for the following year. That would keep Kris busy.

She had lived out of a hotel for the first few months, then rented a flat in Chelsea. It made it easier for those trips over to see Diana at the university, and then over to France.

She had gone over last fall to visit Albert and Valentine. It was apple season, and she had helped Valentine at the roadside stand, selling apples and some of her apple pastries. Her website was doing well, and a market in Arras, along with three bakeries, had committed to carry her apple products.

Those trips to the French countryside had filled the weekends when she wasn't working overtime or heading off to one of the book fairs to promote Cate's book. She'd needed that, to lose herself in the countryside, to heal, Albert called it, even though the cast was off and her arm had healed a long time ago, leaving only a hairline scar where they took out the pin a few weeks earlier.

She had returned to the farmhouse, and then walked through the orchards, trying to understand who Micheleine was, what had it taken for a young girl to join the Resistance and then go off to fight a brutal enemy.

Like so many during the war, she had simply disappeared, a number among so many numbers of casualties. But her impact had been enormous. Albert was the last connection to her, someone who had known her during that time.

"She was like most young people," he told her as they had walked together through the orchards on another trip, the apple crop finally in, red and gold leaves drifting down around them.

"Idealistic, passionate, in the beginning. Later, after she had seen and done some of those things, the last time...I noticed a change in her," he spoke, then stopped to remember, pulling those memories out of decades past.

"There was a sadness too. I think she knew she would not be coming back."

"Why did she go back when she could have been safe with Angeline and their mother, and the war was almost over," she had asked, wanting to understand, needing to understand.

He thought about that as they walked that fall day.

"Faith," he finally answered. Just that one word. Then he had explained, "She had enormous faith. She knew what she must do, that she could not hide and let others go as her father and brothers had gone in the early years. It was the same with the tapestry," he had continued.

"She knew that she must save it from falling into Nazi hands. To lose it would have been to lose not only an important part of our history, but part of herself. She fought for what she believed in, like the young woman in the tapestry, yes?" He had paused again, and looked at her.

"Not unlike your search to find the reason your friend died, that brought you here. And it was the same for your brother, I think." He had reached out then and touched her cheek.

"Something he believed in, that was part of him." He had pointed to himself then.

"I understand this, and your friend, James Morgan, he also understands."

They had continued to walk through the orchard. Albert was silent for a long time, then he was thoughtful.

"I think we do not need a church to pray in. I have prayed in the forest as a boy, and here in this orchard. God hears us wherever we are. But I think if we lose our faith, then we lose ourselves."

She thought about that afterward, in the quiet sounds of the farmhouse, Valentine talking with her grandfather as she put more wood on the fire, Ju-Ju snoring at Albert's feet as he smoked his pipe.

Was that what it was like for Isabel Raveneau, a story that had played out against the backdrop of another war in another time and place? For Micheleine hundreds of years later, then for her brother, and James Morgan?

In a world where everything had sped up—communication, instant answers on the internet, reality programs that in reality showed lives no one could identify with, where the meaning of everyday life depended on the next sound-bite or video from the media to make choices and decisions—what were the things that mattered?

Faith in a higher power? God?

Diana had said much the same thing in those quiet after-hours at the university where the tapestry was taken after it was found, after the student photographers, professors from the historical department, and restoration experts had gone home for the day.

They walked together through that enormous workshop, the tapestry laid out on long tables, the images Isabel Raveneau had created telling their own story—of love, war, and death, and another young girl who had donned armor and taken up the sword.

"She had enormous faith," Diana explained. "It was her strength. You see, this image woven throughout, the trinity knot and thistle, like your medallion, the things she believed in—God, and the man she loved."

If we lose our faith, we lose ourselves.

She stared at those images in the tapestry in the quiet stillness of the university museum. She had lost her faith when Mark died. She had walked away from it, in pain, angry. And for a long time she had lost herself.

She continued to think about that when she returned to London and she threw herself into work on the book with Trevor Allen, coordinating the marketing for the launch.

She had dinner meetings with Alec and Trevor, working weekends, and she met Danny when he first returned to London.

"I thought I picked up the scent of perfume at my flat after you were there," he had teased her.

"'Splendor,' is it?" he asked with a grin. "In the bath and on the sheets." He had given her that look then. "Nice."

She hadn't worn that scent or any perfume since that horrific evening at the Blue Anchor. In that way that something stayed in one's memory—a sound, a song, or a particular scent—it reminded her of that horrible night and the chaos on the patio where four people had died. Things that mattered.

Over the months, she and Danny met occasionally for drinks, or supper when they were both in London. He became a connection to James, someone who understood the reasons he had to go back, who had experienced some of the same things.

"He'll be all right, you know," he tried to reassure her. "But he needed to go back, you see. It wasn't finished, and that's the hardest thing for all of us. It's not the risk that it might be us one day, it's the ones we leave behind."

Danny became a good friend, someone who understood in ways that Alec Cameron didn't.

On a trip to New York a couple of months earlier, she had connected back with a client they had worked with a few years before. He was an avid rock-and-roll collector and the book had been about some of the rock artists he had worked with. He had a rare, original studio recording of 'Running on Empty.'

It took several conversations and her agreement to take a look at another book project he was working on, in exchange for that original recording. She had it sent to Danny, a way of saying 'thank you.'

Then, in that way that things had of speeding up, everything happening at once, even with the best-laid plans, Cate's book went into production, marketing kicked into high gear, and it was coming out in twelve different languages, with the e-book version available in thirty days.

They had been burning the midnight oil for weeks, and now it was on the shelves with that line out the door and down the street in the drizzling rain eight days before Christmas.

Everything that could go wrong hadn't materialized, except for that delayed delivery. Clerks appeared rolling book carts from the back of the store. Copies of Cate's books were stacked on the table, and Trevor Allen smiled at the next customer. He was successful in his own right, but the collaboration would boost his career to the next level. Cate would have liked that.

Editors didn't usually attend book signings. Those were all about the book and the author. But she had wanted to make certain every detail had been handled, and it was the same location where Cate had her first book signing.

"Has anyone ever mentioned that you can be very stubborn about things?" Trevor had asked as she had gone down the mental checklist again, ticking off each item—plenty of copies of the book now, several pens in front of Trevor, bottled water, several staff on hand to assist customers.

She smiled to herself. She could probably exit now, leave the rest to Trevor and the store managers, grab something to eat, then head back to the office. She turned toward the entrance, and suddenly stopped.

Customers pushed past her—students with backpacks, older men who waited in line for a copy, several women, older people, younger people who had never known Cate but identified with the stories she had written and with a woman who had kicked down barriers for women in journalism, stopping in for a copy their teacher or mother had recommended, chatting among themselves with cups of coffee from the coffee bar in their hands.

And a face in the crowd.

The long military overcoat with brass buttons and the uniform just visible at the collar, had replaced jeans, the sweatshirt, and the leather jacket.

He was leaner, older, even though it had been less than a year. It was there in the expression on his face, in his eyes, of things he had seen and done, and had spoken about only once in the middle of the night, the raw and dark places that had brought them together.

There had been no text message, no Skype conversation, no hastily sent e-mail that he was back. It didn't matter.

Thank you, God, she silently whispered, then took a deep breath and slowly walked toward him.

"Danny didn't mention that you were back."

A tired smile, and some other expression behind the smile—weariness and the shadows of other things.

"The last few days have been chaos. Communication was sketchy until we got to Germany, a late flight, then debrief..."

He knew he was staring at her, but he needed to see the deep blue of her eyes that he'd thought about a hundred times, convincing himself they weren't that color. They were. And a hundred other things he remembered from that time in France.

Running on empty, things he would tell her about later, and other things that he wouldn't, couldn't share. Not yet, maybe not ever.

"I know someone who might be able to help with that communication problem," she said. Keep it light, she told herself. Don't ask any questions. He was there. It was enough.

"Innis?" he replied, almost a smile.

The crowd moved around and past them, a curious look from an older gentleman, then a different look from a young woman—definite invitation, the sort of look that usually ended in bed. He didn't seem to notice.

"It might have to wait," she told him. "He's on vacation. He thought it was probably a good idea to keep some distance between them and Paris, something about having broken a few laws with his hacking skills."

"The need to be invisible for a while."

There was something in the way he said it. He knew about that sort of thing. Being invisible. That silence again as more customers made their way toward the author table.

"I heard the new book made the bestseller list."

The media, even in those dark places, she thought.

Kris nodded. "The press has been all over it, one of their own and all that. And with the added publicity about the accident and finding the tapestry. I wish she could have been here for that."

She knew exactly what Cate would have thought about all of it, something about the tabloid press not knowing their ass from a real story, and then something else about finding a good bar nearby when the crowd cleared.

She wanted to ask him about all of it, and at the same time she was afraid to ask. She had asked her brother once. Just once.

He watched the emotions that played across her face, the way she kept everything under control, like the first time at the airport, and a dozen times afterward in France, then when they returned to London. Strength.

Strength to survive the loss of someone she had loved deeply, strength to track down a friend's killer.

His fingers closed gently around her wrist. He traced the scar where surgeons had put in the pin, and then removed it. Strength enough.

"It's almost healed," he said, his fingers lightly stroking over the scar. He would have taken her pain if he could have that day in the quarry. He would take all of it.

"The doctor at hospital said I won't even notice it in a few months."

Scars, wounds that had healed. And other wounds that would take more time.

"You did it," he said, looking around the bookstore, then at the desk where Trevor signed copies of the book.

"A lot of hard work. Cate would be proud."

She breathed past the sudden emotion that came.

"There will be more work. I'll be spending a lot of time in London."

"The tapestry?"

"Diana and her team are continuing their work on it. They hope to have it ready to go on display by June."

Casual conversation.

How did they do this? she thought. Who were they, after almost a year with those brief Skype and text messages half a world away? After everything that had happened?

Could she do this? Could she take whatever time he had and not lose herself when he left again? Waiting for that call from Anne, or a text message from Danny?

She took a deep breath, holding on.

"How much time do you have?"

That look, an expression that she knew so well, the weariness, the lines at the corners of his eyes as he stared down at her wrist, that dark gaze as he looked up.

"Several years now."

Not a week, or a few days...?

"There's the usual paperwork to make everything official. That will take some time, but it's finished for me."

It was the way he said it, that accent that had a way of slipping through, wrapping around the words, something he shared with her as if it was just the two of them in spite of the crowd that moved around them.

"My time is my own now."

There was more that was left unsaid, but it was there in that dark gaze that watched her, filled with the shadows of those raw and dark places he'd been.

She looked down at his hand, still wrapped around her wrist, the tip of the sword at the tattoo just visible at the edge of his sleeve.

"There's a place I know," he said, watching her.

"Are you asking me out on a date?"

Did people date any more, or just hook up?

A real smile then, tired, but it was there for the first time since she saw him standing in the entrance of the bookstore.

"There's a fine single malt I'm told the owner always keeps behind the bar."

The Tavern.

"It's a long drive," she replied.

"There's an inn along the way. The place is a bit rowdy at the end of the day, but the bartender is a good sort, and the fire is warm on a cold night."

He touched her cheek, the way he had that first night in London almost a year ago. She had held on then, needed to hold on. Needed it now, needed him.

The wounds were still there, for both of them—the things he had seen and done, the pain of loss, the men he had served with. For her, the loss of her brother, friends she would like to have known—a young girl called Jehanne, Isa Raveneau, Vilette Moreau. And the one person who had brought them all together.

Cate.

She would always miss her—the first time they met at that writers' conference, their work together over those books that had become bestsellers, discussions about character and plotting, late night conversations over her favorite whisky in a hotel bar after her latest book signing.

But there were new friends — Danny, Trevor Allen with so much raw talent that it was almost frightening, Diana Jodion and her passion for the tapestry, Valentine with her faith in a woman she had never met or known but loved, and Albert with his own story that needed to be told.

Things that mattered.

Her hand wrapped around his, holding on.

It was a very long drive, and a very fine whisky.

AUTHOR'S NOTE

People and places...

The characters in *Blood Game* are a blend of real and fiction. I've tried to respect and do justice to all of them.

Bill Dunnett was a war-time photographer during World War II. I've added the character of Paul Bennett for the benefit of the story.

Micheleine Robillard is fictional as is Albert Marchand. They are composites of so many, young and old, who joined the Resistance during the war. It has been written that without their struggle and contributions, in the very least the war would have gone on much longer, and France might have been lost. All of them provided invaluable knowledge, courage, and sacrifice to the Allied cause.

Vilette Moreau is also a composite of different personalities from that time period, from an actress who lured several of the German high command to her bed and extracted valuable information during the war that she passed on to the Allies, to a well-known chanteuse in a French nightclub, and a young woman who claimed to be descended from French aristocracy, all rolled into one.

Simon Fraser, Lord Lovat, was real, and there are many accounts that have been written about his participation in the landing at Normandy, France, June, 1944, when he instructed his personal piper to play 'Highland Laddies' as they scrambled from the landing craft onto the beach. I created that brief encounter with the character of Paul Bennett to put him front and center of that part of the story.

CB Ross is also a composite in her brief but integral appearance, a pioneer as a female war correspondent in a time when there were few, and like others who have come after and have made their own sacrifices for 'the story.' Brave, gutsy women who too often have been overlooked.

Innis, bless him, with all his tattoos and a generous, if grumbling nature. He is also fictional, but resembles someone I know very well. The disguise was necessary to protect the not-so-innocent.

Kris McKenna—her pain and her loss, are real in so many women who have experienced some of the same things, and struggle on a daily basis, redefining their lives as partners, mothers, daughters, to find the things in life that matter.

James Morgan—I will simply say that there is a man out there with the tattoo of a stag's head, who has been in hard places and has made hard choices, the warrior who represents so many who have gone into other hard places, and some who have made the ultimate sacrifice. James' character is to honor all of them.

The memorial at Lochaber, Scotland, is real and a very moving place to visit. It's the sort of place where everyone is usually very quiet, reading the inscriptions, seeing the mementoes left there, a memorial to those who have made hard choices through several wars.

The Abbey Mont St. Michel with its rich history as an abbey, a hospital, and a refuge for pilgrims fleeing the Holy Land centuries past, is also real, visited by thousands every year. The legend of St. Michael's spire is true. There is a bridge now that connects the abbey to the mainland of France, but there was a time when it could only be accessed at low tide on a land bridge of sand.

The village of Montigny is a composite of small French villages throughout France, steeped in rich history, including World Wars I and II, when they sat at the edge of those great conflicts.

The 'hospital' in the quarry mine is real, discovered a few years ago. It was once an active limestone quarry, with chambers and tunnels, and resembled an underground village. There are photographs on-line of the rooms that were found still intact, with cots for the injured and other furnishings, along with a rail line once used by miners, explosives still in crates, and images carved in stone walls by the injured soldiers who were taken there—the perfect hiding place for a rare artifact.

The Tavern is based on a photograph of a two-hundred-year-old inn on an abandoned coach road in the Scottish Highlands, the perfect retreat for a former war correspondent and best-selling author, working on her next novel.

The old abandoned church at the end of *Blood Game* is like so many places all over Britain, with grave slabs carved with inscriptions in Latin and likenesses of the knights buried beneath them. They are being discovered all the time. This particular knight was buried in the kirkyard of a small, crumbling, long-abandoned church beside a stone wall. I've borrowed that knight's story for James of Montfort.

James Morgan's stag-head tattoo is real, as stated before, and part of what defines who he is and what he's done, like someone I know.

The Raveneau Tapestry represents thousands of pieces of art, sculptures, and other artifacts possibly including a legendary gold train, that were confiscated during World War II, and hidden. Some pieces have been found in private collections, in attics, with some returned to the families of their rightful owners. Many others may never be found.

The secret in the tapestry is based on an actual account about that fateful last crusade to the Holy Land in 1335, that ended at Teba, Spain, where many were slaughtered including two sons of St. Clair, who were taking the heart of Robert the Bruce of Scotland to the Holy Land.

Those who survived were executed or held for ransom, while a handful of others escaped.

ALSO BY CARLA SIMPSON

Angus Brodie and Mikaela Forsythe Murder Mystery

A Deadly Affair

Deadly Secrets

A Deadly Game

Deadly Illusion

A Deadly Vow

Deadly Obsession

A Deadly Deception

Merlin Series

Daughter of Fire

Daughter of the Mist

Daughter of the Light

Shadows of Camelot

Dawn of Camelot

Daughter of Camelot

The Young Dragons, Blood Moon

Clan Fraser

Betrayed

Revenge

Outlaws, Scoundrels & Lawmen

Desperado's Caress

Passion's Splendor

Silver Mistress

Memory and Desire

Desire's Flame

Silken Surrender

Angels, Devils, Rebels & Rogues

Ravished

Always My Love

Seductive Caress

Seduced

Deceived

Standalone Contemporary Supense

Blood Game

ABOUT THE AUTHOR

"I want to write a book... " she said.

"Then do it," he said.

And she did, and received two offers for that first book proposal.

A dozen historical romances later, and a prophecy from a gifted psychic and the Legacy Series was created, expanding to seven additional titles.

Along the way, two film options, and numerous book awards.

But wait, there's more a voice whispered, after a trip to Scotland and a visit to the standing stones in the far north, and as old as Stonehenge, sign posts the voice told her, and the Clan Fraser books that have followed that told the beginnings of the clan and the family she was part of...

And now... murder and mystery set against the backdrop of Victorian London in the new Angus Brodie and Mikaela Forsythe series, with an assortment of conspirators and murderers in the brave new world after the Industrial Revolution where terrorists threaten and the world spins closer to war.

When she is not exploring the Darkness of the fantasy world, or pursuing ancestors in ancient Scotland, she lives in the mountains near Yosemite National Park with bears and mountain lions, and plots murder and revenge.

And did I mention fierce, beautiful women and dangerous, handsome men?

They're there, waiting...

Join Carla's Newsletter

www.ingramcontent.com/pod-product-compliance
Lightning Source LLC
Chambersburg PA
CBHW020008120726
47903CB00004B/1185